# the elephant in the room

zubaan

Spring

# Contents

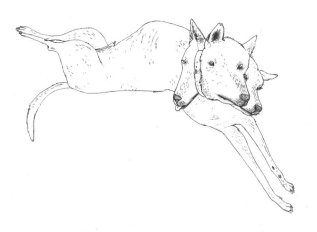

*Manjula Padmanabhan:*
*author, artist, cartoonist, playwright.*

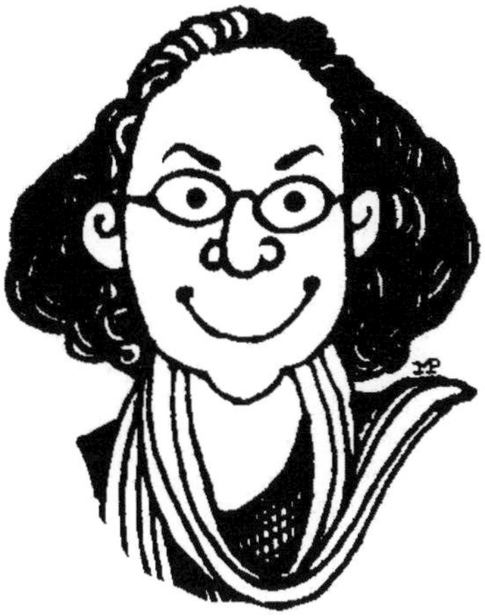

# Foreword

WHY do so many of us still fret about our secret hair? Our never-to-be-born babies? Our grandmother's opinions? The size of our bums? WHY are so many of us defined by our shapes and our body parts, rather than the worlds we build through our knowledge, experience and talent? WHY are so many of us crushed by social pressure until we ourselves no longer believe in ourselves?

The answer is: elephants.

Not real elephants, of course, but the giant, unexamined and unmentionable issues that deform—and sometimes augment—the dreams of so many girls and women.

There have always been highly acclaimed women illustrators amongst us. Beatrix Potter comes to mind. Claire Bretécher in France. Japan's comic industry is maintained by armies of women artists. Yet it was really only when Marjane Satrapi published her graphic memoir *Persepolis* in 2000, that a giant portal was punched open for many other women artists to flood through.

Publishers began to consider the possibility that women represented a market opportunity. And then—hallelujah! The Internet! The World Wide Web combined with easy-to-use graphic software and fingertip-friendly electronic screens really brought the revolution home to girls and young women. Alison Bechdel in the US and Amruta Patil in India have built their success on the foundation of their highly refined artistic sensibilities. But it's the unschooled techniques of thousands of amateur cartoonists exploring the digi-verse on their tablets and iPhones which truly revolutionized the visual landscape.

In *Drawing the Line*, Zubaan's previous collection of graphic narratives, that freedom from artistic and stylistic constraint came through in stories drawn and written by young urban Indian women.

In this fresh collection the focus has shifted to... elephants. Indian as well as European. The book came into being when a group of German and Indian artist-authors travelled to Nrityagram, in Karnataka, India to spend time thinking, writing, drawing and sharing across the cultural spectrum to capture the experience of being women.

The resulting stories and styles are as varied as the spices that make up a curry. A curry made of tears and hair, menstrual blood and secrets, bitter arguments and sweet memories, dogs, cats and babies, moons and stars. Some are tasty, some are medicinal, some are magical. All are vivid.

Go on then. Go see the elephants.

Manjula Padmanabhan

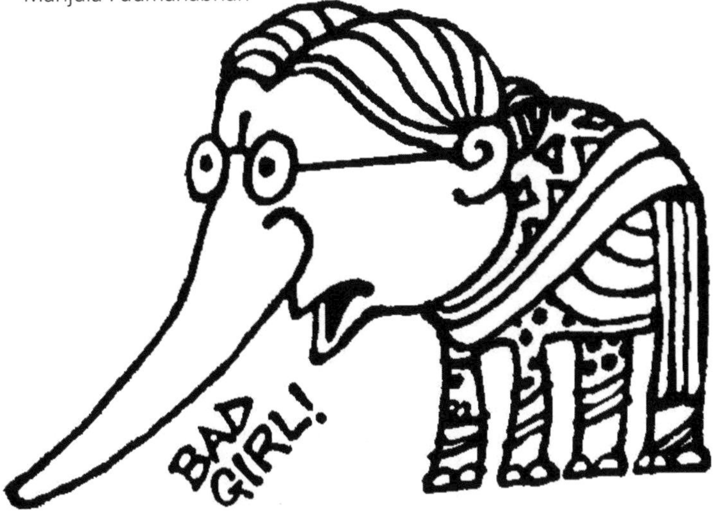
BAD GIRL!

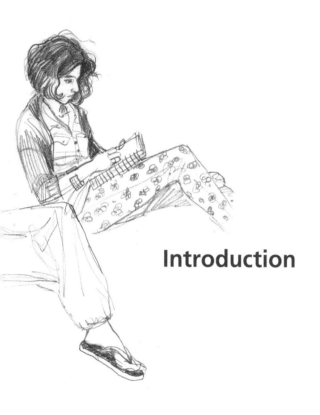

# Introduction

In 2016, a group of German cartoonists met with eight Indian colleagues in Nrityagram, Bangalore, to create this book. It all started two years earlier when the Goethe-Institut New Delhi and Zubaan organised a workshop for Indian women cartoonists led by Larissa Bertonasco, Ludmilla Bartscht and Priya Kuriyan. This resulted in a book, *Drawing the Line*, published by Zubaan in India. Larissa was so enthusiastic about the intercultural collaboration, she developed a joint volume of SPRING with all of the participants collaborating on an egalitarian basis in the spirit of direct democracy as the group had always done. The result is the book you now hold in your hands.

We lived together at a place for writers' residencies around 30 kilometres from Bangalore. The building is on the site of Nrityagram, a school for classical Indian dance. The huge property felt like paradise: different buildings scattered around the complex like in a village with gardens in between where fruit and vegetables were grown.

Our time together consisted of intense interaction, with discussions among the entire group or in smaller groups. The two resident dogs, Guru and Swami, liked to visit us, and took their naps next to us in the shade, where it was a pleasant 30°C. Each woman drew her story and presented it to the group, resulting in lively discussions. Every morning, we worked on our drawings together, and a small library for comics provided considerable inspiration.

Our first working title was *Role Models*—which in addition to its literal meaning in English also conveys the meaning of "setting a pattern." We wanted to make conscious reference to our roles as women in our respective societies as the idea was to juxtapose Indian and German women's experiences. Our final title, *The Elephant in the Room,* is an expression that describes an important and obvious fact that no one wants to talk about as it is considered uncomfortable.

While women in Germany seem to live relatively self-determined lives with many possibilities, in a non-homogeneous country like India things are a little more complex. India is a nation of paradoxes and women in India today reflect that paradox. Rapid economic changes have had a profound impact on womens' roles in Indian society. Social relations change, love marriages gain acceptance, women pursue careers in business,

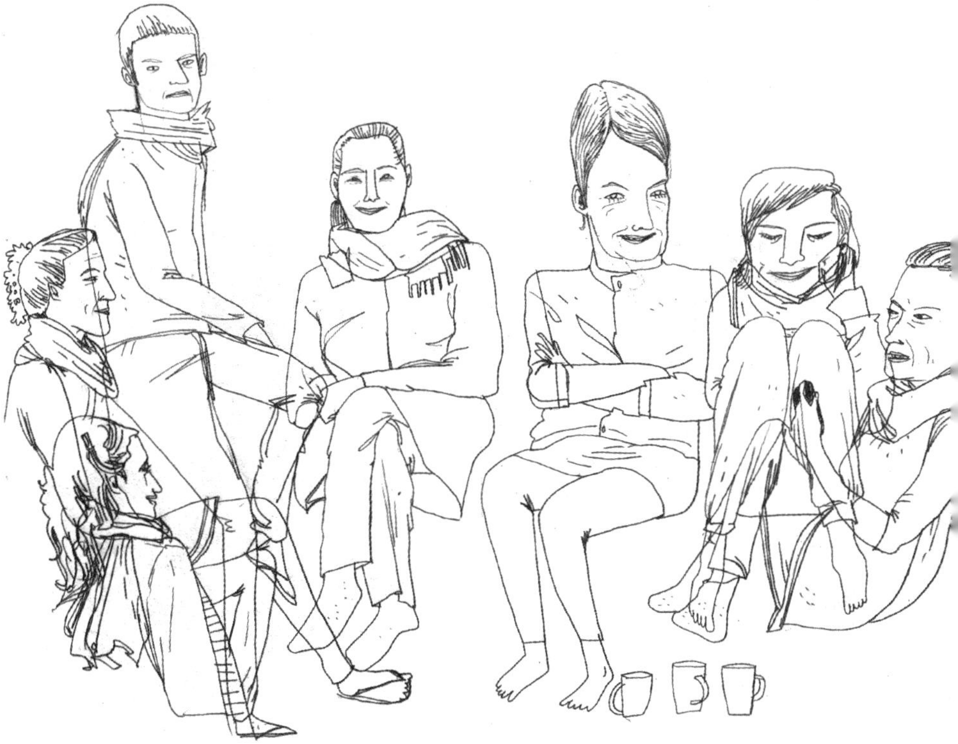

politics or cultural affairs—the women's movement is generally strong. But this does not apply everywhere or for everyone in India. Sexual violence, domestic violence, rape and female foeticide continue to be huge problems. Deeply entrenched inequities of caste and class add to the complexities of conversations around gender and choices for women in India.

What has changed over the past few years though, is that conversations around gender and violence against women—which are often lead by young women of diverse cultural backgrounds and faiths—are no longer easily brushed under the carpet.

The differences of our living environment filled whole evenings of lively discussions, but it showed also how much we have in common that matters to us and connects us. The question of our identity as female artists and the relationship between freedom and responsibility was more relevant in our discussions than ever before.

On the last evening before we headed home, we lay on the stone floor of the amphitheatre in which the heat of the day could still be felt, and warmed our backs. We gazed up at the moonlit sky, and watched the clouds as their shapes shifted. The texture that could be seen on the surface of the moon appeared twisted, somehow different from the familiar view from Europe.

The SPRING group would like to thank the Maecenia Foundation and the Goethe-Institute for financial support, particularly Ute Reimer Böhner and Sohani Sachdeva (Goethe-Institute New Delhi) for their organisational support; Isabelle Erler for her help regarding applications; Sandra Meifarth for the layout, her patience and staying on top of things; and finally the initiator Larissa Bertonasco, along with Priya Kuriyan, without whose tireless commitment to the group this project would not have been possible.

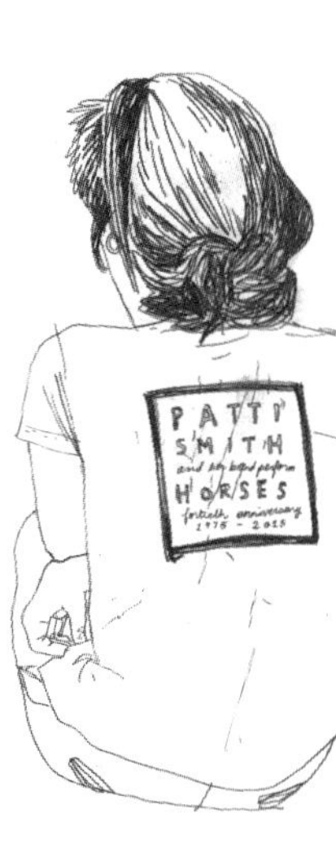
PATTI
SMITH
HORSES

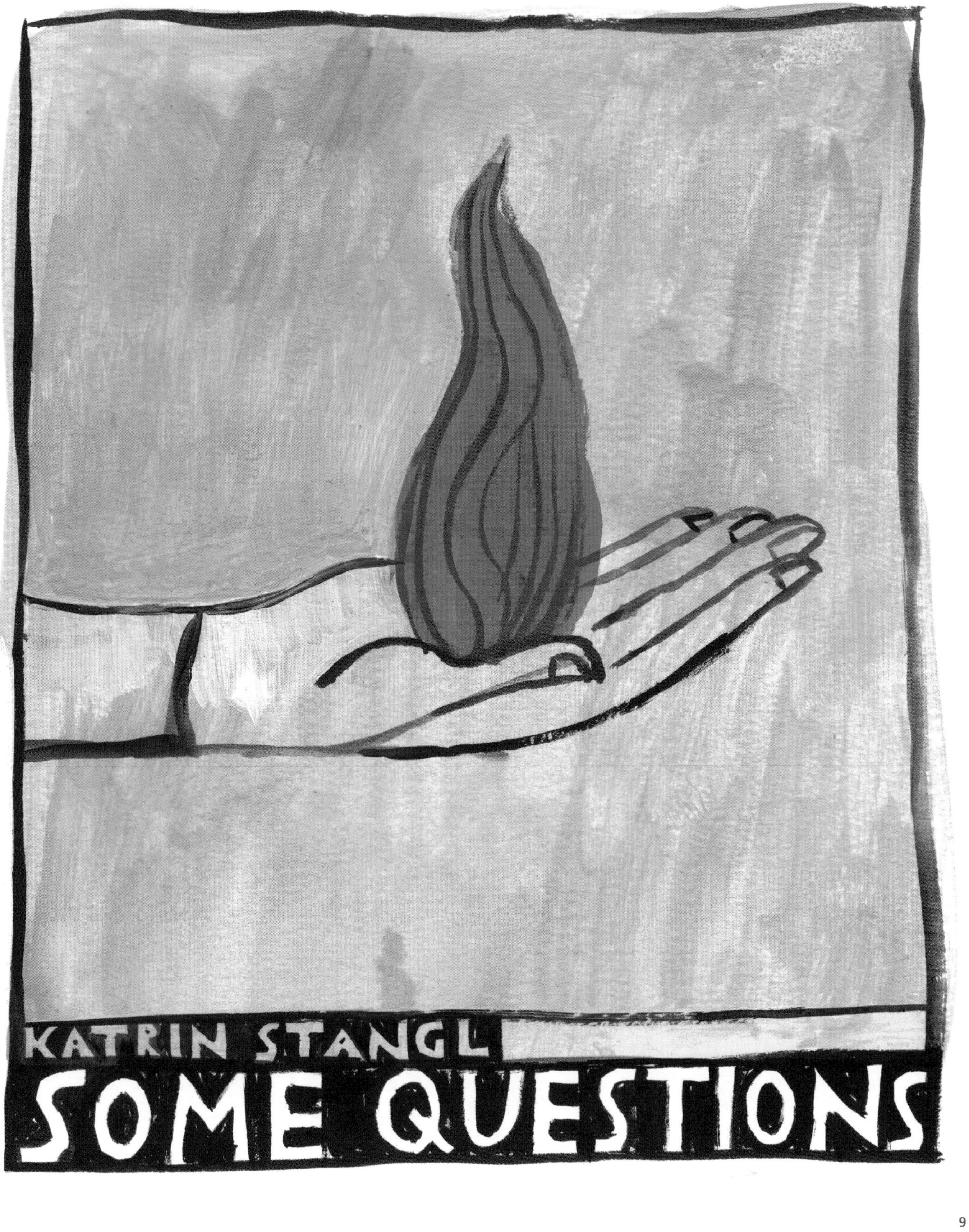

KATRIN STANGL

# SOME QUESTIONS

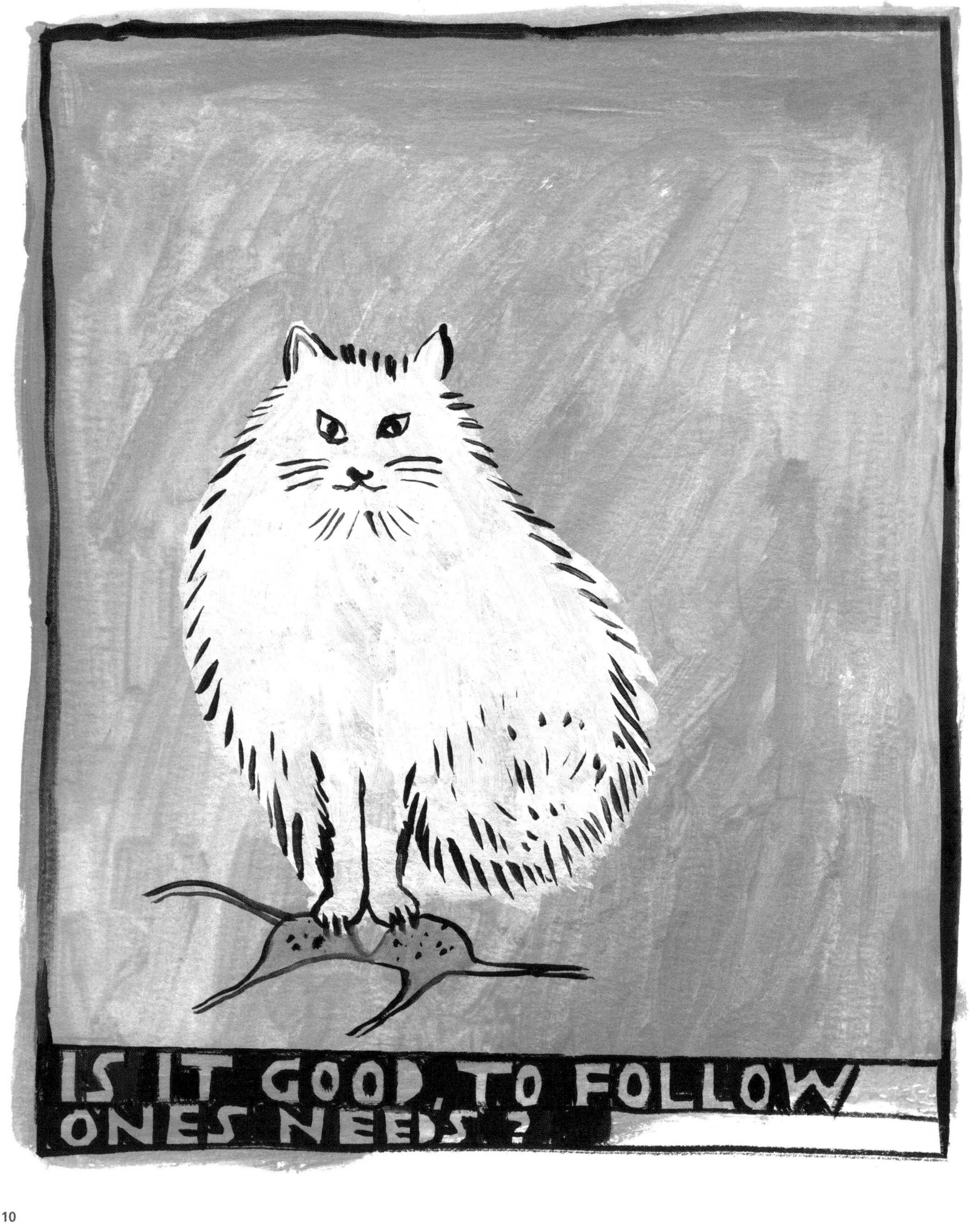
IS IT GOOD, TO FOLLOW
ONES NEEDS ?

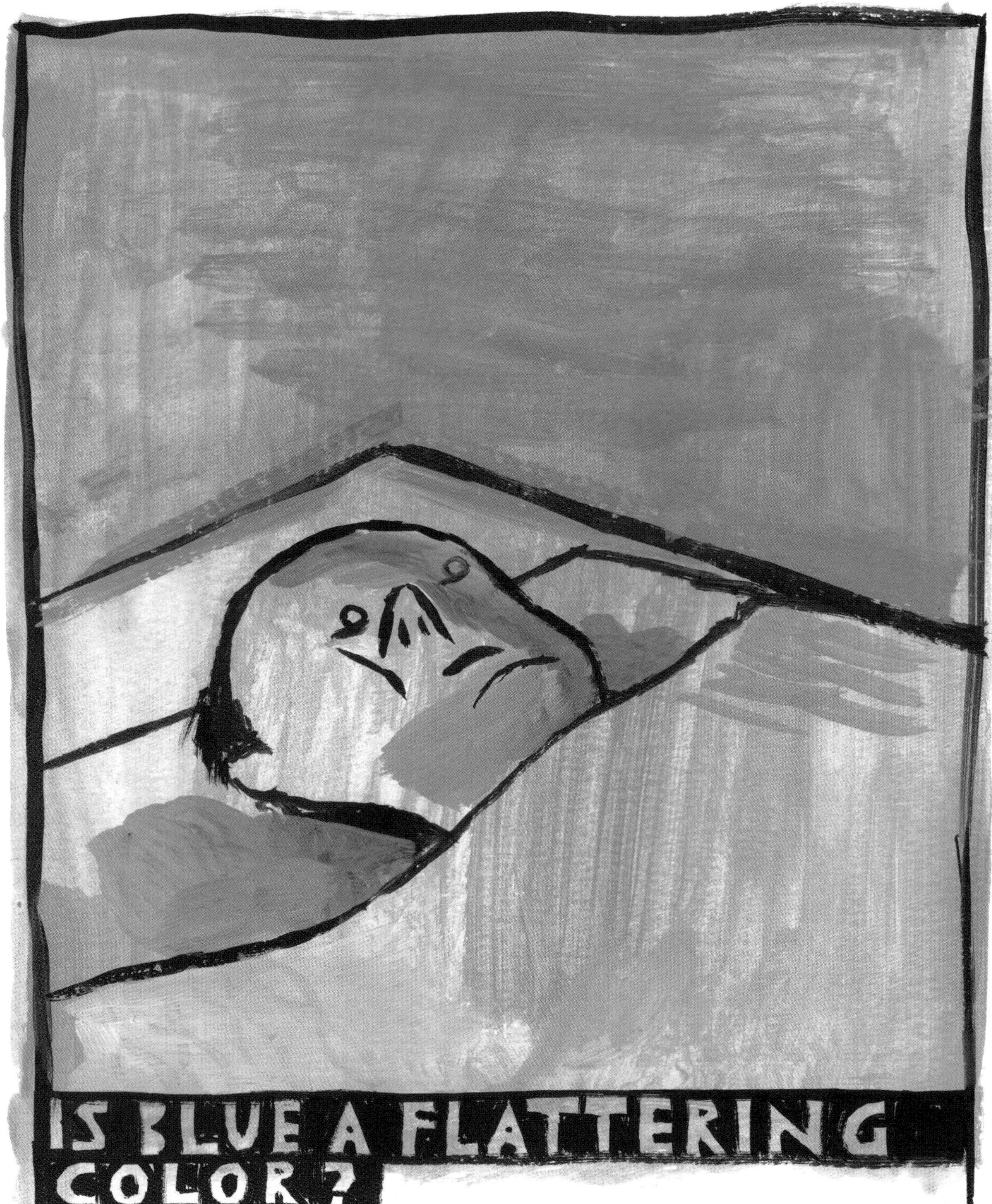
IS BLUE A FLATTERING
COLOR?

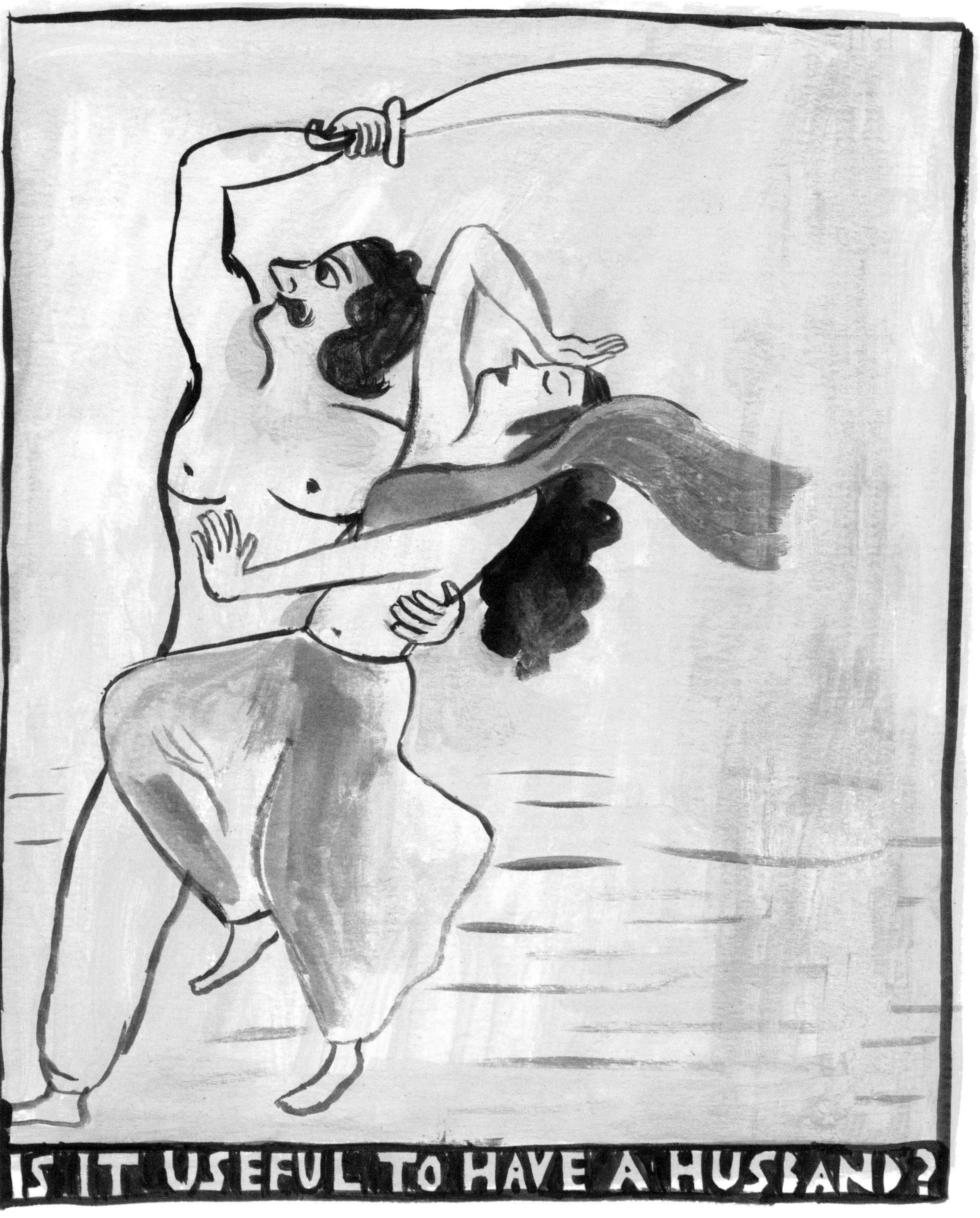
IS IT USEFUL TO HAVE A HUSBAND?

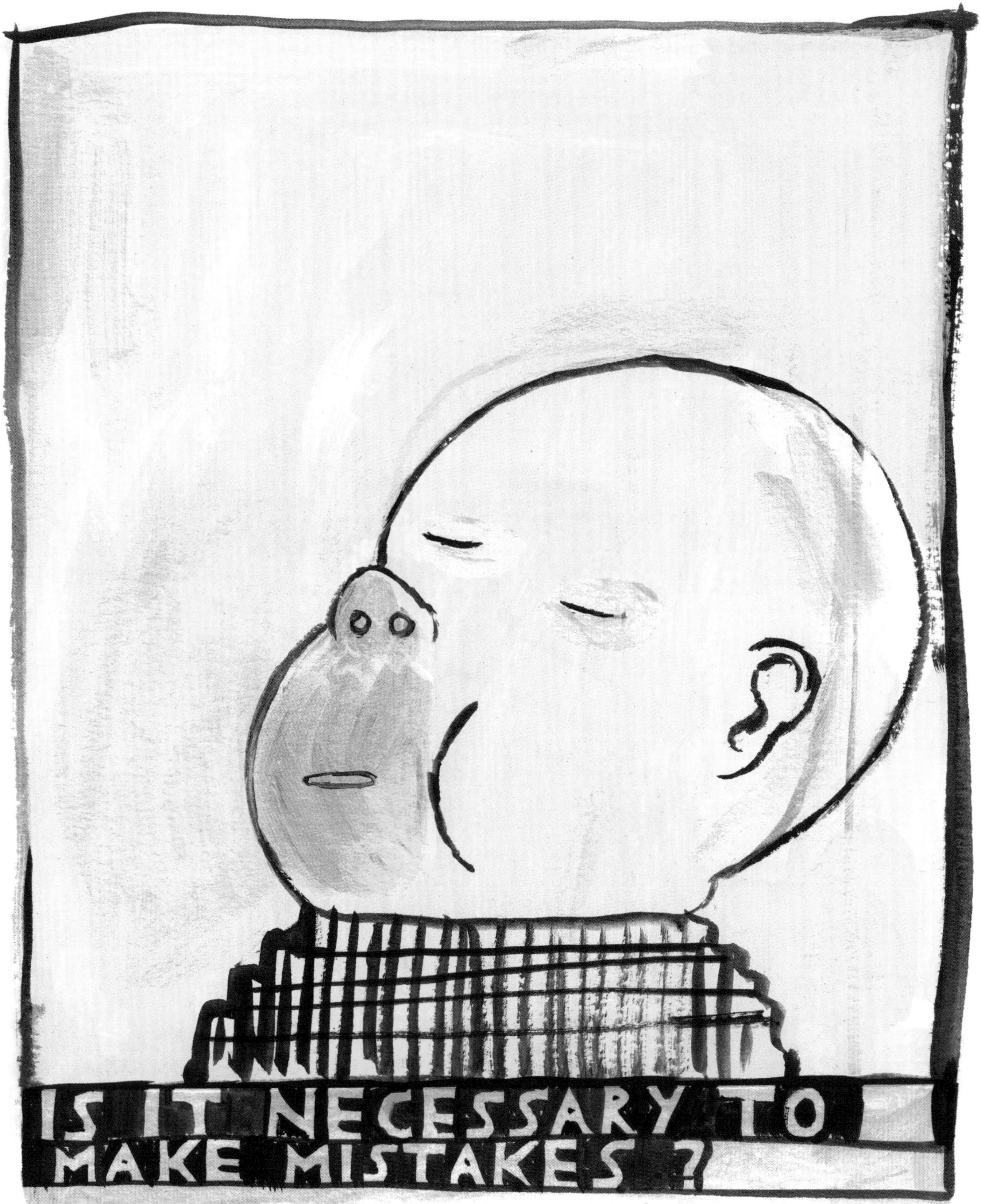
IS IT NECESSARY TO
MAKE MISTAKES ?

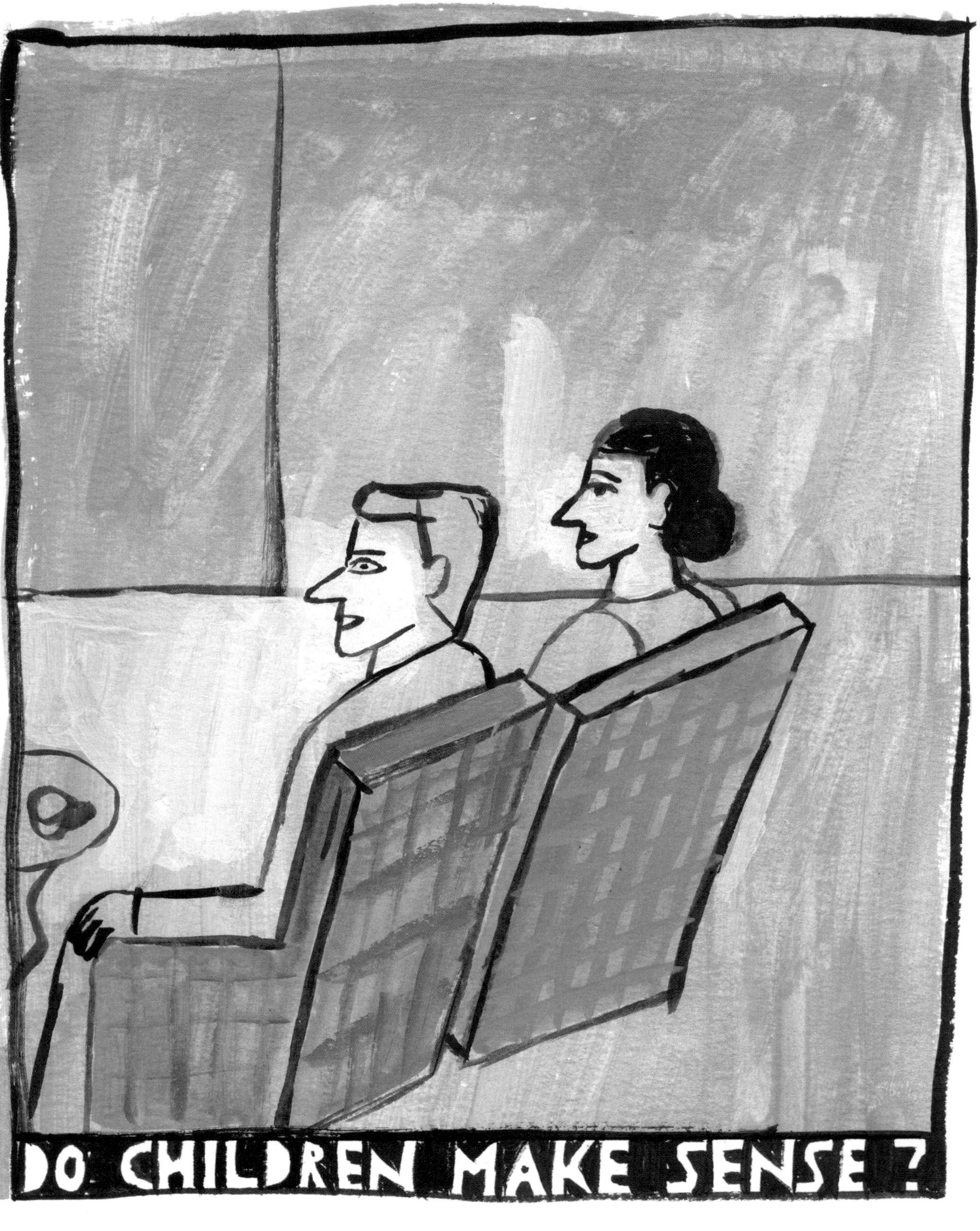
DO CHILDREN MAKE SENSE ?

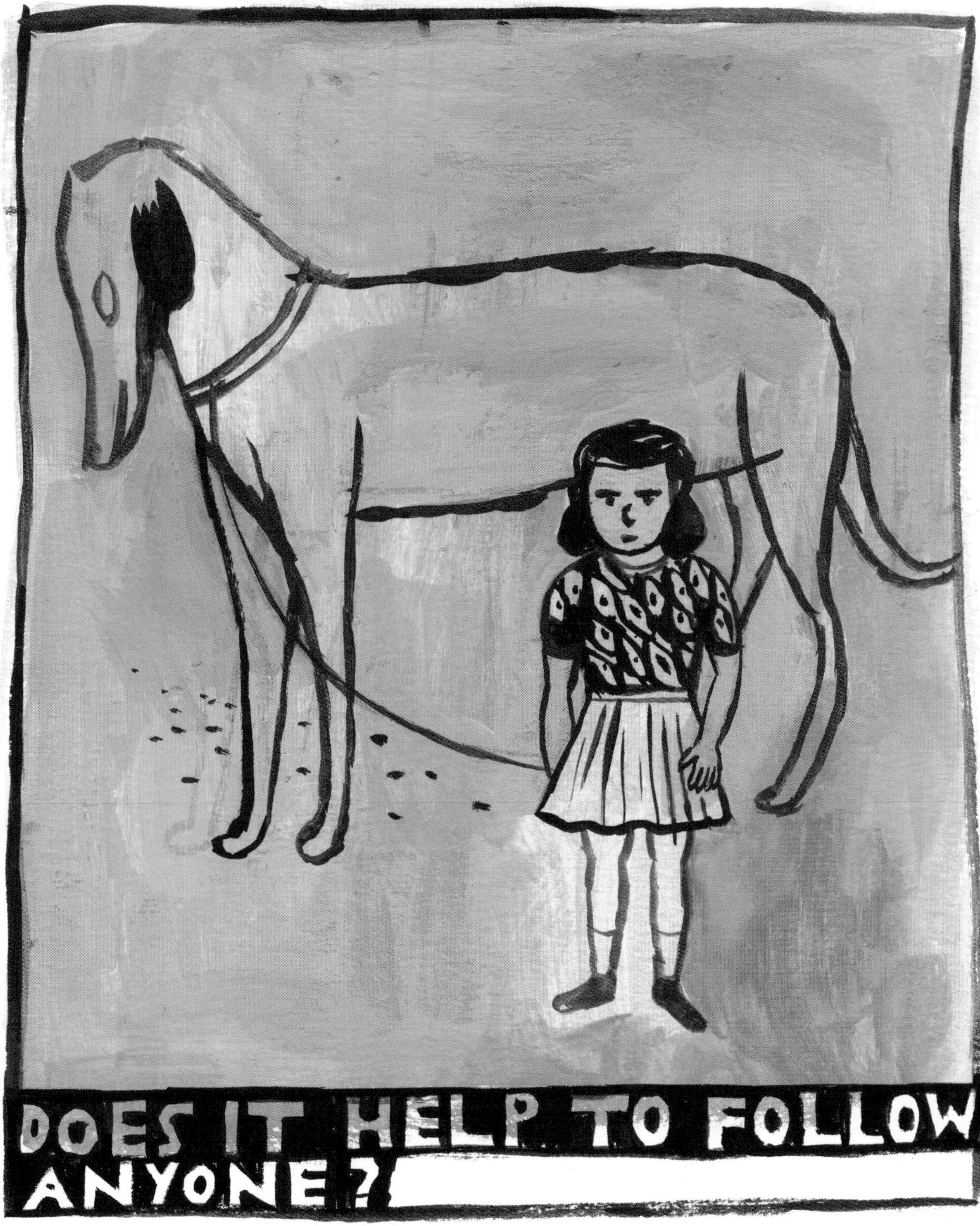
DOES IT HELP TO FOLLOW
ANYONE?

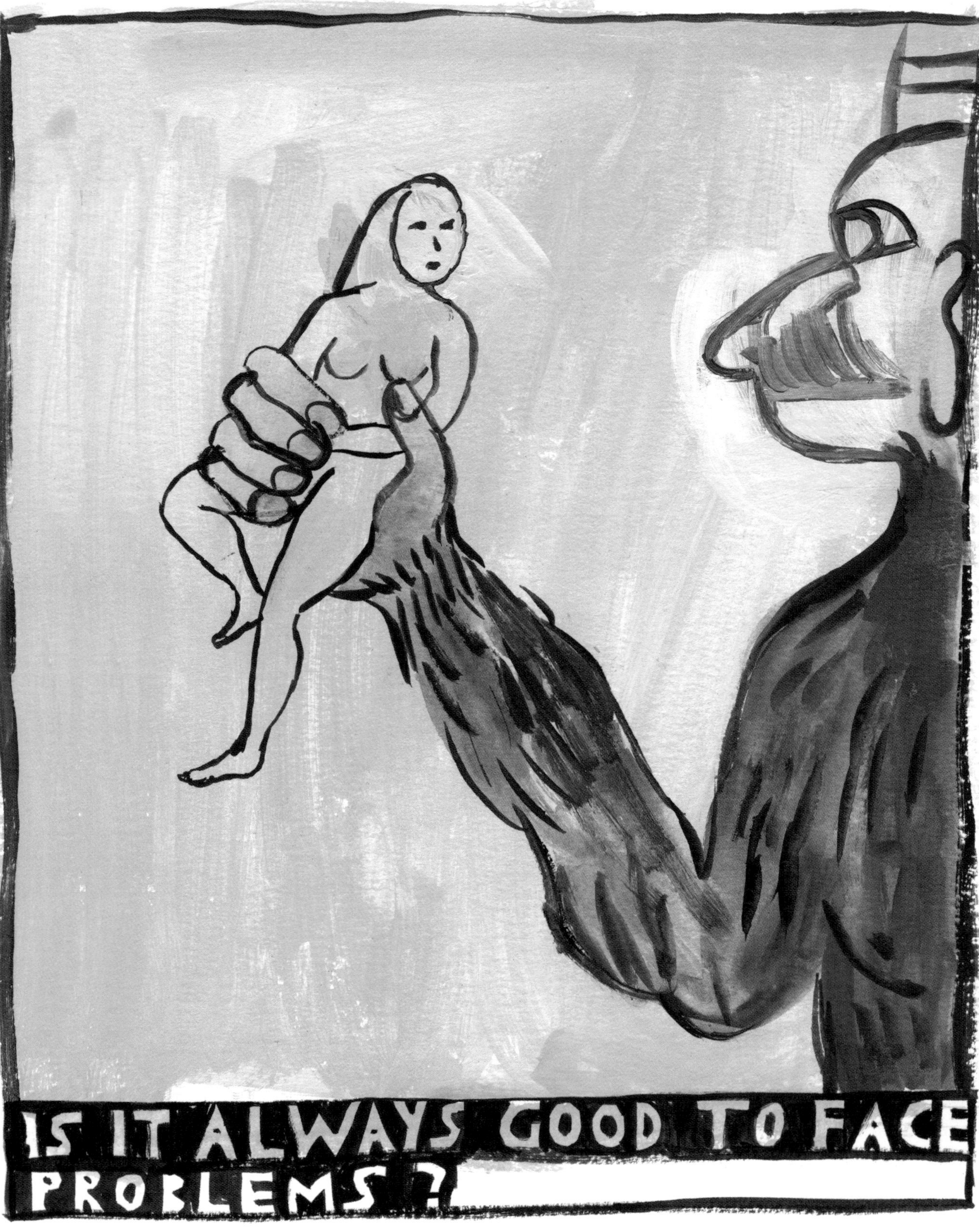
IS IT ALWAYS GOOD TO FACE
PROBLEMS ?

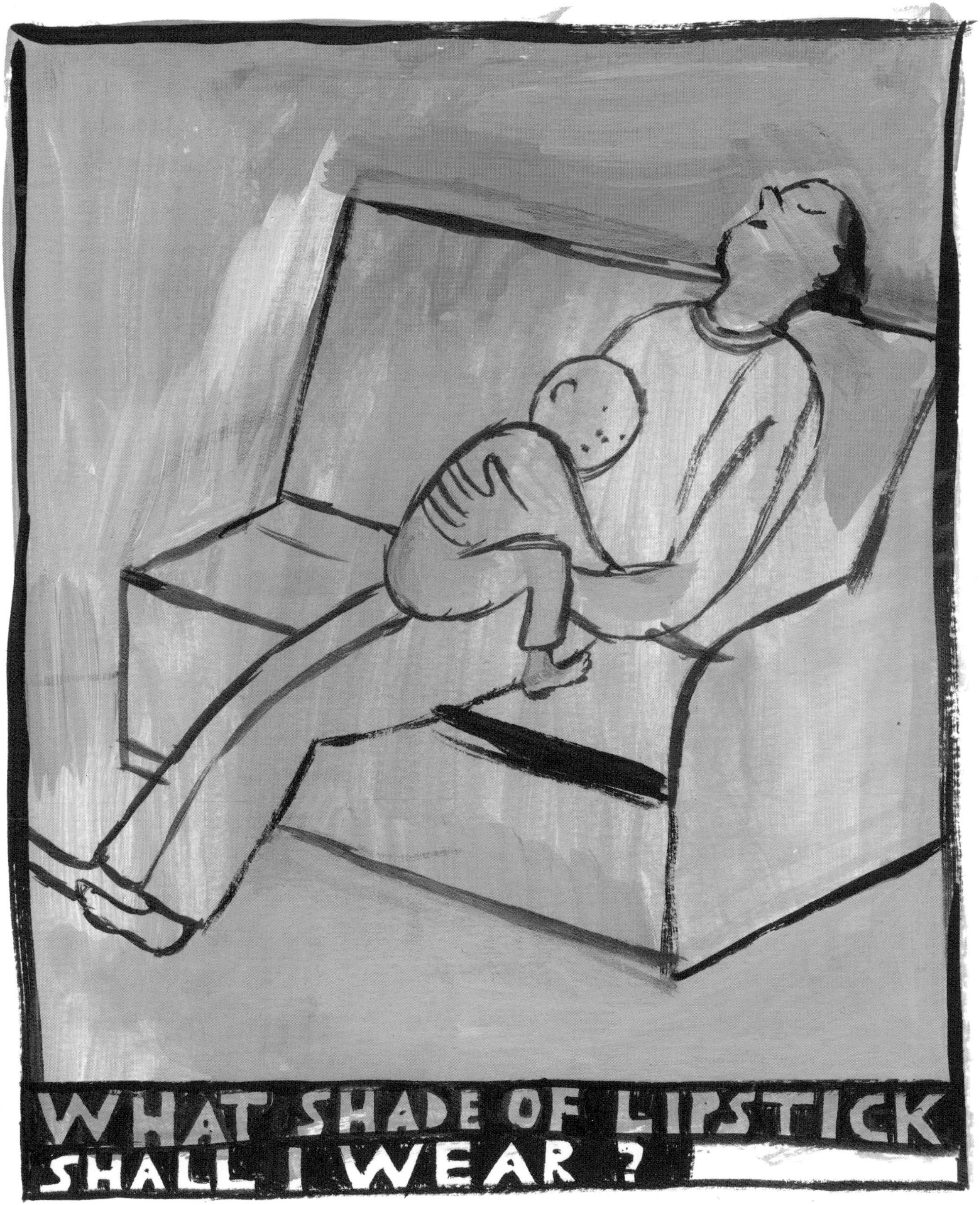
WHAT SHADE OF LIPSTICK
SHALL I WEAR ?

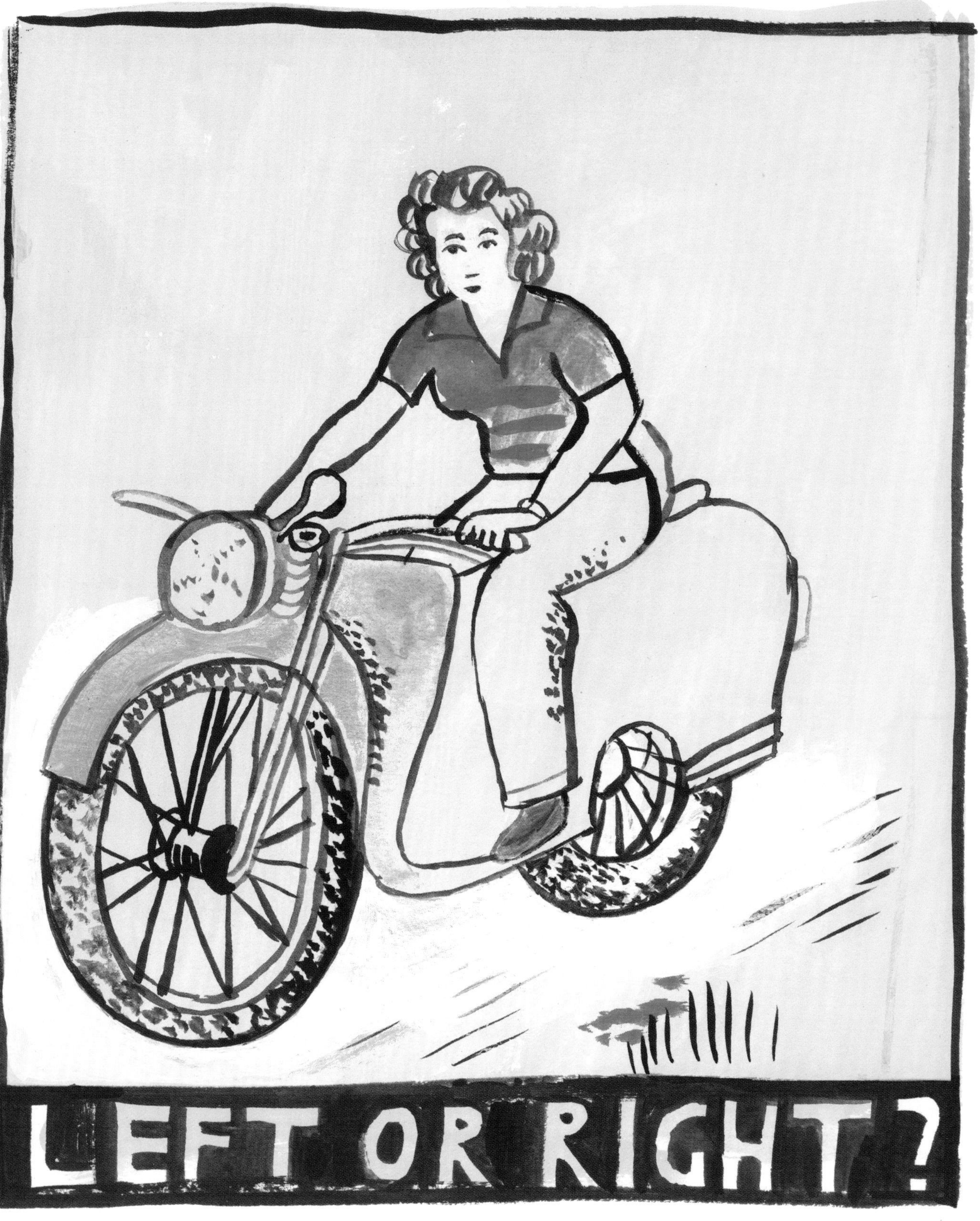
LEFT OR RIGHT?

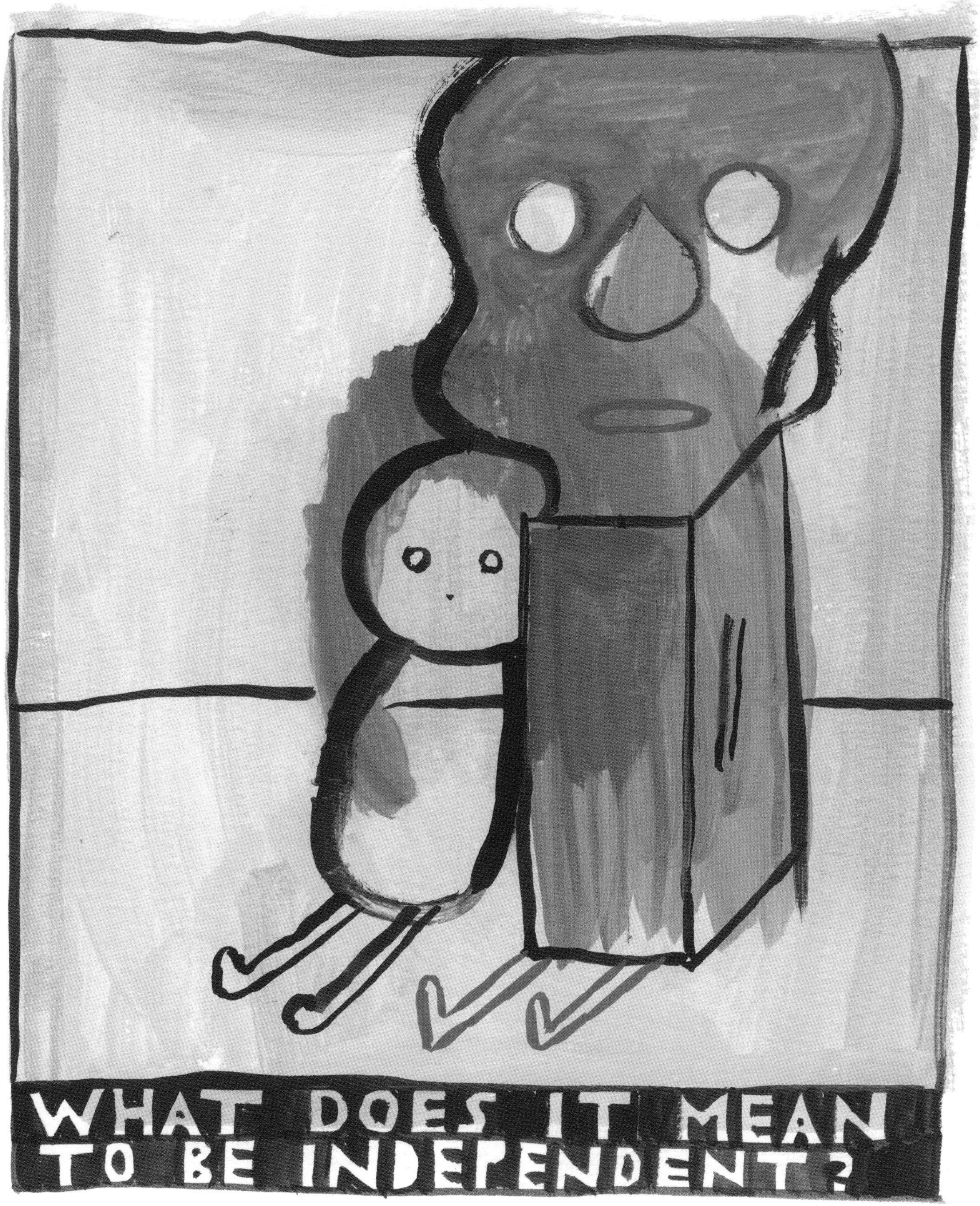
WHAT DOES IT MEAN
TO BE INDEPENDENT?

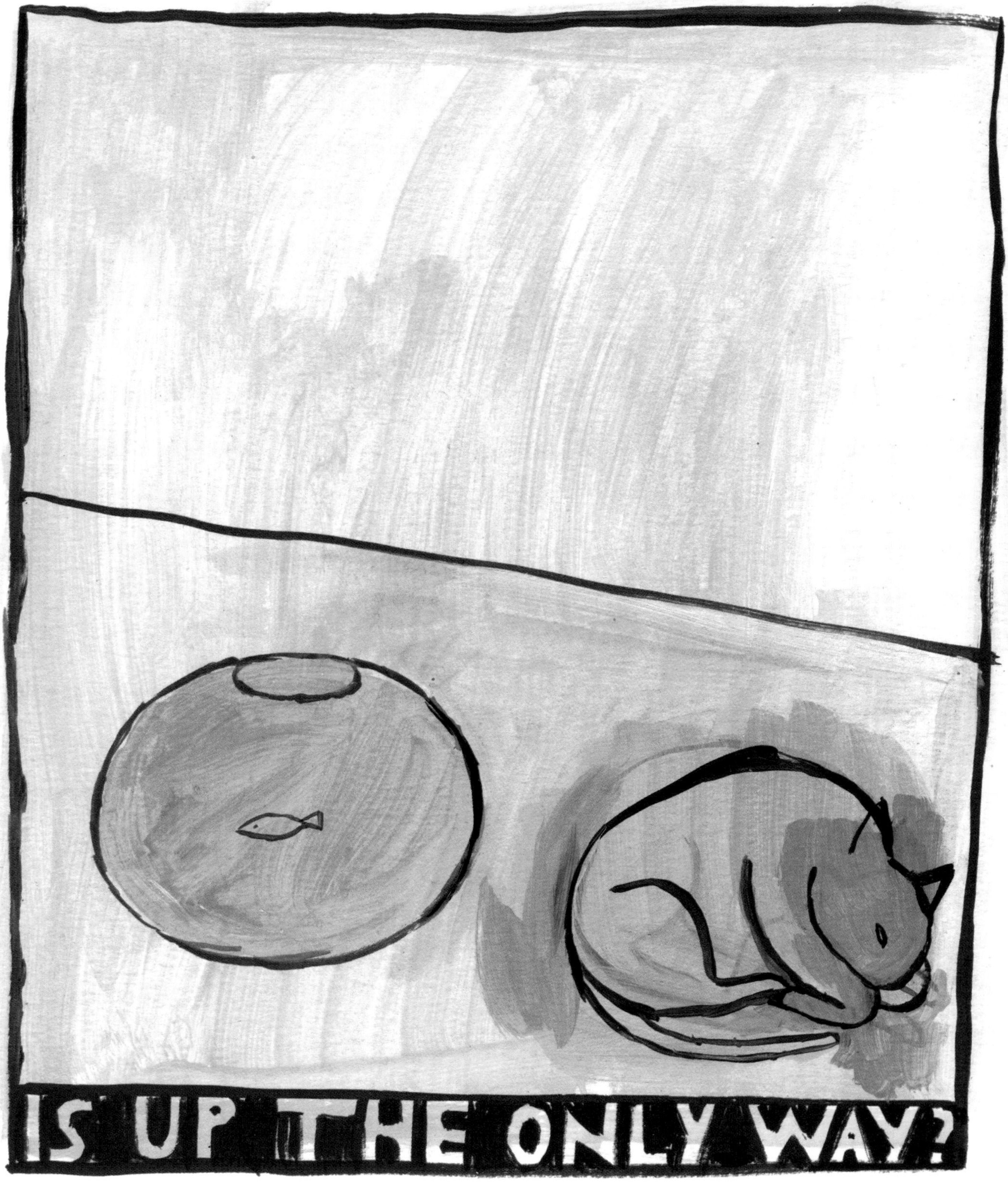
IS UP THE ONLY WAY?

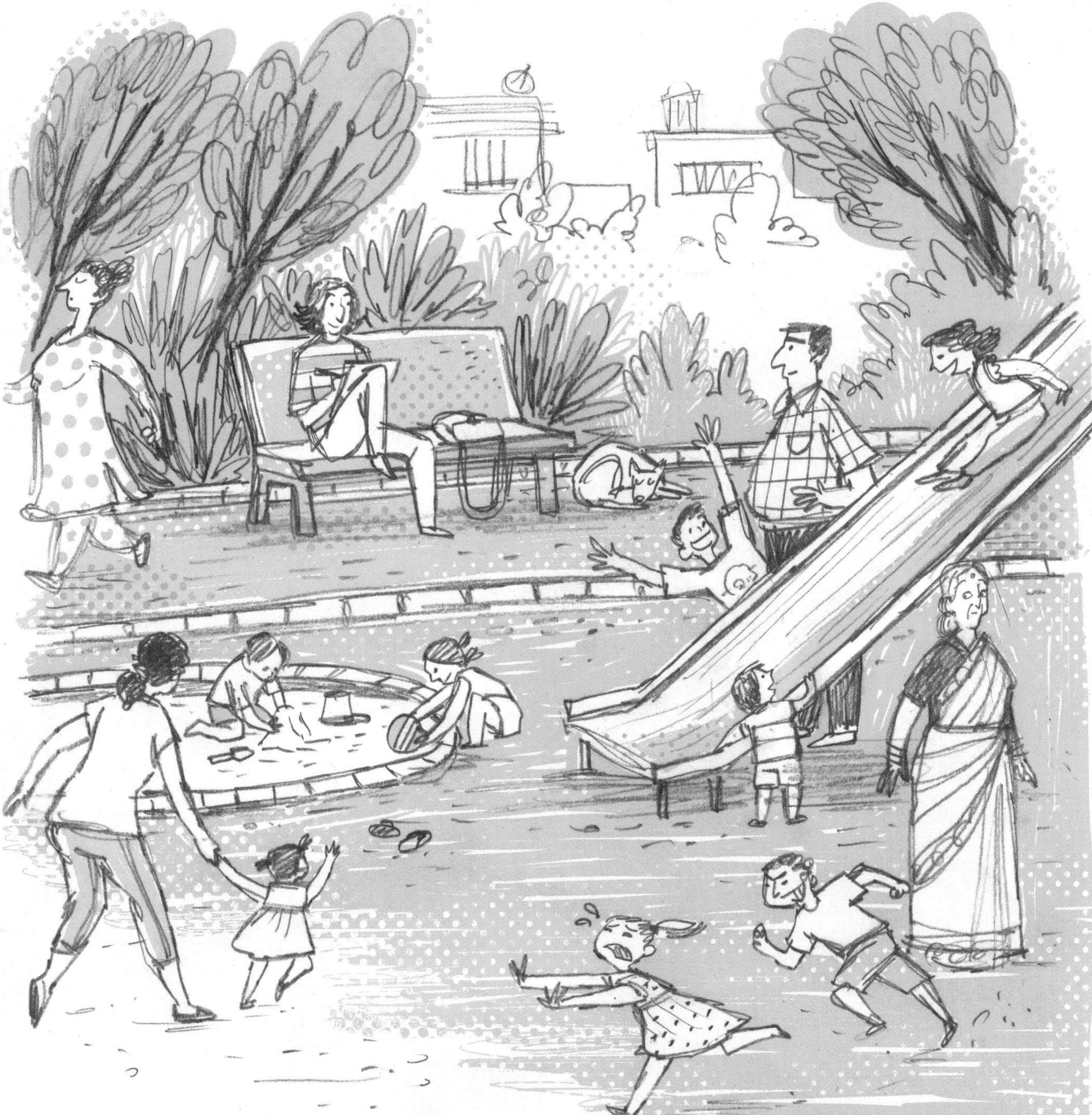

# OTHERLY URGES

- ARCHANA SREENIVASAN

IF I REMEMBER RIGHT, EVEN FROM THE AGE OF 17, I HAD NO DESIRE TO EVER BE A MOTHER.

ME AT 17

WHEN THE TIME IS RIGHT, YOU WILL WANT A CHILD.

YUCK!

LATE TWENTIES...

TRY IT WITH AN OPEN MIND YA! YOU DON'T HAVE TO MARRY IF YOU STILL DON'T WANT TO!

GULP!

MATRIMONY .COM

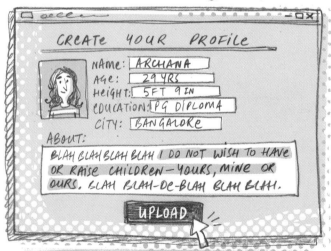

CREATE YOUR PROFILE

NAME: ARCHANA
AGE: 29 YRS
HEIGHT: 5 FT 9 IN
EDUCATION: PG DIPLOMA
CITY: BANGALORE

ABOUT:
BLAH BLAH BLAH BLAH I DO NOT WISH TO HAVE OR RAISE CHILDREN — YOURS, MINE OR OURS. BLAH BLAH-DE-BLAH BLAH BLAH.

UPLOAD

TO MY SURPRISE, A FEW POTENTIAL SUITORS STILL CONTACTED ME!

IN CASE YOU'RE WONDERING... YES, I'M MARRIED. AND NO, WE DIDN'T MEET ON A MATRIMONY SITE.

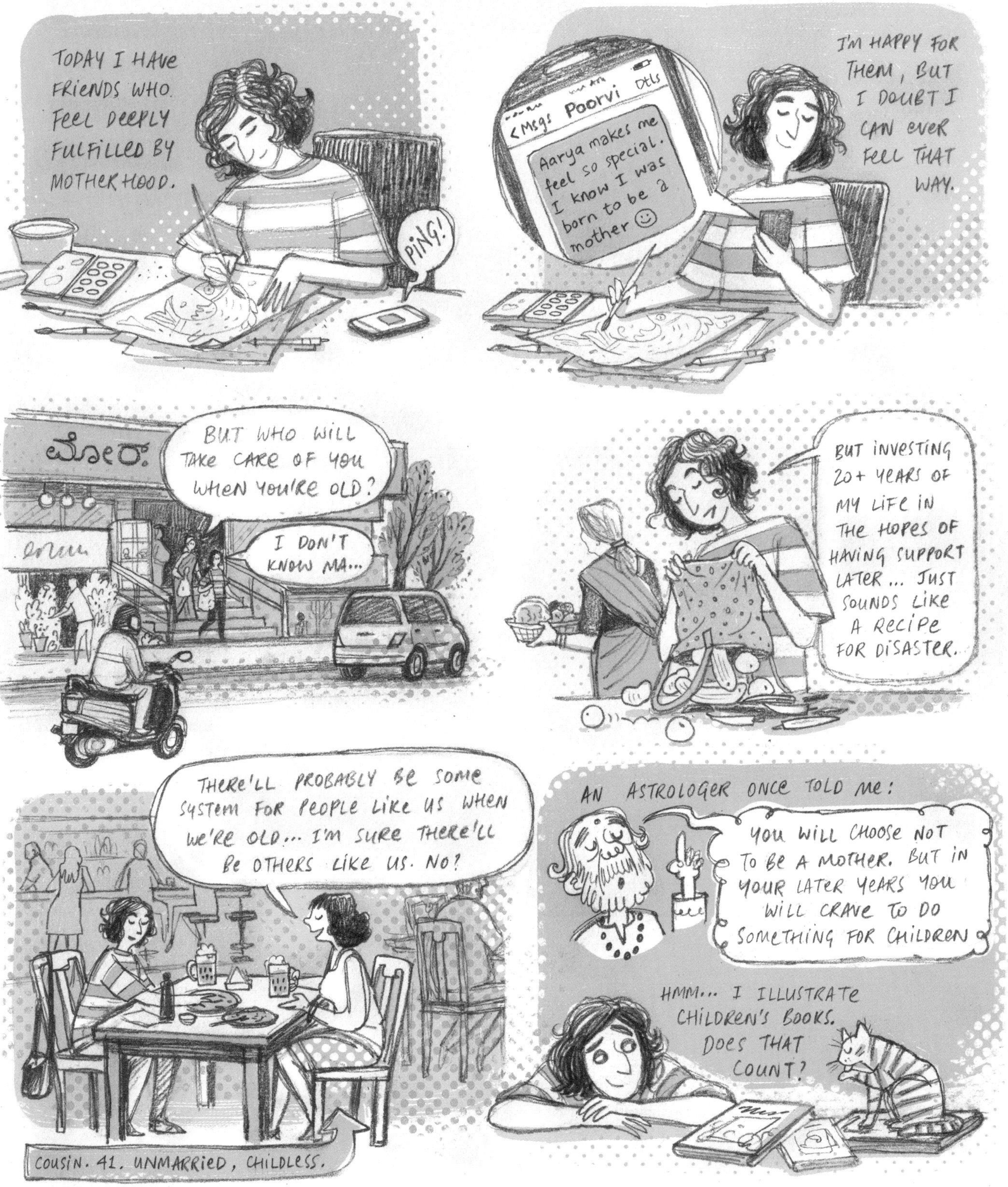
TODAY I HAVE FRIENDS WHO FEEL DEEPLY FULFILLED BY MOTHERHOOD.
PING!
I'M HAPPY FOR THEM, BUT I DOUBT I CAN EVER FEEL THAT WAY.
<Msgs Poorvi Dtls
Aarya makes me feel so special. I know I was born to be a mother ☺
BUT WHO WILL TAKE CARE OF YOU WHEN YOU'RE OLD?
I DON'T KNOW MA...
BUT INVESTING 20+ YEARS OF MY LIFE IN THE HOPES OF HAVING SUPPORT LATER... JUST SOUNDS LIKE A RECIPE FOR DISASTER.
THERE'LL PROBABLY BE SOME SYSTEM FOR PEOPLE LIKE US WHEN WE'RE OLD... I'M SURE THERE'LL BE OTHERS LIKE US. NO?
COUSIN. 41. UNMARRIED, CHILDLESS.
AN ASTROLOGER ONCE TOLD ME:
YOU WILL CHOOSE NOT TO BE A MOTHER. BUT IN YOUR LATER YEARS YOU WILL CRAVE TO DO SOMETHING FOR CHILDREN
HMM... I ILLUSTRATE CHILDREN'S BOOKS. DOES THAT COUNT?

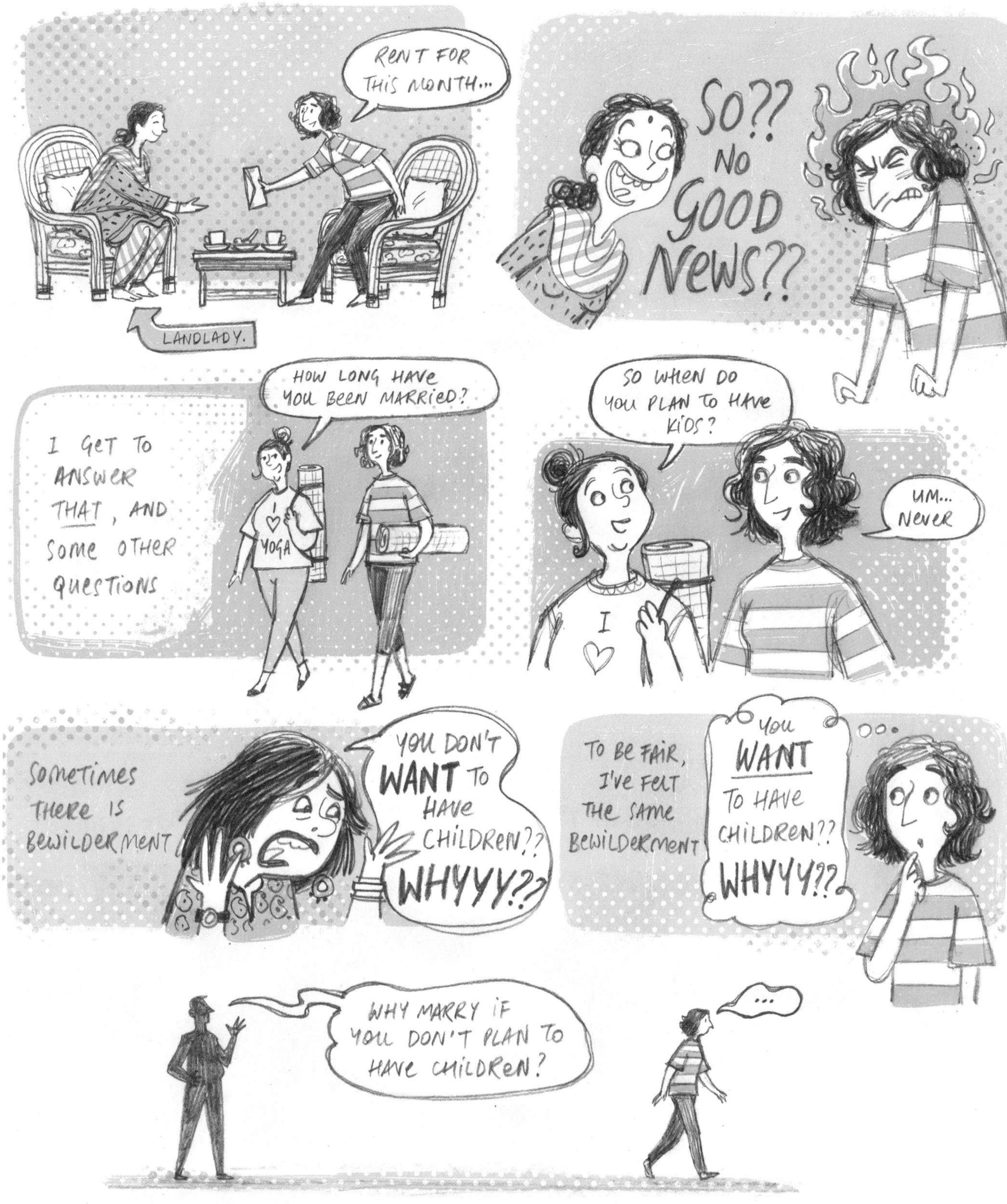
RENT FOR THIS MONTH...
LANDLADY.
SO?? NO GOOD NEWS??
HOW LONG HAVE YOU BEEN MARRIED?
I GET TO ANSWER THAT, AND SOME OTHER QUESTIONS
I ♥ YOGA
SO WHEN DO YOU PLAN TO HAVE KIDS?
UM... NEVER
I ♥
SOMETIMES THERE IS BEWILDERMENT
YOU DON'T WANT TO HAVE CHILDREN?? WHYYY??
TO BE FAIR, I'VE FELT THE SAME BEWILDERMENT
YOU WANT TO HAVE CHILDREN?? WHYYY??
WHY MARRY IF YOU DON'T PLAN TO HAVE CHILDREN?
...

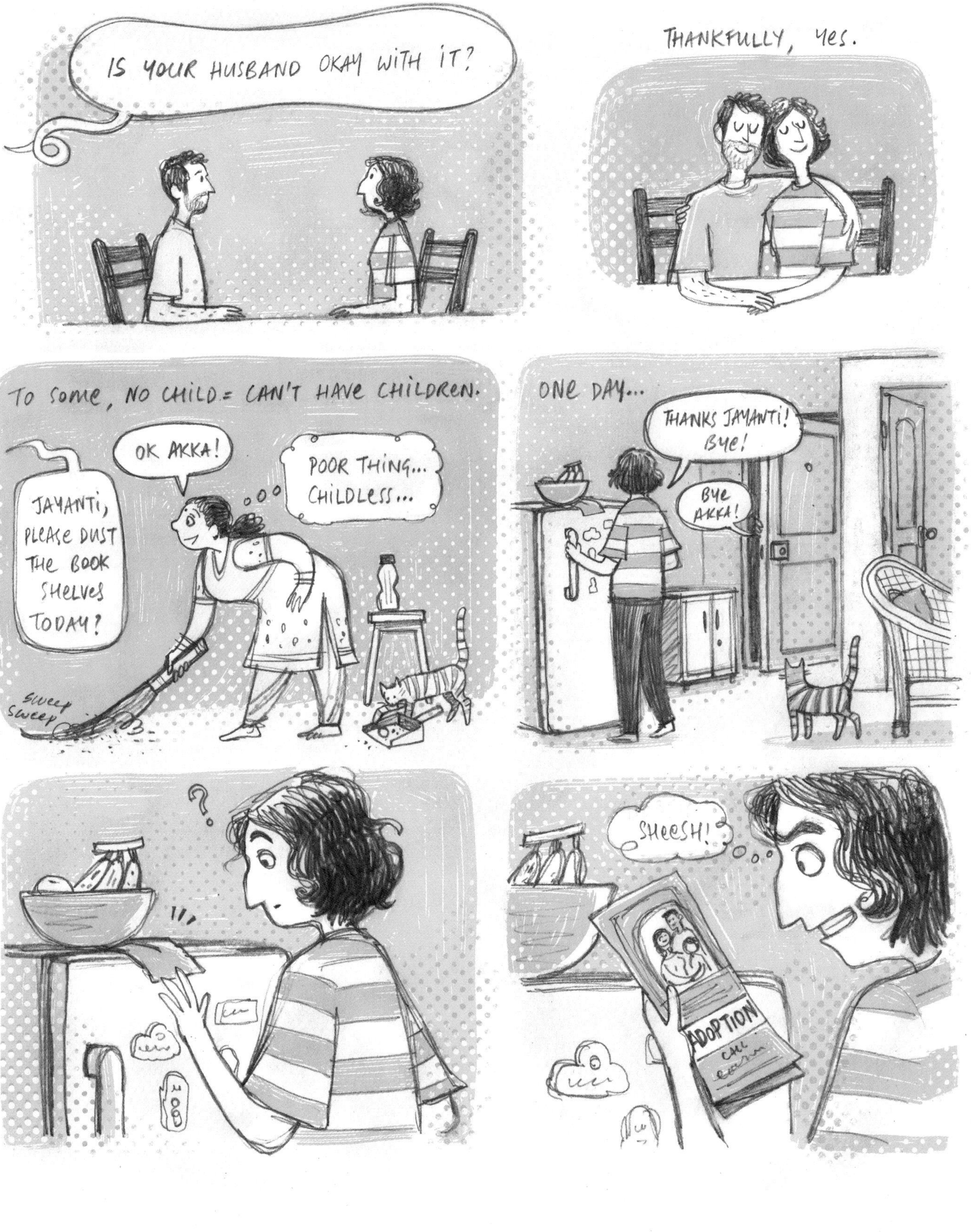
IS YOUR HUSBAND OKAY WITH IT?
THANKFULLY, YES.
TO SOME, NO CHILD = CAN'T HAVE CHILDREN.
JAYANTI, PLEASE DUST THE BOOK SHELVES TODAY?
OK AKKA!
POOR THING... CHILDLESS...
SWEEP SWEEP
ONE DAY...
THANKS JAYANTI! BYE!
BYE AKKA!
?
SHEESH!
ADOPTION
CALL

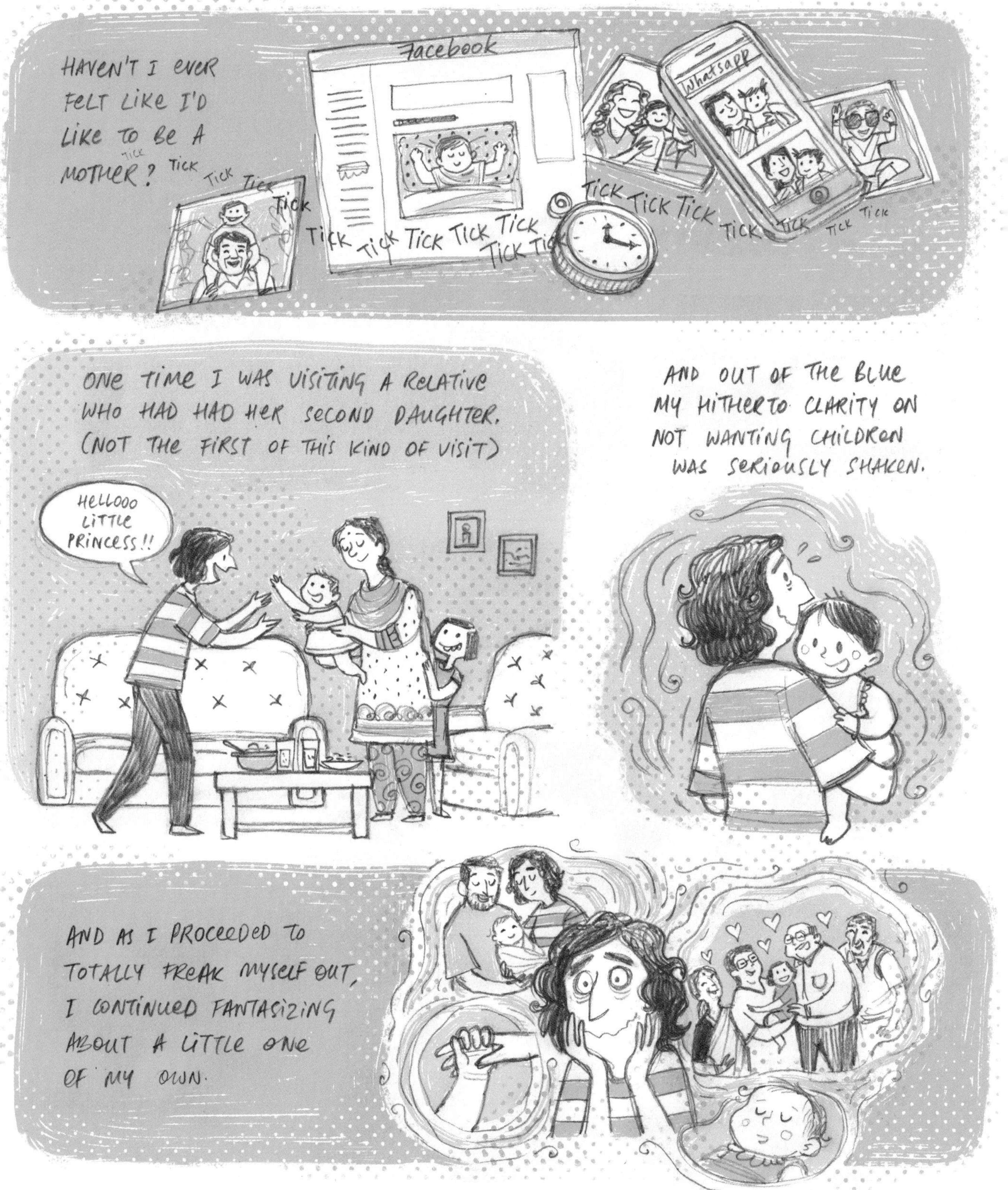
HAVEN'T I EVER FELT LIKE I'D LIKE TO BE A MOTHER?
Facebook
Whatsapp
Tick Tick Tick Tick Tick Tick Tick Tick Tick Tick Tick Tick Tick Tick Tick Tick Tick
ONE TIME I WAS VISITING A RELATIVE WHO HAD HAD HER SECOND DAUGHTER. (NOT THE FIRST OF THIS KIND OF VISIT)
HELLOOO LITTLE PRINCESS!!
AND OUT OF THE BLUE MY HITHERTO CLARITY ON NOT WANTING CHILDREN WAS SERIOUSLY SHAKEN.
AND AS I PROCEEDED TO TOTALLY FREAK MYSELF OUT, I CONTINUED FANTASIZING ABOUT A LITTLE ONE OF MY OWN.

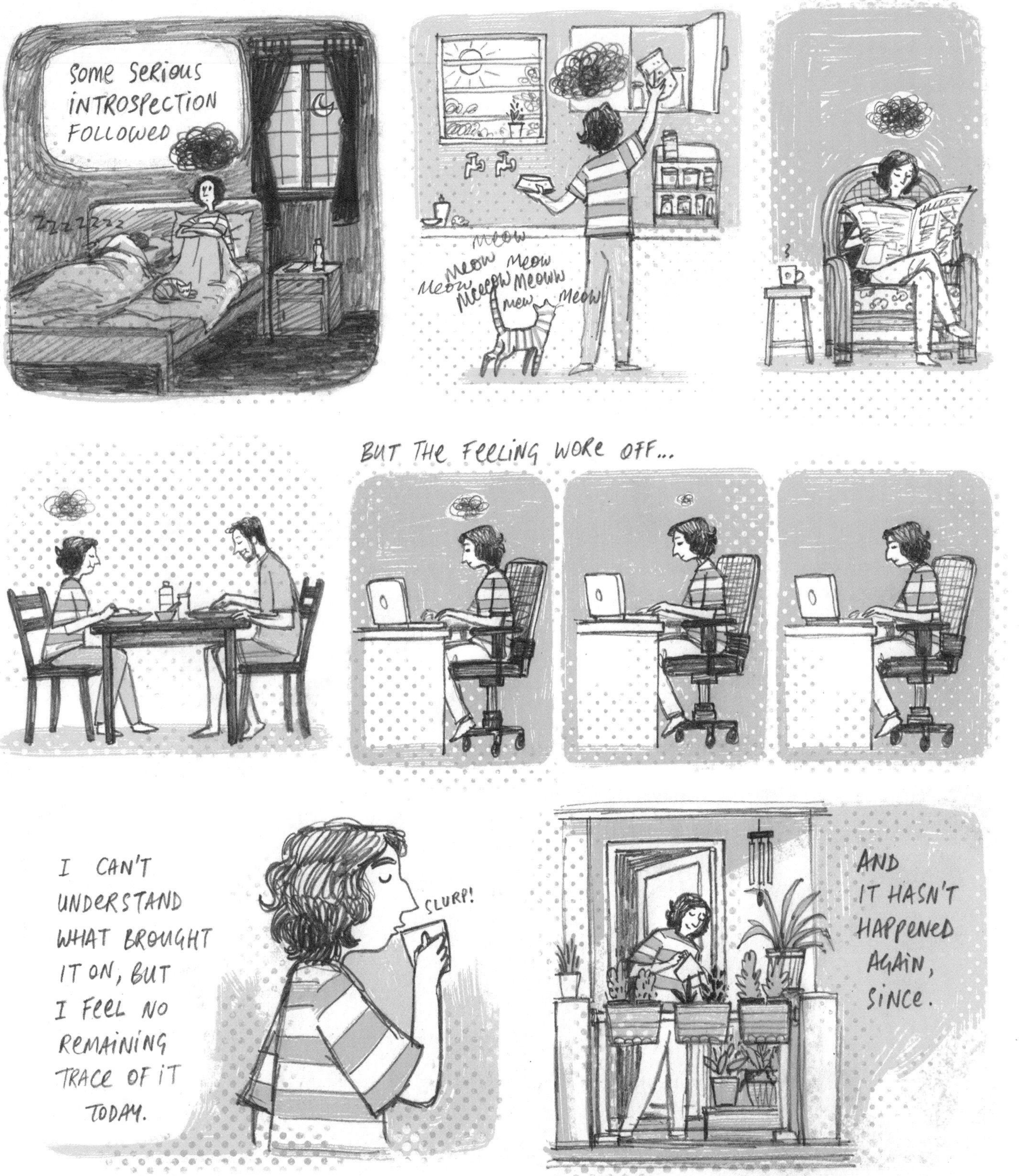
SOME SERIOUS INTROSPECTION FOLLOWED
ZZZZZZZ
MEOW
MEOW
MEOW
MEOW
MEEEOW
MEOWW
MEW
MEOW
BUT THE FEELING WORE OFF...
I CAN'T UNDERSTAND WHAT BROUGHT IT ON, BUT I FEEL NO REMAINING TRACE OF IT TODAY.
SLURP!
AND IT HASN'T HAPPENED AGAIN, SINCE.

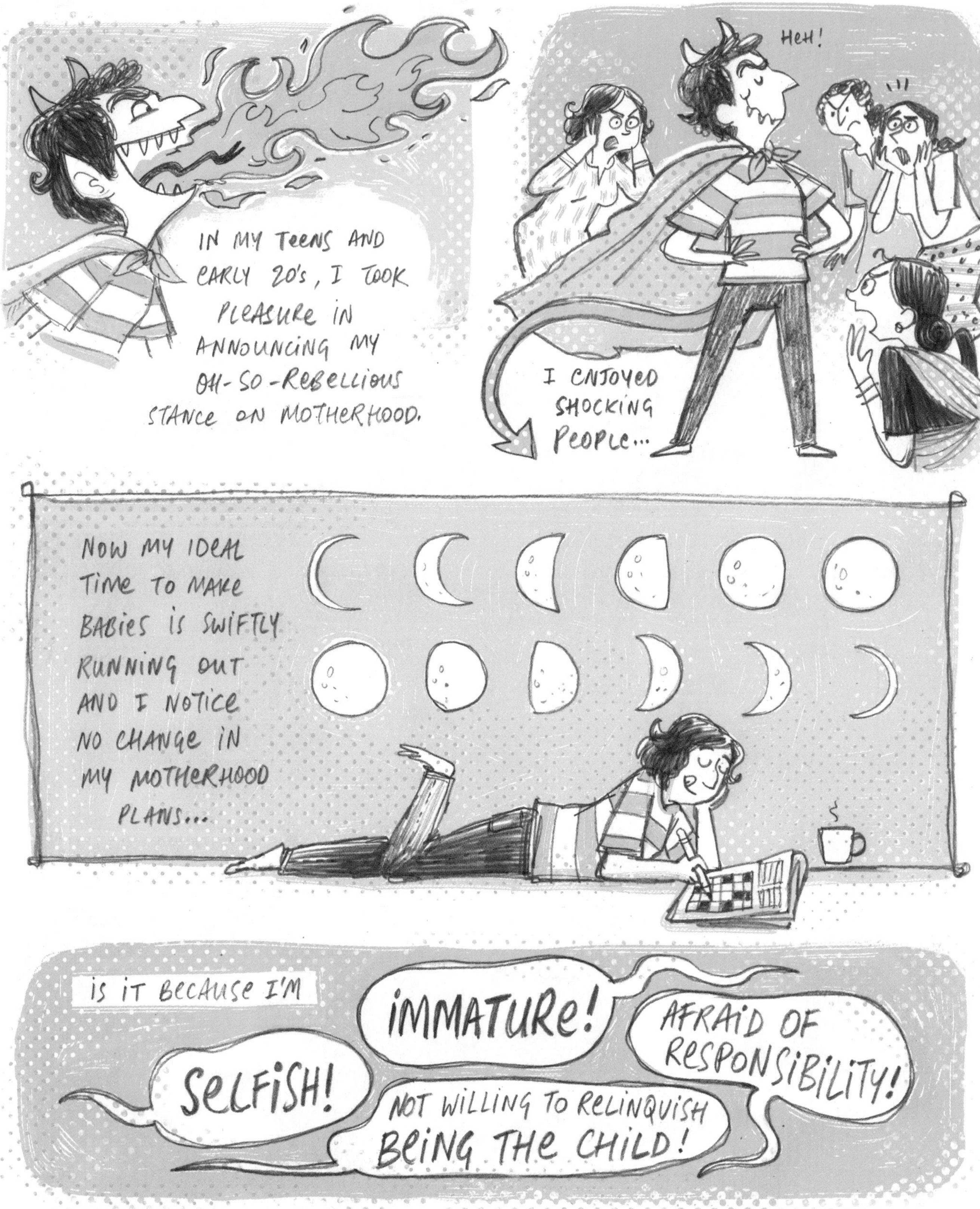
IN MY TEENS AND EARLY 20's, I TOOK PLEASURE IN ANNOUNCING MY OH-SO-REBELLIOUS STANCE ON MOTHERHOOD.
HEH!
I ENJOYED SHOCKING PEOPLE...
NOW MY IDEAL TIME TO MAKE BABIES IS SWIFTLY RUNNING OUT AND I NOTICE NO CHANGE IN MY MOTHERHOOD PLANS...
IS IT BECAUSE I'M
IMMATURE!
AFRAID OF RESPONSIBILITY!
SELFISH!
NOT WILLING TO RELINQUISH BEING THE CHILD!

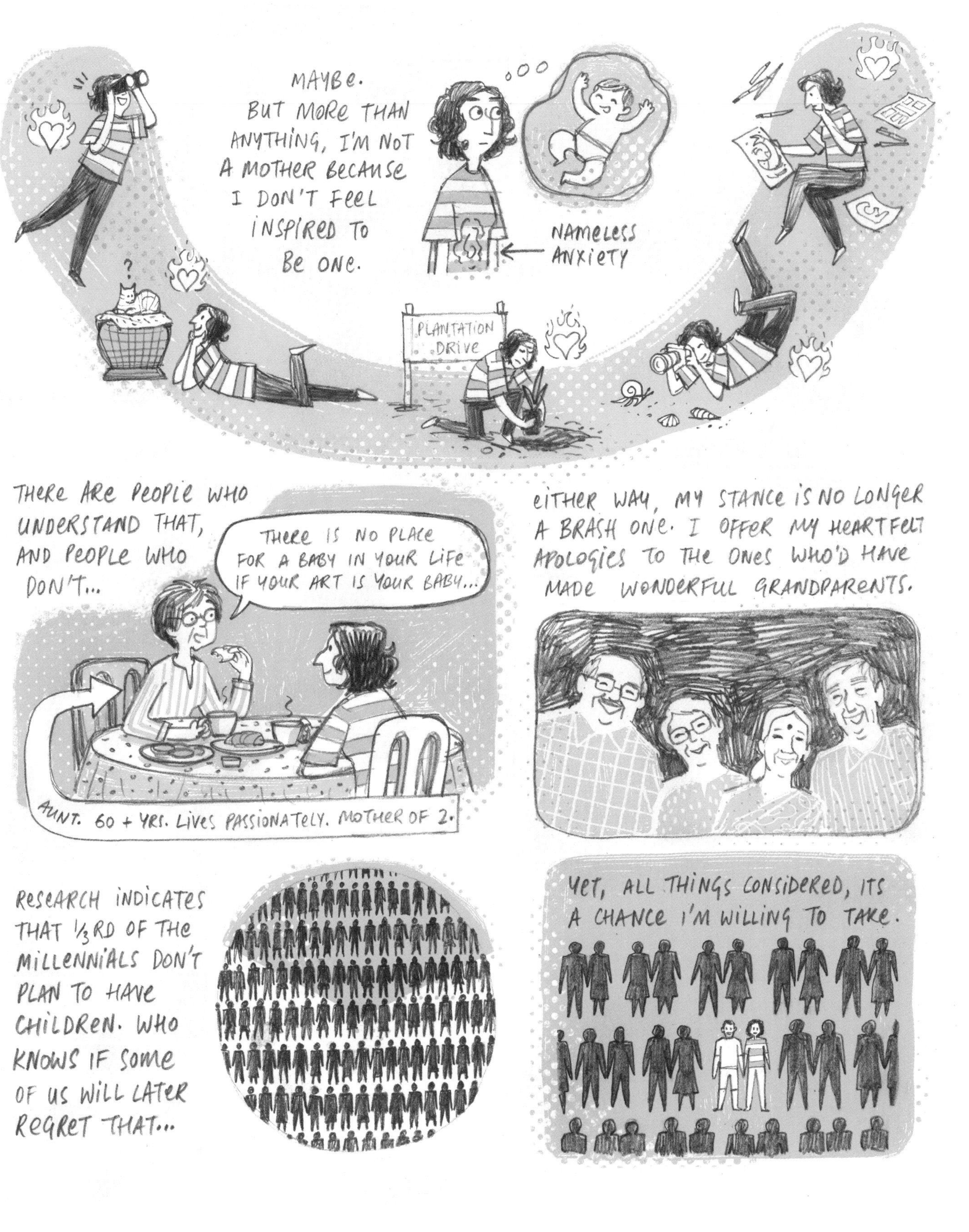
MAYBE.
BUT MORE THAN ANYTHING, I'M NOT A MOTHER BECAUSE I DON'T FEEL INSPIRED TO BE ONE.
NAMELESS ANXIETY
PLANTATION DRIVE
THERE ARE PEOPLE WHO UNDERSTAND THAT, AND PEOPLE WHO DON'T...
THERE IS NO PLACE FOR A BABY IN YOUR LIFE IF YOUR ART IS YOUR BABY...
AUNT. 60 + YRS. LIVES PASSIONATELY. MOTHER OF 2.
EITHER WAY, MY STANCE IS NO LONGER A BRASH ONE. I OFFER MY HEARTFELT APOLOGIES TO THE ONES WHO'D HAVE MADE WONDERFUL GRANDPARENTS.
RESEARCH INDICATES THAT 1/3RD OF THE MILLENNIALS DON'T PLAN TO HAVE CHILDREN. WHO KNOWS IF SOME OF US WILL LATER REGRET THAT...
YET, ALL THINGS CONSIDERED, ITS A CHANCE I'M WILLING TO TAKE.

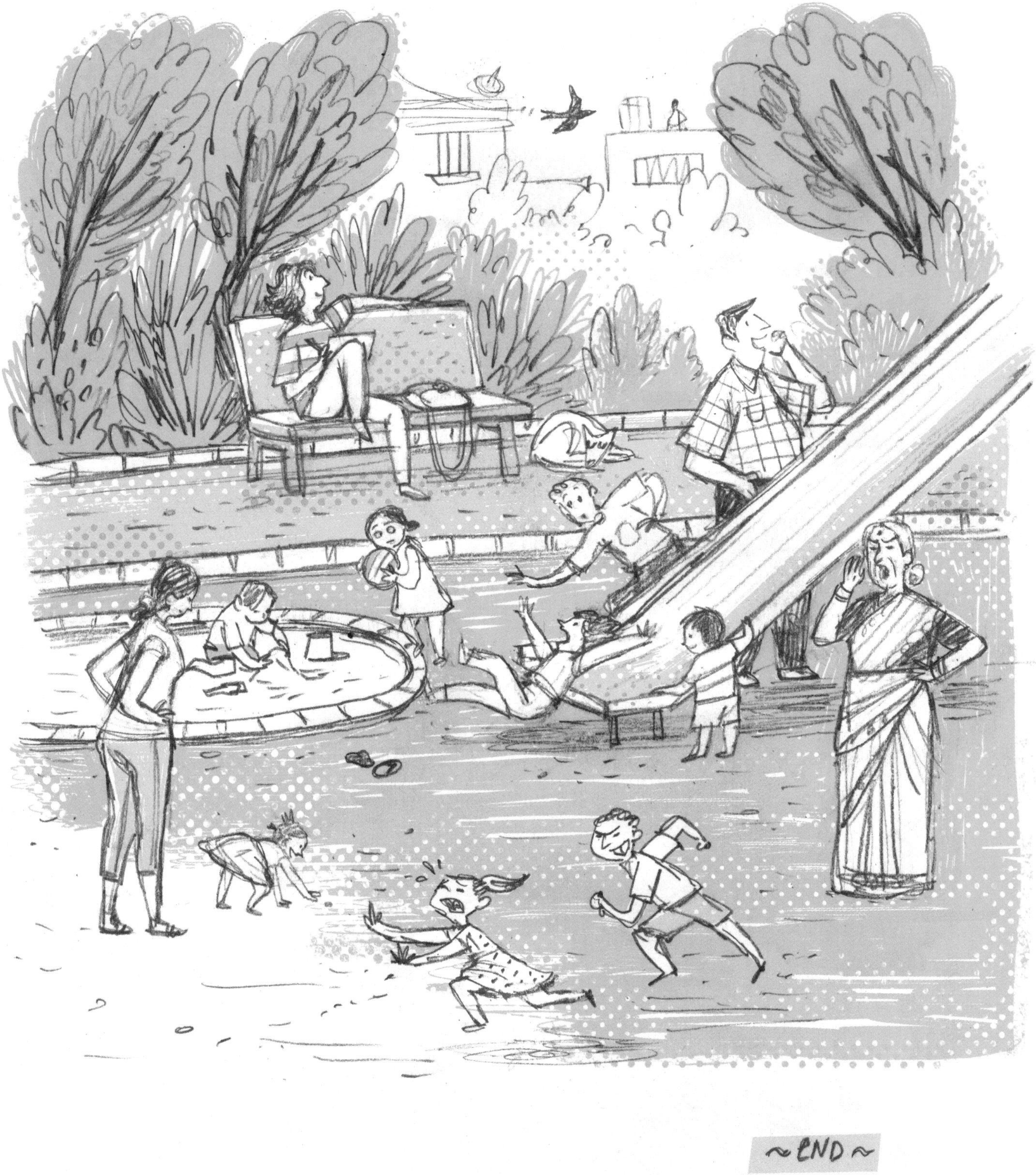

~END~

# WHAT'S WRONG WITH ME

At work, in the kitchen:

Andrea brought her new baby!

You don't want to see it?

Oh-ehm,... no?

What's wrong with wrong with her? Wh Wrong ith her? What's wrong with h wr with h Wha w her? 's w e on th er

## Weekend Mum

yay! Ulli Mama is here!

My son was born shortly after my eighteenth birthday. He lived with his grandparents in the country while I looked for work in the city.

Naturally, I always felt guilty. One day I met a friend who was, of course, raising her child by herself.

I constantly feel guilty. I'm afraid that I'm not a good mum!

ullilu 2015

## The hairy question
My son has fallen in love.

She's American.

Wow, cool!

Apparently, Americans are completely obsessed with shaving their private parts...

... Mum!

What?

For a long time I was constantly asked if I wanted to have children. I always had a different answer, depending on my mood.

  Ha ha, I actually wanted to make my life simpler!

  You know I don't believe in the concept of a "person".

  I don't think I'd be resilient enough.

CLIMATE CHANGE
SPECIES LOSS
ENVIRONMENTAL CATASTROPHE

  Do I want children?

It's bad enough that reincarnation might be real!

Giggle

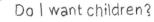

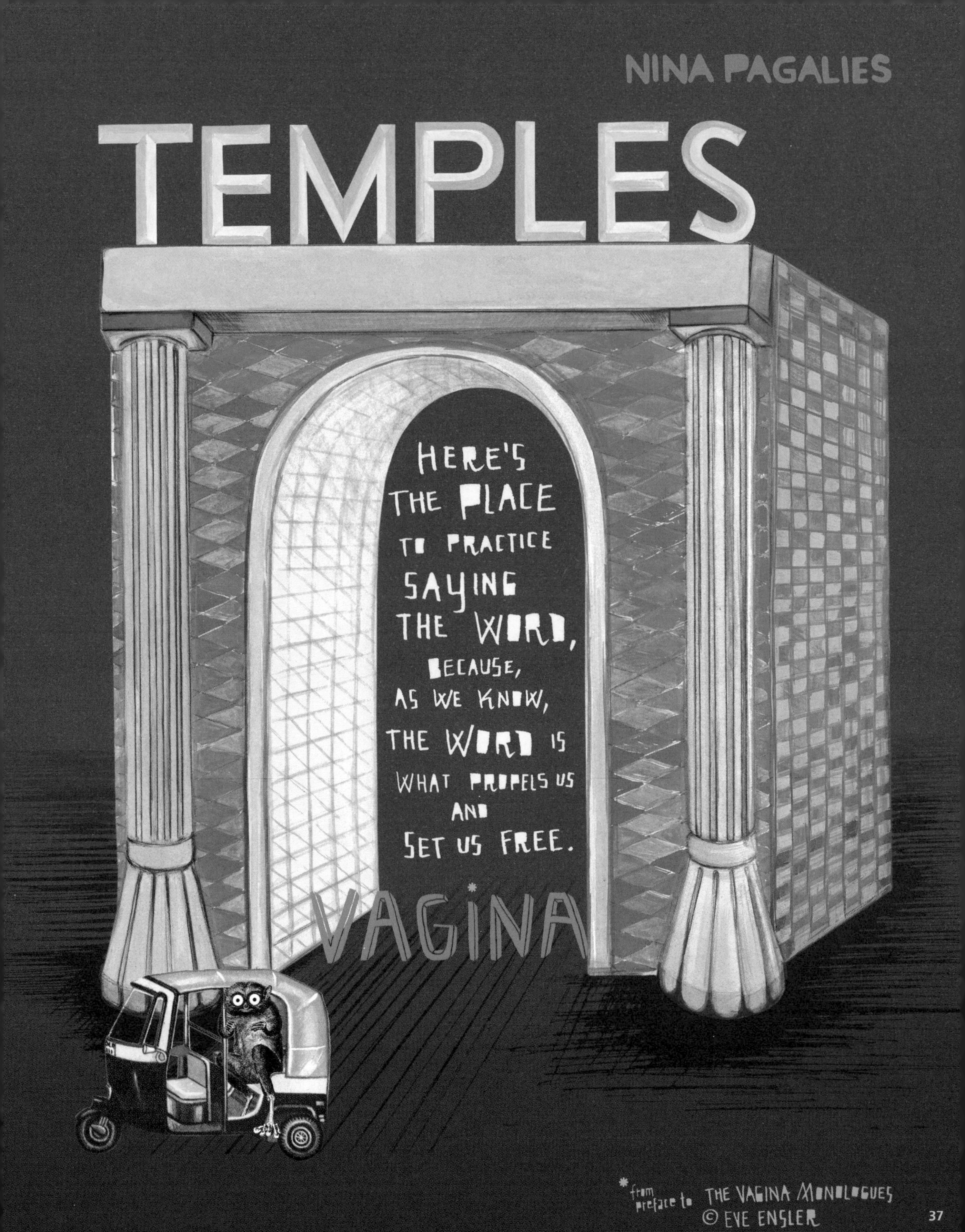
NINA PAGALIES
TEMPLES
HERE'S THE PLACE TO PRACTICE SAYING THE WORD, BECAUSE, AS WE KNOW, THE WORD IS WHAT PROPELS US AND SET US FREE.
VAGINA*
*from preface to THE VAGINA MONOLOGUES © EVE ENSLER

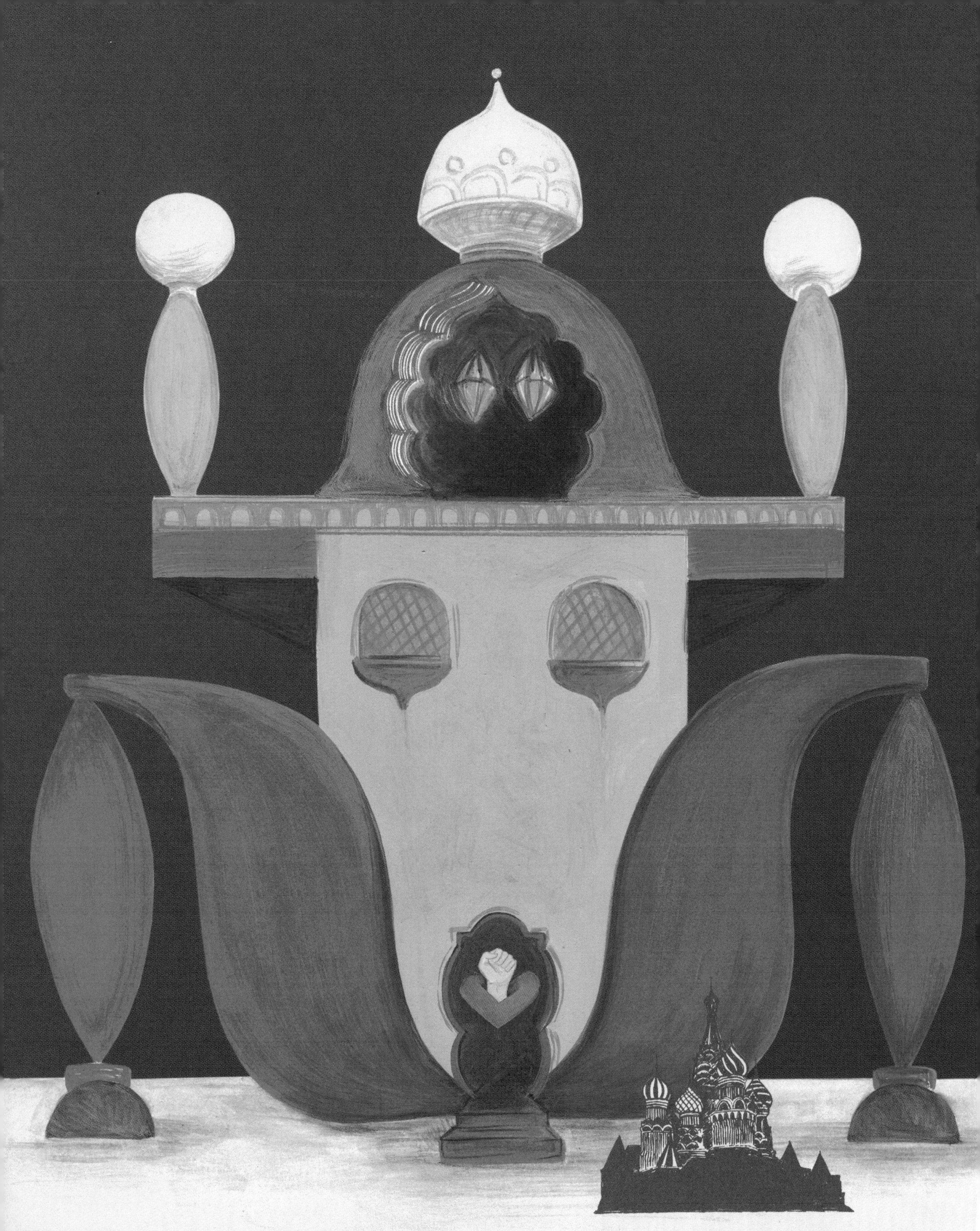

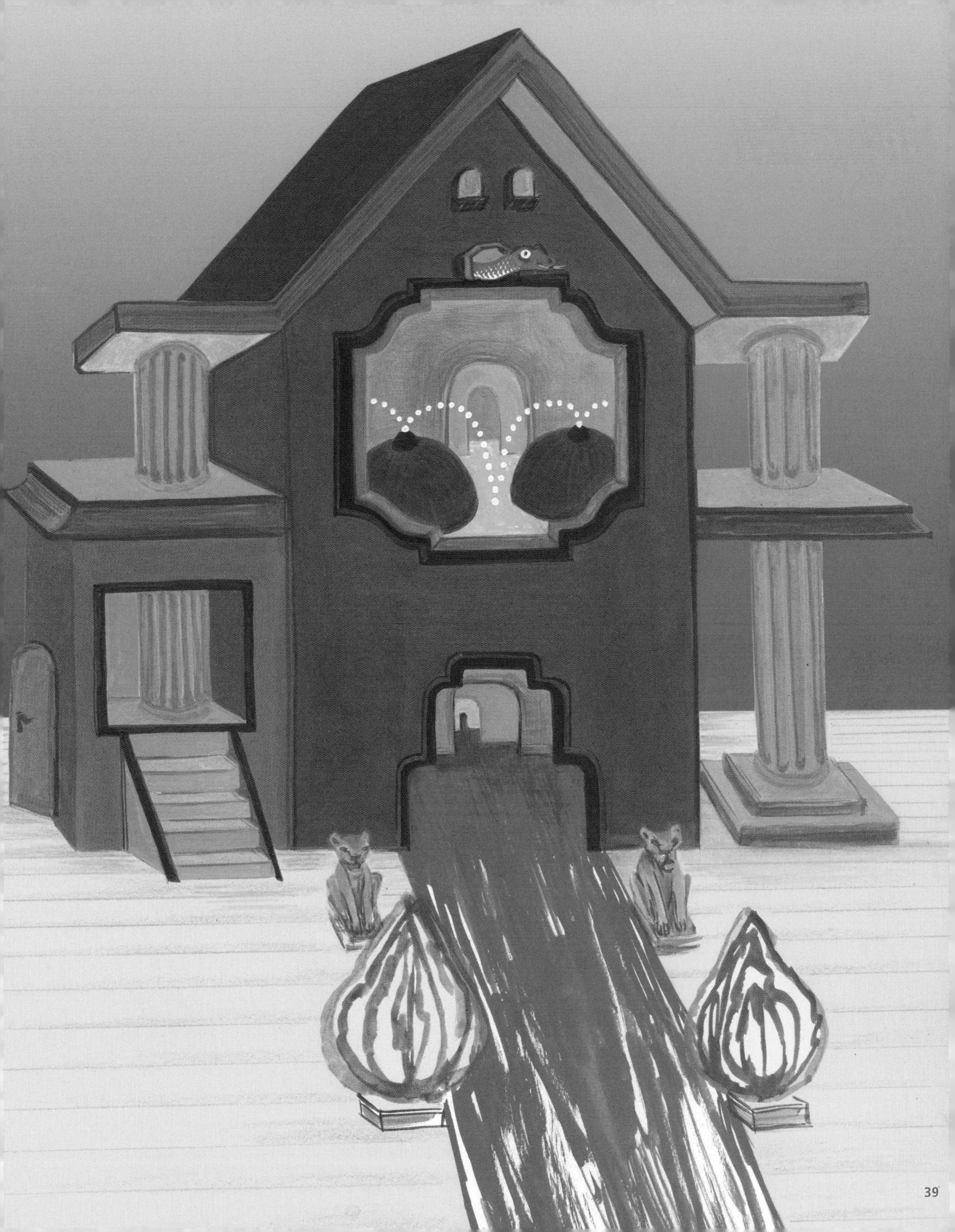

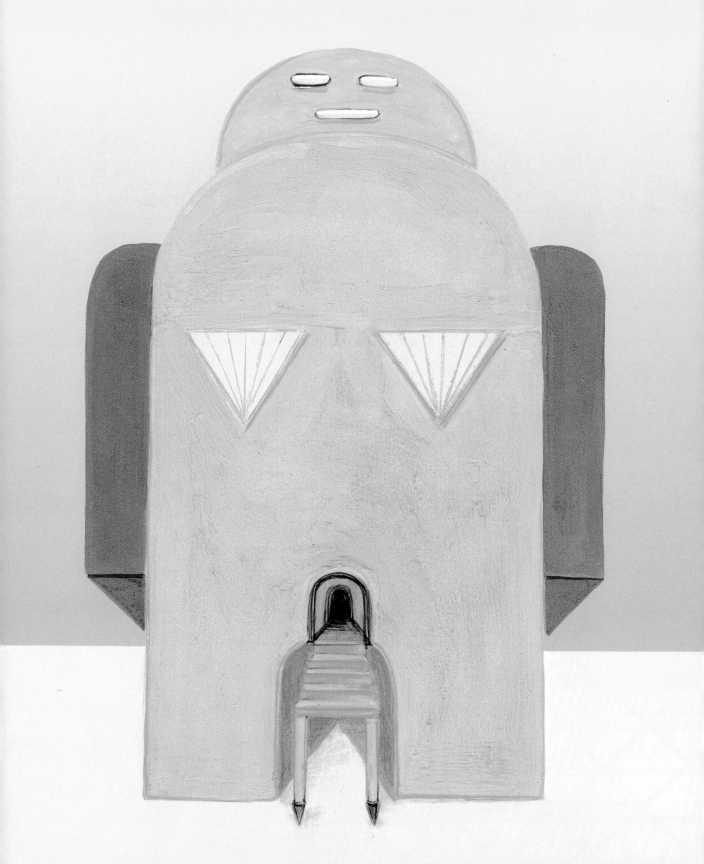

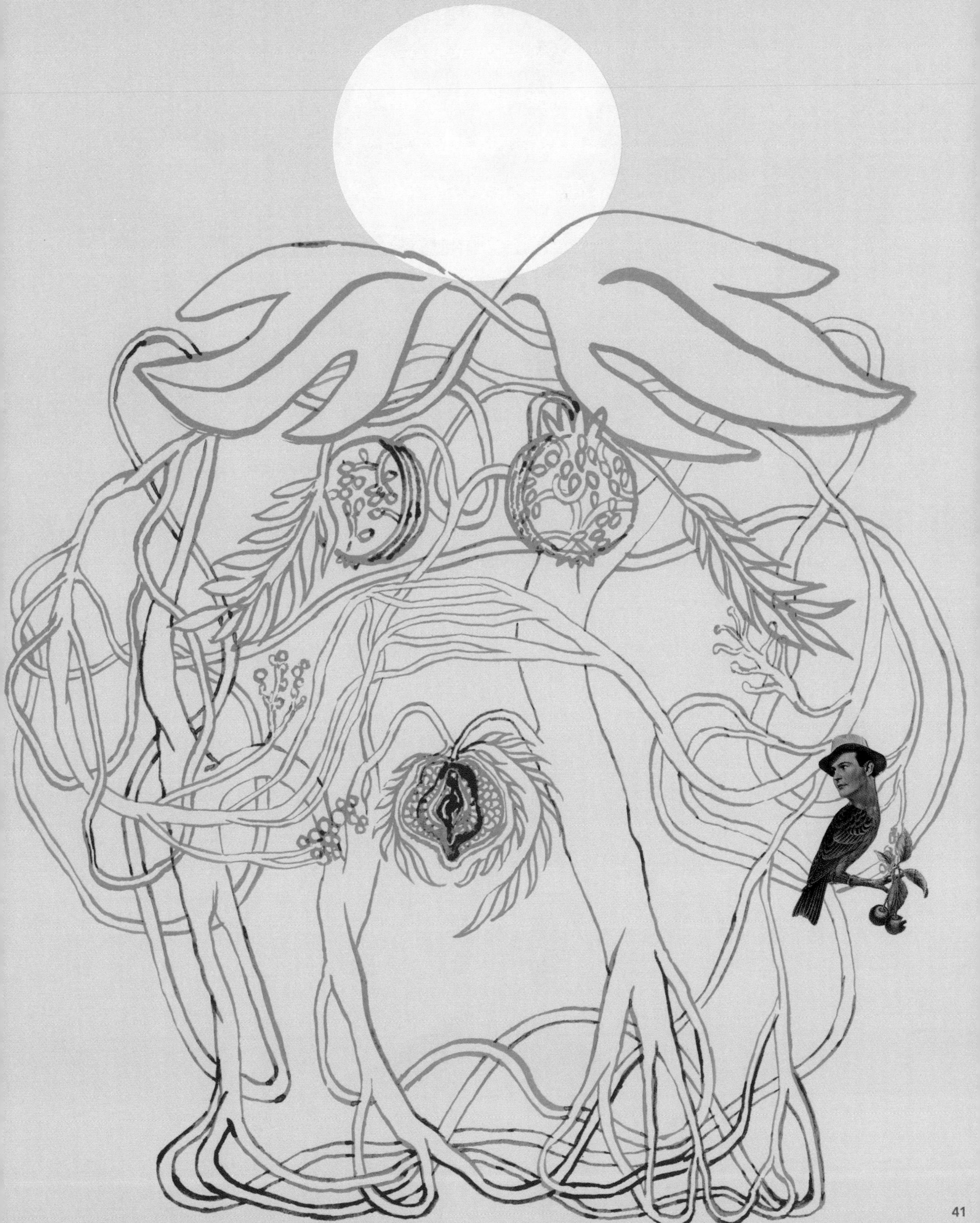

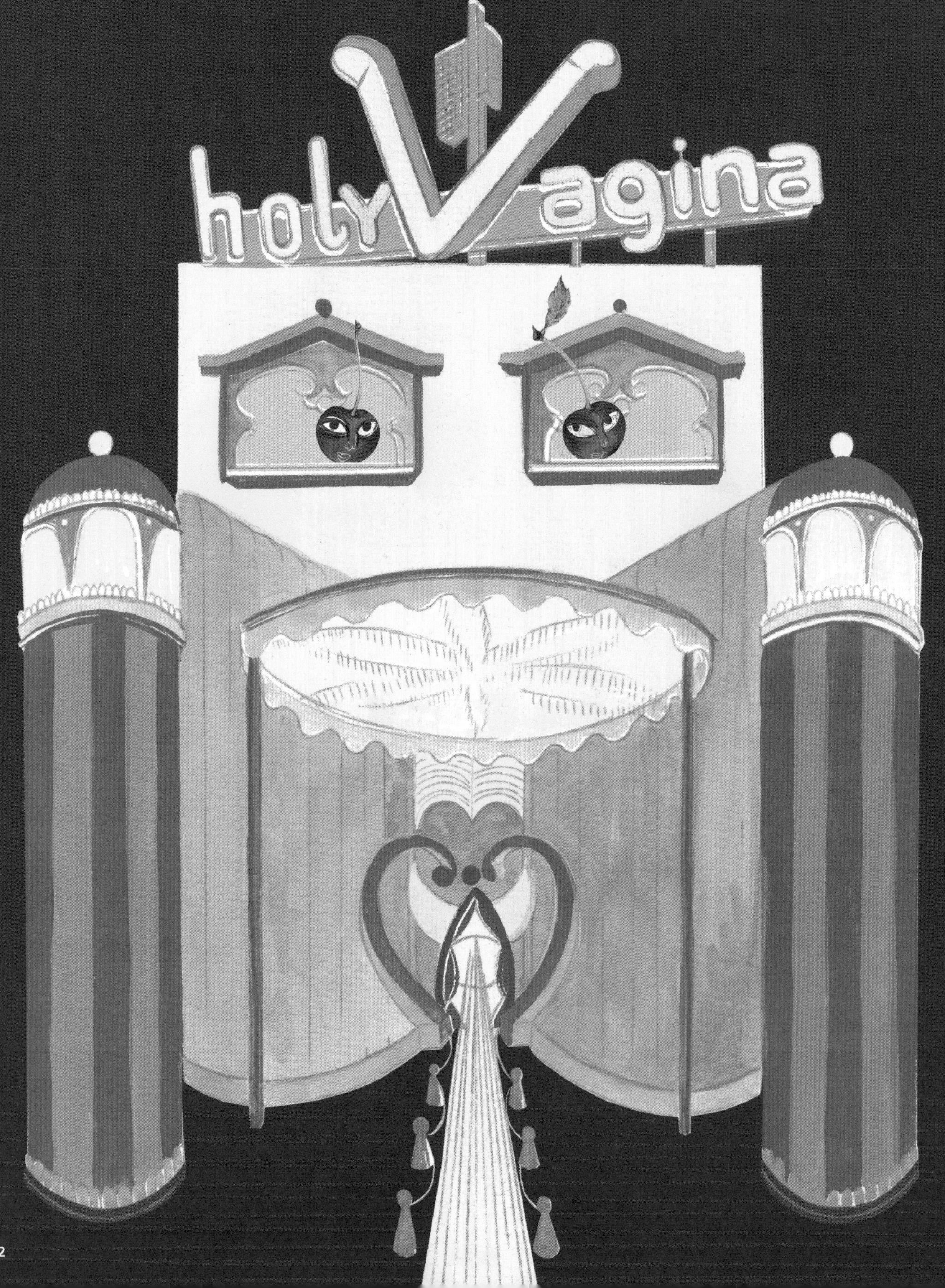
holy Vagina

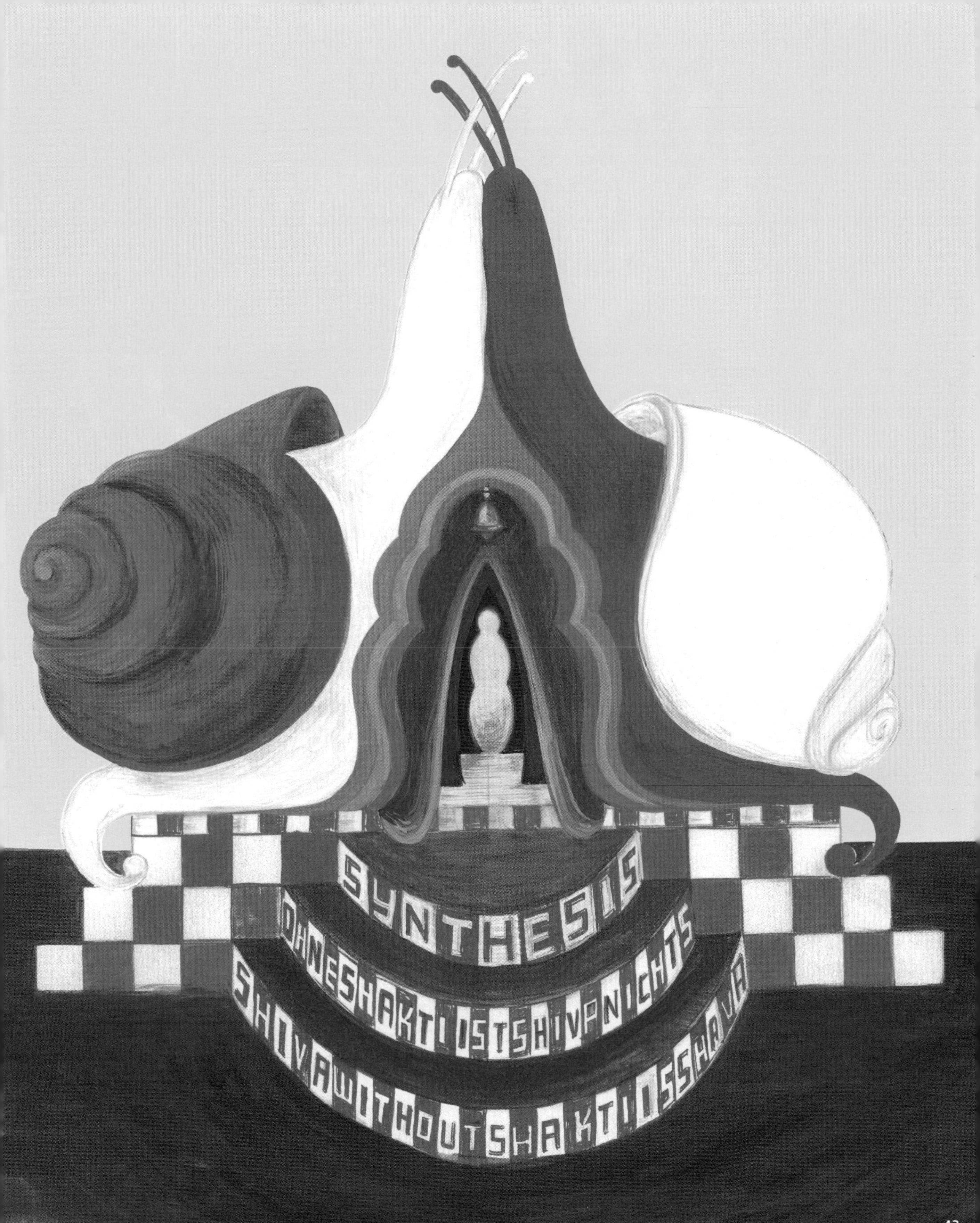
SYNTHESIS
OHNESHAKTIISTSHIVANICHTS
SHIVAWITHOUTSHAKTIISSHAVA

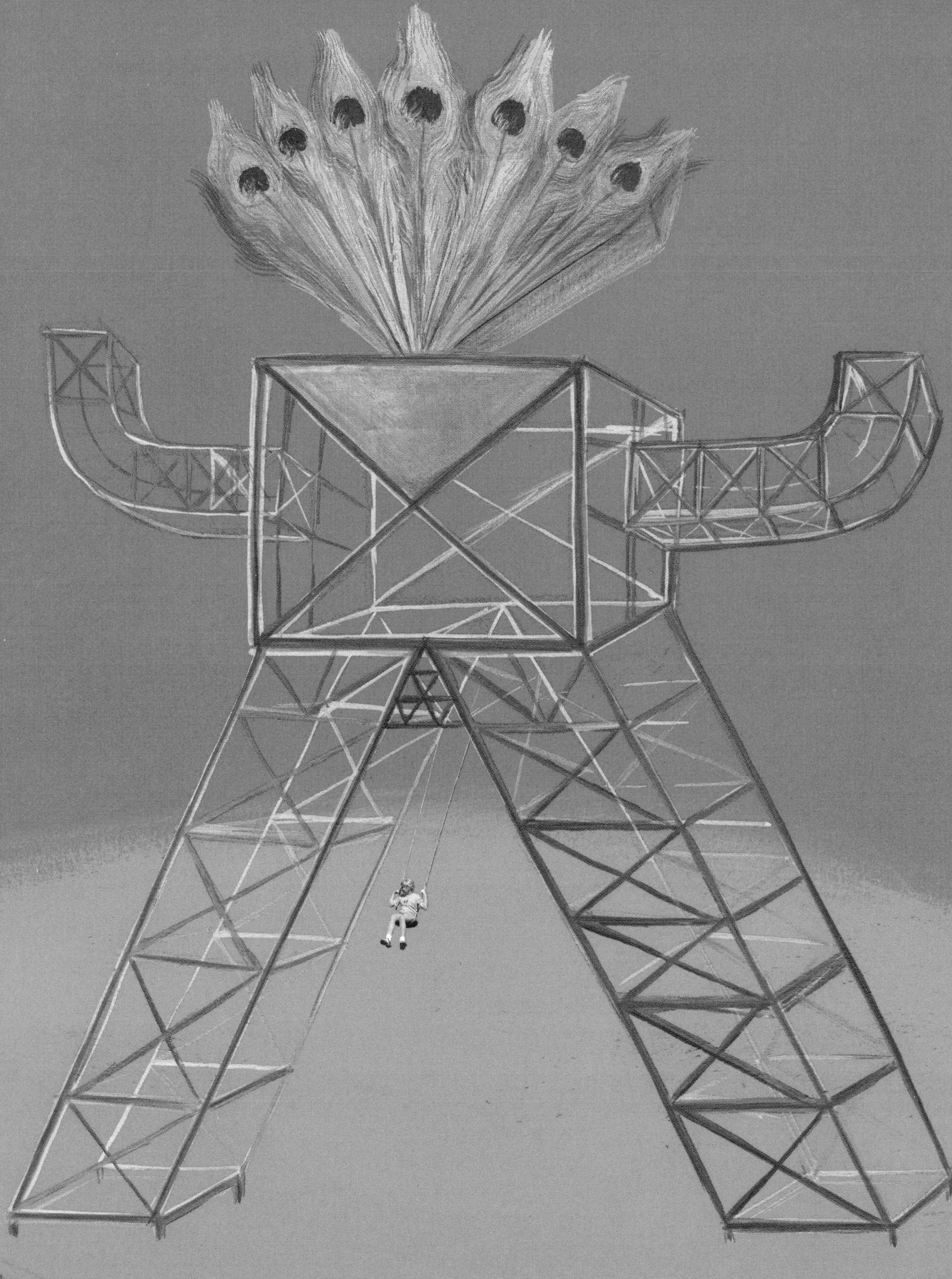

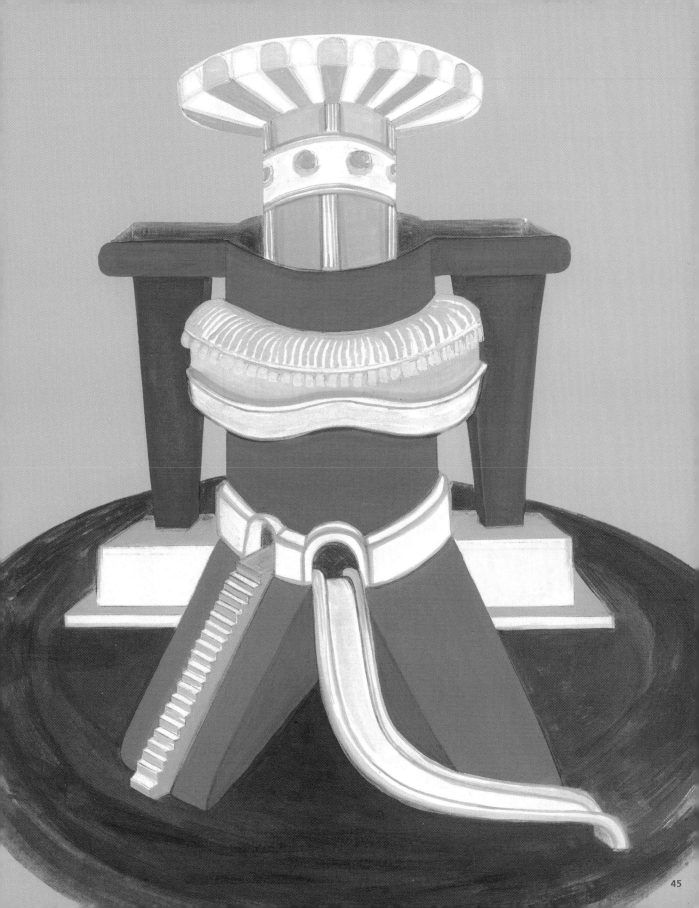

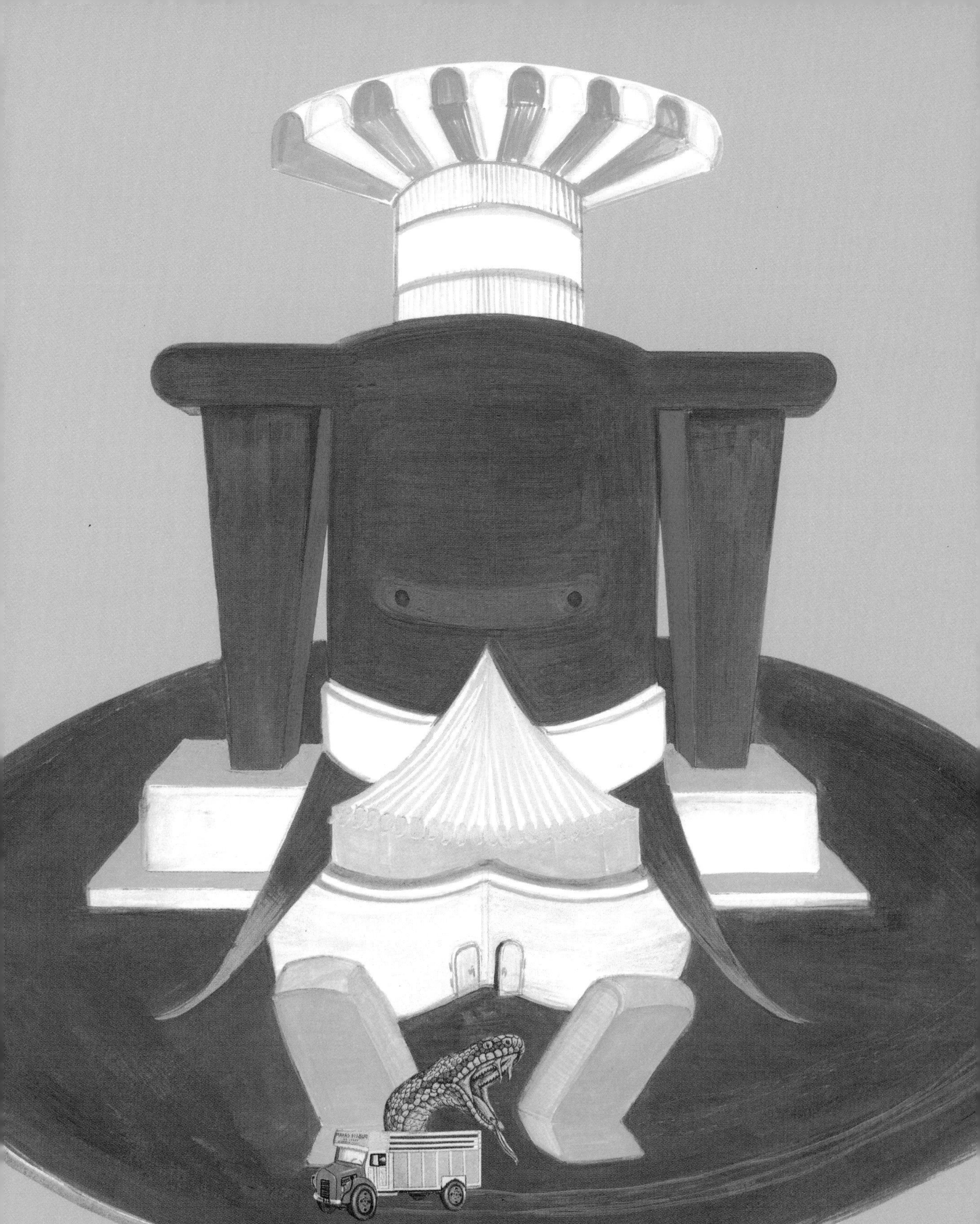

# BUM POWER

LARISSA BERTONASCO

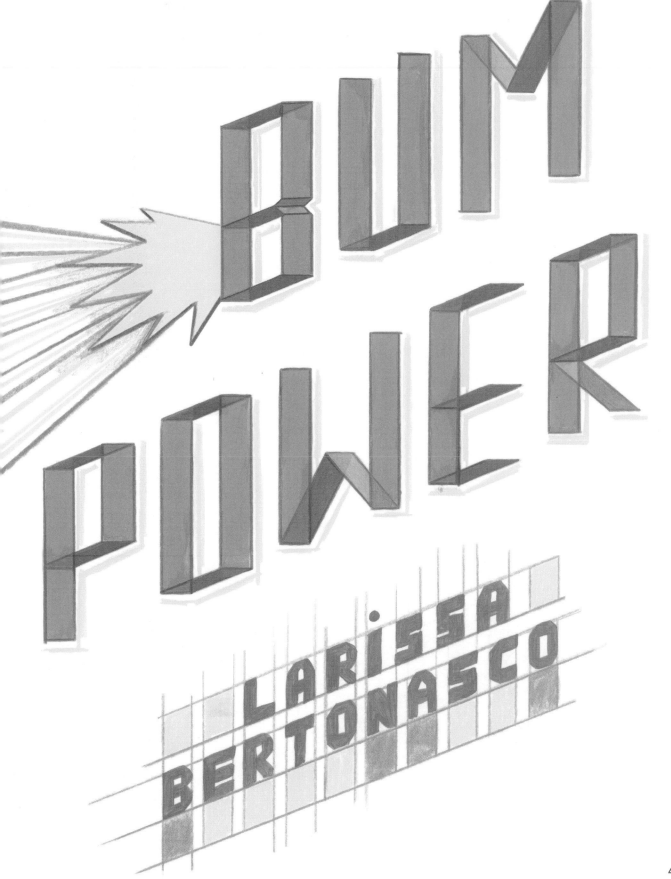

I like to look through boxes of old photographs stored in our attic. Pictures of myself as a teenager are especially striking...

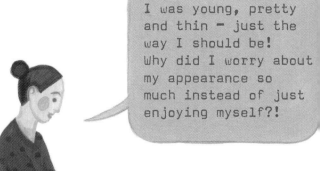

I was young, pretty and thin — just the way I should be! Why did I worry about my appearance so much instead of just enjoying myself?!

My body and I have been through a lot together since then: tears, elation, illnesses, loves, pregnancies, frustration, ageing — 44 years full of life! Even if I don't look any younger, I feel more comfortable now in my own skin. It took a while until I learned about the unique secrets held within my body, until I realised that it was a source of positive energy...

I didn't worry about my body as a child. It was simply there and did its job. I liked to eat ice cream, rode my bicycle and climbed trees.
That changed radically when my body started to change in every possible way, growing and getting out of control. Nothing was the way it used to be.

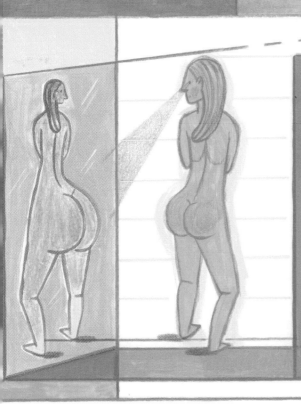

Most worrisome of all was my bum. I thought it was WAY too big. On the other hand, my breasts didn't seem to want to grow at all.
Generally, I only went out with a cardigan knotted around my hips making sure that no one could see me from behind.

51

I was a typical 1980s teenager. My body was the opposite, in every respect, of the ideal notion of beauty then. I was willing to try my best, a bit at least, to live up to the expectations how a teenage girl should look.

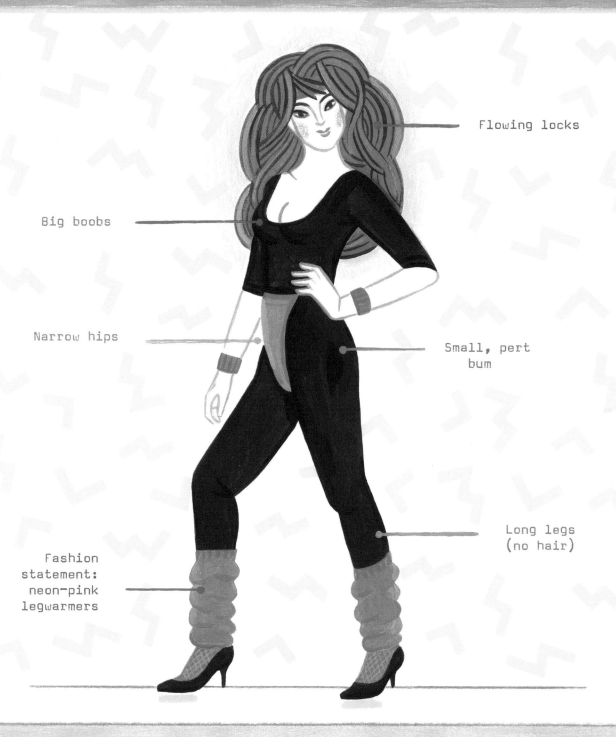

Flowing locks

Big boobs

Narrow hips

Small, pert bum

Long legs (no hair)

Fashion statement: neon-pink legwarmers

This was the beginning of a hopeless, sad battle against my imperfect body...

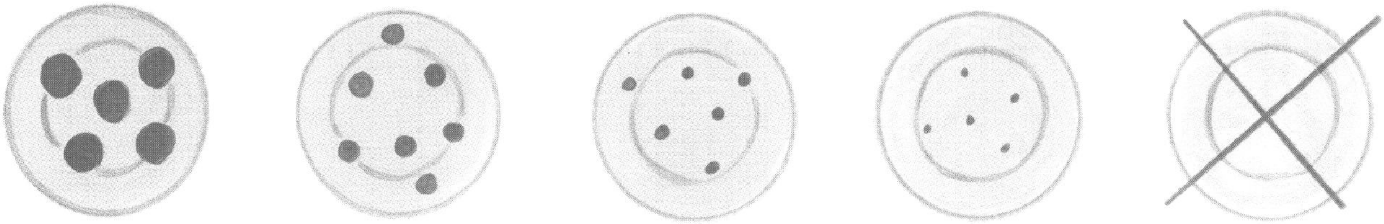

Starving myself didn't help either. Every bite made me feel guilty. I got thinner and thinner, and liked myself less and less.
My already small breasts disappeared completely, but my bottom stayed the same as ever – big and round. I wish I could have done some redistribution. There were several parts of me that could use improvements.

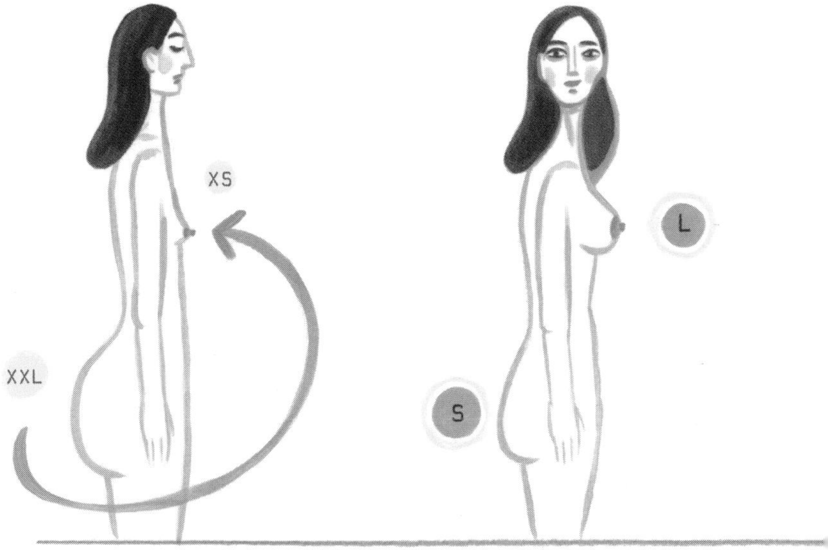
XS
XXL
L
S

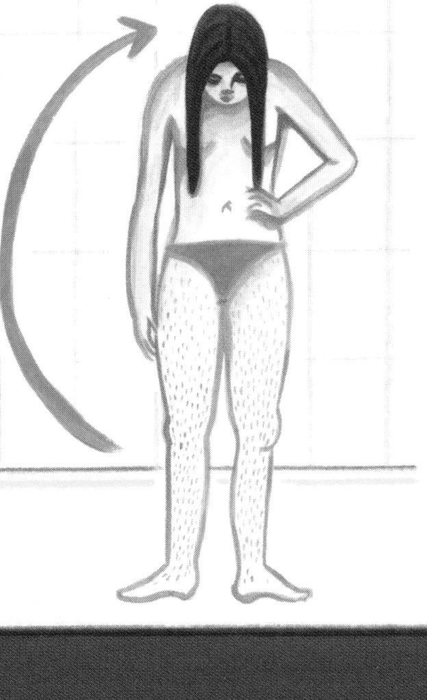

Thanks to my Italian genes, lush hair sprouted in all the wrong places. The hair on my head, though, was the opposite of a mane.
If I could've transplanted my leg hair onto my head, I might've have looked like the perfect '80s diva!

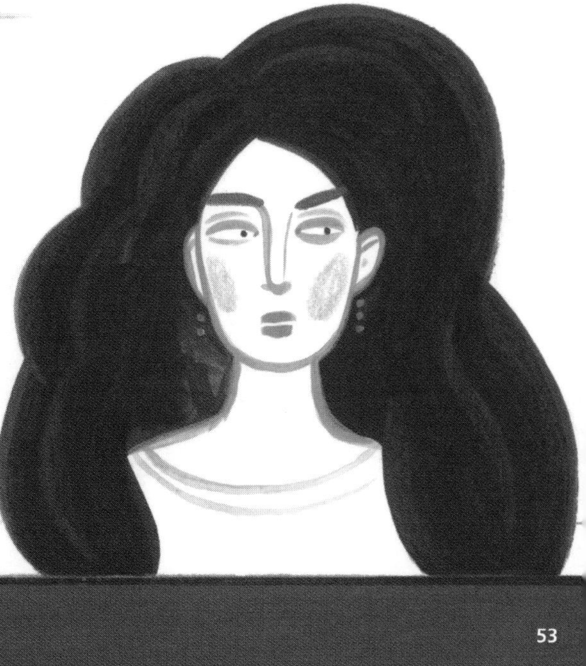

I got pregnant when I was 25. I was right in the middle of my studies at university and the first mother in my circle of friends. I was really looking forward to having the baby and was certain that everything was happening at the right time in my life. Other people seemed more sceptical though...

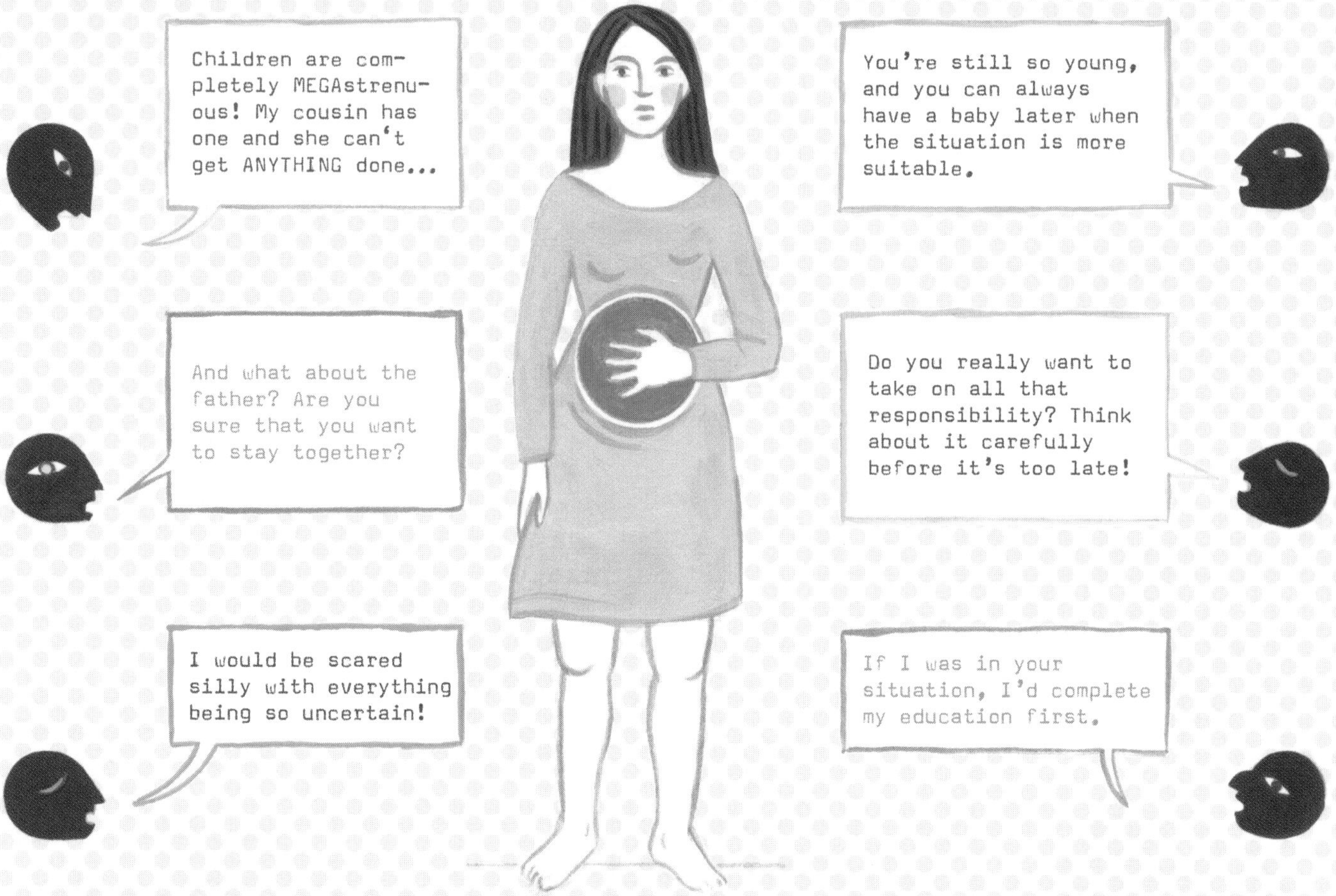

Children are completely MEGAstrenuous! My cousin has one and she can't get ANYTHING done...

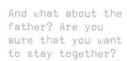

And what about the father? Are you sure that you want to stay together?

I would be scared silly with everything being so uncertain!

You're still so young, and you can always have a baby later when the situation is more suitable.

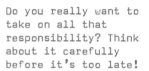

Do you really want to take on all that responsibility? Think about it carefully before it's too late!

If I was in your situation, I'd complete my education first.

I asked my mother for her advice. She raised me and my brother alone and ran her own business all the while. (My mother also has a big bottom.)

Mami, have I got news for you — I'm pregnant!

Oh, how wonderful, my dear! Children are simply the best! I know that you'll be a good mother. The challenges that I faced in life just made me stronger!

During my pregnancy, I learned to trust my body in ways that I hadn't known about before. My body was performing this miracle without ever torturing or straining me. I was finally able to make peace with my own body.

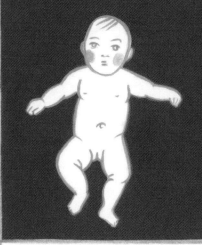

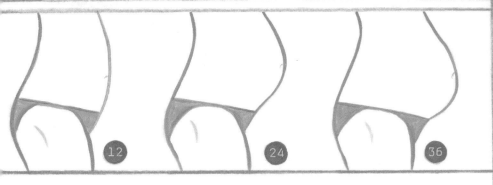

Amazing! My body simply made this sweet creature? Painting is much more difficult! My breasts were finally as big as I had always wanted them to be while also serving an important function - all without any extra effort!

I can't go out much any more, but when I do, I really make the most of it!

After a brief break, I went back to my studies. Life with my daughter helped me discipline myself to deal with my daily routine better now that it had set parameters. The windows of time I had for myself took on additional value and I learned how to make the most of them and work more efficiently. Before, I had more energy to fret and worry and waste time thinking about my bottom. Afterwards, I just didn't have time for all that. At that point, I wanted to complete my studies and earn money.

After completing my studies, I worked
as a freelance illustrator, fell in love
again and had a sweet little boy. I split
childcare between each of their fathers.
Of course, it wasn't always easy to
get everything done that needed to be.
In general though, I'd say that my life
was better than ever.
I escaped from the children into my work
and from my work with the children.

I noticed, as time went by, that I'd
developed more stamina for a wide range
of activities.

I could
cycle around
for hours ...

... or hike my way alon[g]
for days on end ...

... or dance
the night away ...

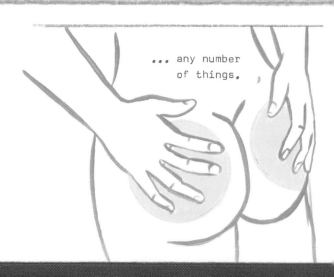

... any number
of things.

Recently, I began to wonder where all this power came from.
I thought long and hard. And then the penny dropped!
All this life-force is stored in my bum! No wonder it's the size it is!
Since I realised that, there's not an ounce of it I would give up.

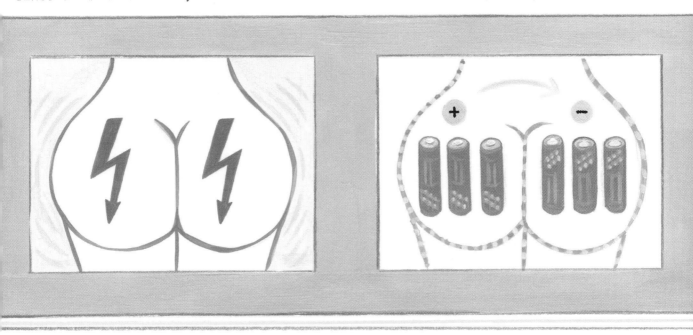

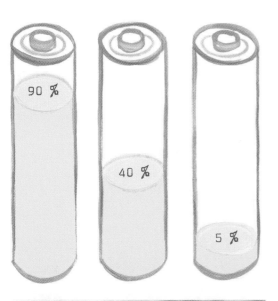

The most important thing is to remember to recharge those batteries regularly.

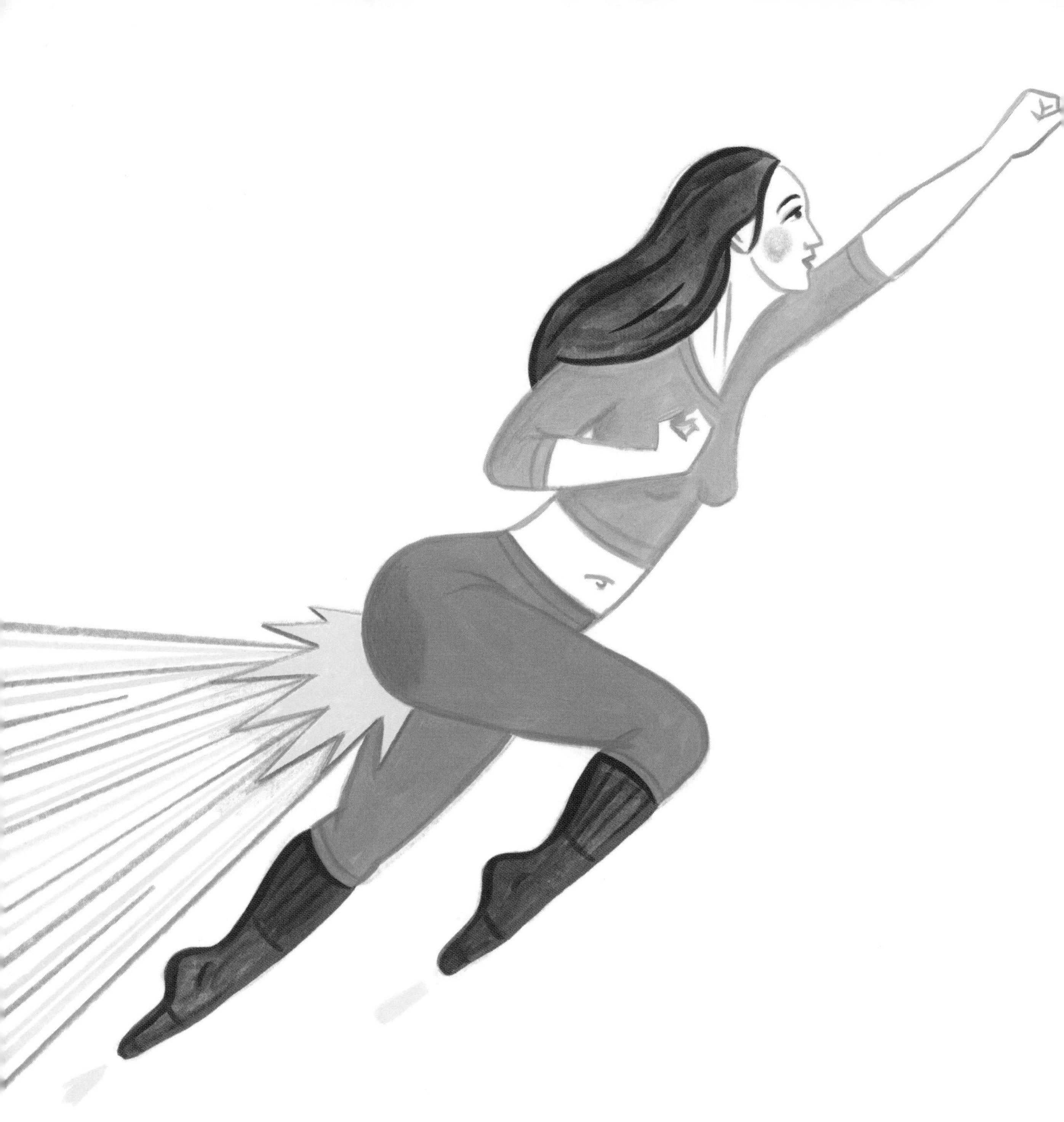

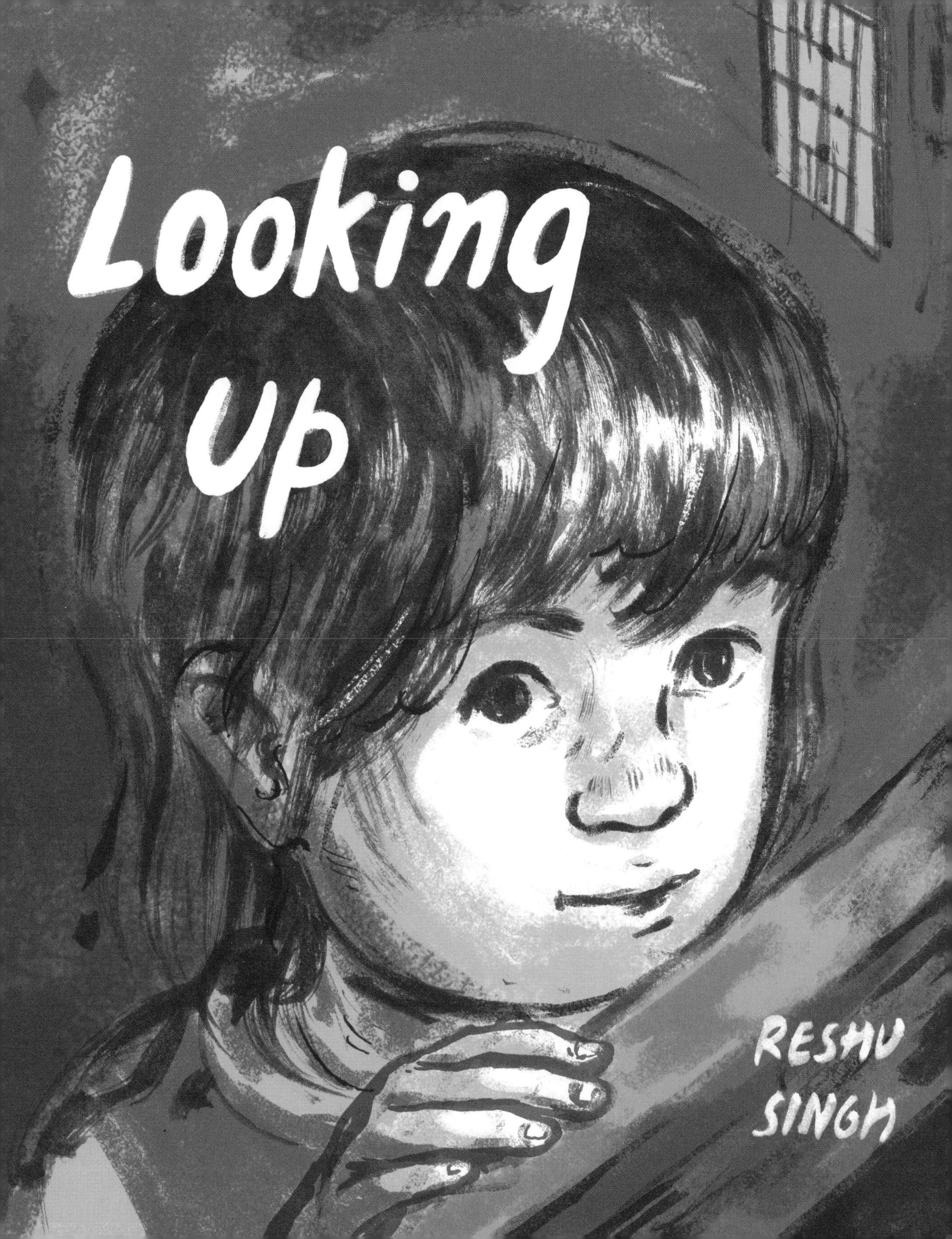
Looking
Up
RESHU
SINGH

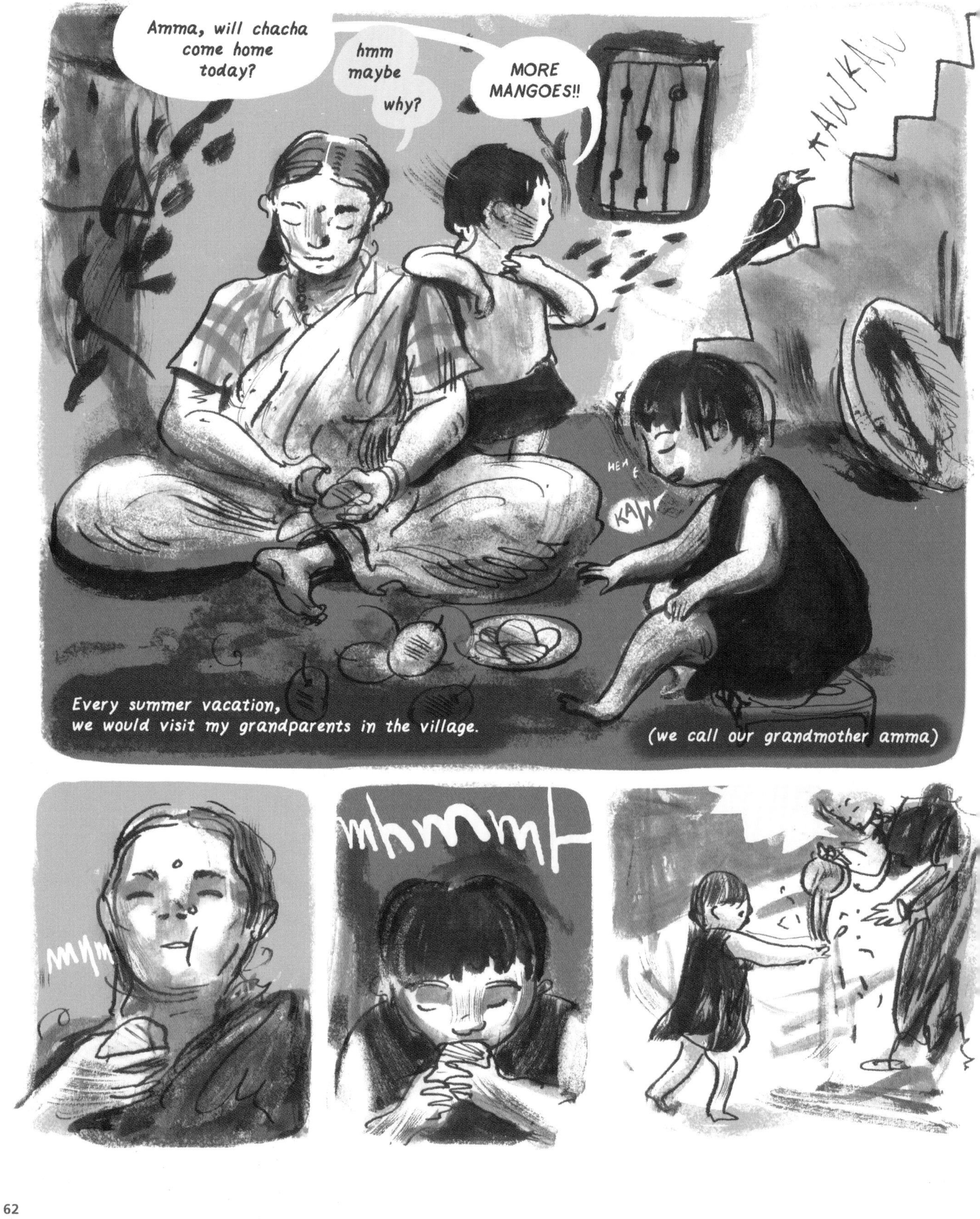
Amma, will chacha come home today?
hmm maybe
why?
MORE MANGOES!!
HEH E
KAW
Every summer vacation,
we would visit my grandparents in the village.
(we call our grandmother amma)

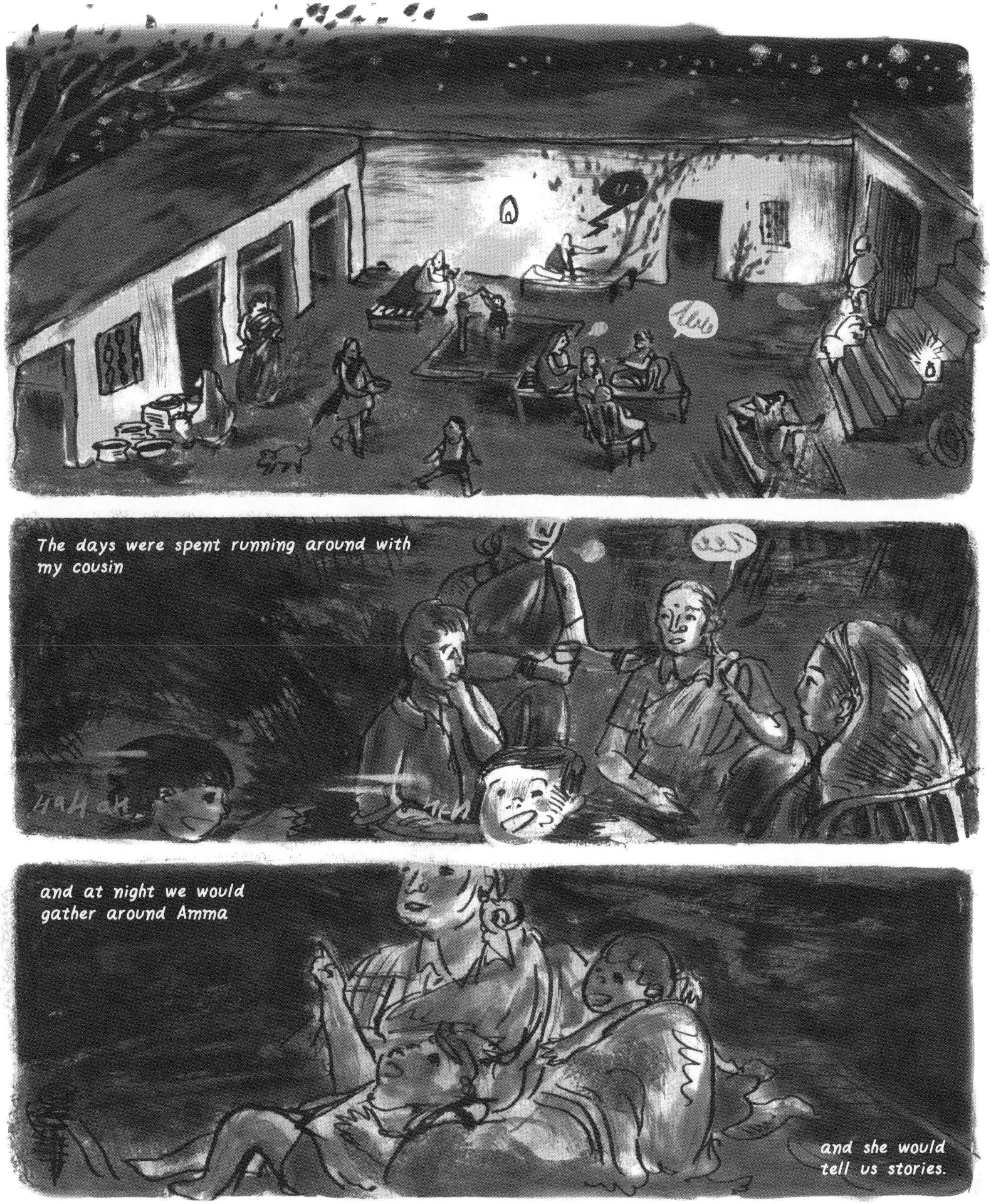
The days were spent running around with my cousin
and at night we would gather around Amma
and she would tell us stories.

She was keen to study, but wasn't allowed to go to school.

Of all wonderful tales she told me

I loved her own, the most.

So secretly at night she would light a lamp inside an earthen pot

so the light didn't spill out and she read her brother's books.

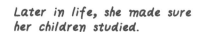

Later in life, she made sure her children studied.

In the begining, she had to sell her saris to pay their school fees as her in-laws opposed the schooling.

They must have believed that education gives people 'wings' and that it would scatter their children away from home and 'family values'.

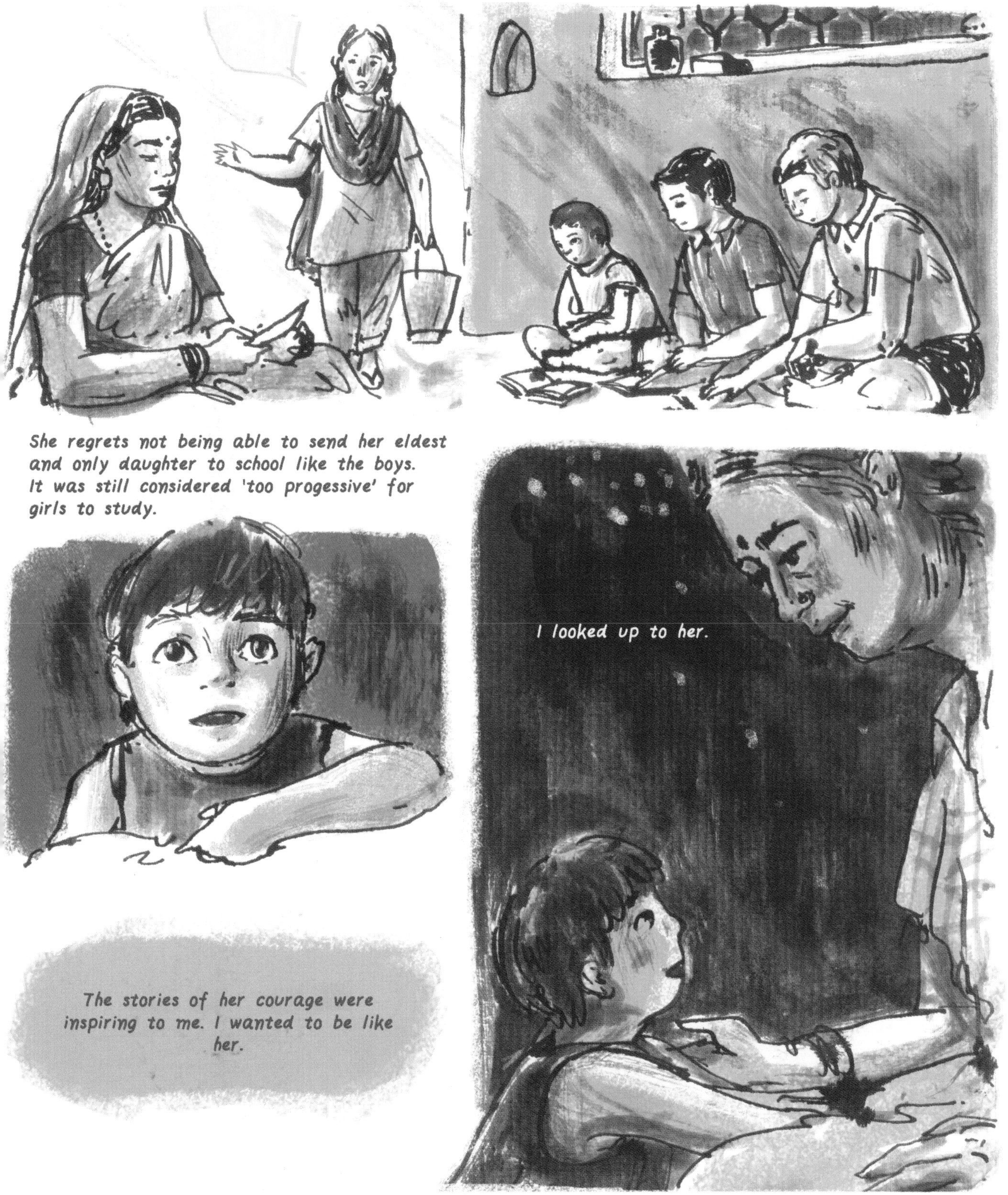
She regrets not being able to send her eldest and only daughter to school like the boys. It was still considered 'too progessive' for girls to study.
I looked up to her.
The stories of her courage were inspiring to me. I wanted to be like her.

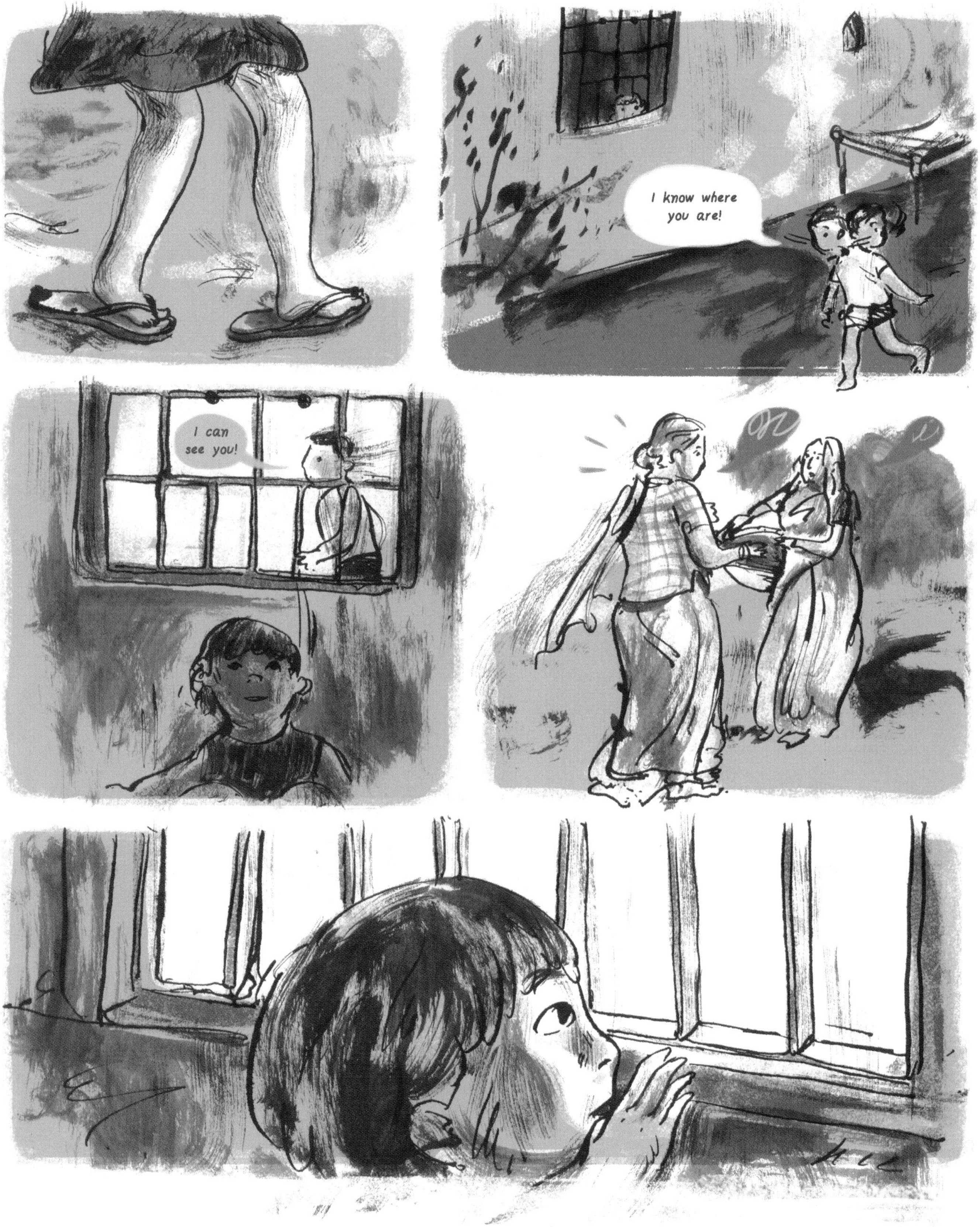
I know where you are!
I can see you!

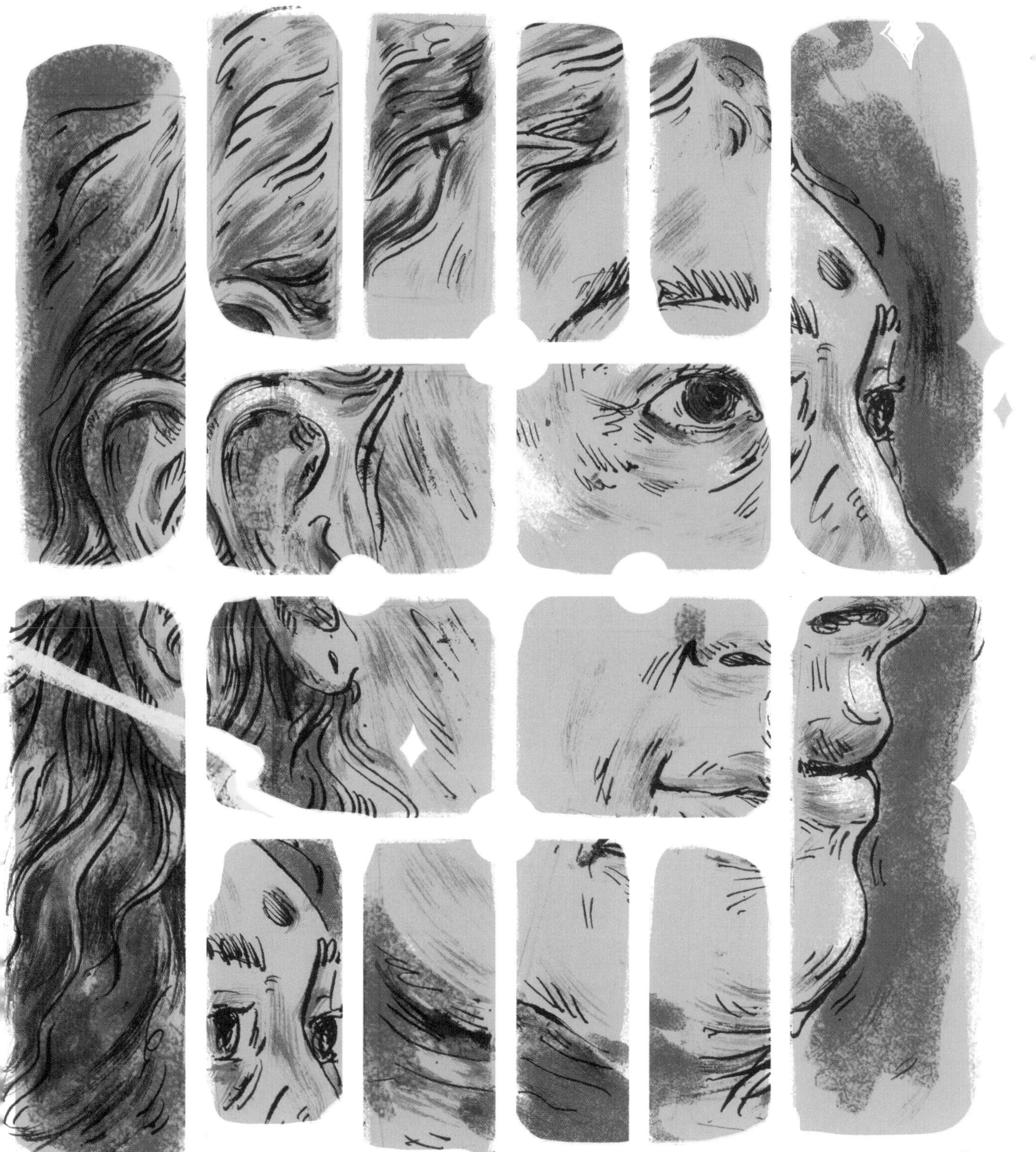

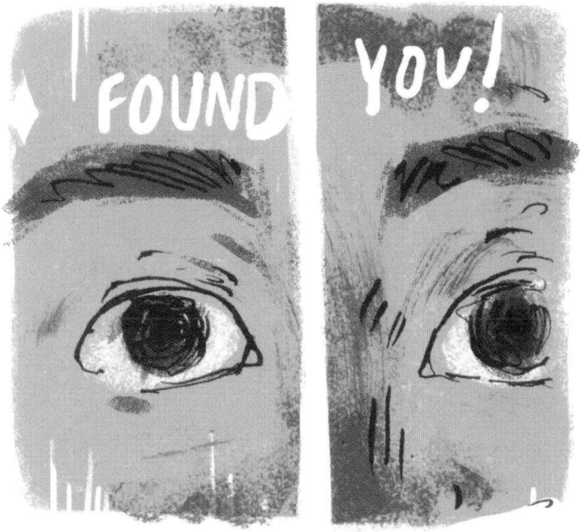
FOUND YOU!

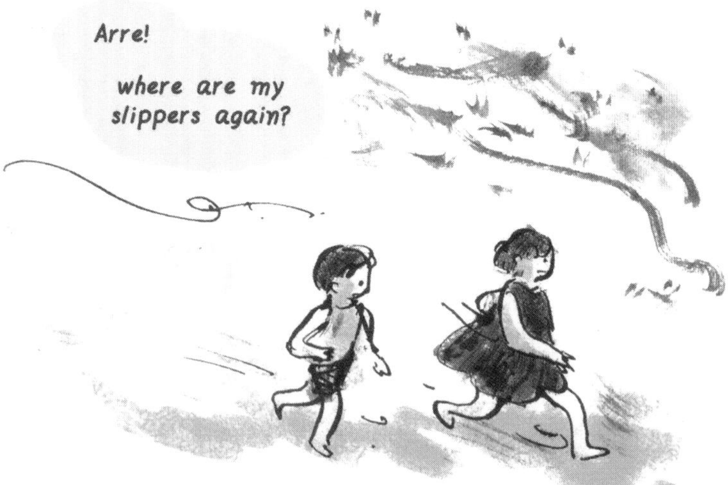
Arre!
where are my slippers again?

Some years later, my sister was born. And my cousin got a little brother.

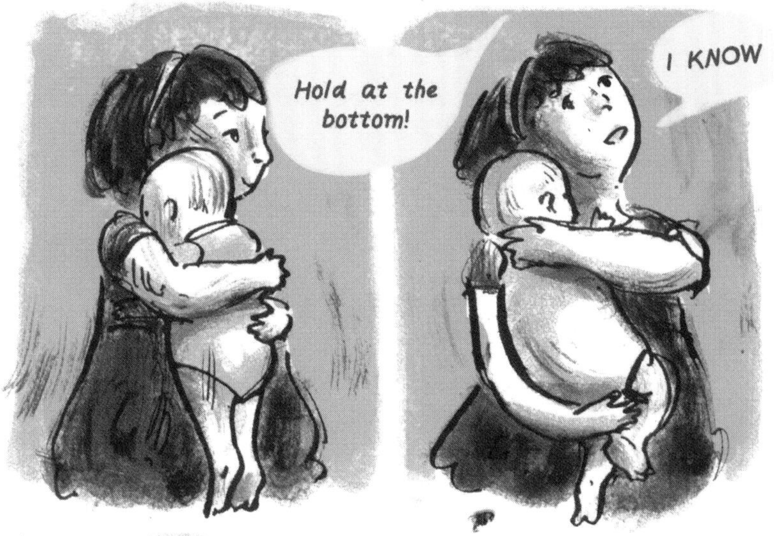
Hold at the bottom!
I KNOW

Now we had new games to play.

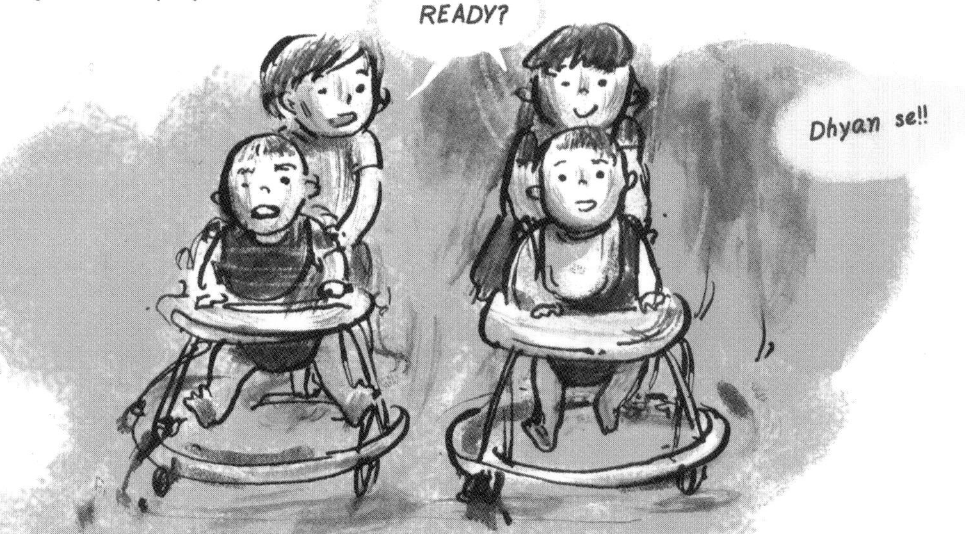
READY?
Dhyan se!!

One day, Amma called me.

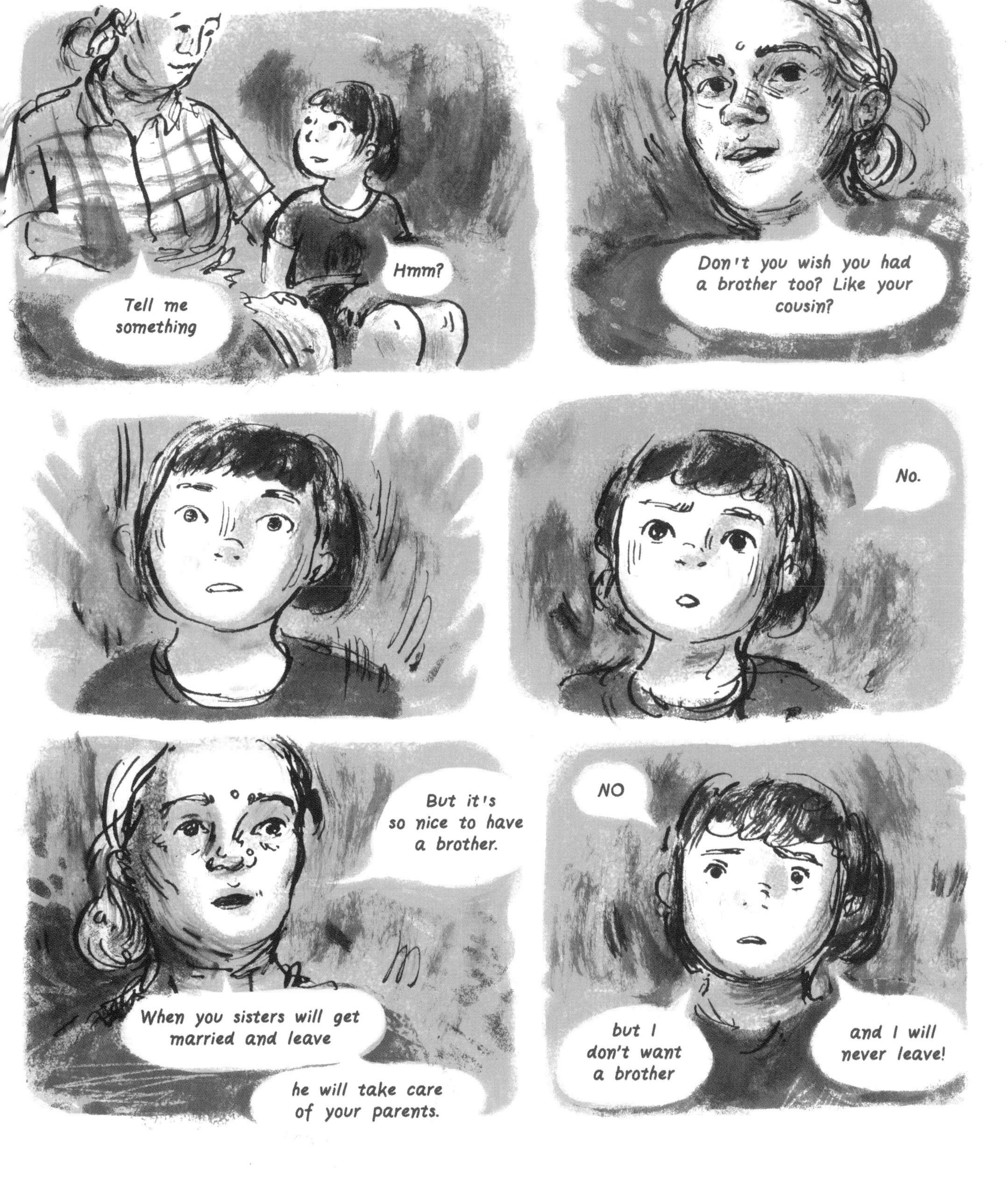

Tell me something
Hmm?
Don't you wish you had a brother too? Like your cousin?
No.
But it's so nice to have a brother.
When you sisters will get married and leave
he will take care of your parents.
NO
but I don't want a brother
and I will never leave!

I didn't like that at all.

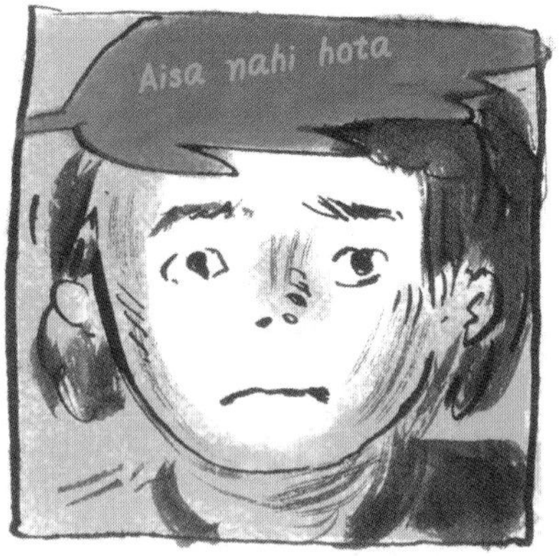
Aisa nahi hota

And to think she might even wish I was a boy?

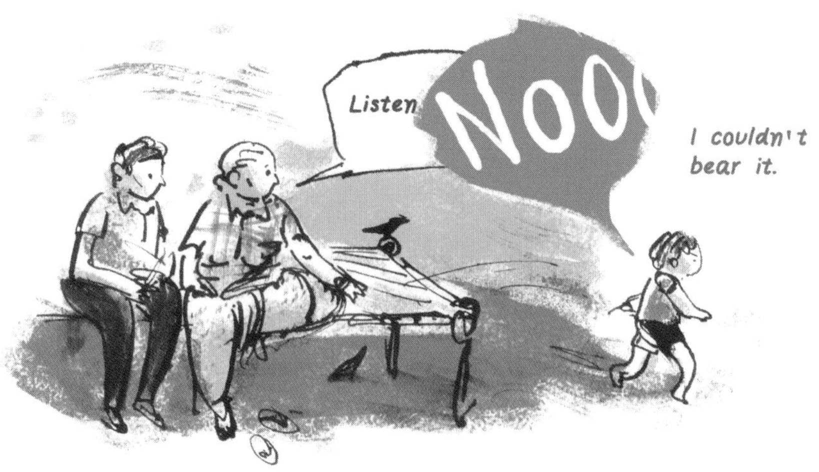
Listen
Noo
I couldn't bear it.

I began to resent her.

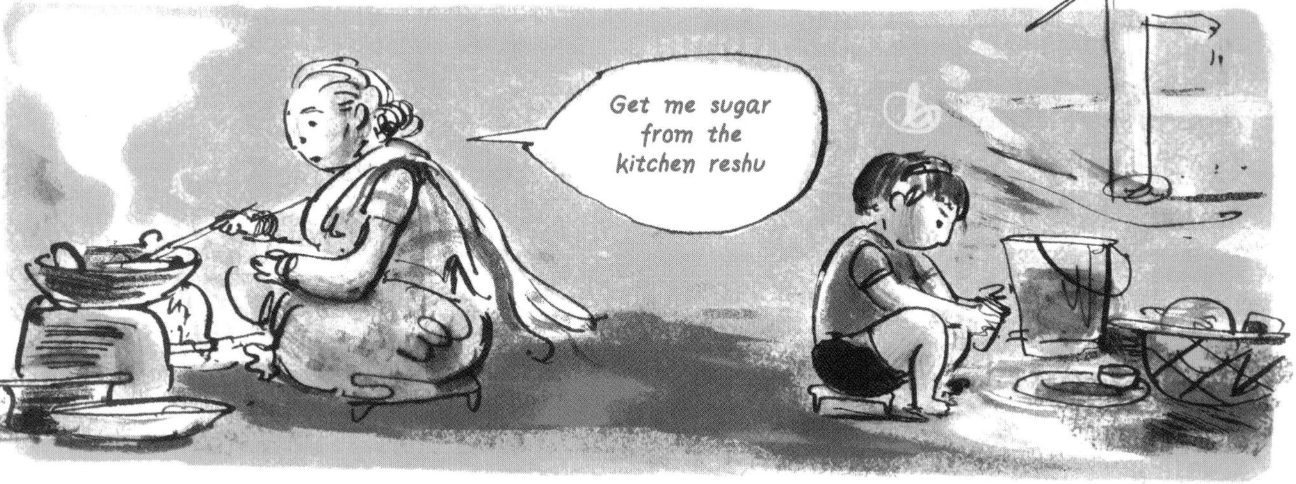
Get me sugar from the kitchen reshu

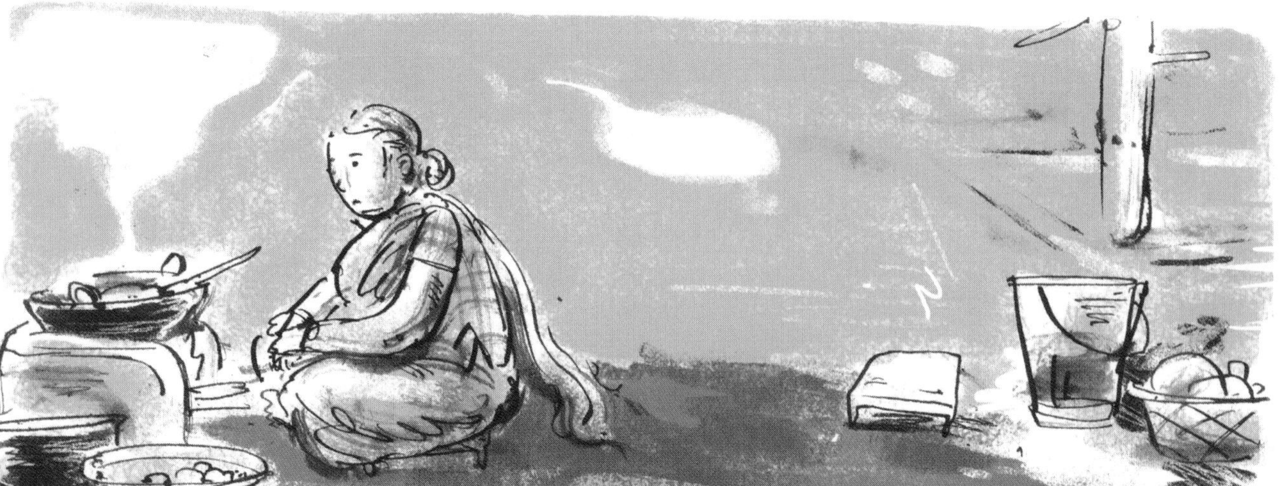

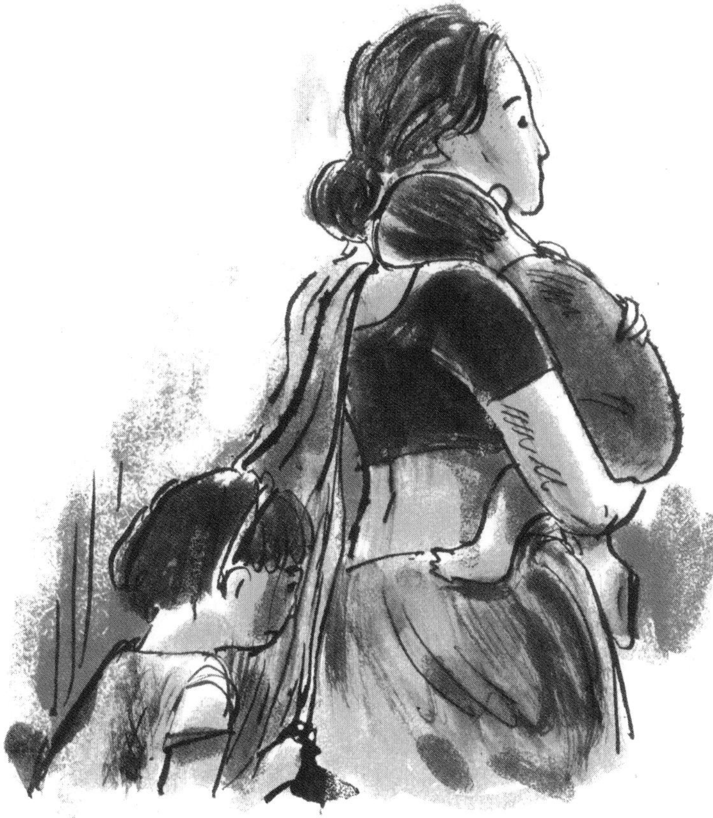

I found out from my mother
years later that she was
constantly pressured by
Amma to have another child,
a boy.

Amma kept believing that
only a son could complete
a family,
even though she stood up
against these very issues
growing up.

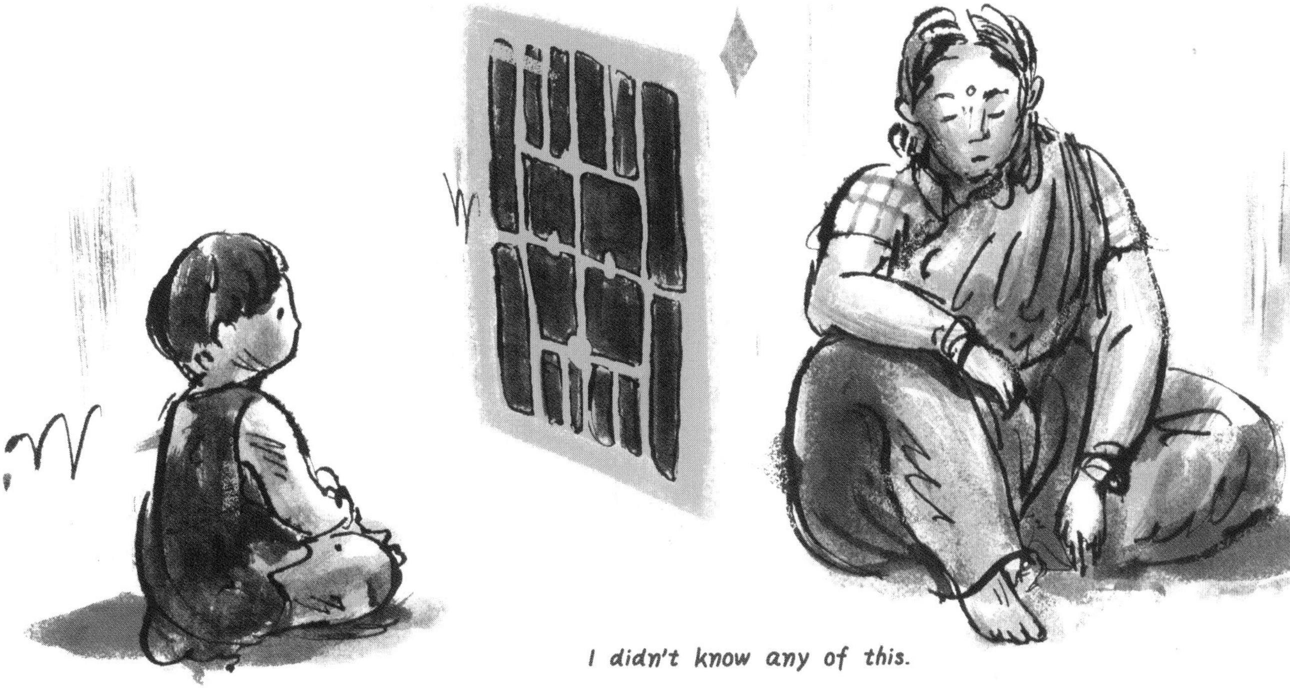

I didn't know any of this.

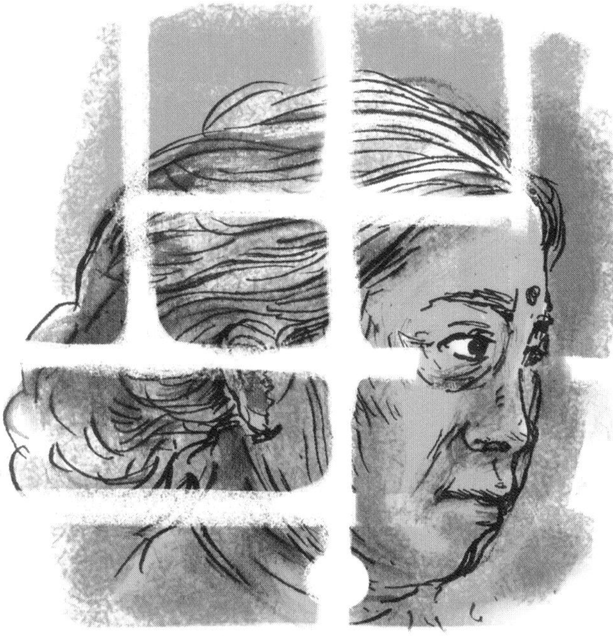

I was only looking at parts.

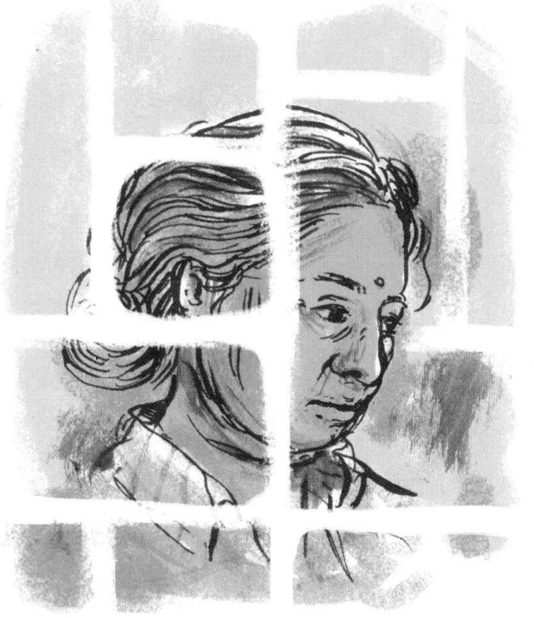

To me, she seemed to treat us kids the same.

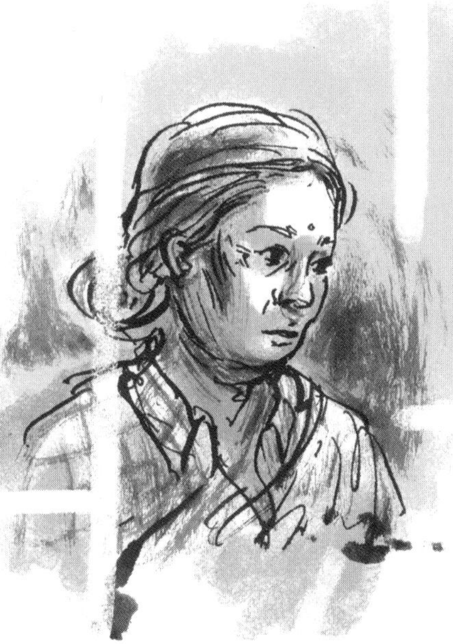

But I could free her now

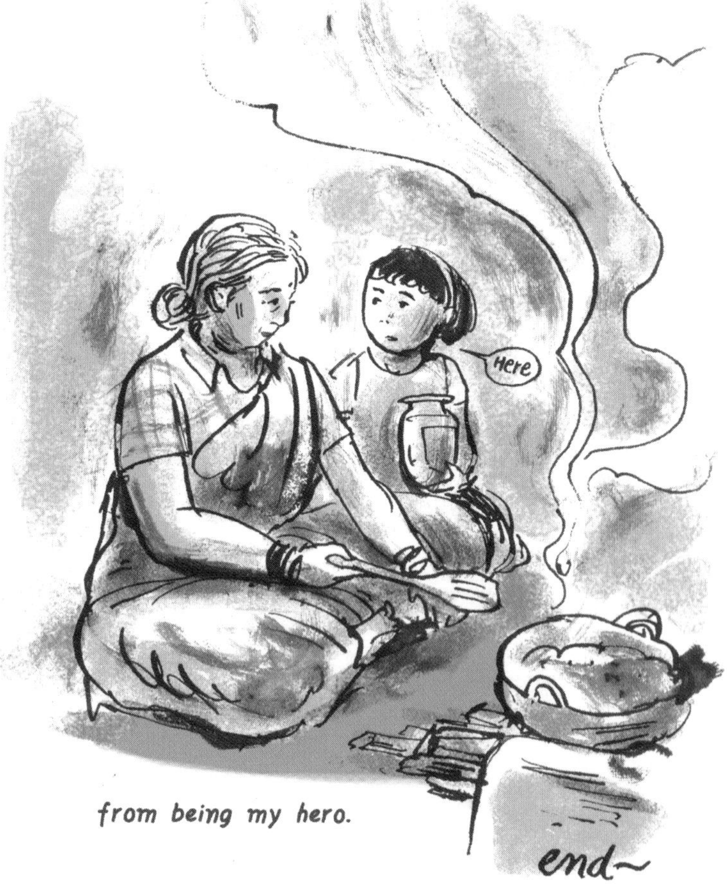
Here

from being my hero.

end~

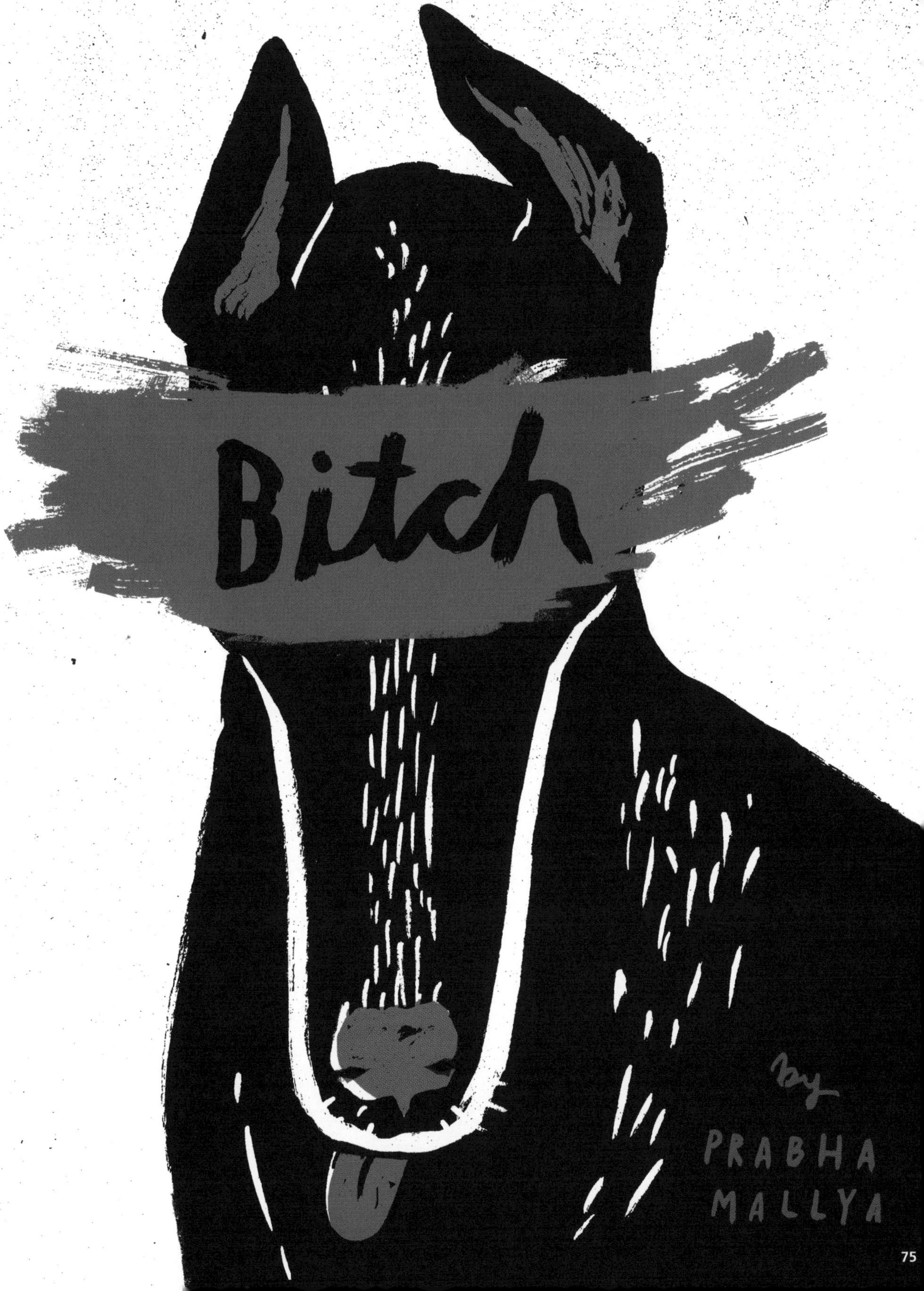
Bitch
by
PRABHA
MALLYA

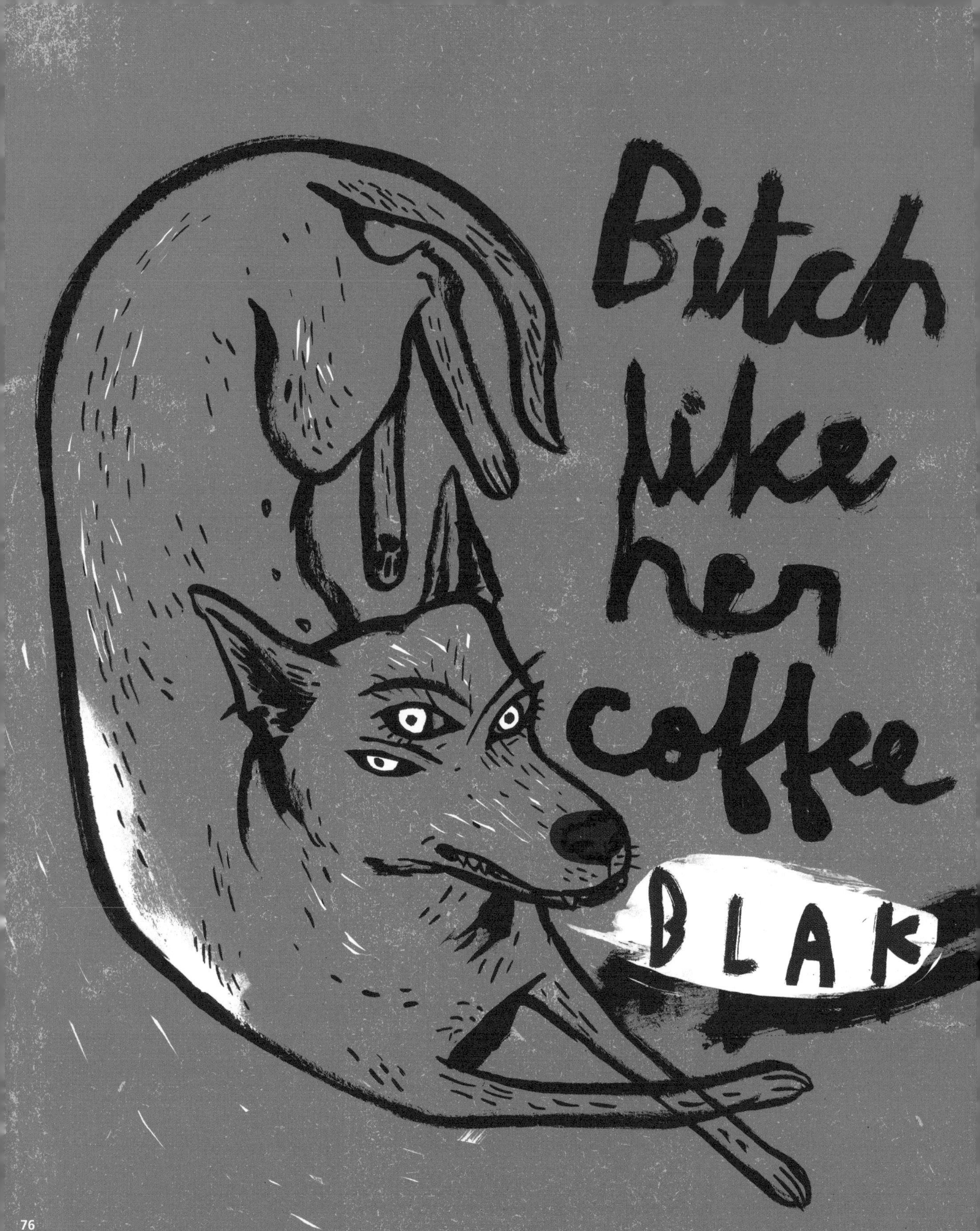
Bitch
like
her
coffee
BLAK

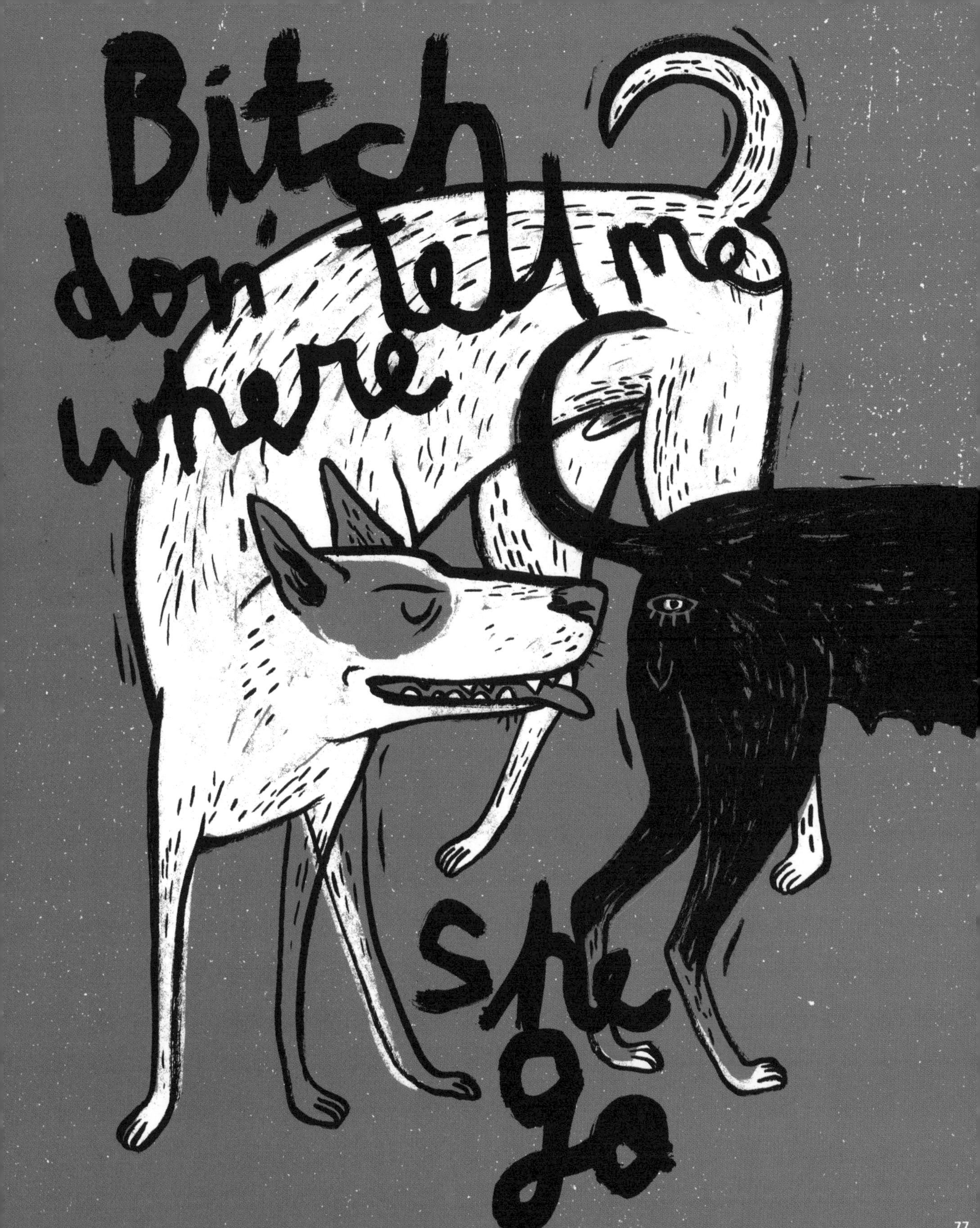
Bitch
don tell me
where
She
go

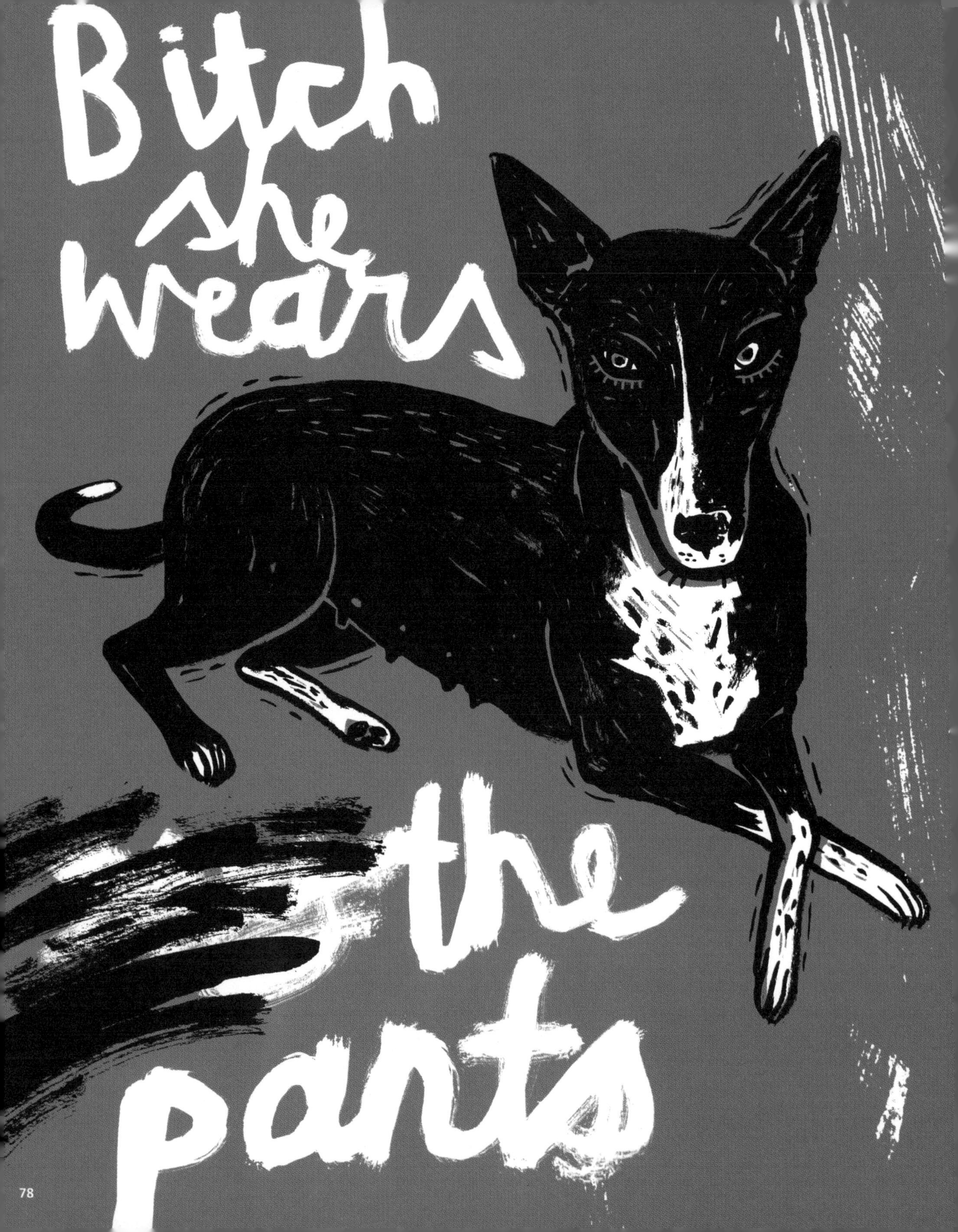
Bitch she wears the pants

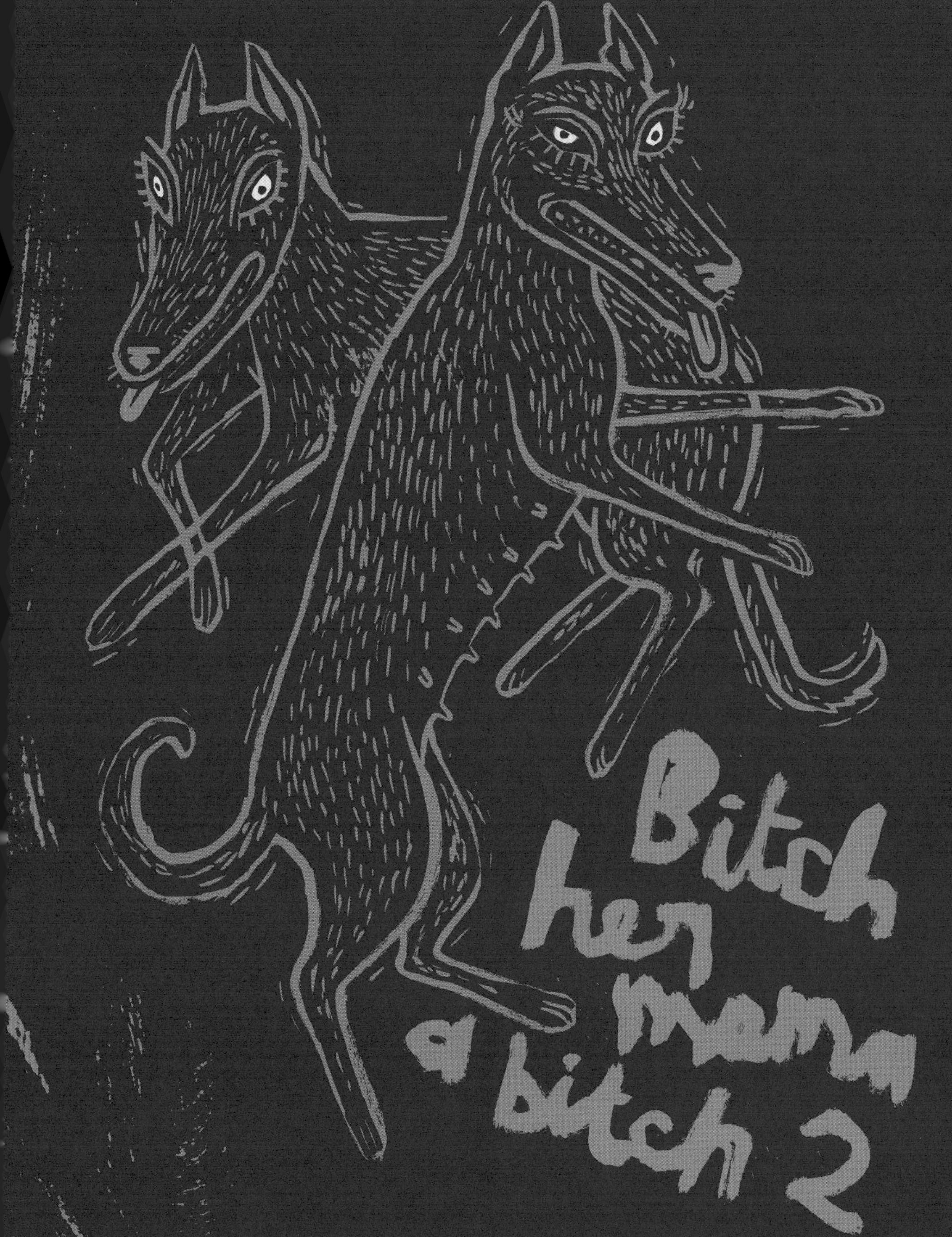
Bitch
her mama
a bitch 2

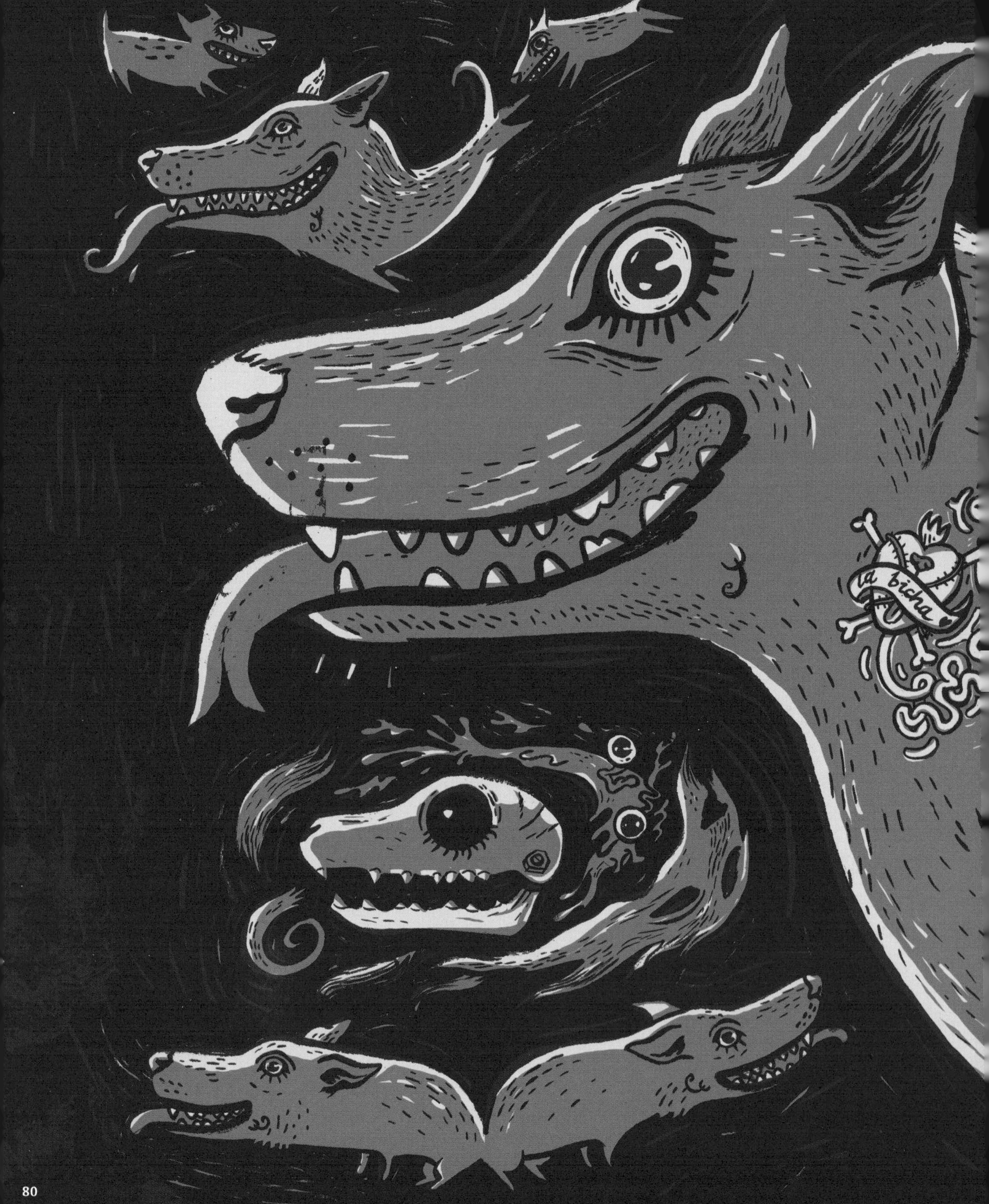
la bicha

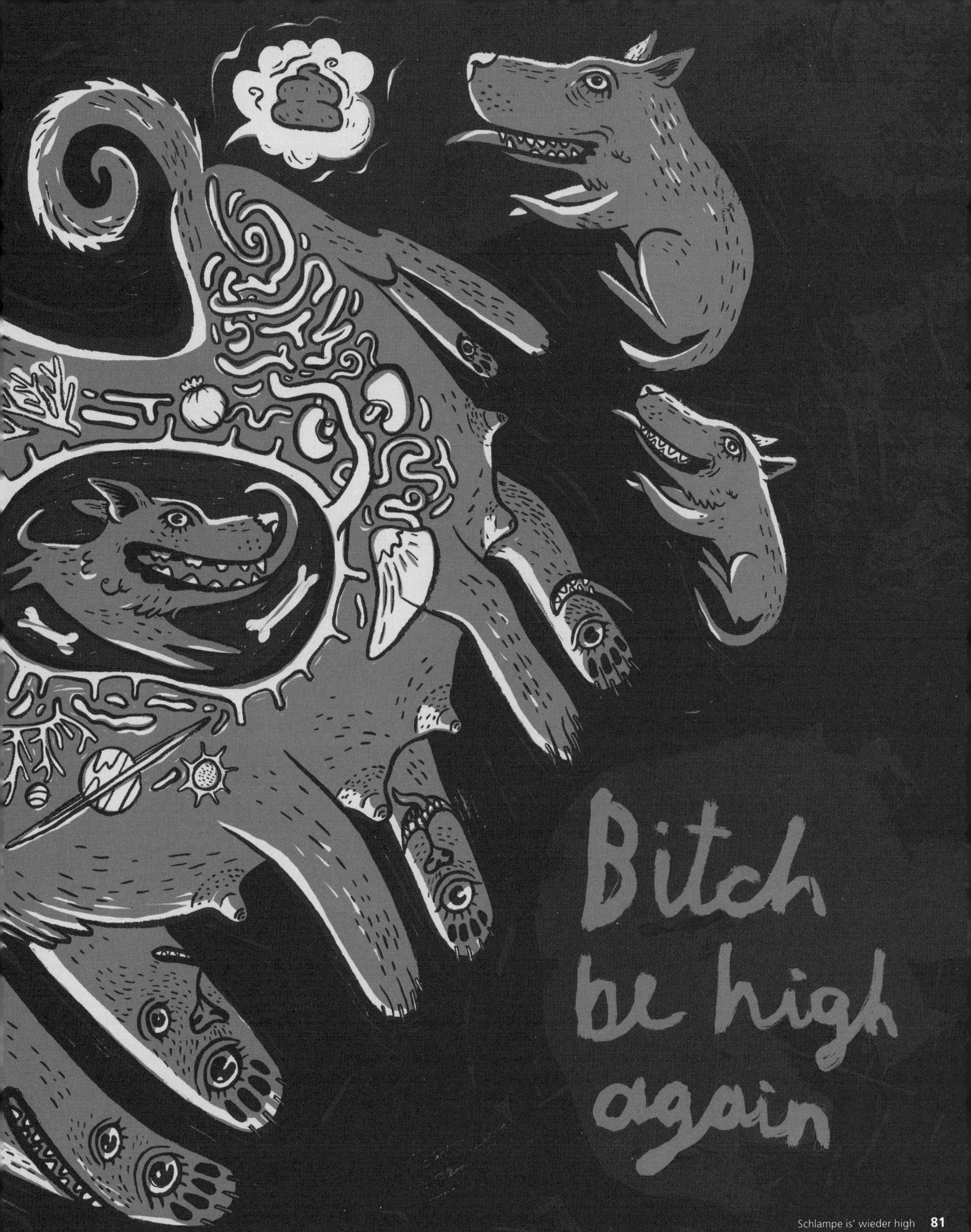
Bitch
be high
again

# Bitch where's your bra

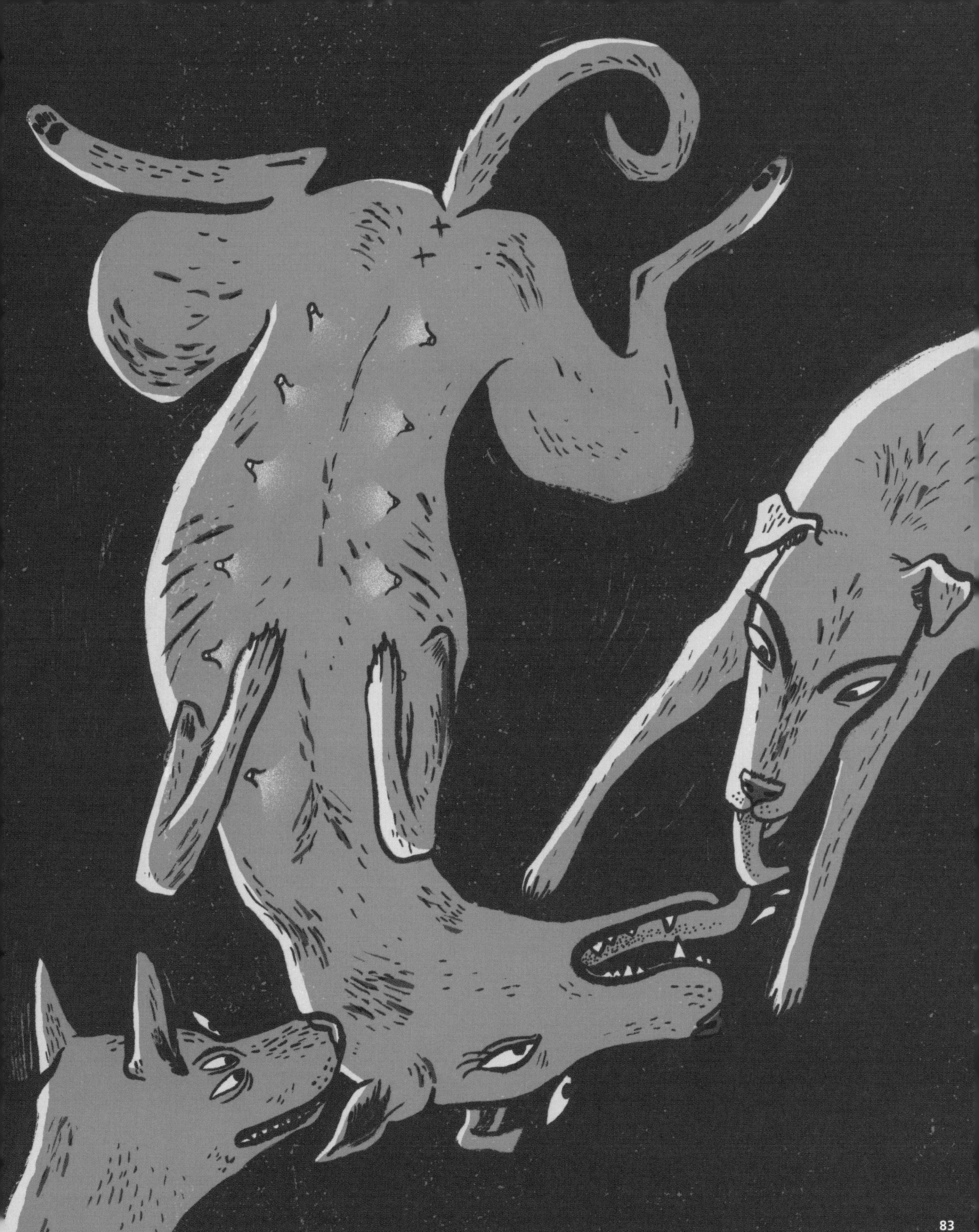

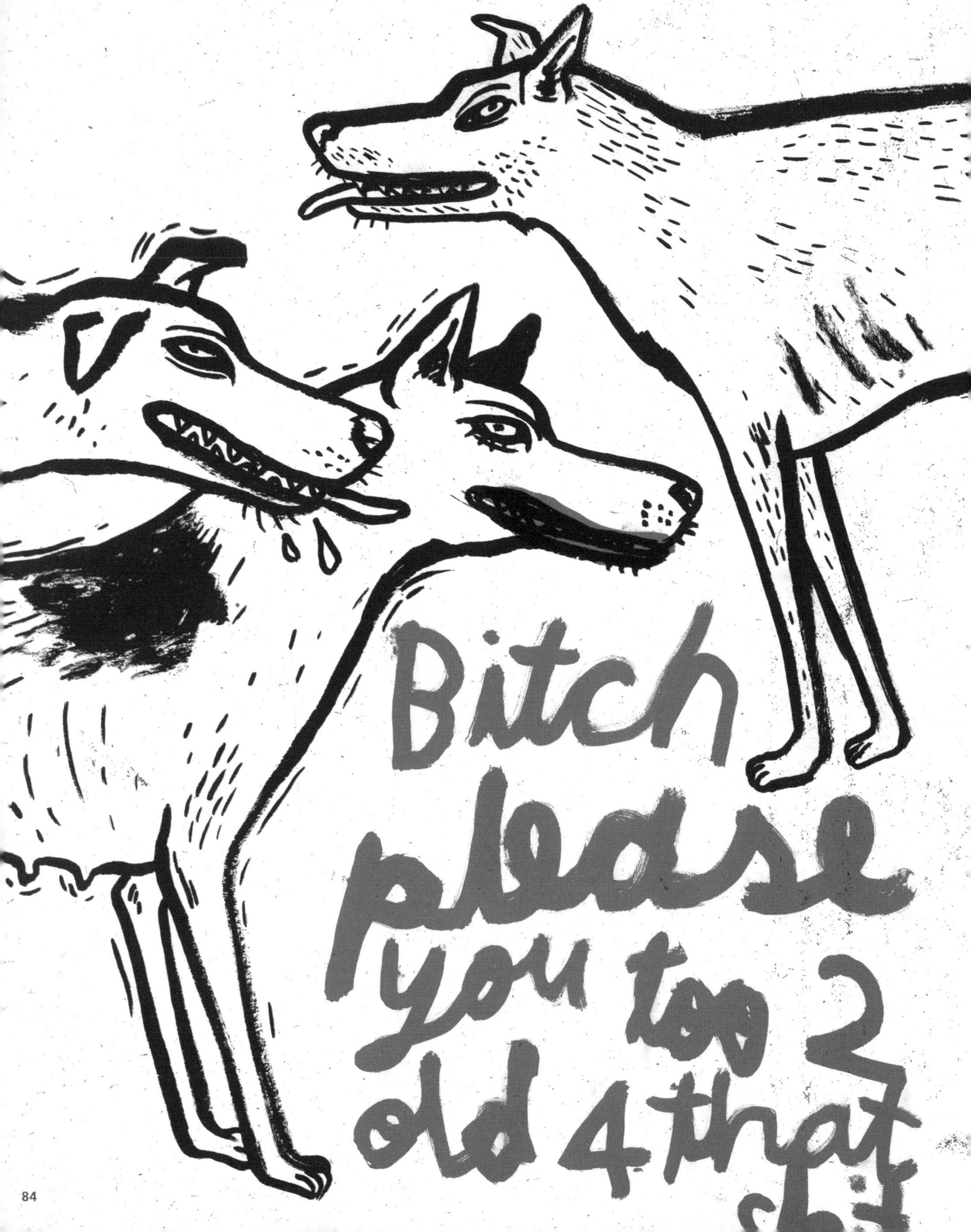
Bitch
please
you too 2
old 4 that

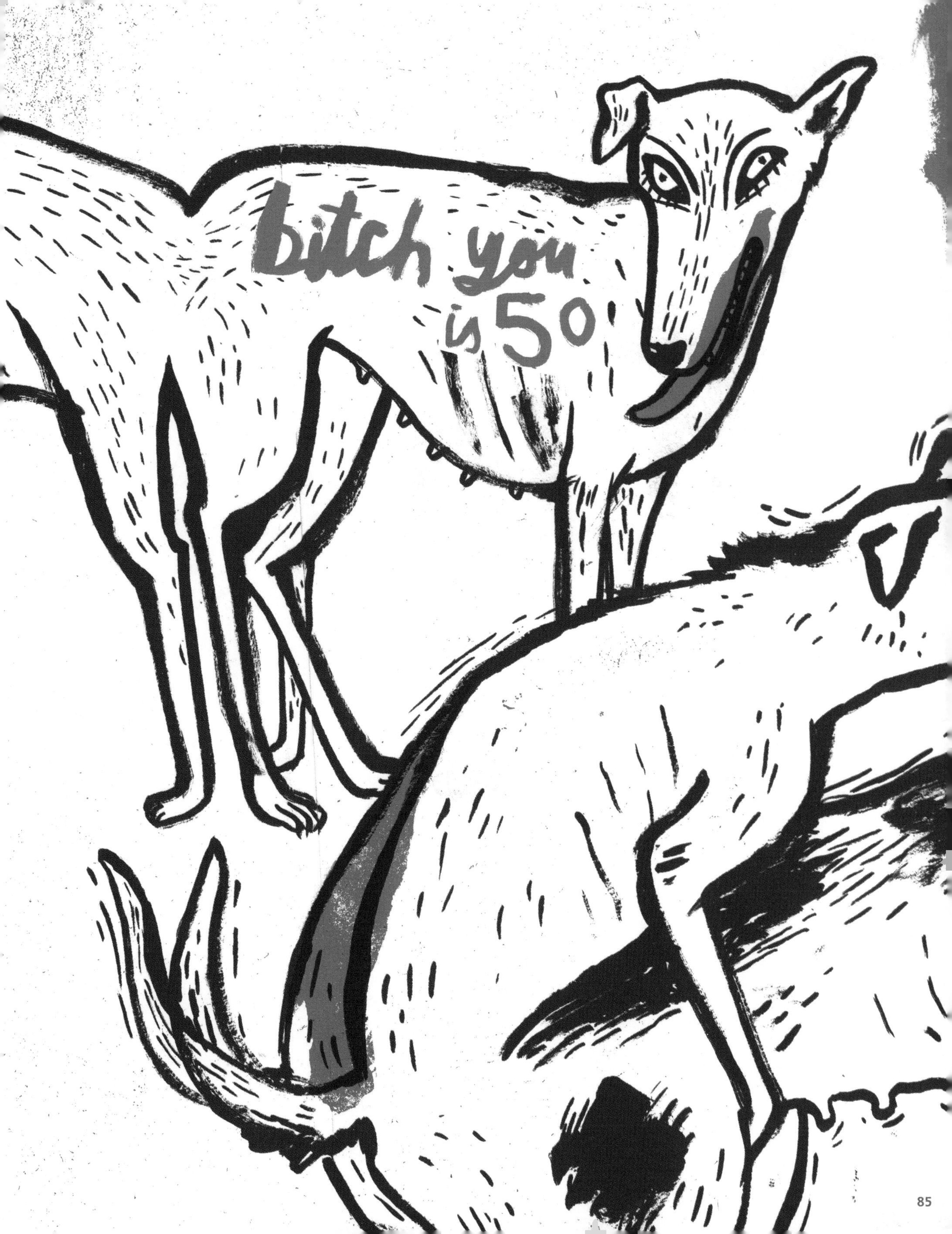
bitch you
is 50

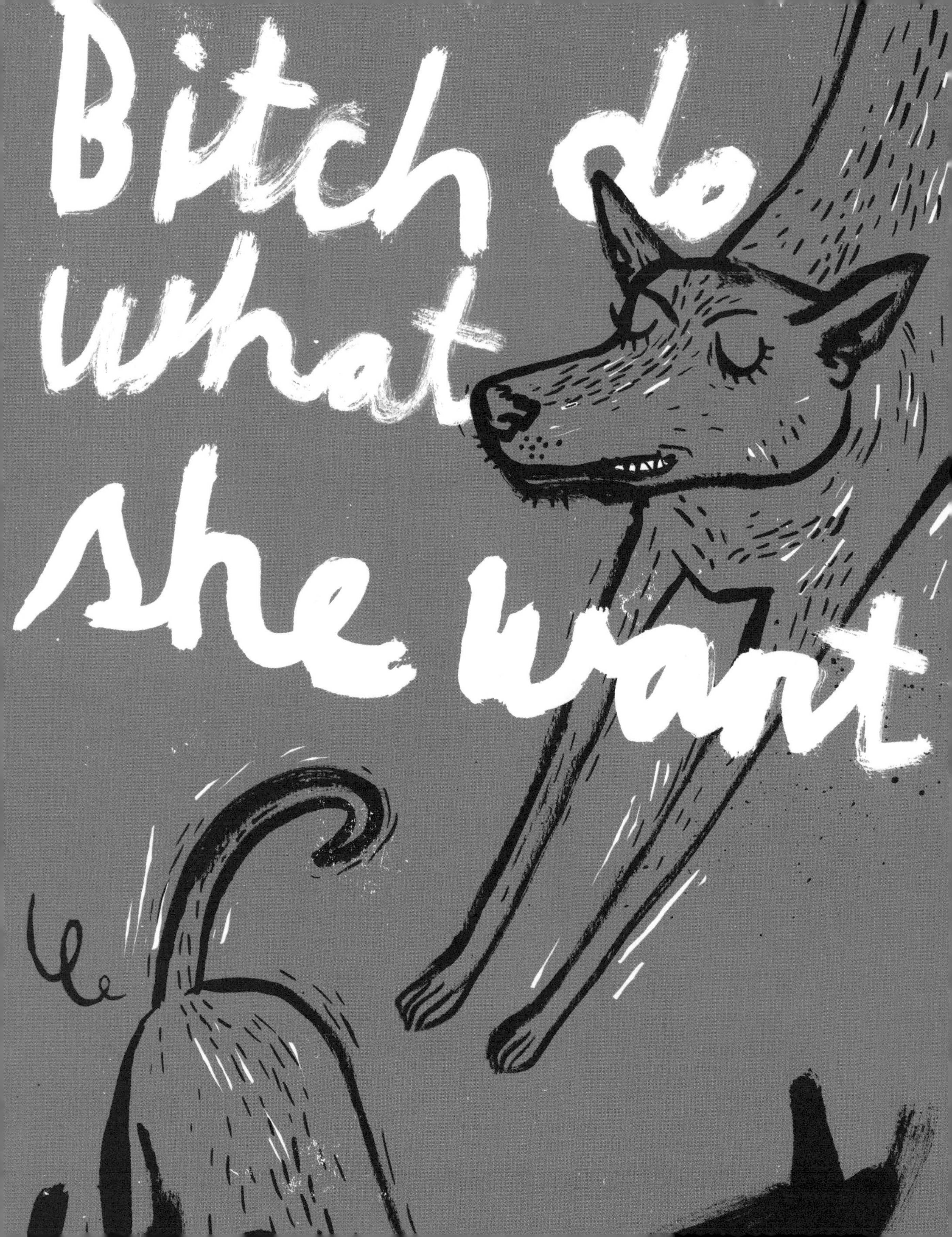
Bitch do what she want

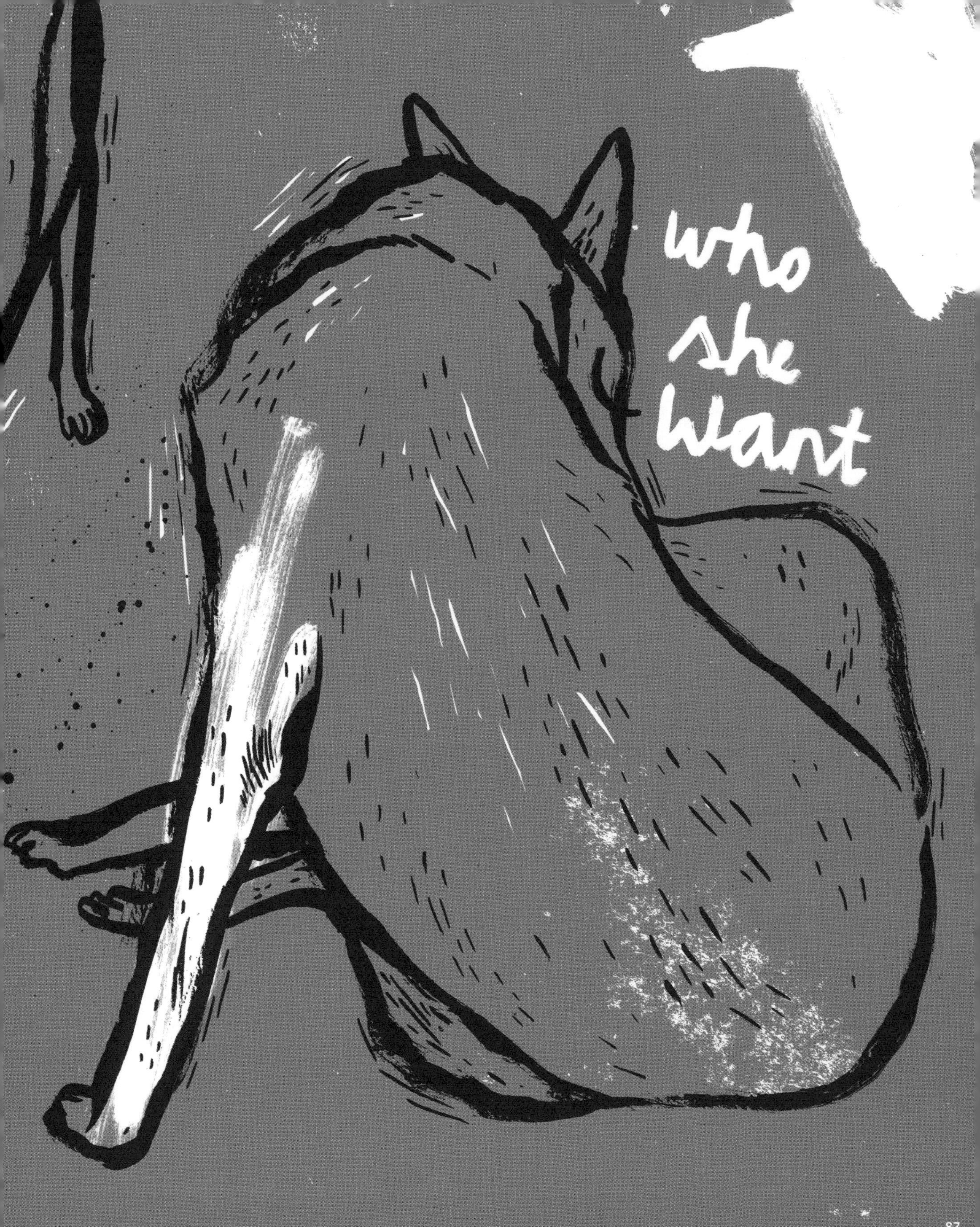
who
she
want

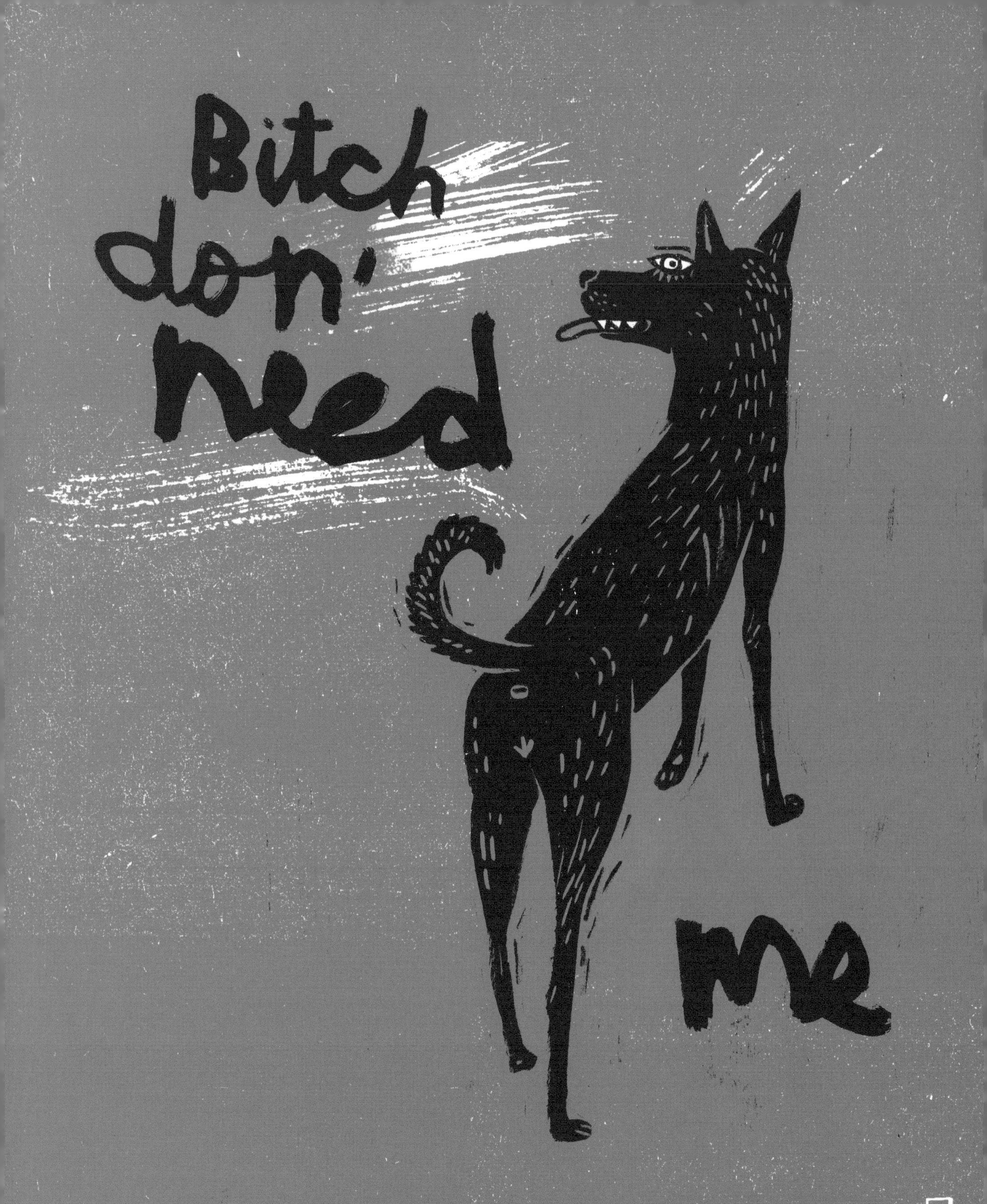
Bitch
don'
need
me

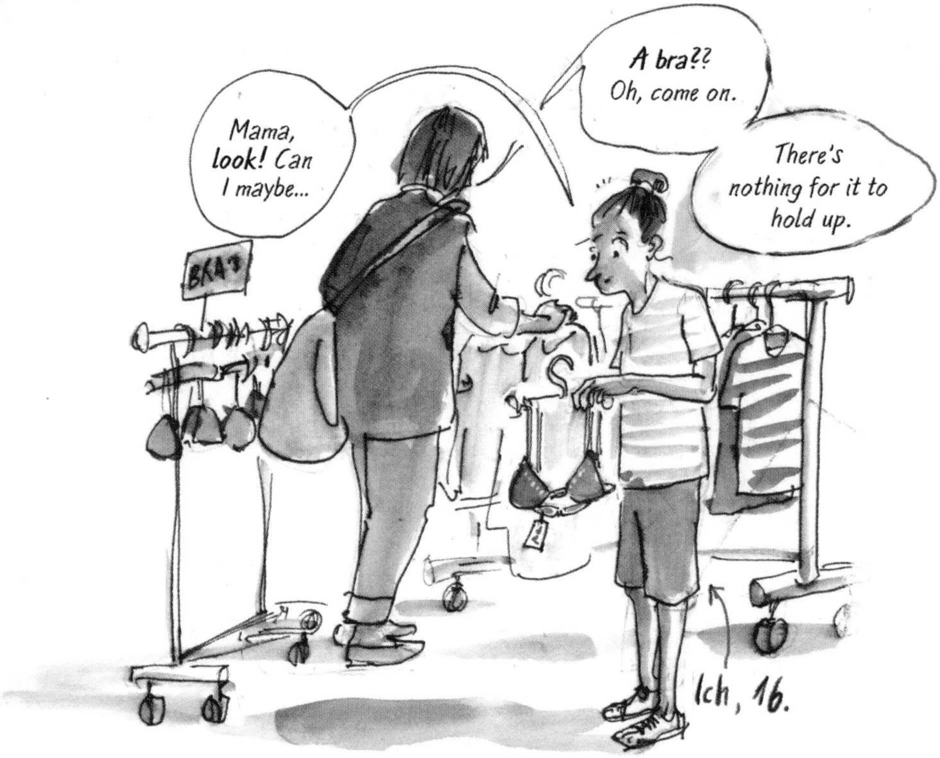
Mama, look! Can I maybe...
A bra?? Oh, come on.
There's nothing for it to hold up.
BRAS
Ich, 16.

I had **ALWAYS** wanted one.
If only for the feeling that there was something there to support.

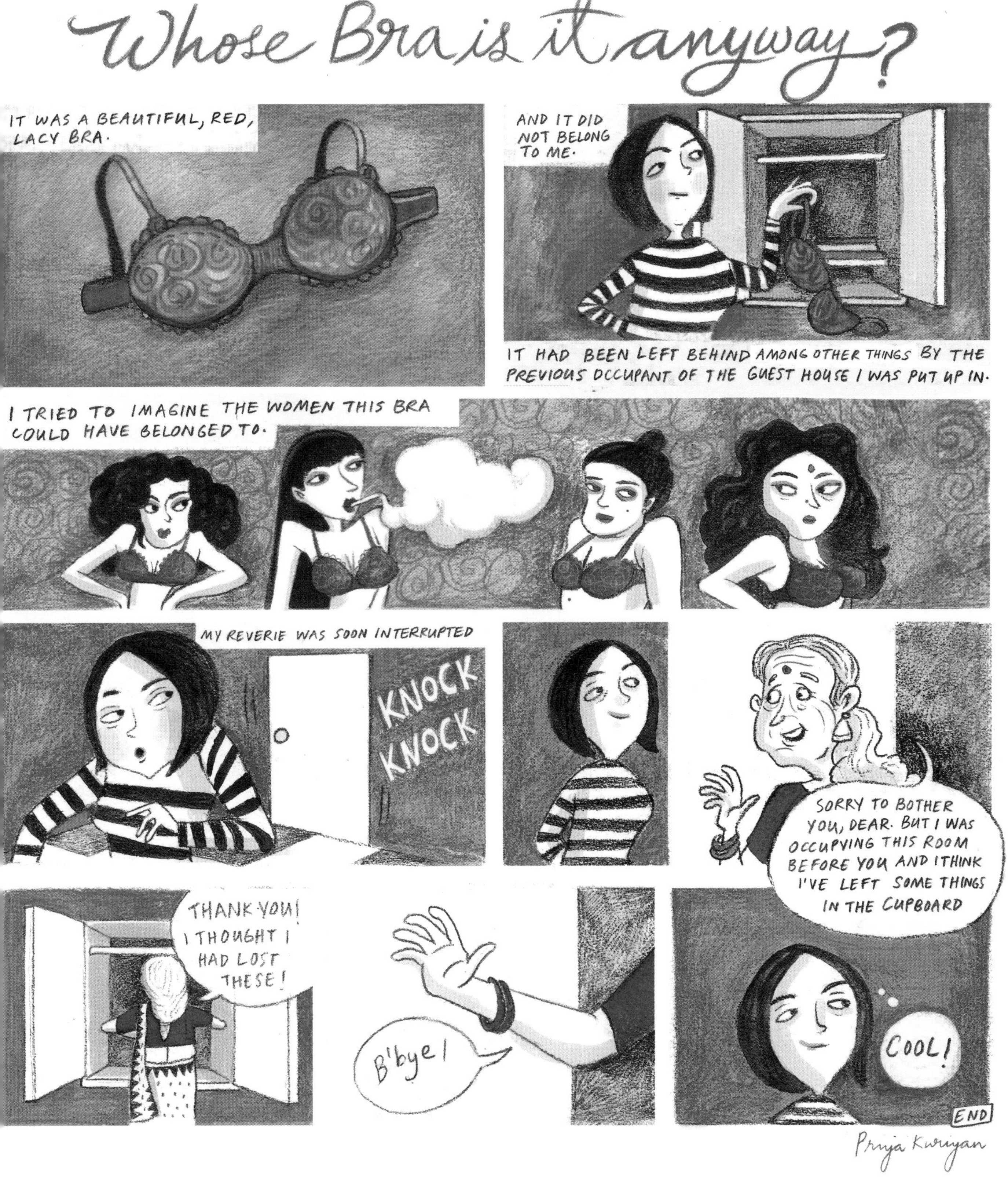
Whose Bra is it anyway?
IT WAS A BEAUTIFUL, RED, LACY BRA.
AND IT DID NOT BELONG TO ME.
IT HAD BEEN LEFT BEHIND AMONG OTHER THINGS BY THE PREVIOUS OCCUPANT OF THE GUEST HOUSE I WAS PUT UP IN.
I TRIED TO IMAGINE THE WOMEN THIS BRA COULD HAVE BELONGED TO.
MY REVERIE WAS SOON INTERRUPTED
KNOCK KNOCK
SORRY TO BOTHER YOU, DEAR. BUT I WAS OCCUPYING THIS ROOM BEFORE YOU AND I THINK I'VE LEFT SOME THINGS IN THE CUPBOARD
THANK YOU! I THOUGHT I HAD LOST THESE!
B'bye!
COOL!
END
Priya Kuriyan

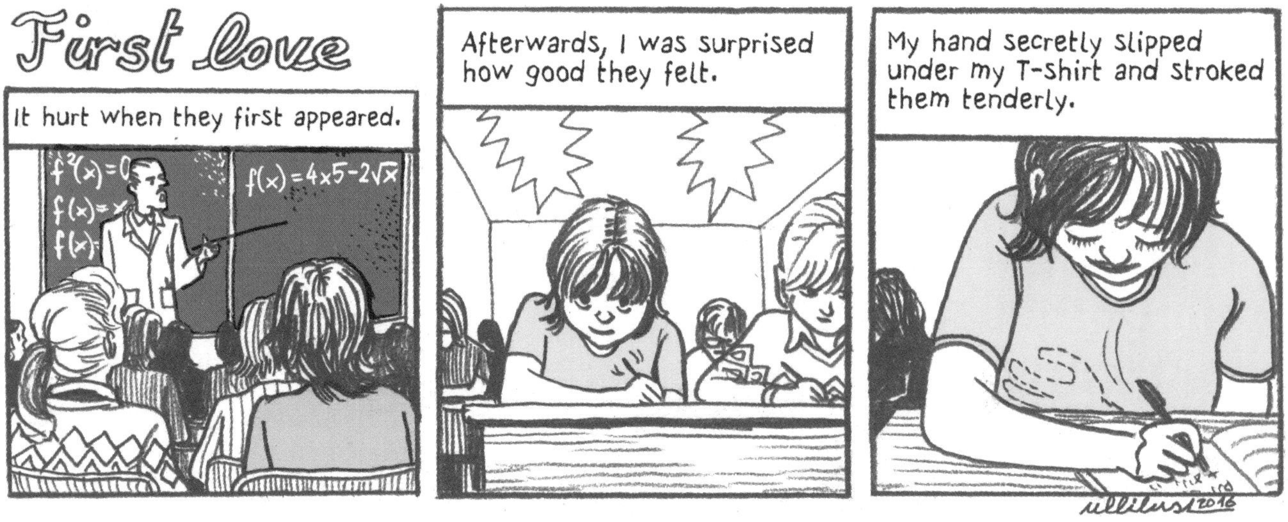
First love
It hurt when they first appeared.
f(x) =4x5−2√x
Afterwards, I was surprised how good they felt.
My hand secretly slipped under my T-shirt and stroked them tenderly.
ullilust 2016

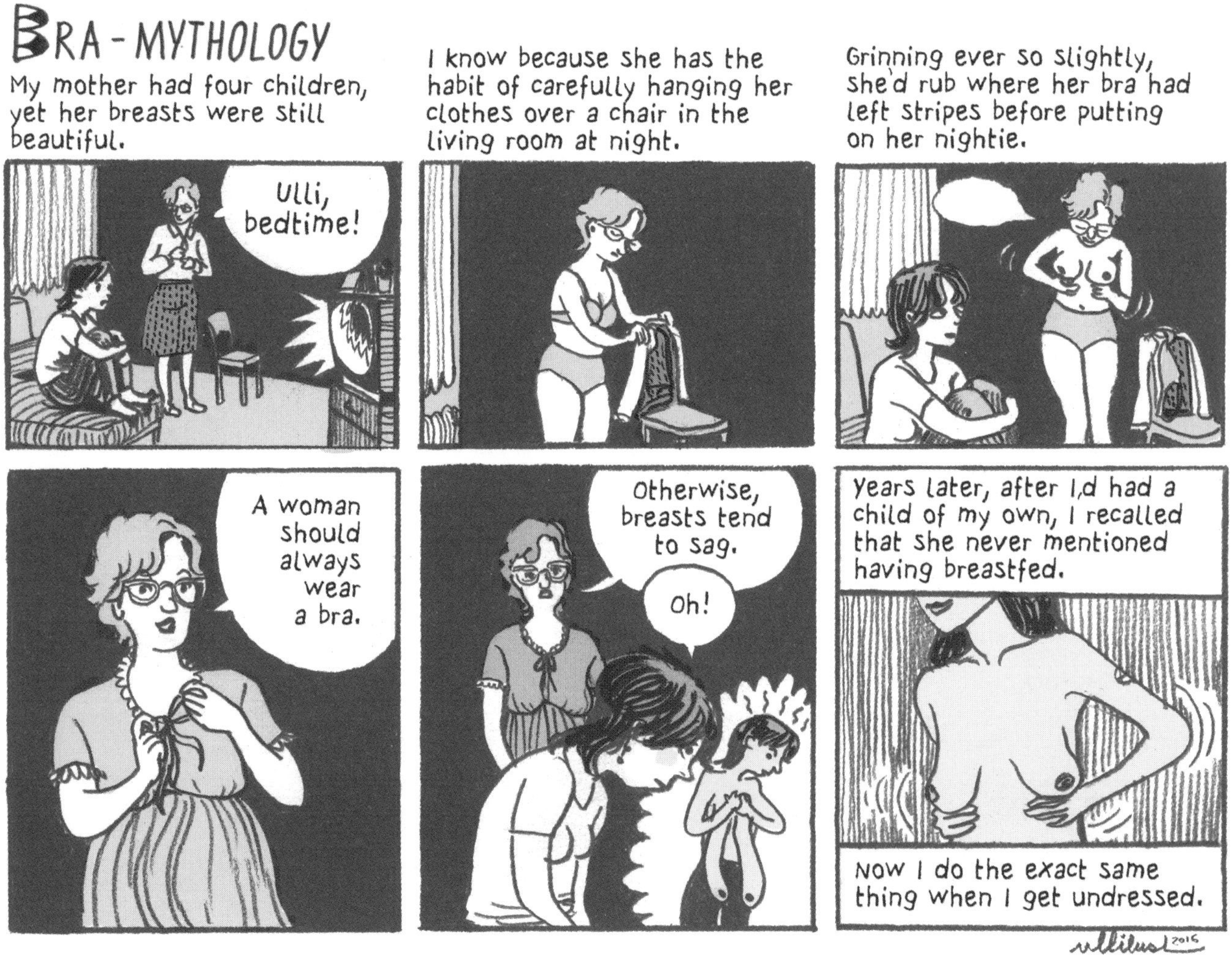
BRA-MYTHOLOGY
My mother had four children, yet her breasts were still beautiful.
Ulli, bedtime!
I know because she has the habit of carefully hanging her clothes over a chair in the living room at night.
Grinning ever so slightly, she'd rub where her bra had left stripes before putting on her nightie.
A woman should always wear a bra.
Otherwise, breasts tend to sag.
Oh!
Years later, after I,d had a child of my own, I recalled that she never mentioned having breastfed.
Now I do the exact same thing when I get undressed.
ullilust 2016

# sometimes

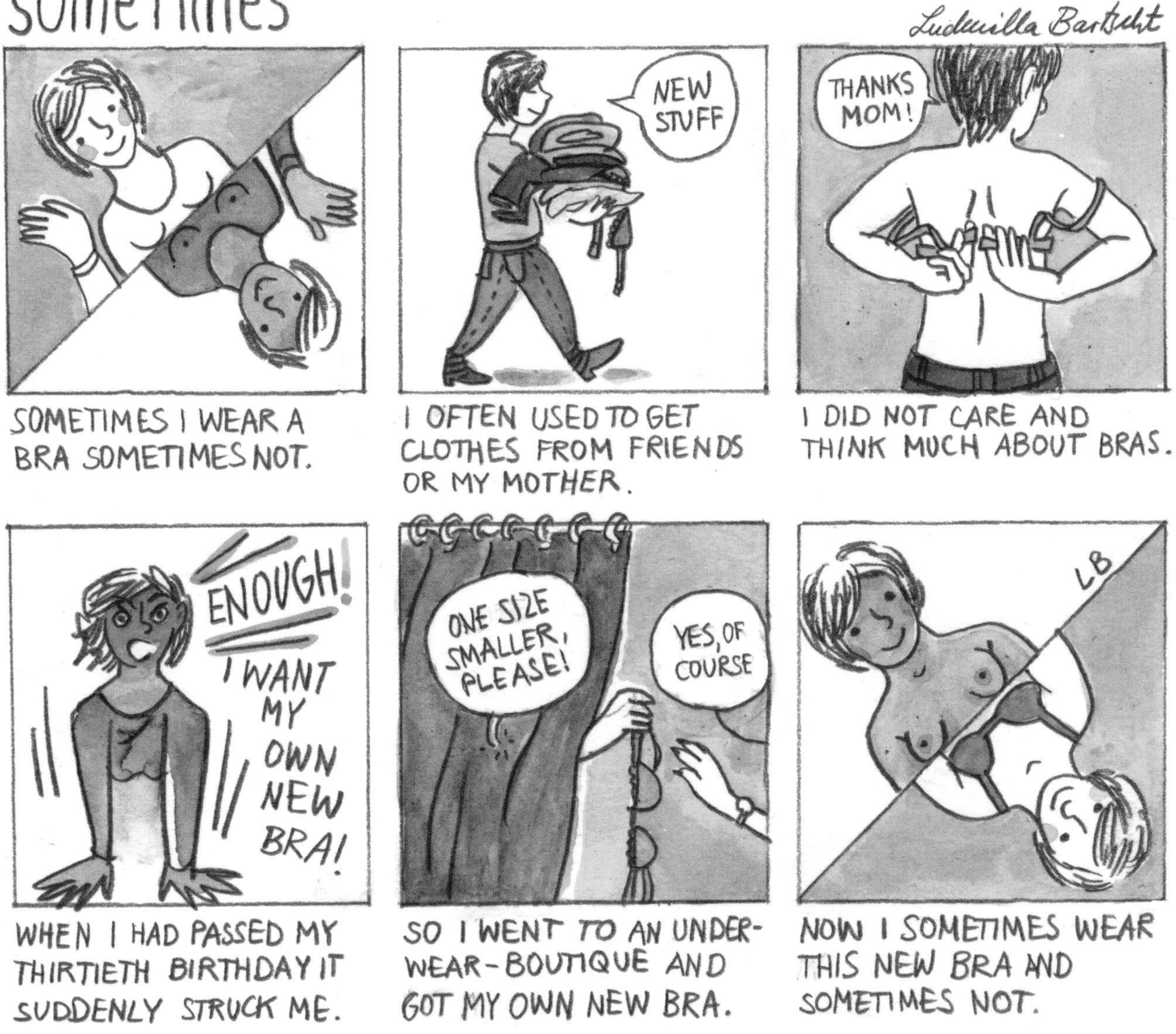
Ludmilla Bartscht
SOMETIMES I WEAR A BRA SOMETIMES NOT.
NEW STUFF
I OFTEN USED TO GET CLOTHES FROM FRIENDS OR MY MOTHER.
THANKS MOM!
I DID NOT CARE AND THINK MUCH ABOUT BRAS.
ENOUGH!
I WANT MY OWN NEW BRA!
WHEN I HAD PASSED MY THIRTIETH BIRTHDAY IT SUDDENLY STRUCK ME.
ONE SIZE SMALLER, PLEASE!
YES, OF COURSE
SO I WENT TO AN UNDER-WEAR-BOUTIQUE AND GOT MY OWN NEW BRA.
LB
NOW I SOMETIMES WEAR THIS NEW BRA AND SOMETIMES NOT.

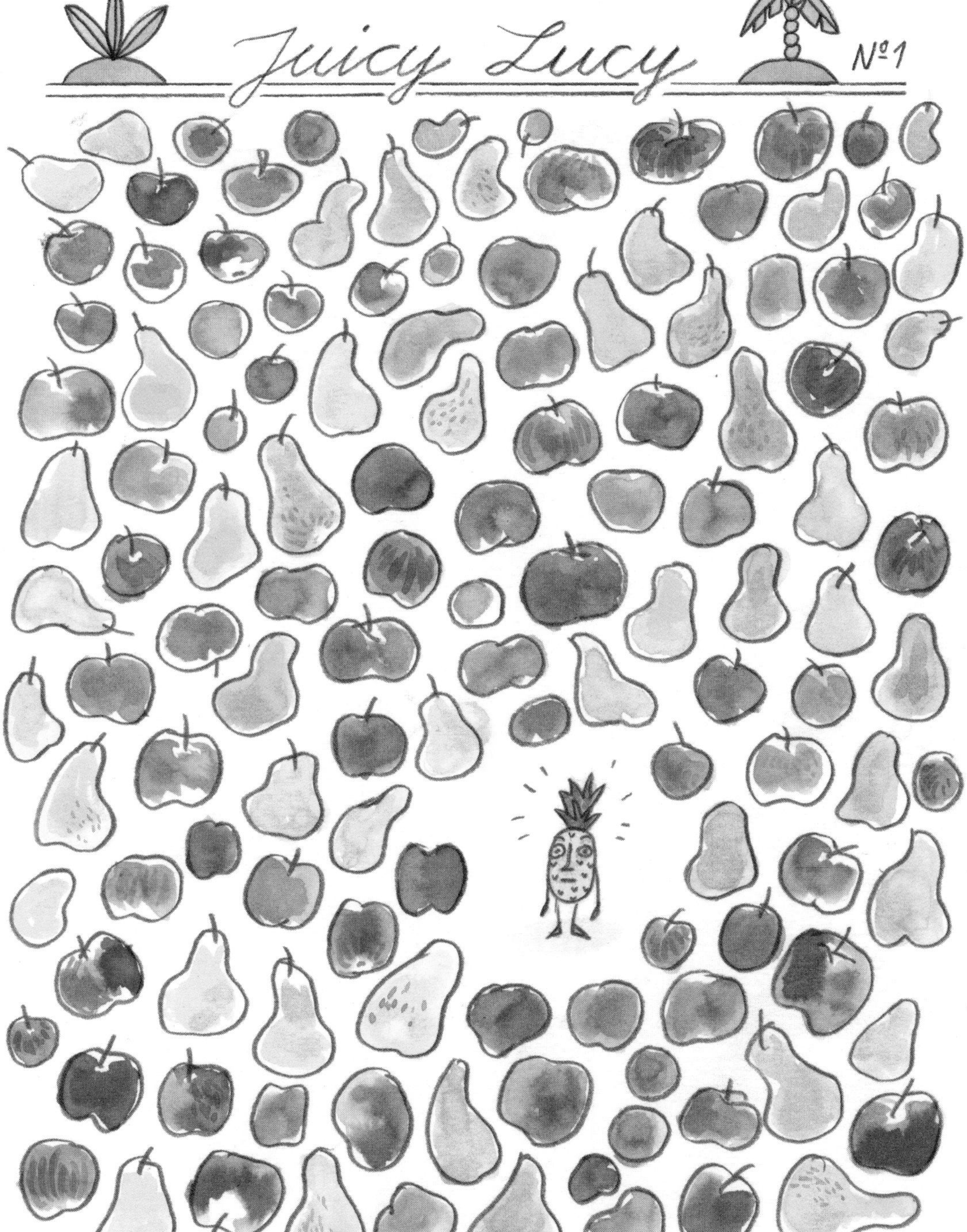
Juicy Lucy
№1
Ludmilla Bartscht

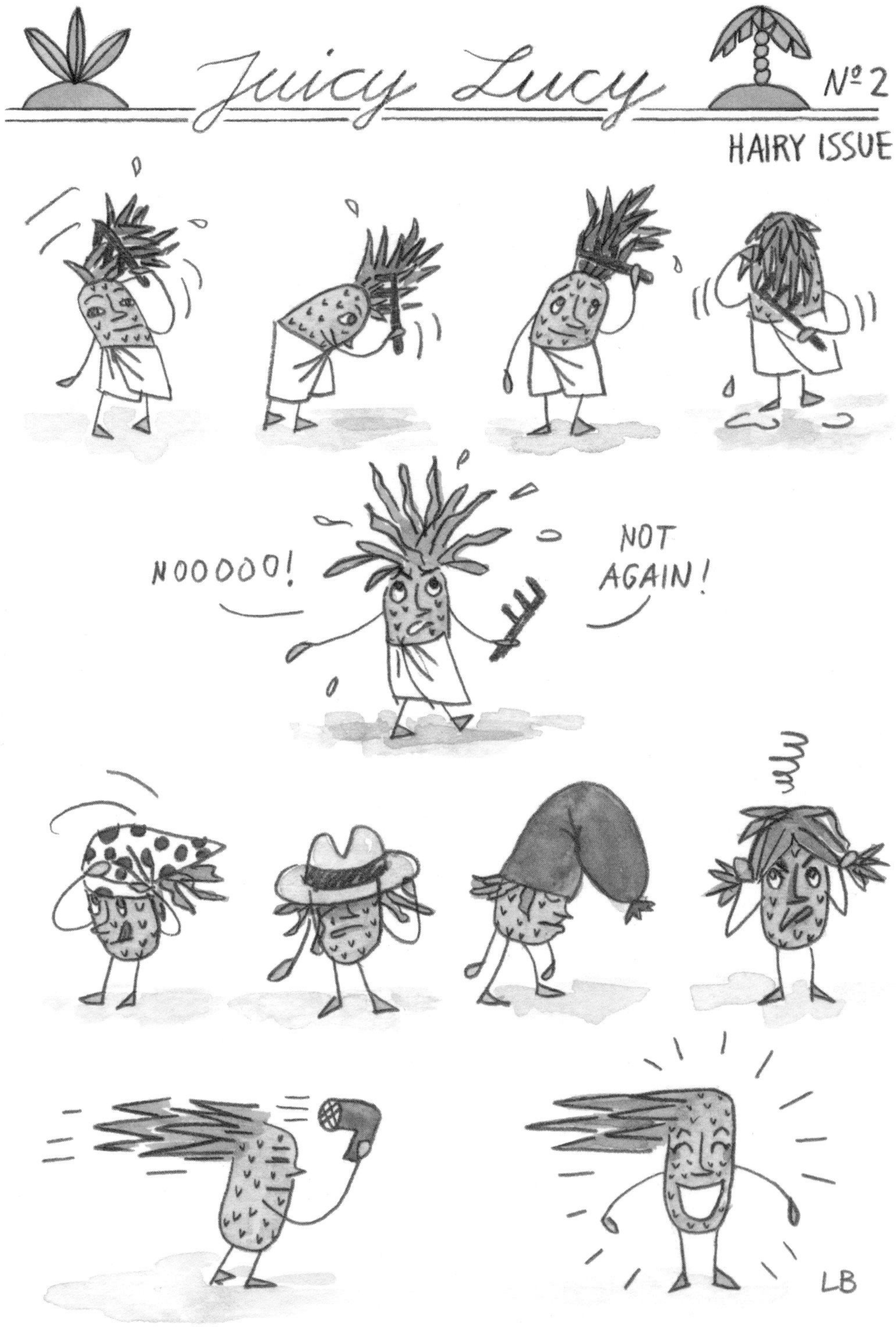
Juicy Lucy
Nº2
HAIRY ISSUE
NOOOOO!
NOT AGAIN!
LB

# Juicy Lucy Nº 3

HI BRA LO BRA

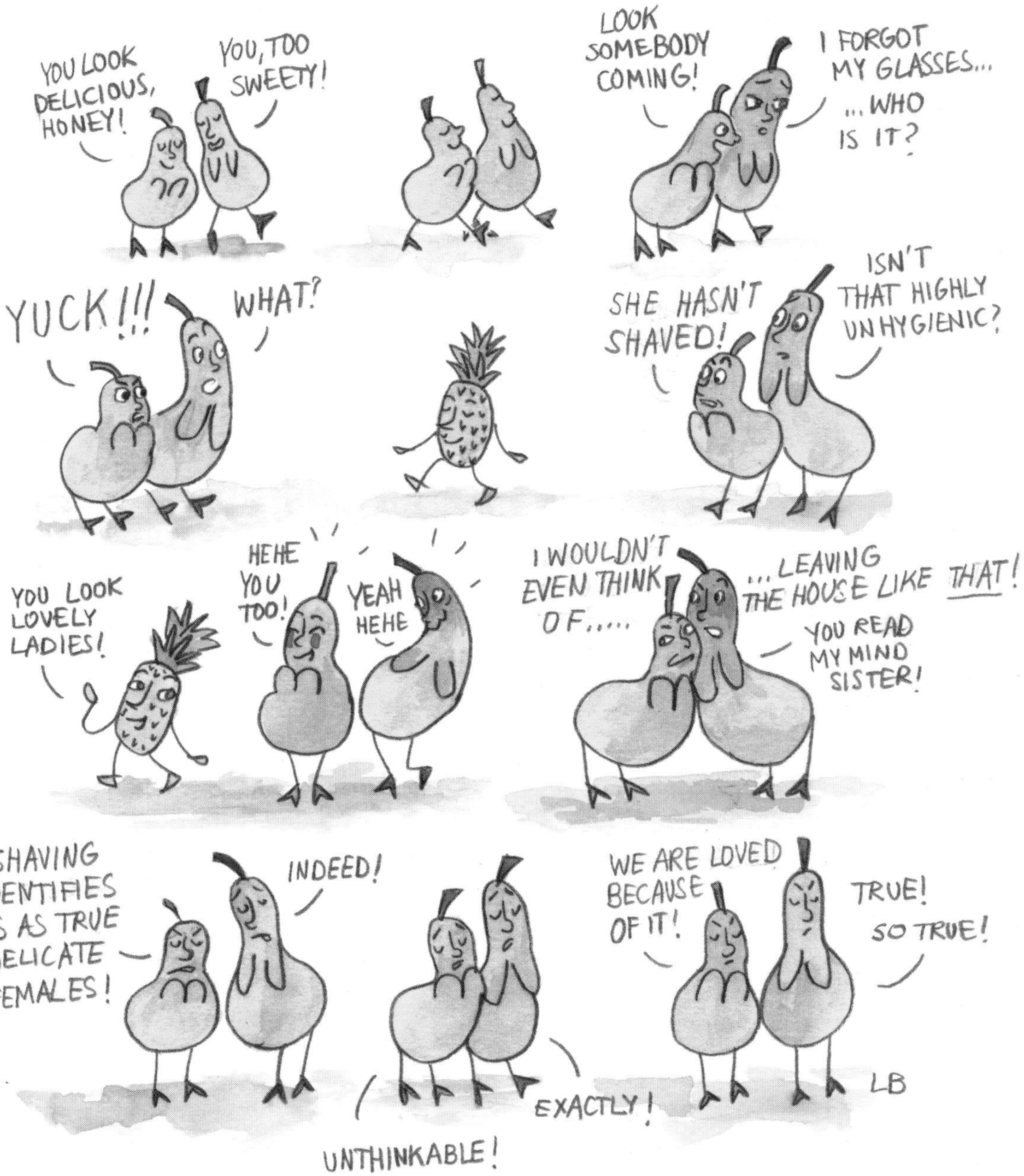
YOU LOOK DELICIOUS, HONEY!
YOU, TOO SWEETY!
LOOK SOMEBODY COMING!
I FORGOT MY GLASSES...
...WHO IS IT?
YUCK!!!
WHAT?
SHE HASN'T SHAVED!
ISN'T THAT HIGHLY UNHYGIENIC?
YOU LOOK LOVELY LADIES!
HEHE YOU TOO!
YEAH HEHE
I WOULDN'T EVEN THINK OF.....
...LEAVING THE HOUSE LIKE THAT!
YOU READ MY MIND SISTER!
SHAVING IDENTIFIES US AS TRUE DELICATE FEMALES!
INDEED!
UNTHINKABLE!
EXACTLY!
WE ARE LOVED BECAUSE OF IT!
TRUE!
SO TRUE!
LB

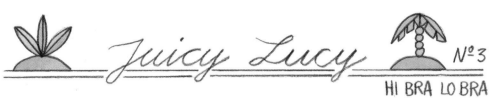

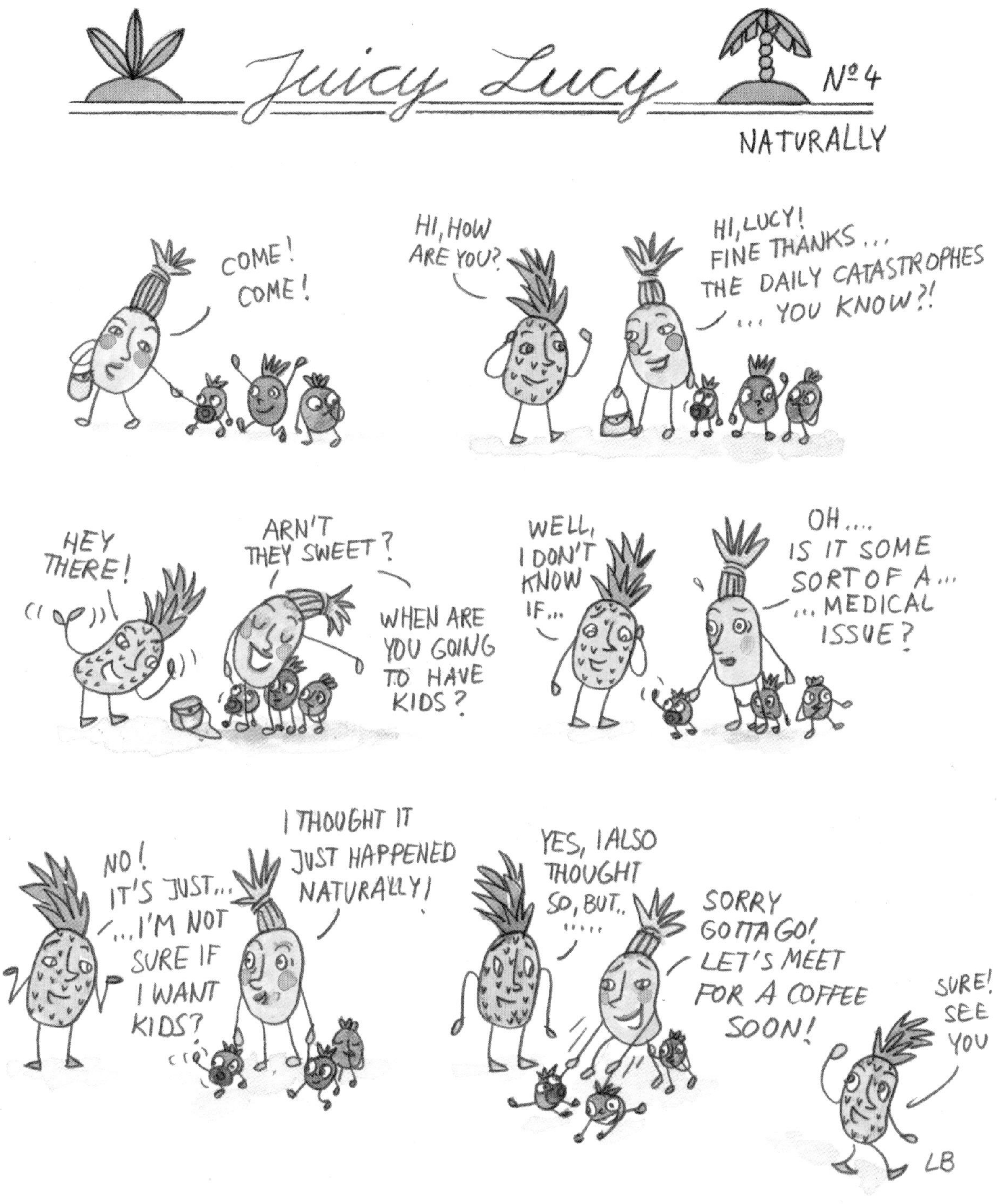
Juicy Lucy
Nº4
NATURALLY
COME! COME!
HI, HOW ARE YOU?
HI, LUCY! FINE THANKS... THE DAILY CATASTROPHES ... YOU KNOW?!
HEY THERE!
ARN'T THEY SWEET?
WHEN ARE YOU GOING TO HAVE KIDS?
WELL, I DON'T KNOW IF...
OH.... IS IT SOME SORT OF A... ...MEDICAL ISSUE?
NO! IT'S JUST... ...I'M NOT SURE IF I WANT KIDS?
I THOUGHT IT JUST HAPPENED NATURALLY!
YES, I ALSO THOUGHT SO, BUT.. .....
SORRY GOTTA GO! LET'S MEET FOR A COFFEE SOON!
SURE! SEE YOU
LB

Juicy Lucy
Nº5
PROMISES
loved & sexy
EVERYTHING YOU DREAM OF
LB

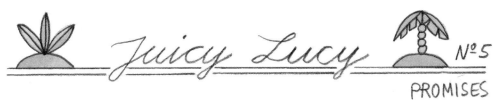

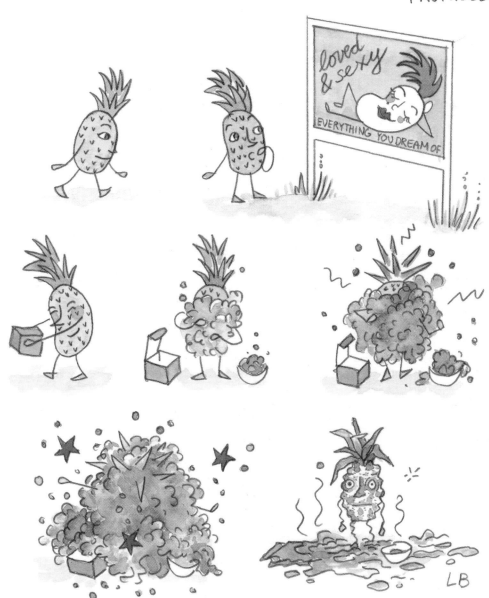

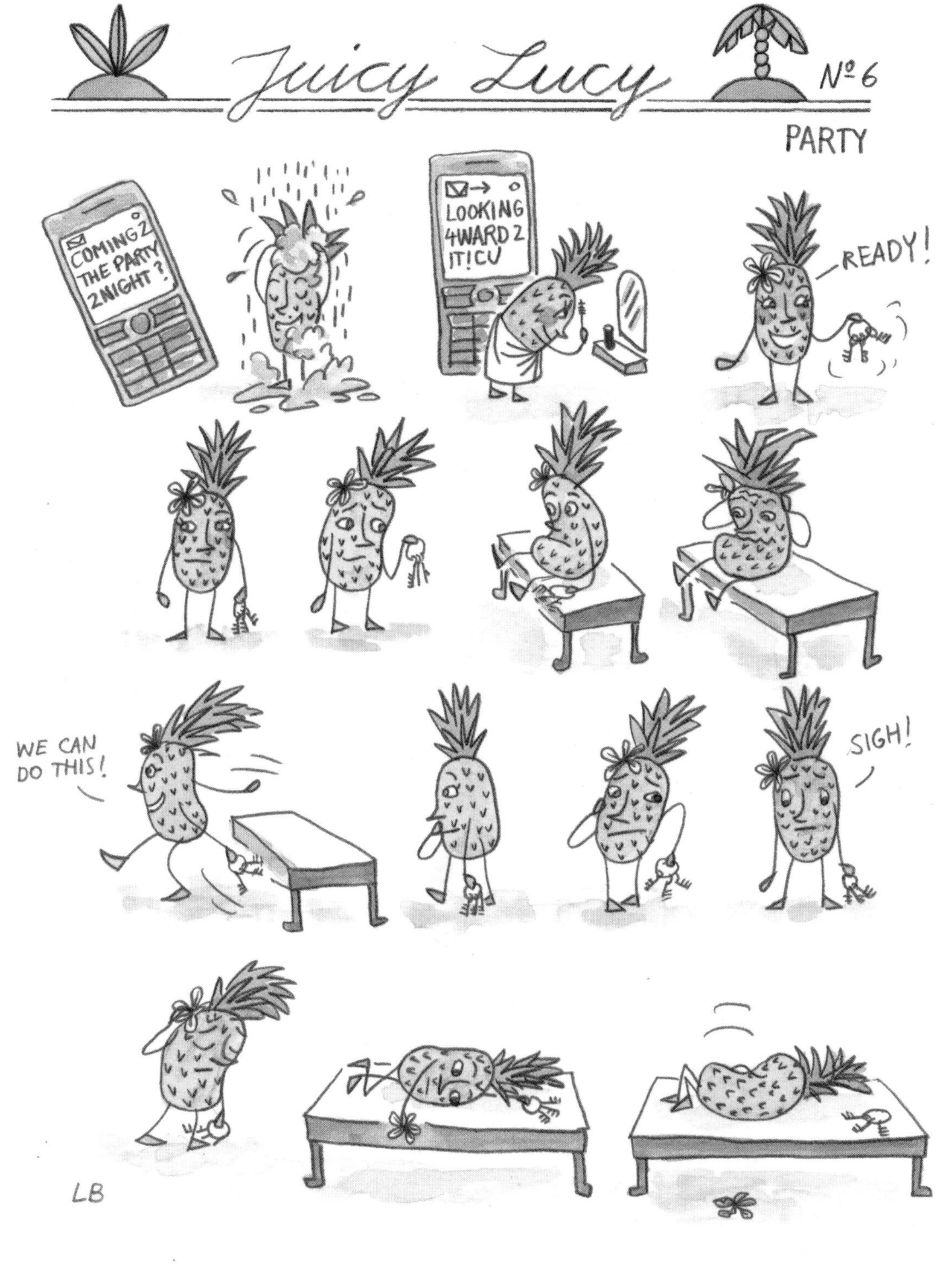
Juicy Lucy
Nº6
PARTY
COMING 2 THE PARTY 2NIGHT?
LOOKING 4WARD 2 IT! CU
READY!
WE CAN DO THIS!
SIGH!
LB

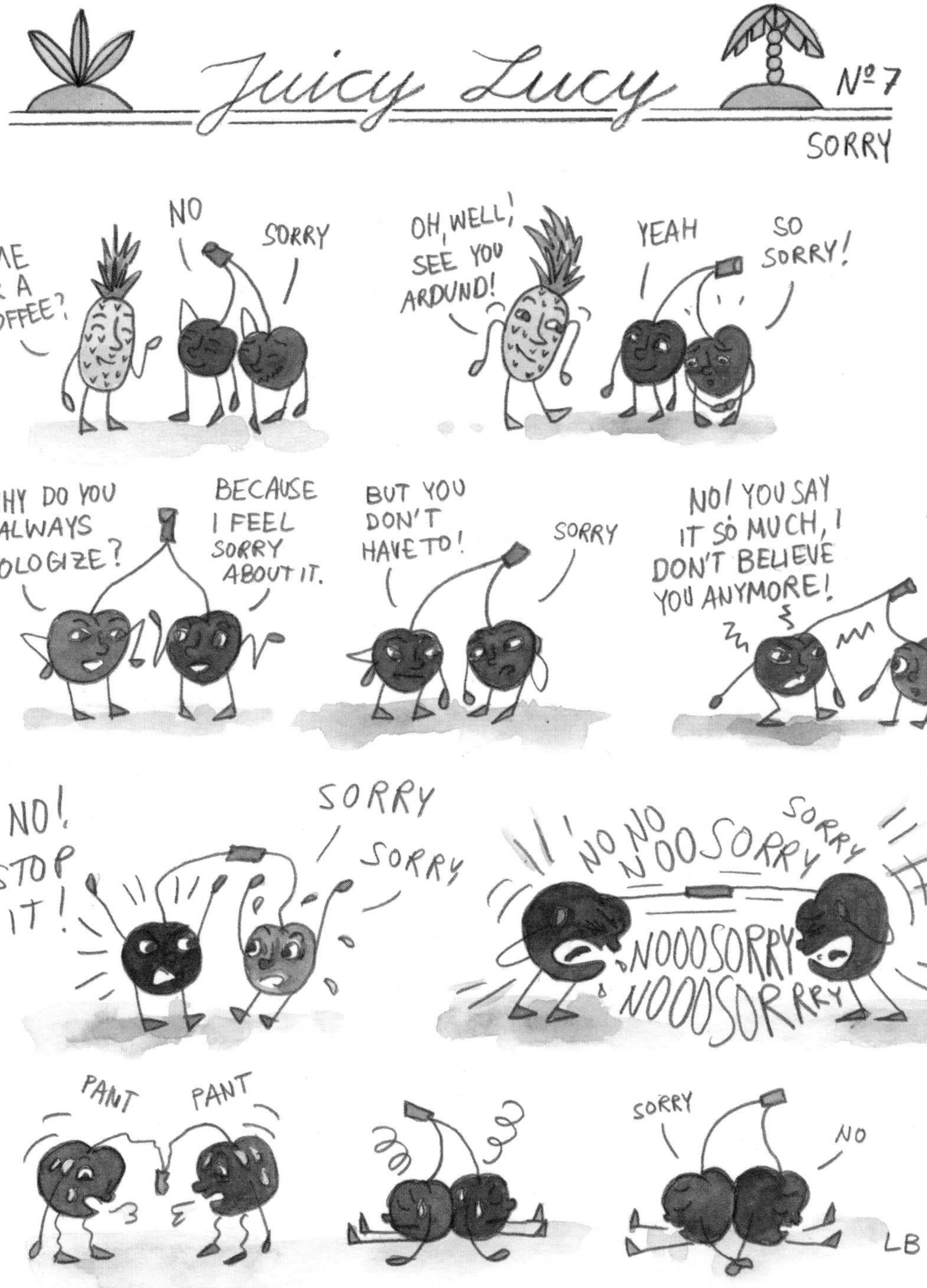
Juicy Lucy
№ 7
SORRY
TIME FOR A COFFEE?
NO
SORRY
OH, WELL! SEE YOU AROUND!
YEAH
SO SORRY!
WHY DO YOU ALWAYS APOLOGIZE?
BECAUSE I FEEL SORRY ABOUT IT.
BUT YOU DON'T HAVE TO!
SORRY
NO! YOU SAY IT SO MUCH, I DON'T BELIEVE YOU ANYMORE!
OH NO! SORRY!
NO! STOP IT!
SORRY
SORRY
NO NO NOO SORRY
SORRY
NOOOSORRY
NOOOSORRRY
PANT
PANT
SORRY
NO
LB

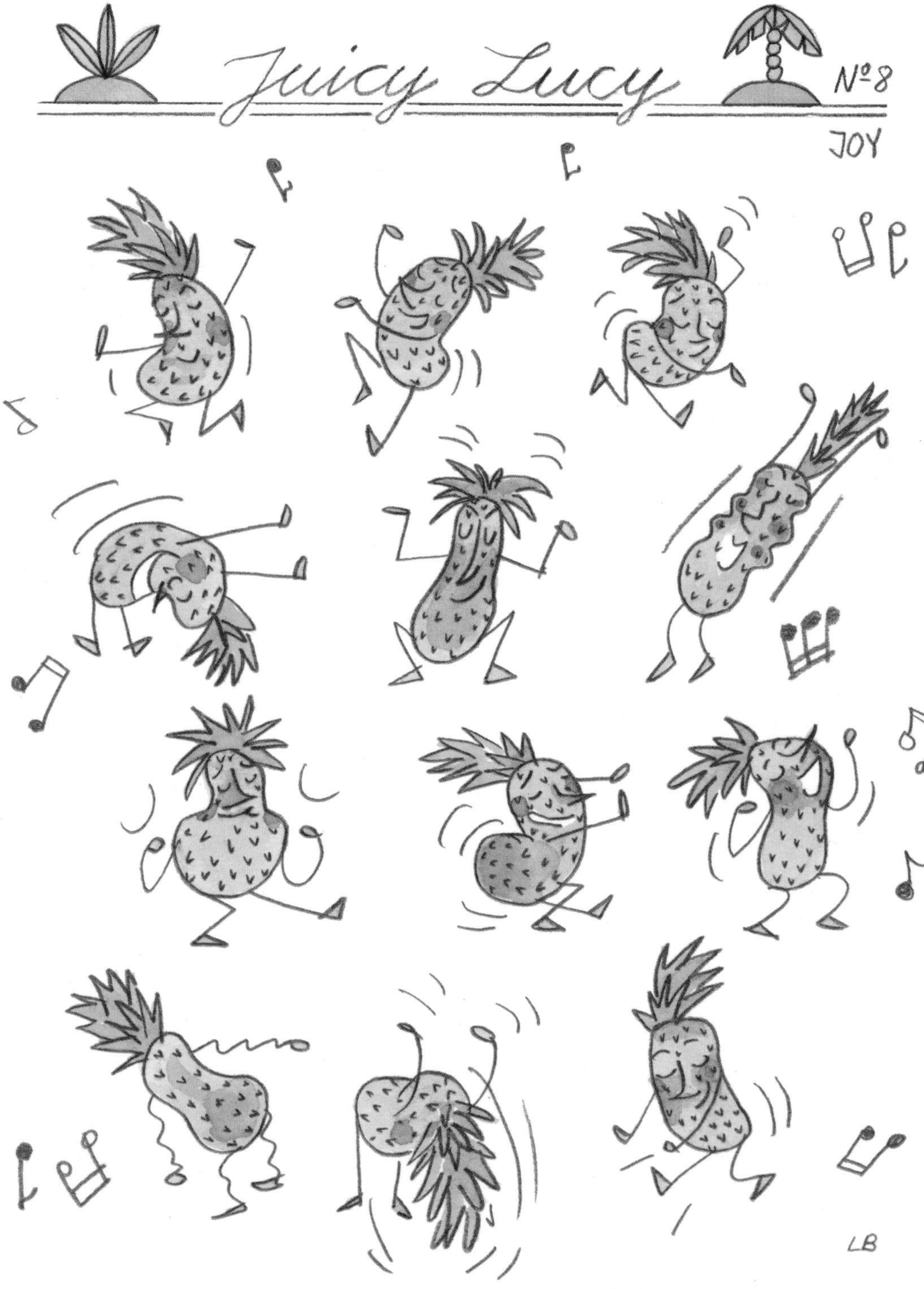
Juicy Lucy
№ 8
JOY
LB

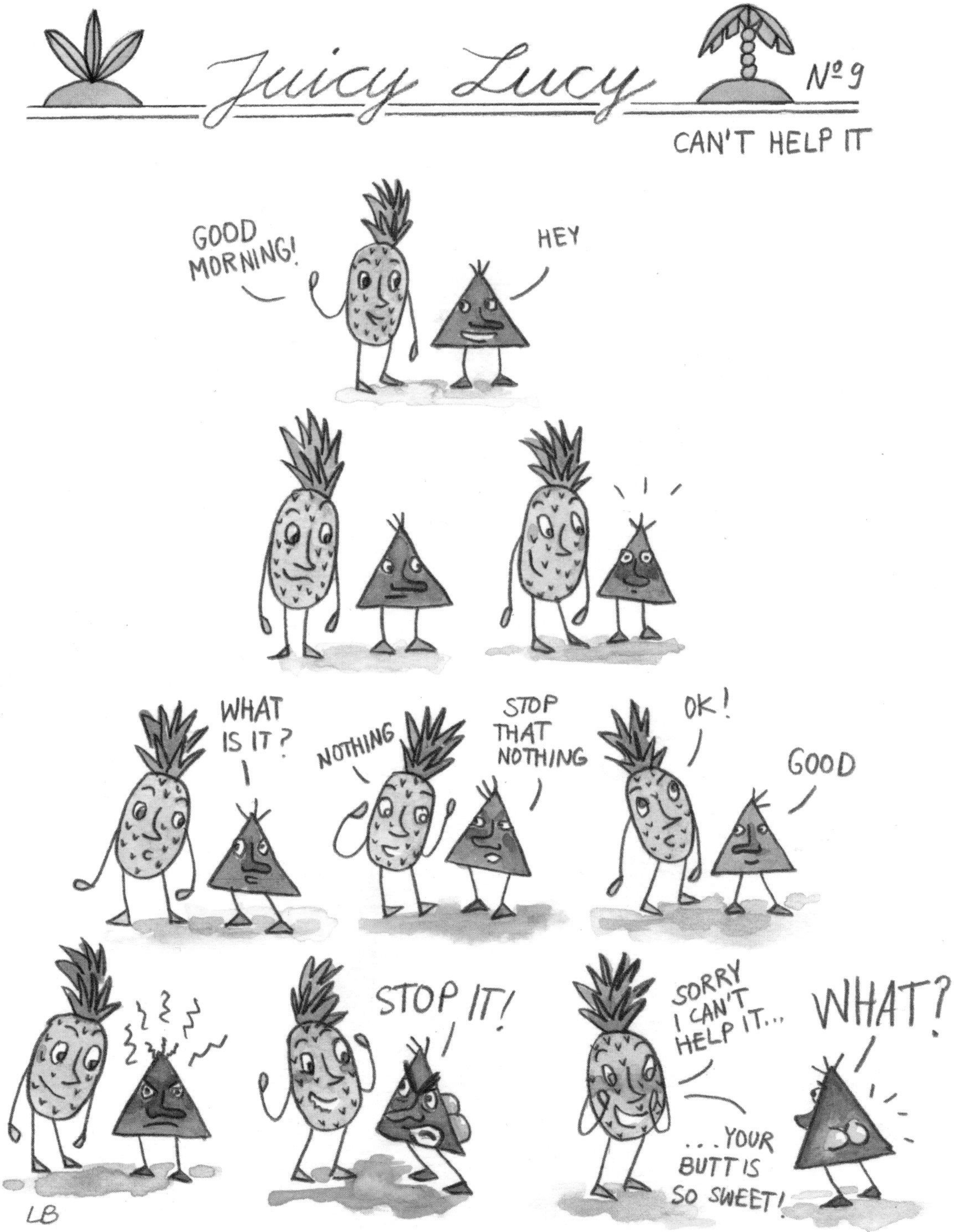
Juicy Lucy
№ 9
CAN'T HELP IT
GOOD MORNING!
HEY
WHAT IS IT?
NOTHING
STOP THAT NOTHING
OK!
GOOD
STOP IT!
SORRY I CAN'T HELP IT...
...YOUR BUTT IS SO SWEET!
WHAT?
LB

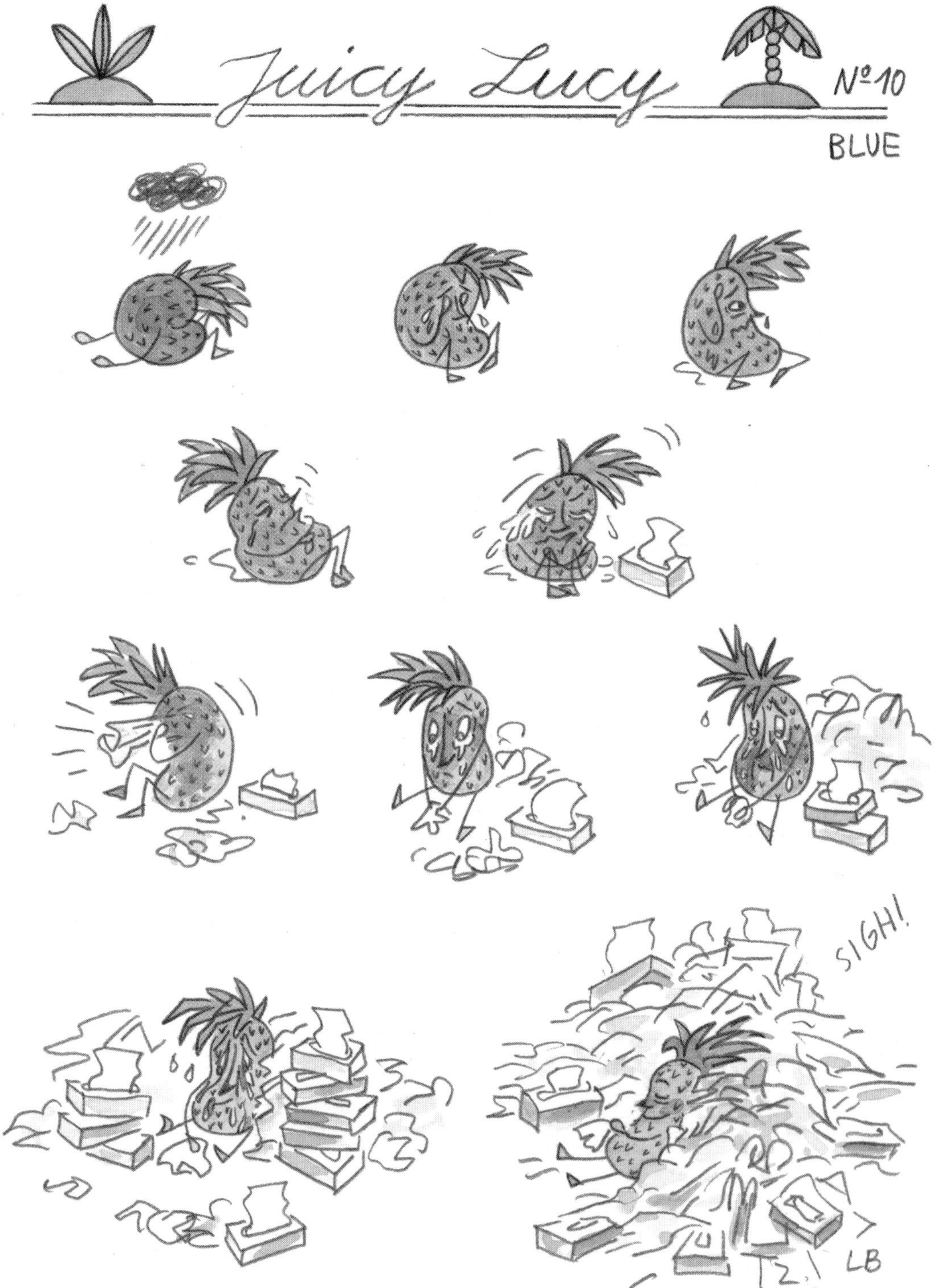
Juicy Lucy
Nº10
BLUE
SIGH!
LB

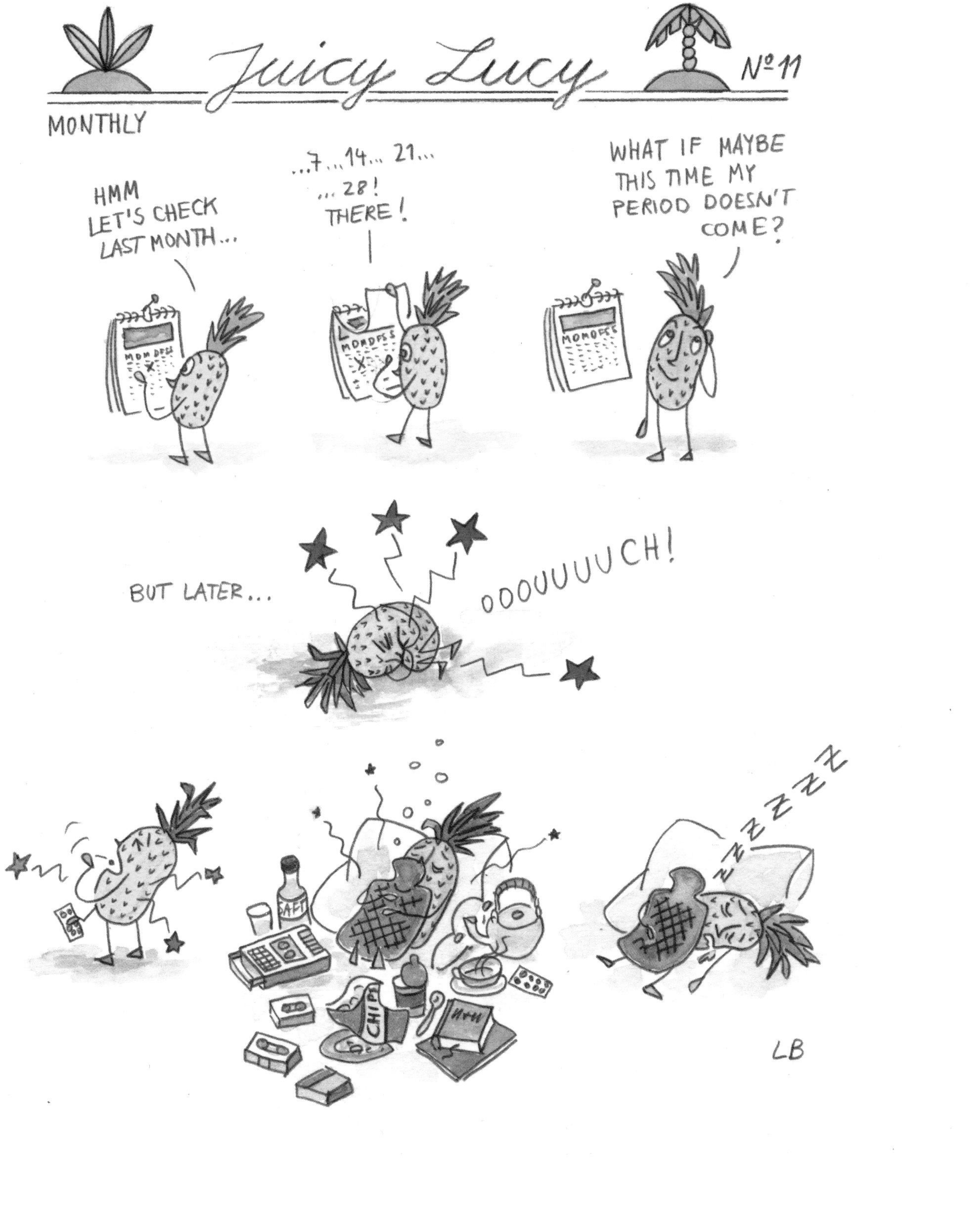
Juicy Lucy
№ 11
MONTHLY
HMM
LET'S CHECK
LAST MONTH...
...7...14... 21...
...28!
THERE!
WHAT IF MAYBE
THIS TIME MY
PERIOD DOESN'T
COME?
BUT LATER...
OOOUUUUCH!
SAFT
CHIPS
ZZZZZZ
LB

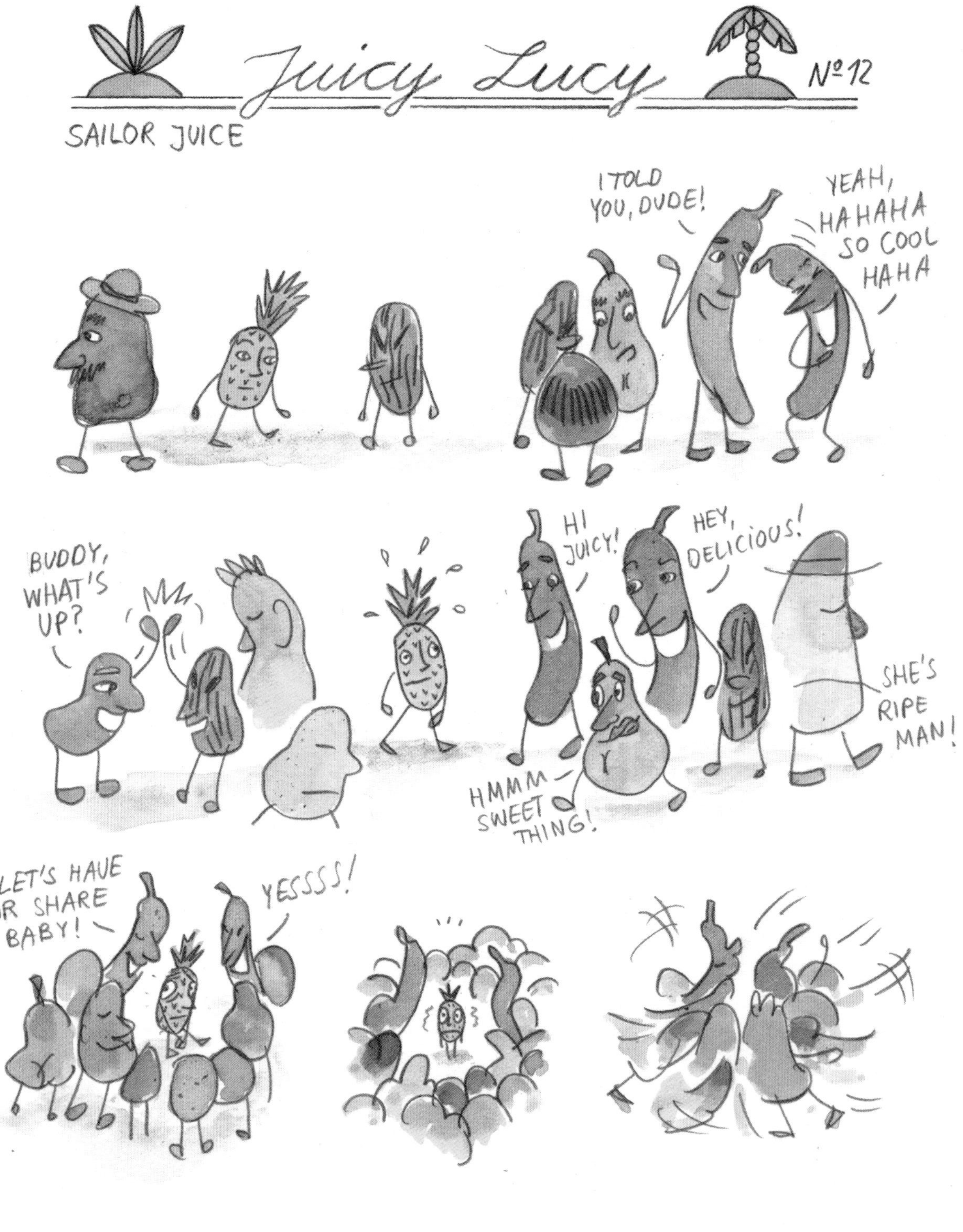
Juicy Lucy
№12
SAILOR JUICE
I TOLD YOU, DUDE!
YEAH, HAHAHA SO COOL HAHA
BUDDY, WHAT'S UP?
HI JUICY!
HEY, DELICIOUS!
SHE'S RIPE MAN!
HMMM SWEET THING!
LET'S HAVE OUR SHARE BABY!
YESSSS!

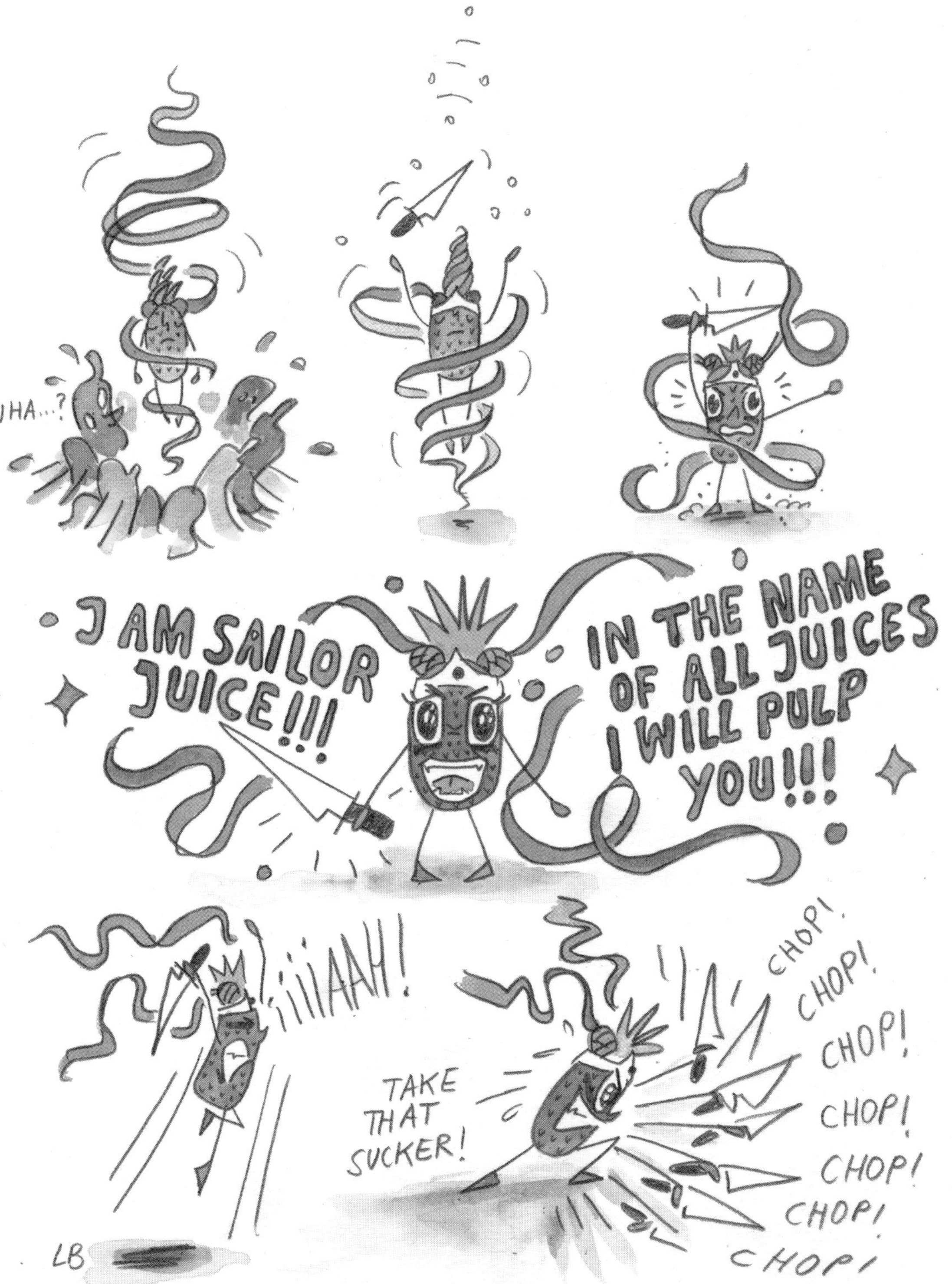
WHA...?
I AM SAILOR JUICE!!!
IN THE NAME OF ALL JUICES I WILL PULP YOU!!!
¡¡¡IAAH!
TAKE THAT SUCKER!
CHOP!
CHOP!
CHOP!
CHOP!
CHOP!
CHOP!
CHOP!
LB

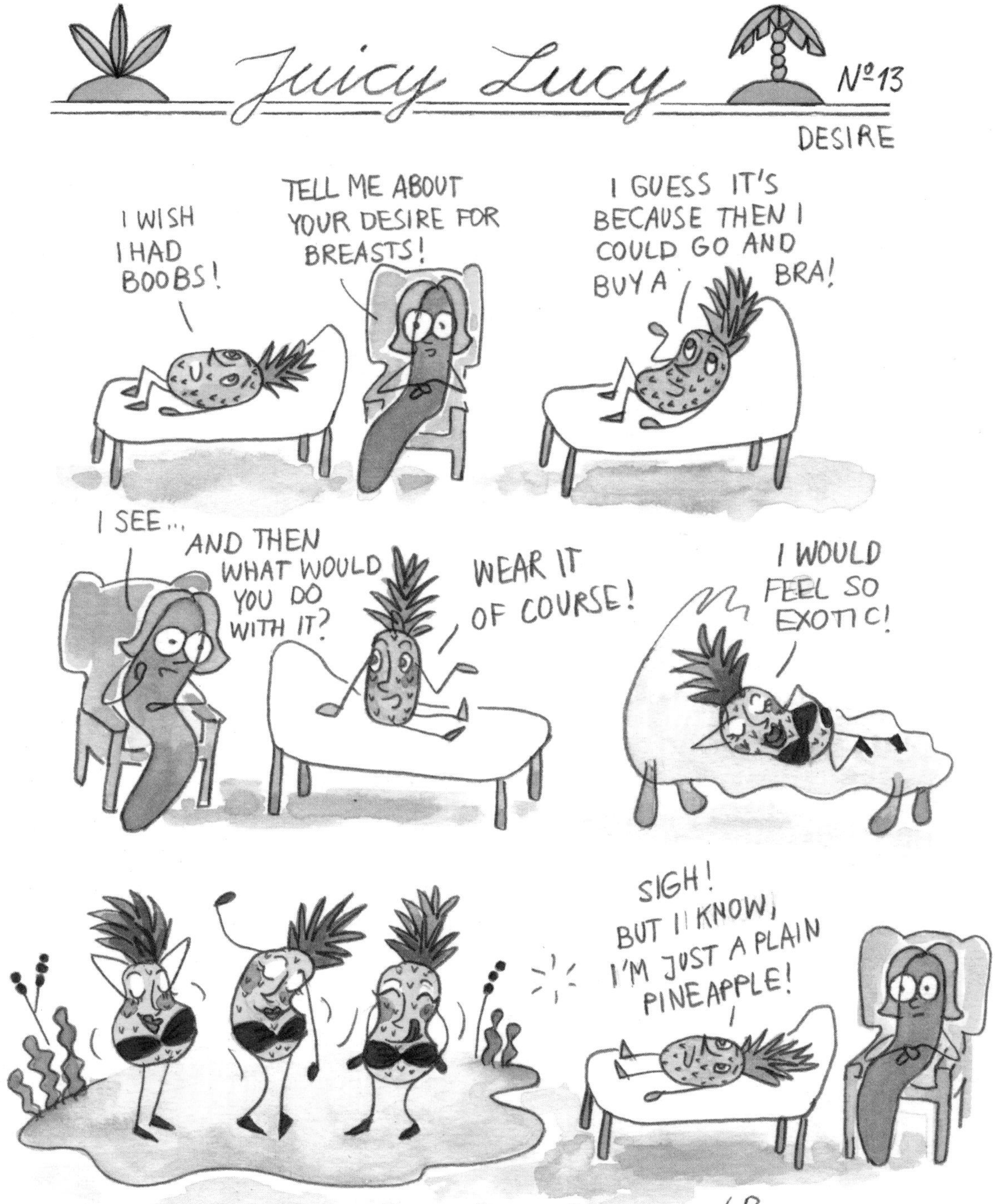
Juicy Lucy
№13
DESIRE
I WISH I HAD BOOBS!
TELL ME ABOUT YOUR DESIRE FOR BREASTS!
I GUESS IT'S BECAUSE THEN I COULD GO AND BUY A BRA!
I SEE...
AND THEN WHAT WOULD YOU DO WITH IT?
WEAR IT OF COURSE!
I WOULD FEEL SO EXOTIC!
SIGH! BUT I KNOW, I'M JUST A PLAIN PINEAPPLE!
LB

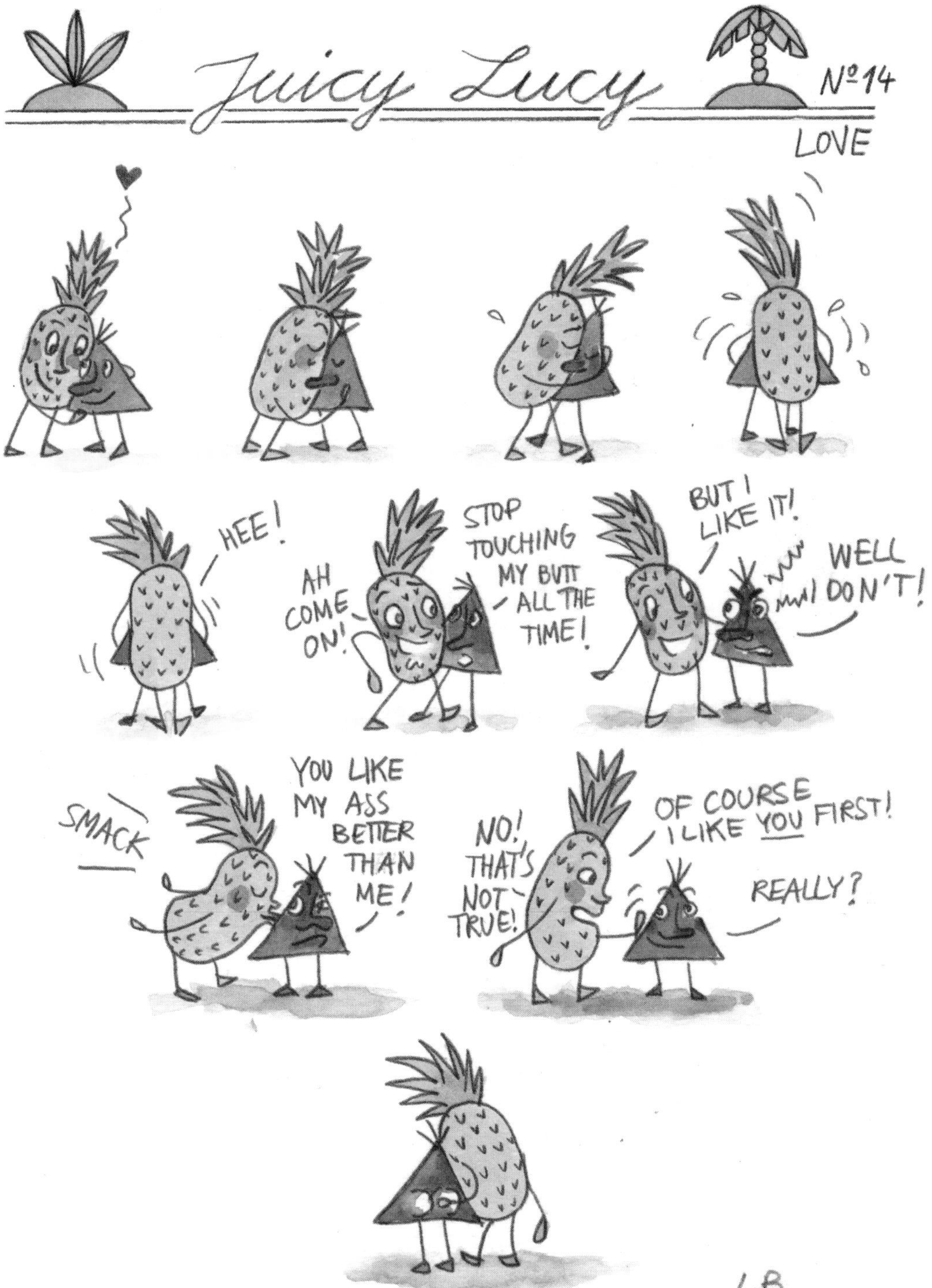
Juicy Lucy
№ 14
LOVE
HEE!
AH COME ON!
STOP TOUCHING MY BUTT ALL THE TIME!
BUT I LIKE IT!
WELL I DON'T!
SMACK
YOU LIKE MY ASS BETTER THAN ME!
NO! THAT'S NOT TRUE!
OF COURSE I LIKE YOU FIRST!
REALLY?
LB

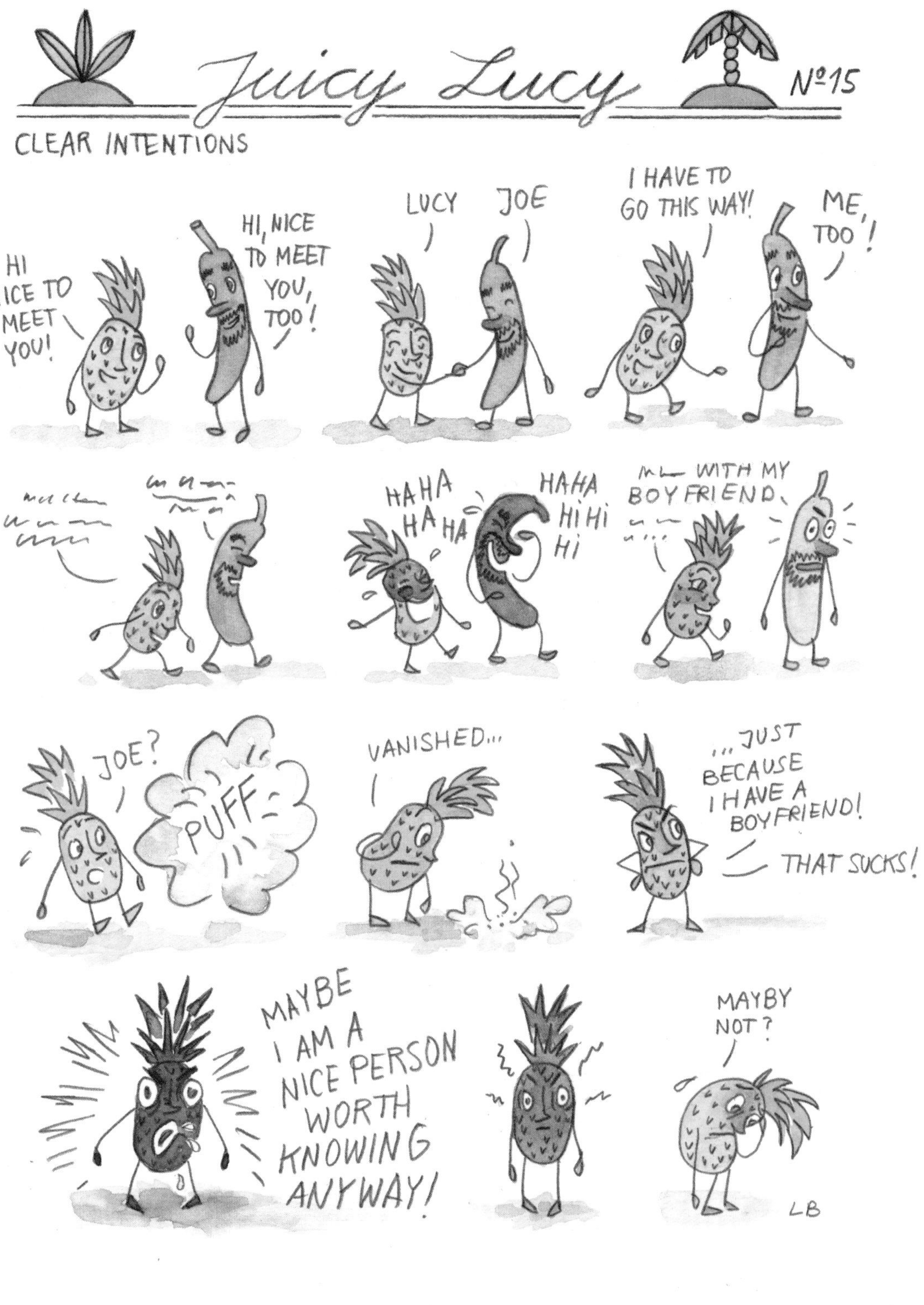

Juicy Lucy
Nº15
CLEAR INTENTIONS
HI NICE TO MEET YOU!
HI, NICE TO MEET YOU, TOO!
LUCY
JOE
I HAVE TO GO THIS WAY!
ME, TOO!
HAHA HA HA
HAHA HI HI HI
WITH MY BOYFRIEND.
JOE?
PUFF
VANISHED...
...JUST BECAUSE I HAVE A BOYFRIEND!
THAT SUCKS!
MAYBE I AM A NICE PERSON WORTH KNOWING ANYWAY!
MAYBY NOT?
LB

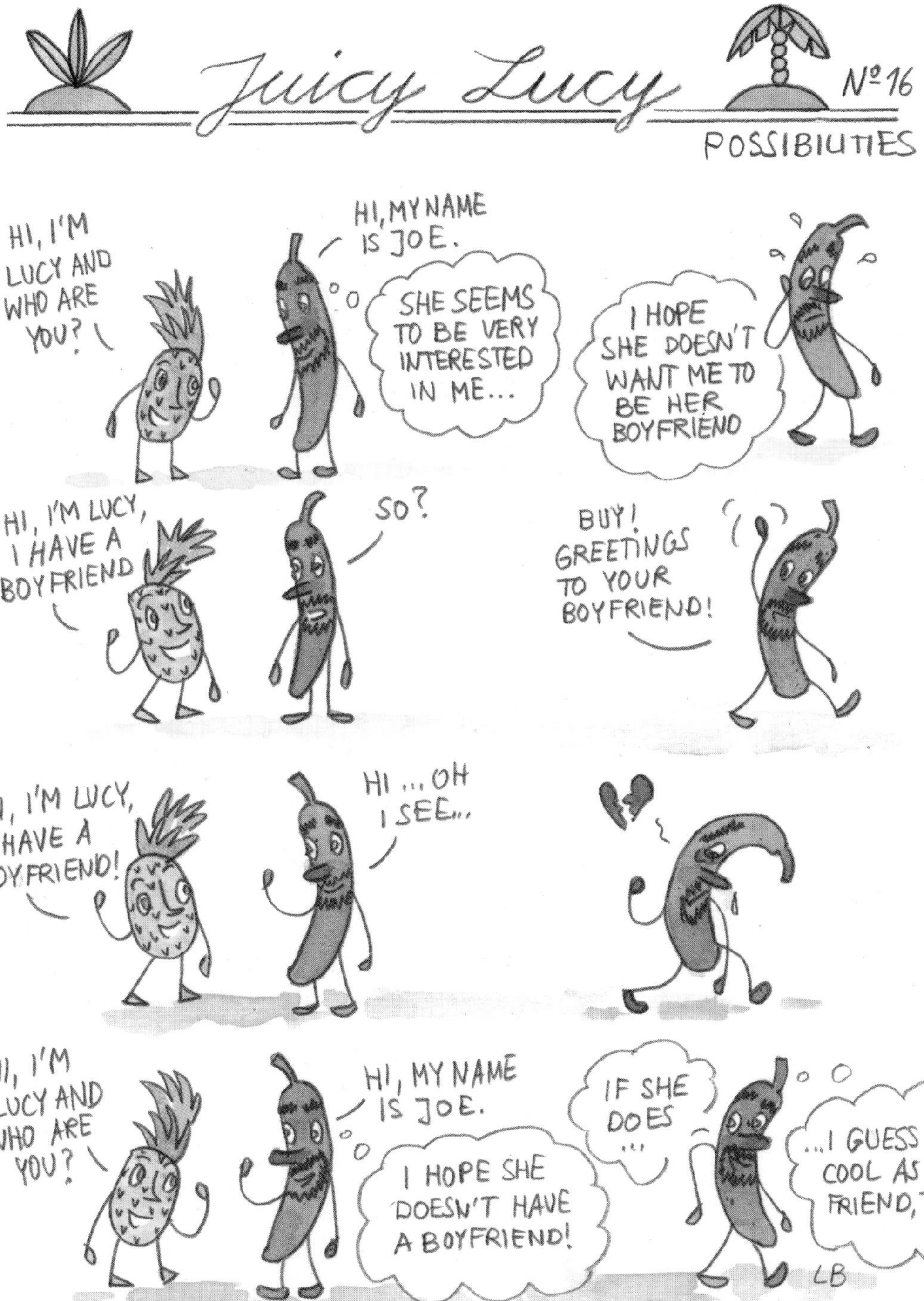
Juicy Lucy
Nº 16
POSSIBILITIES
HI, I'M LUCY AND WHO ARE YOU?
HI, MY NAME IS JOE.
SHE SEEMS TO BE VERY INTERESTED IN ME...
I HOPE SHE DOESN'T WANT ME TO BE HER BOYFRIEND
HI, I'M LUCY, I HAVE A BOYFRIEND
SO?
BUY! GREETINGS TO YOUR BOYFRIEND!
HI, I'M LUCY, I HAVE A BOYFRIEND!
HI ... OH I SEE...
HI, I'M LUCY AND WHO ARE YOU?
HI, MY NAME IS JOE.
I HOPE SHE DOESN'T HAVE A BOYFRIEND!
IF SHE DOES ...
...I GUESS SHE'S COOL AS A FRIEND, TOO!
LB

WHAT'S THE POINT?

WHAT ELSE WOULD YOU LIKE TO BE?

WHAT IF I DON'T WANT TO BE JUICY?

IT'S EASIER TO TELL WHAT I DON'T WANT!

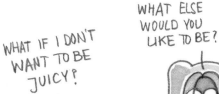

THEN START WITH THAT!

I DON'T WANT TO BE SEEN JUST AS A SWEET THING, I DON'T WANT TO BE EXPECTED TO DRESS UP, PUT MAKE UP ON OR SHAVE TO BE A REAL PINEAPPLE, I DON'T WANT TO BE TREATED AS THOUGH I CAN'T HANDLE THINGS ON MY OWN, I DON'T WANT TO BE A WOMAN FIRST OR TO BE SEEN AS AN OBJECT, I DON'T WANT TO THINK I HAVE TO BECOME PERFECT, I DON'T WANT FEEL NEVER GOOD ENOUGH, SWEET ENOUGH, RIPE ENOUGH, TENDER ENOUGH, JUICY ENOUGH,... ...NOT ENOUGH!

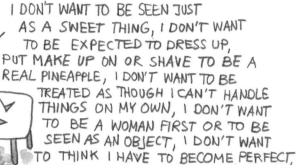

I SEE...

OF COURSE I AM JUICY!

BUT...

...IS THAT THE POINT?

LB

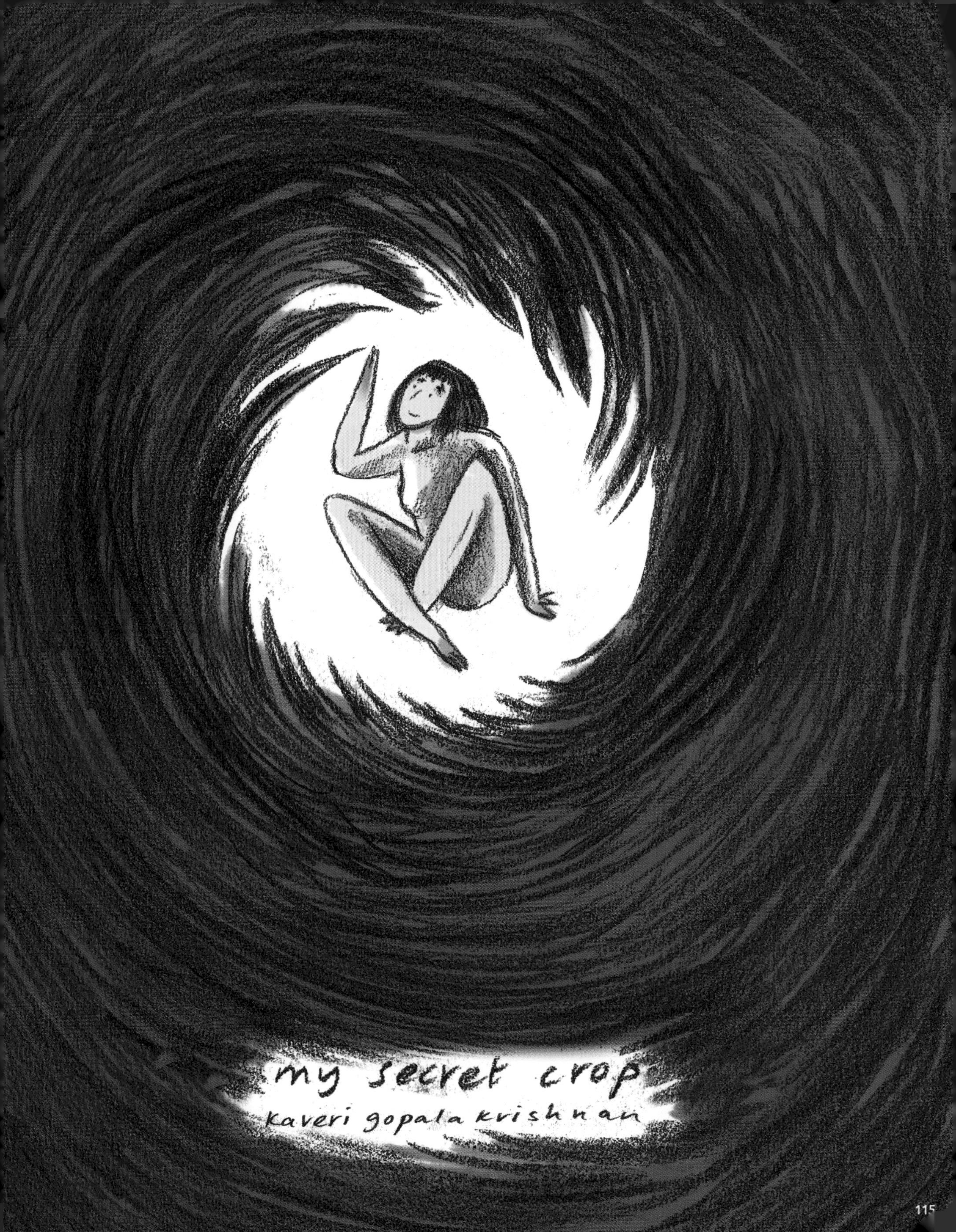
my secret crop
kaveri gopalakrishnan

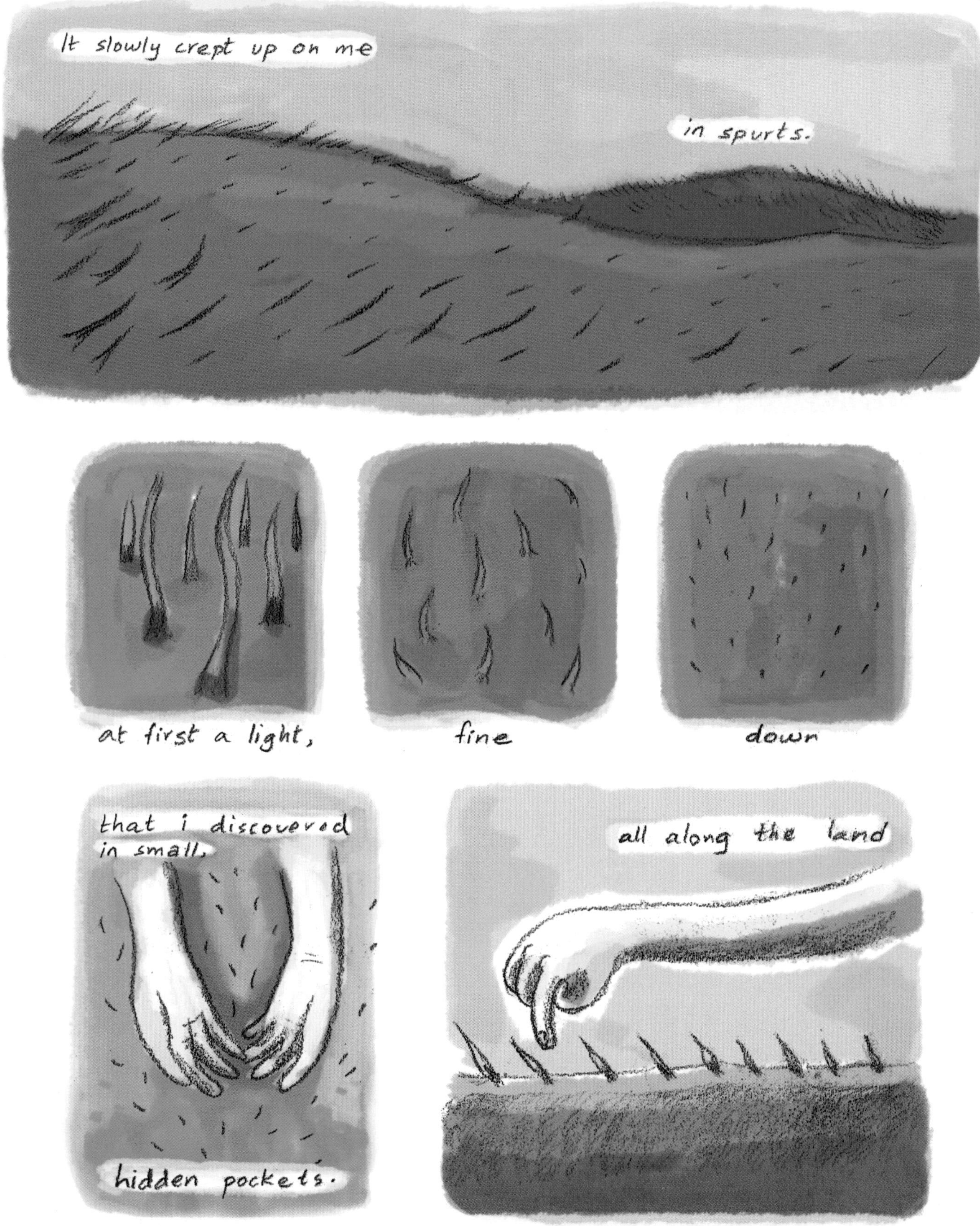
It slowly crept up on me
in spurts.
at first a light,
fine
down
that i discovered in small,
hidden pockets.
all along the land

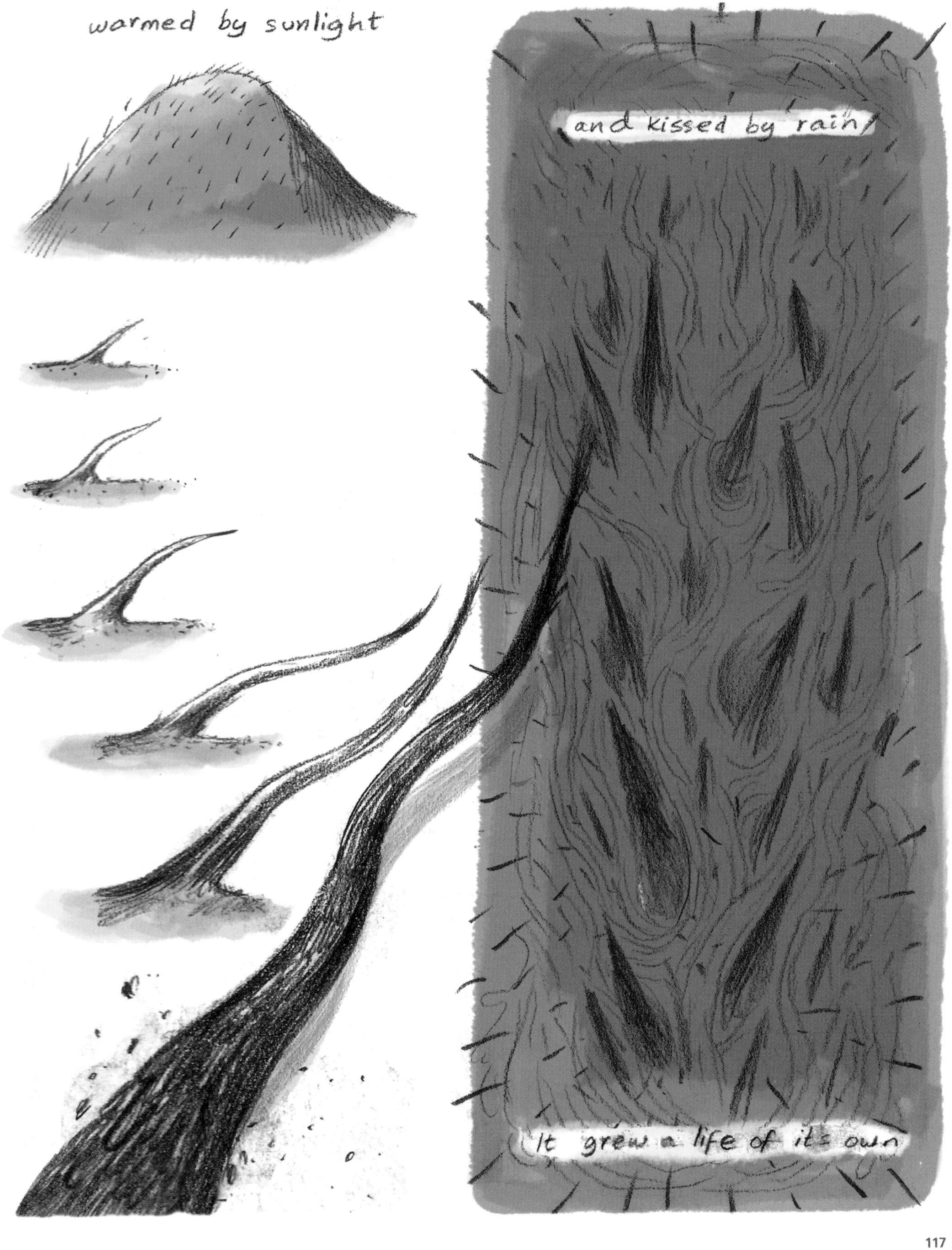
warmed by sunlight
and kissed by rain
It grew a life of its own

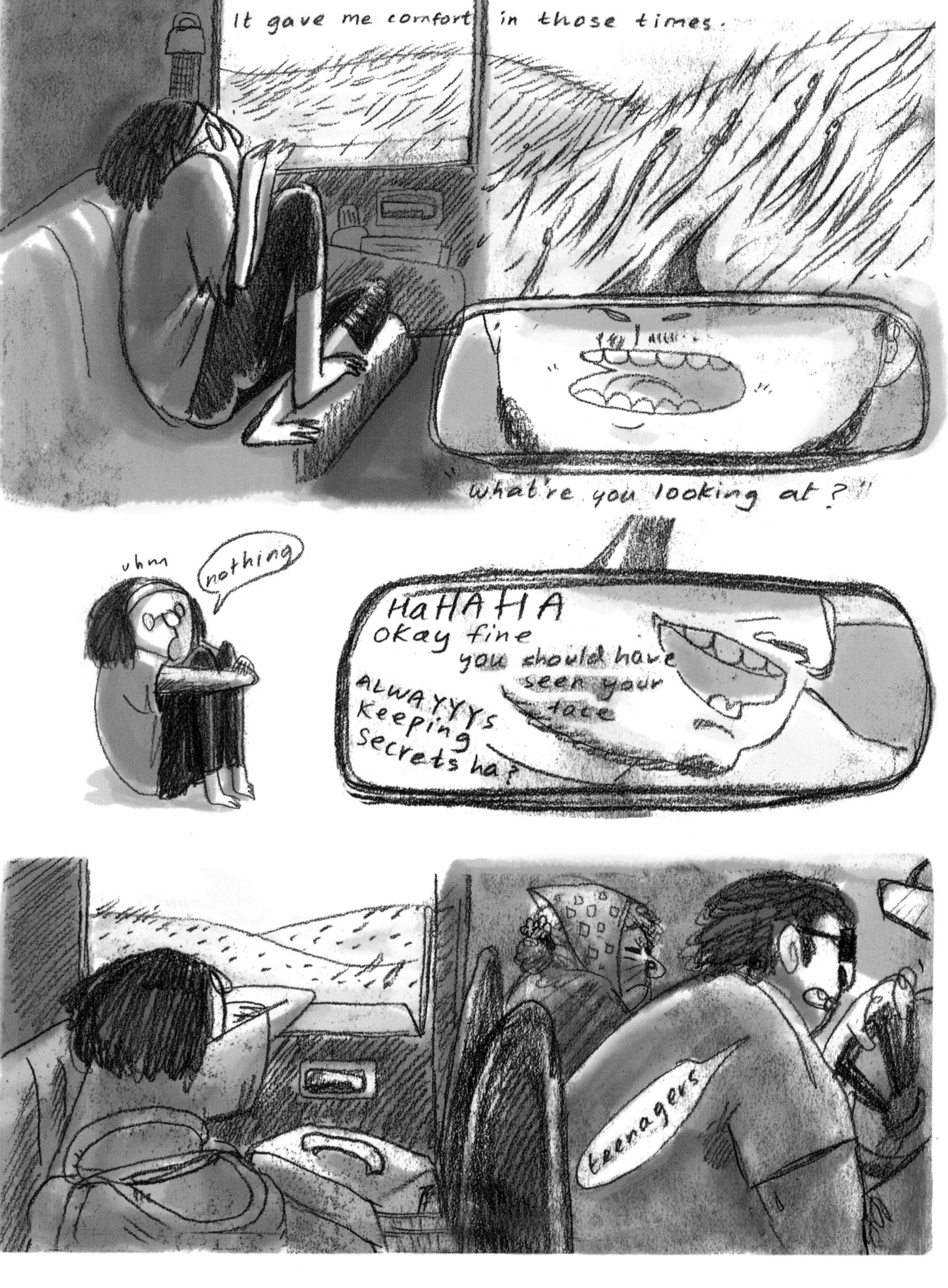
It gave me comfort in those times.
"what're you looking at?"
uhm
nothing
HaHAHA
Okay fine
you should have seen your face
ALWAYYYs Keeping Secrets ha?
teenagers

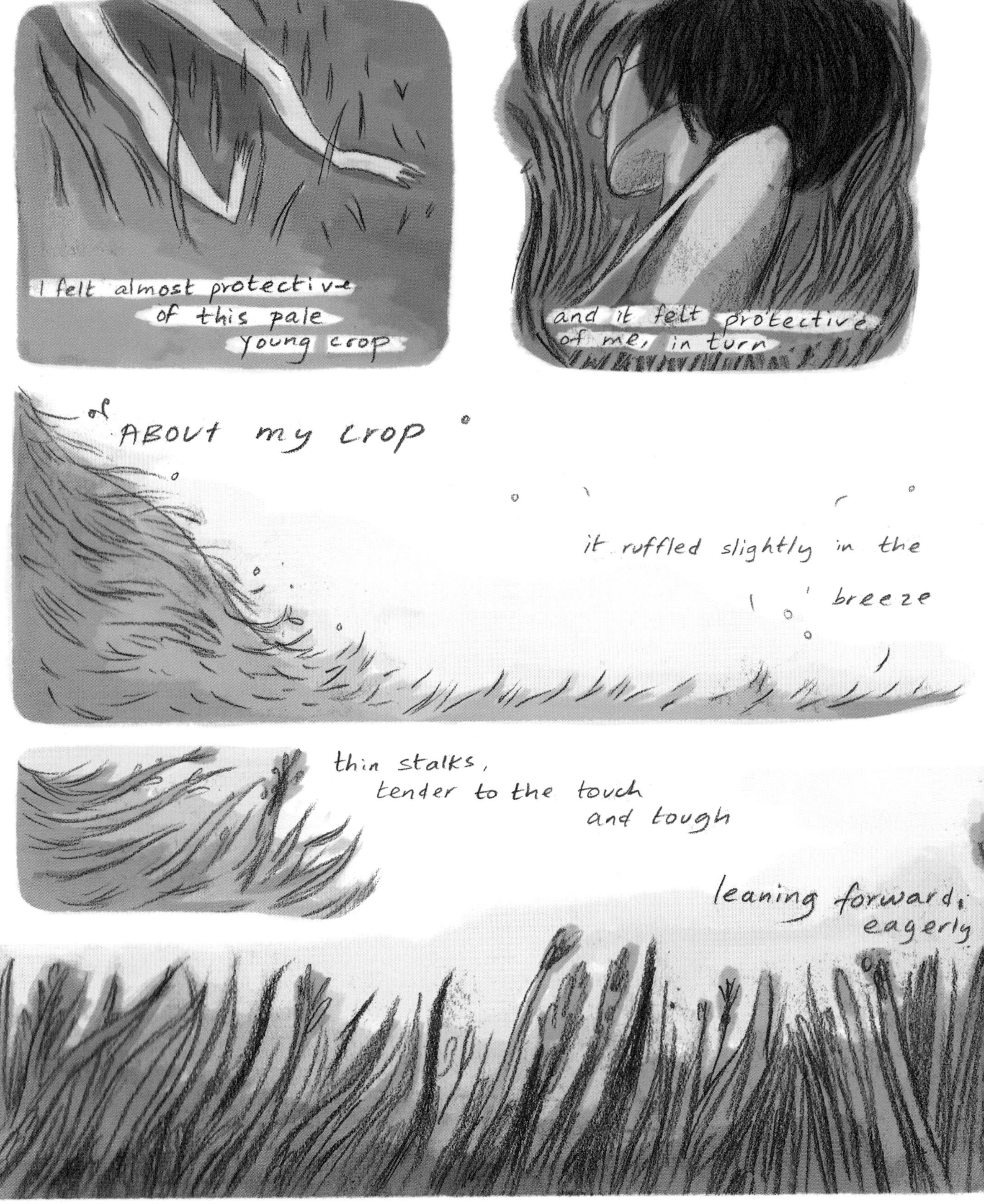
I felt almost protective
of this pale
young crop
and it felt protective
of me, in turn
of ABOUT my crop
it ruffled slightly in the
breeze
thin stalks,
tender to the touch
and tough
leaning forward,
eagerly

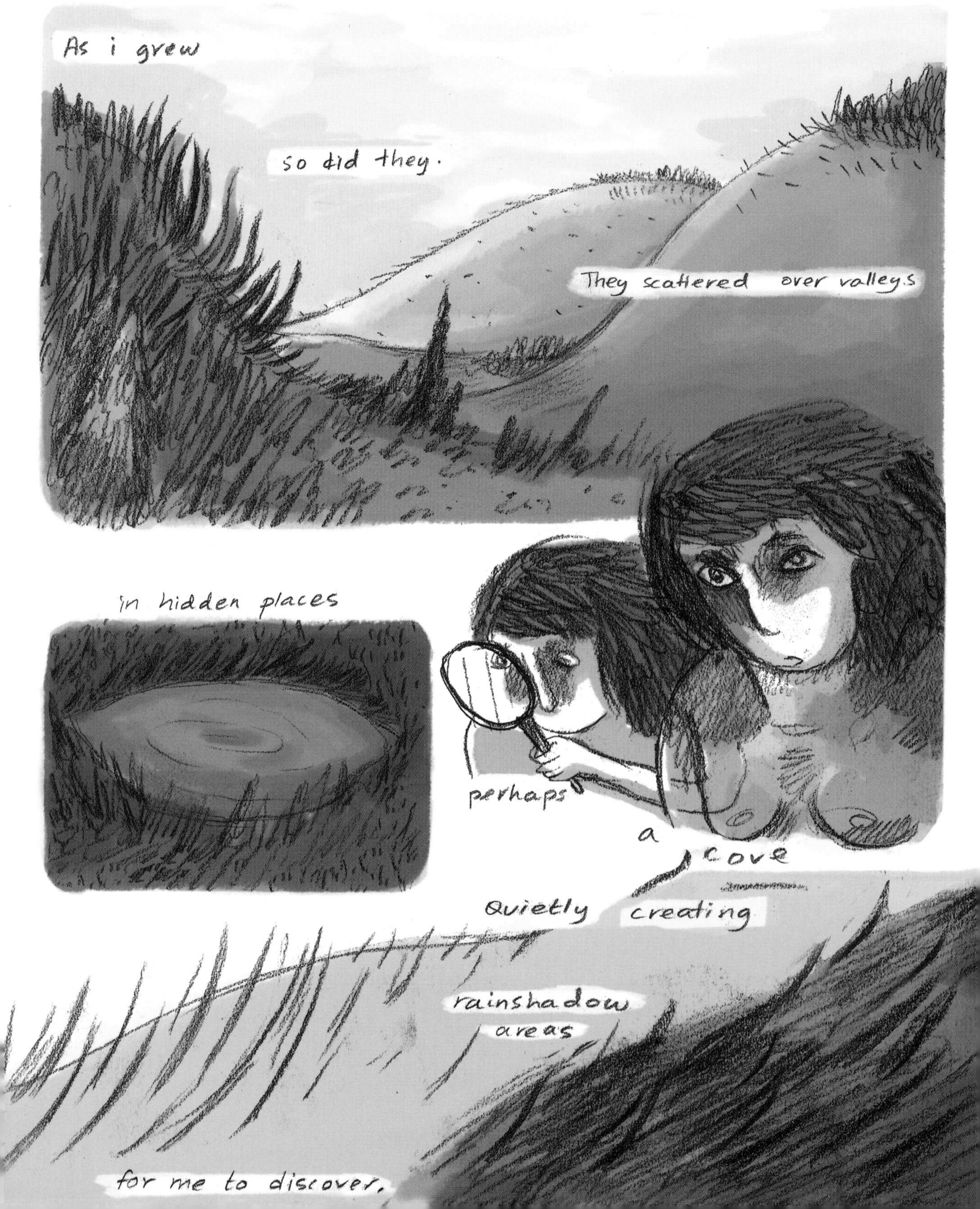
As i grew
so did they.
They scattered over valleys
in hidden places
perhaps
a
cove
Quietly creating
rainshadow
areas
for me to discover.

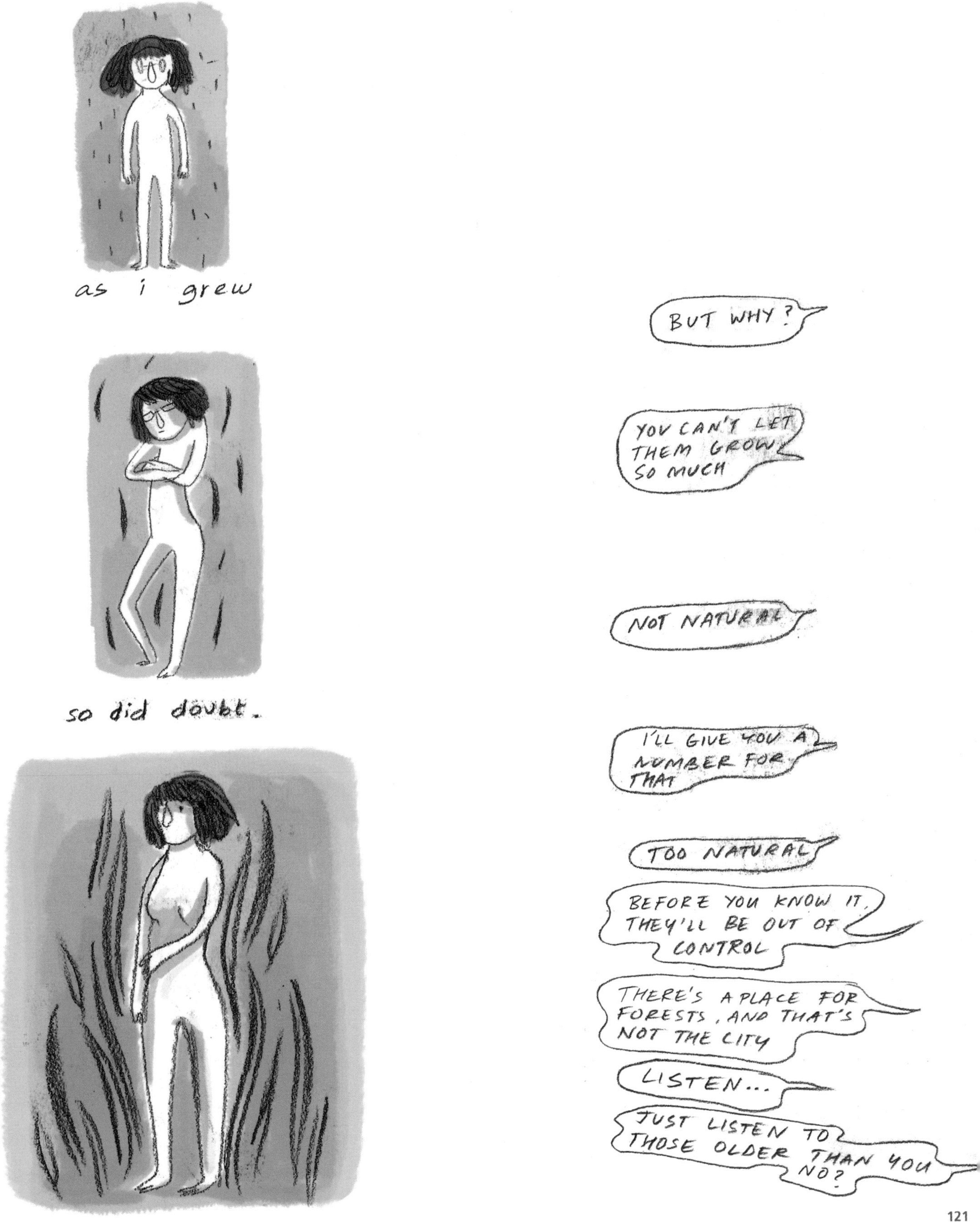
as i grew
BUT WHY?
YOU CAN'T LET THEM GROW SO MUCH
NOT NATURAL
so did doubt.
I'LL GIVE YOU A NUMBER FOR THAT
TOO NATURAL
BEFORE YOU KNOW IT, THEY'LL BE OUT OF CONTROL
THERE'S A PLACE FOR FORESTS, AND THAT'S NOT THE CITY
LISTEN...
JUST LISTEN TO THOSE OLDER THAN YOU NO?

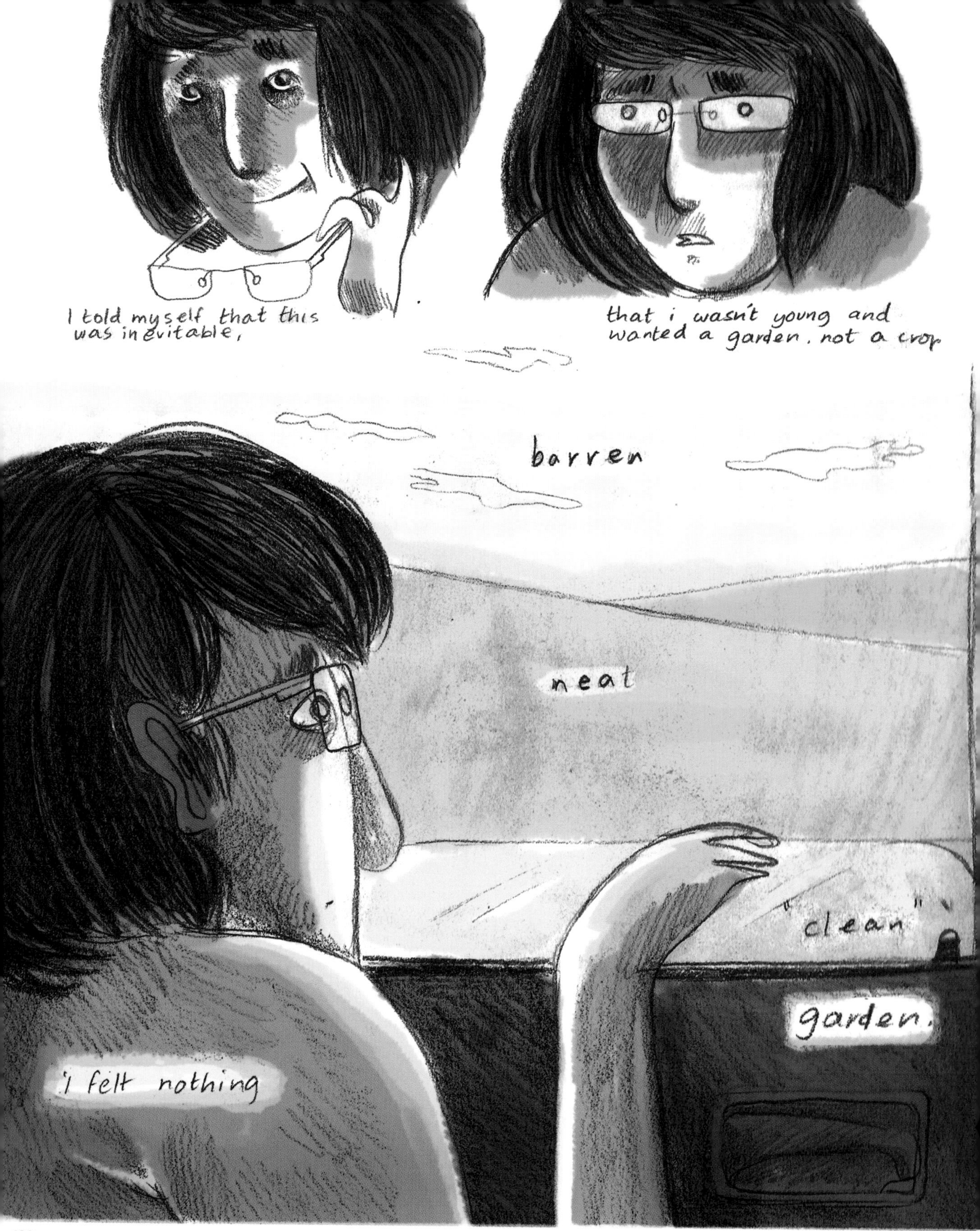
I told myself that this was inevitable,
that i wasn't young and wanted a garden, not a crop
barren
neat
"clean"
garden.
i felt nothing

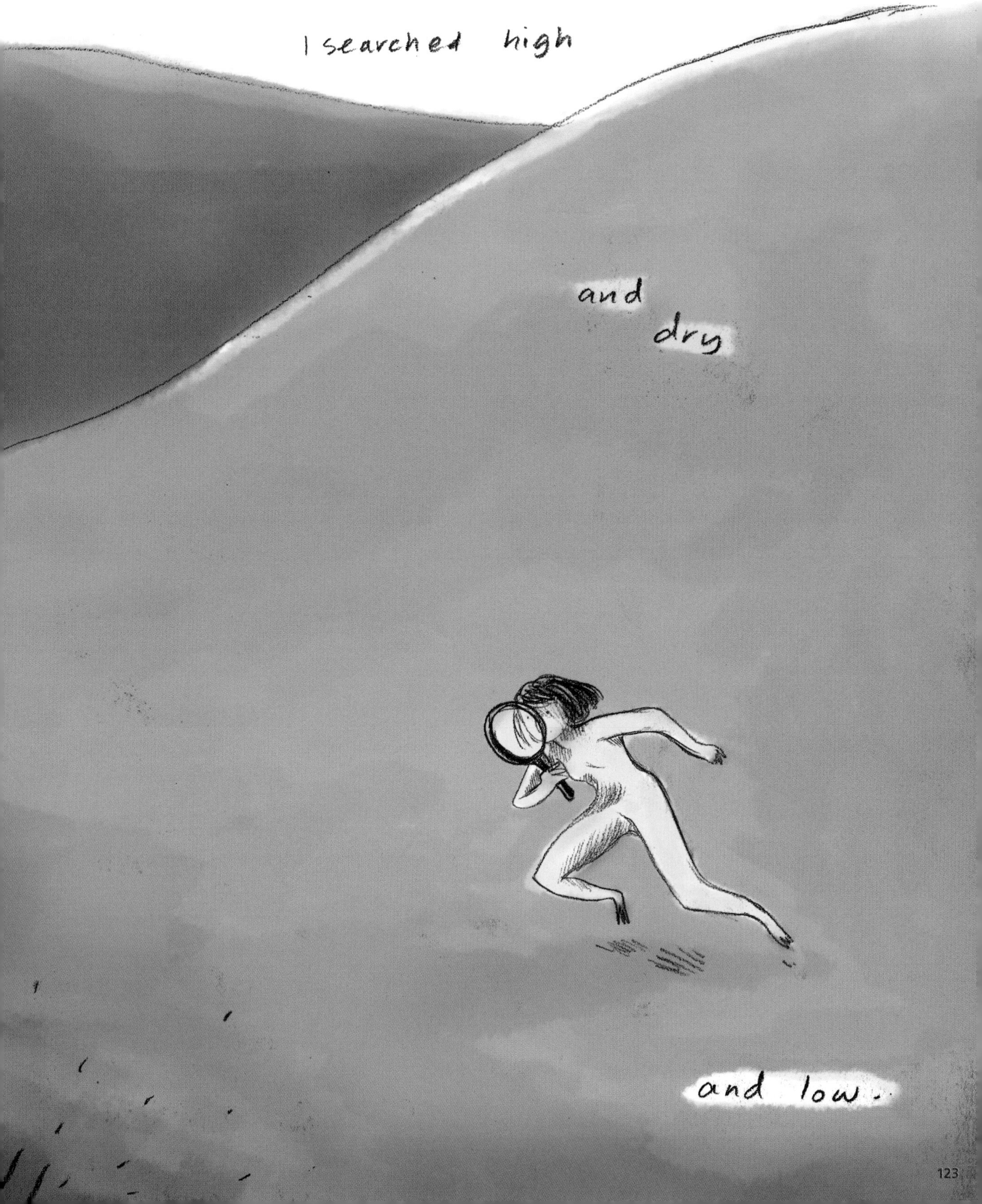
I searched high
and dry
and low.

a new season

a fresh start

wild wonderfully
wild
and all mine

protective

all encompassi

terrifyingly
real
and comfortable

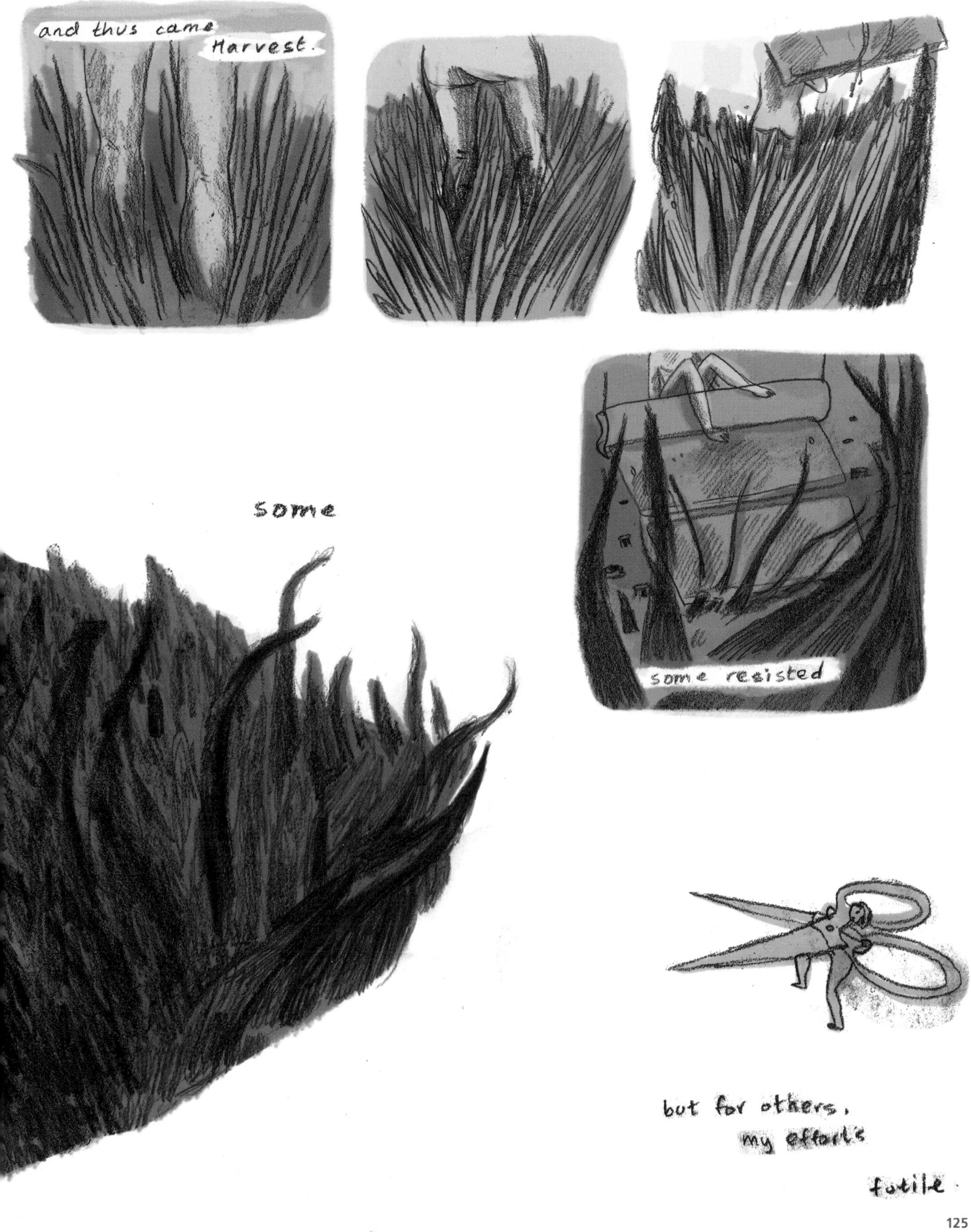
and thus came Harvest.
some
some resisted
but for others, my efforts
futile.

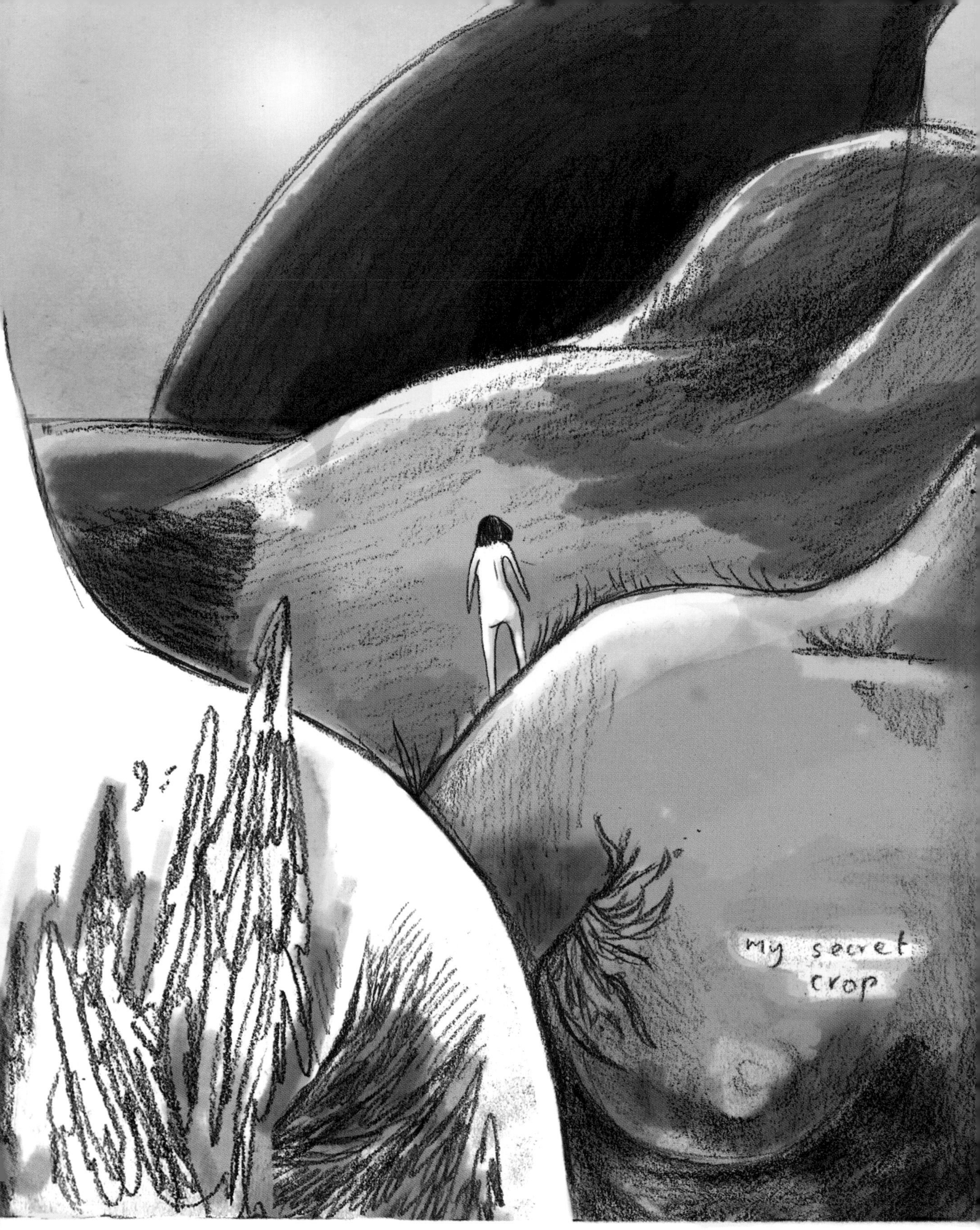
my secret
crop

THE HUNGRY GUEST

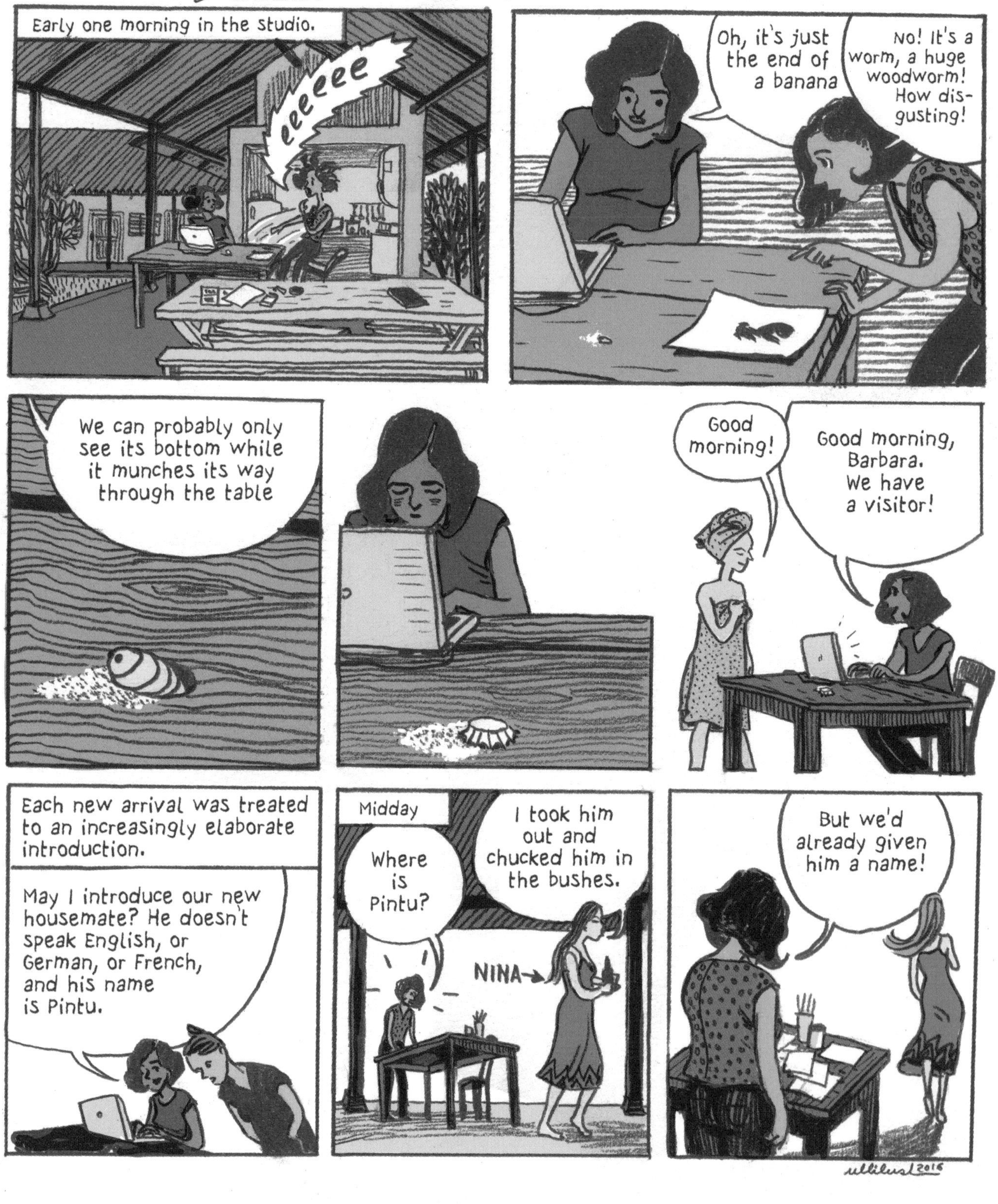

Early one morning in the studio.
eeeeee
Oh, it's just the end of a banana
No! It's a worm, a huge woodworm! How disgusting!
We can probably only see its bottom while it munches its way through the table
Good morning!
Good morning, Barbara. We have a visitor!
Each new arrival was treated to an increasingly elaborate introduction.
May I introduce our new housemate? He doesn't speak English, or German, or French, and his name is Pintu.
Midday
Where is Pintu?
I took him out and chucked him in the bushes.
NINA
But we'd already given him a name!
ullilust 2016

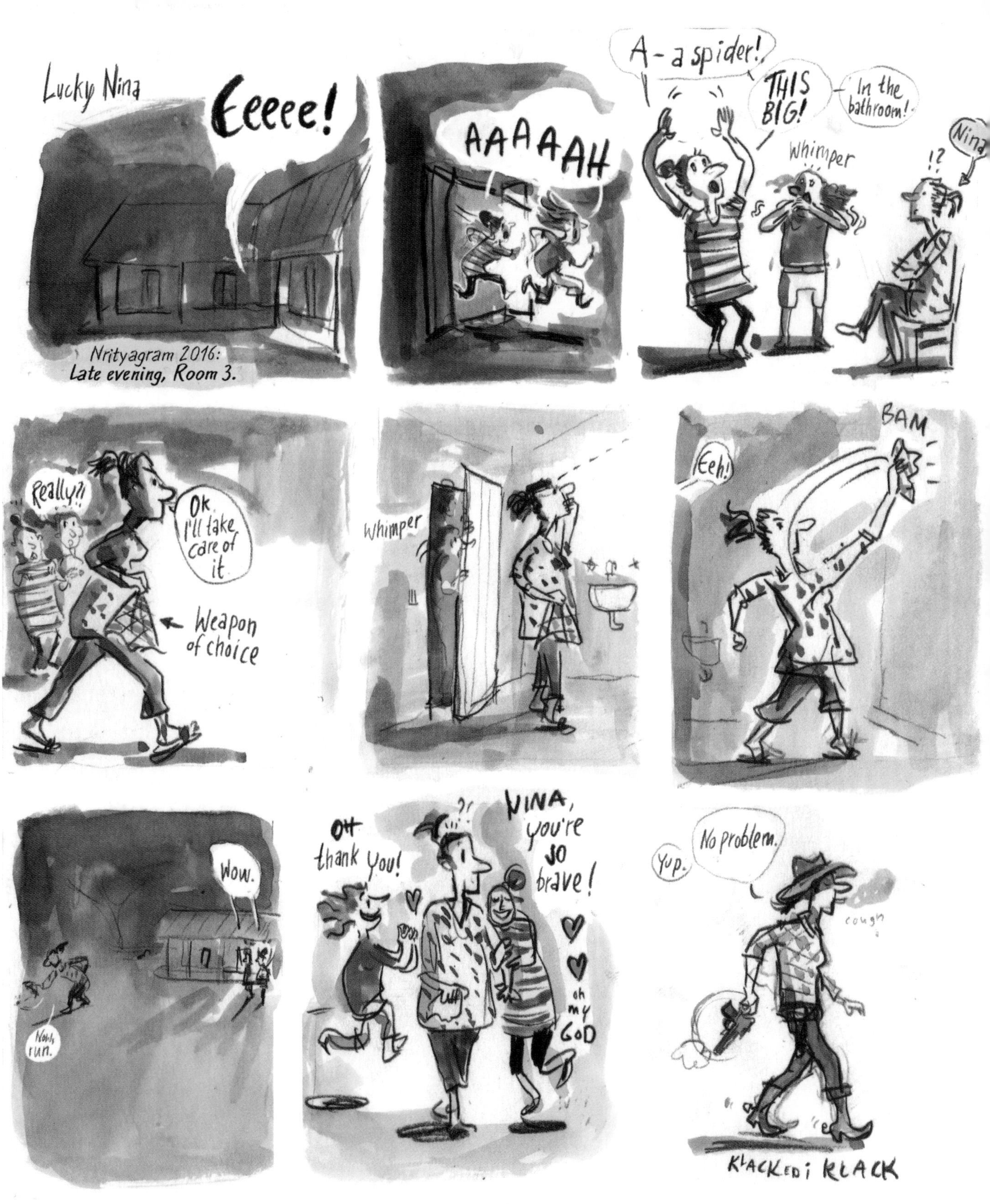

Lucky Nina
Eeeee!
Nrityagram 2016:
Late evening, Room 3.
AAAAAH
A - a spider!
THIS BIG!
In the bathroom!
Whimper
!?
Nina
Really?!
Ok, I'll take care of it
Weapon of choice
Whimper
BAM
Eeh!
Wow.
Now, run.
OH thank you!
?!
NINA, you're SO brave!
oh my GOD
Yup.
No problem.
cough
KLACKEDI KLACK

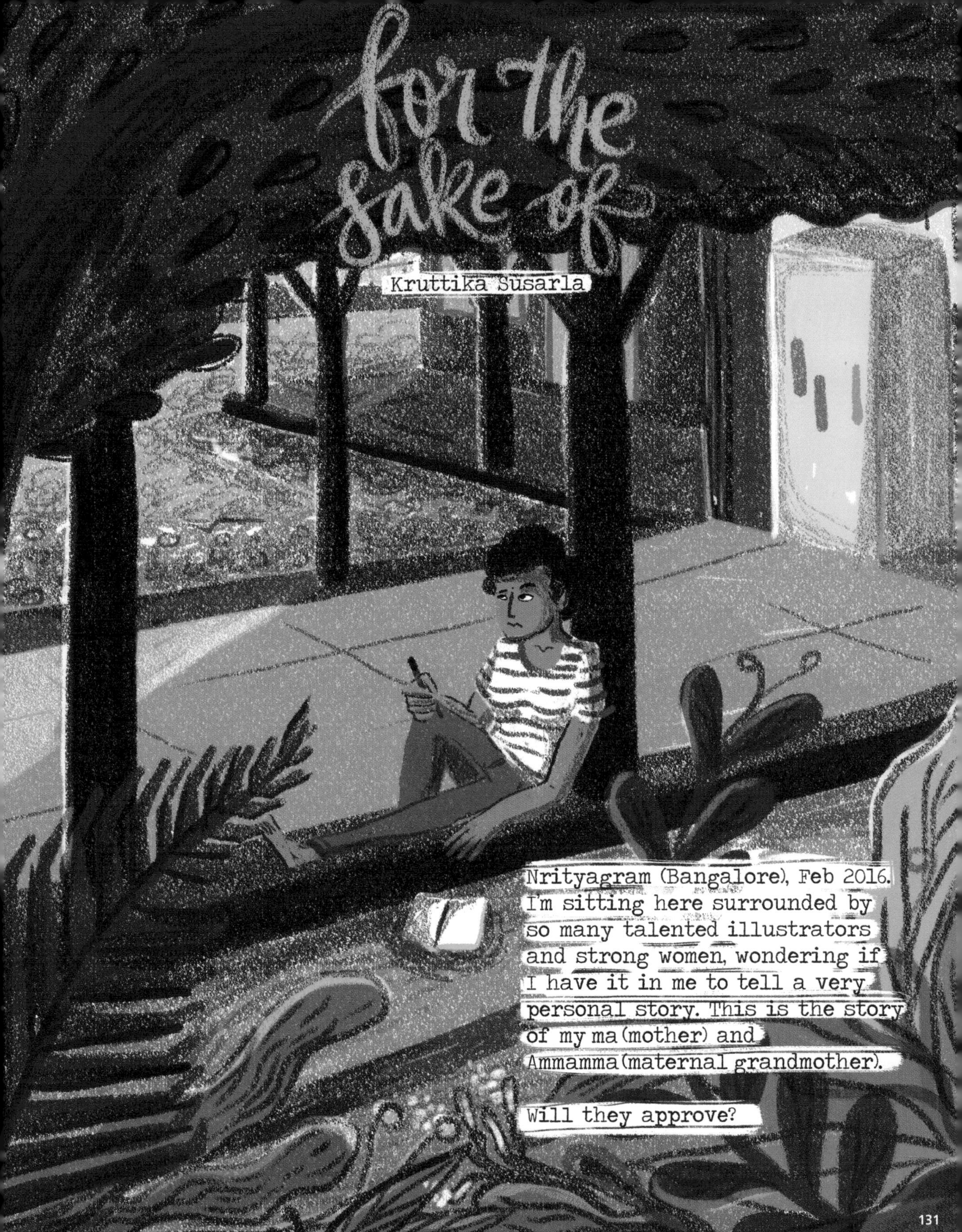
for the sake of
Kruttika Susarla
Nrityagram (Bangalore), Feb 2016. I'm sitting here surrounded by so many talented illustrators and strong women, wondering if I have it in me to tell a very personal story. This is the story of my ma(mother) and Ammamma(maternal grandmother).
Will they approve?

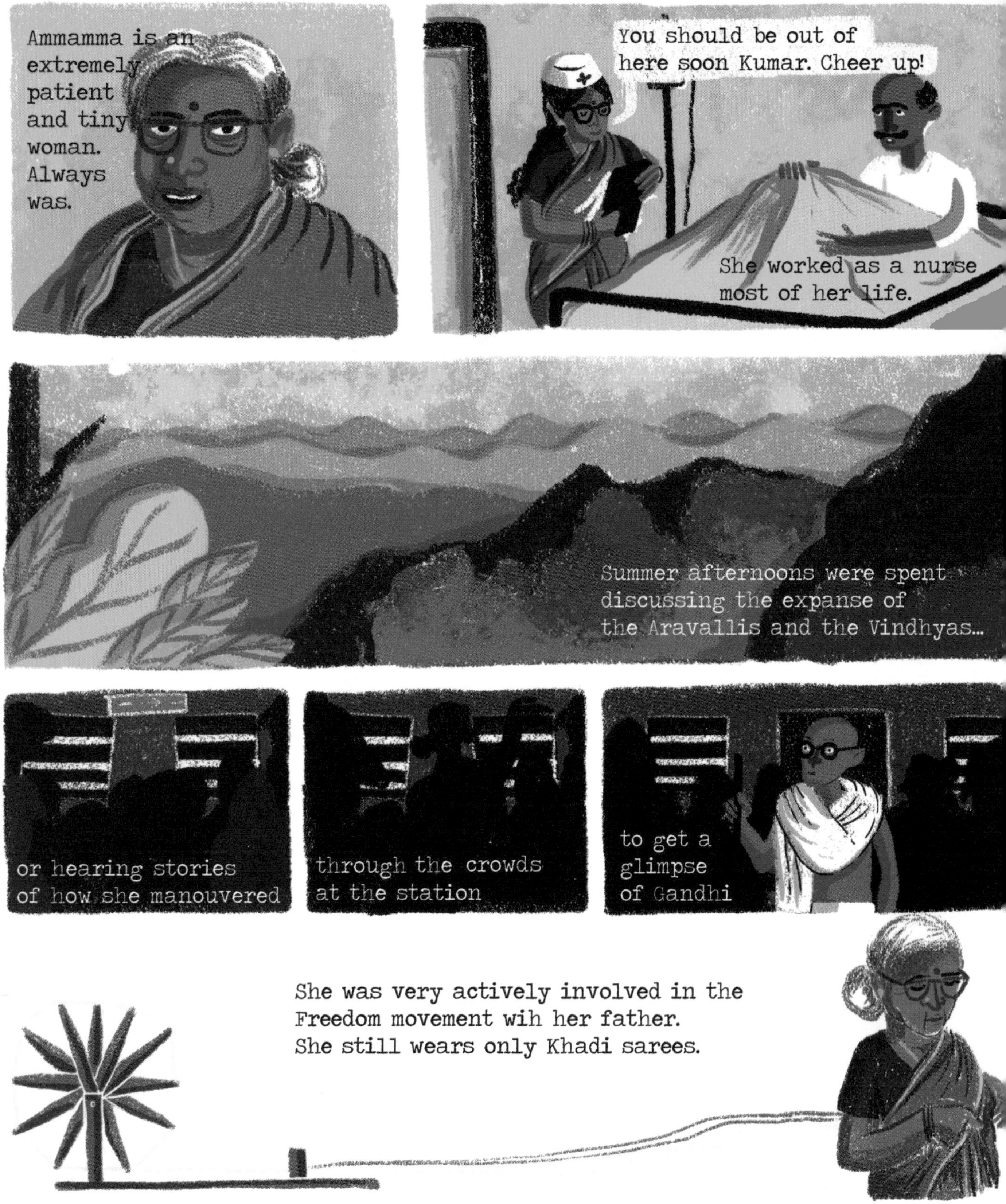
Ammamma is an extremely patient and tiny woman. Always was.
You should be out of here soon Kumar. Cheer up!
She worked as a nurse most of her life.
Summer afternoons were spent discussing the expanse of the Aravallis and the Vindhyas...
or hearing stories of how she manouvered
through the crowds at the station
to get a glimpse of Gandhi
She was very actively involved in the Freedom movement wih her father.
She still wears only Khadi sarees.

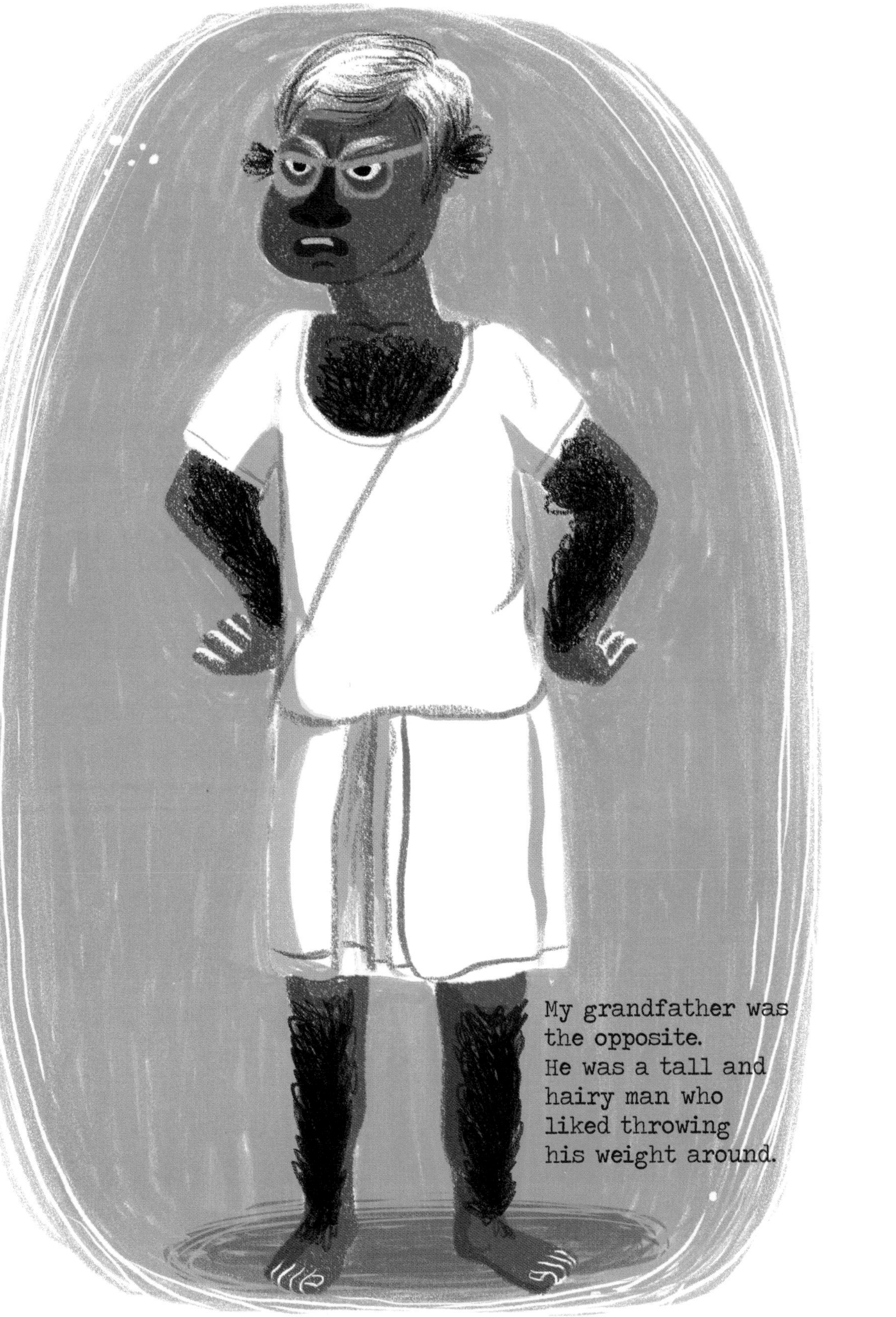
My grandfather was the opposite.
He was a tall and hairy man who liked throwing his weight around.

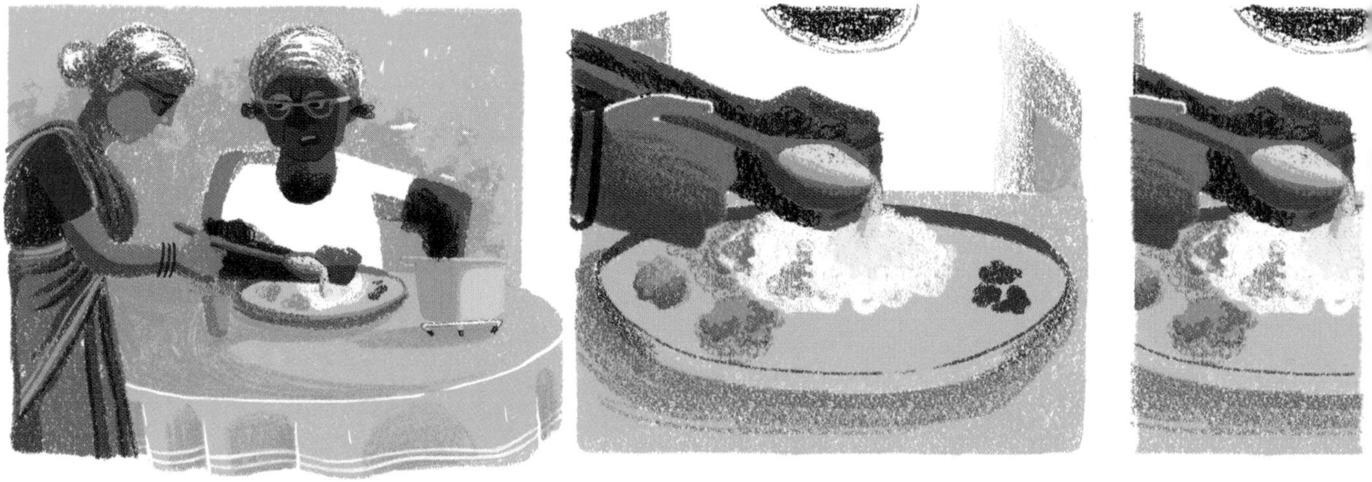

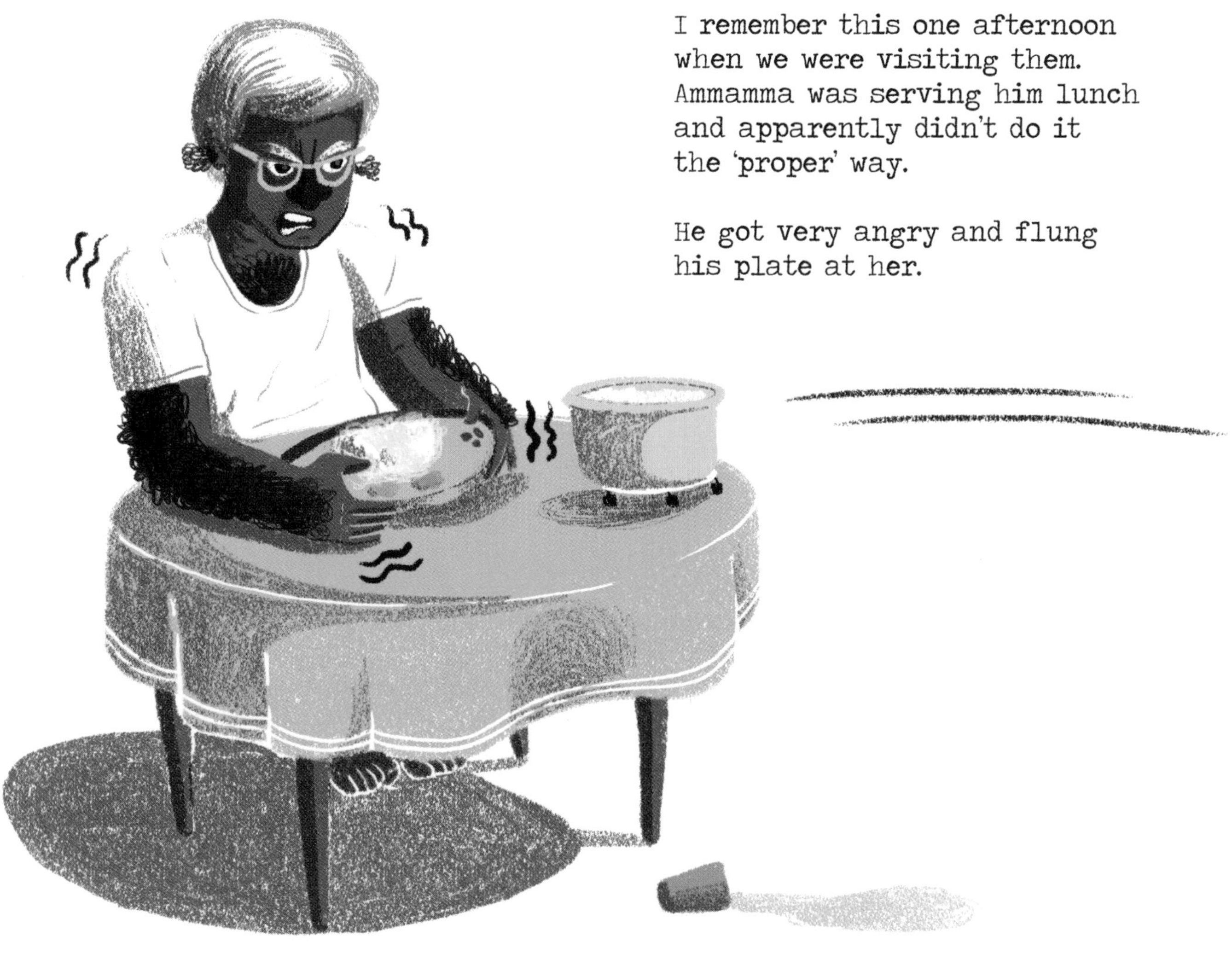

I remember this one afternoon
when we were visiting them.
Ammamma was serving him lunch
and apparently didn't do it
the 'proper' way.

He got very angry and flung
his plate at her.

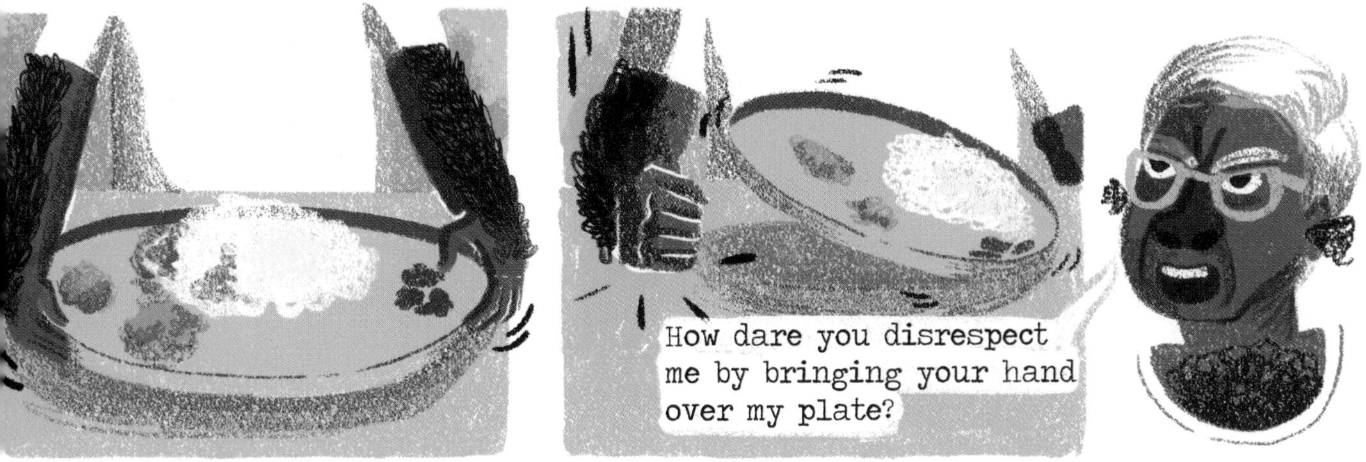
How dare you disrespect me by bringing your hand over my plate?

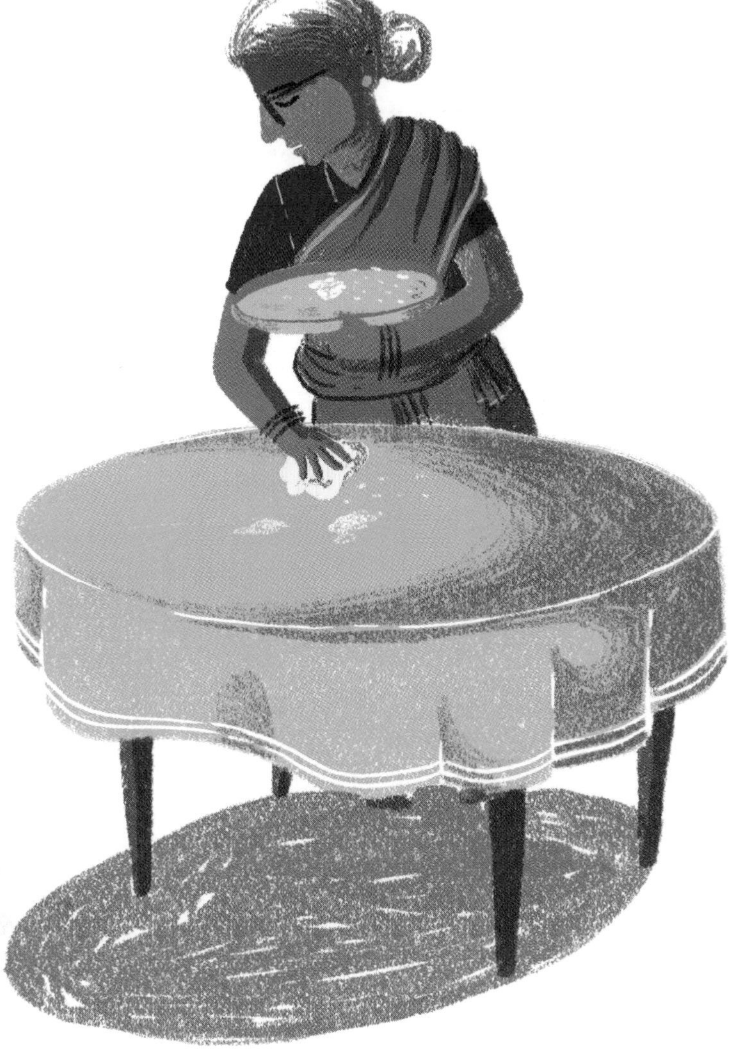

She did not say a word that day.

She 'adjusted' to him.

When I was younger, I thought it was very weak of her to do so, but, was it?

What is strength? Is it the ability to raise your daughters well despite your circumstances?

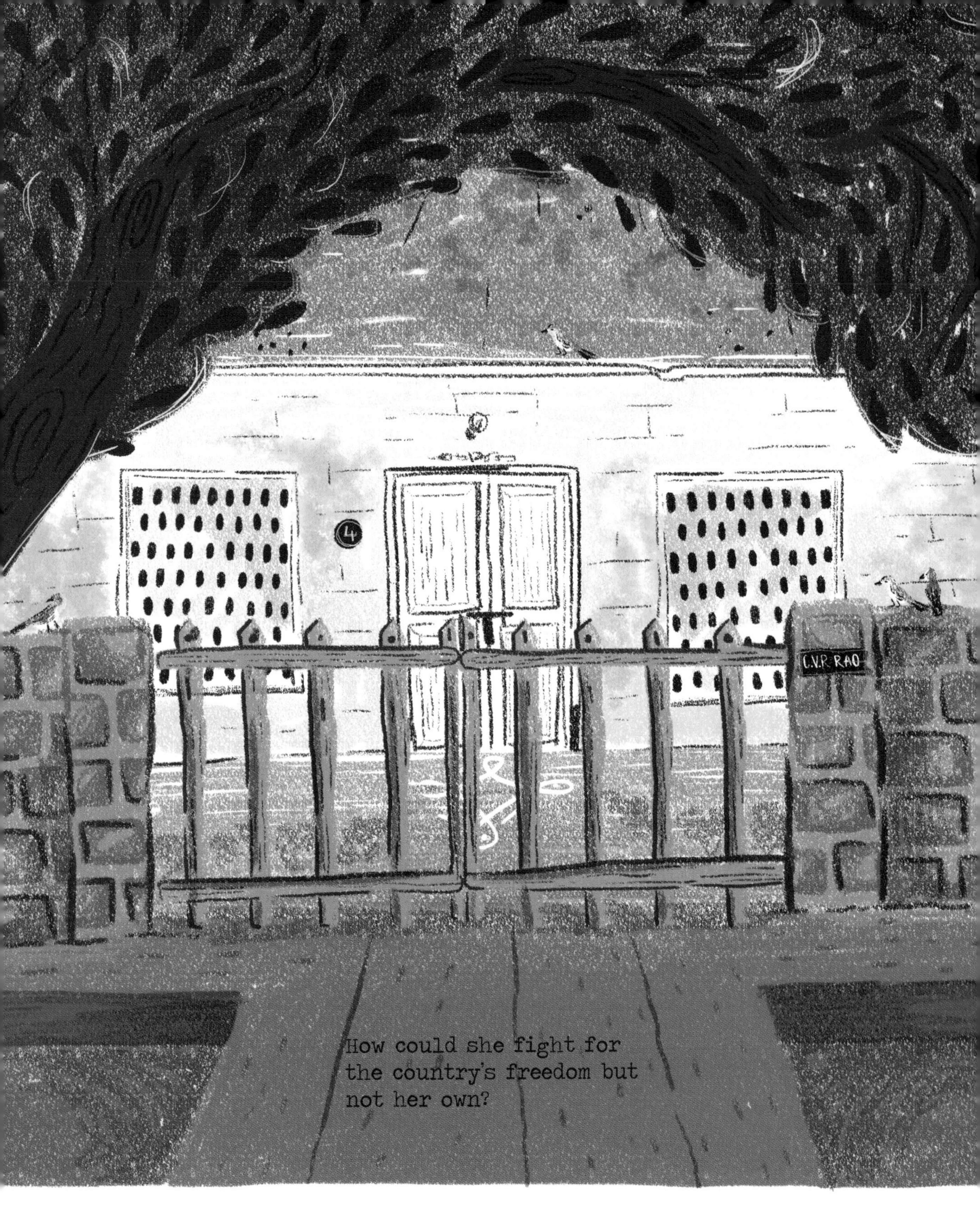
C.V.R. RAO

How could she fight for the country's freedom but not her own?

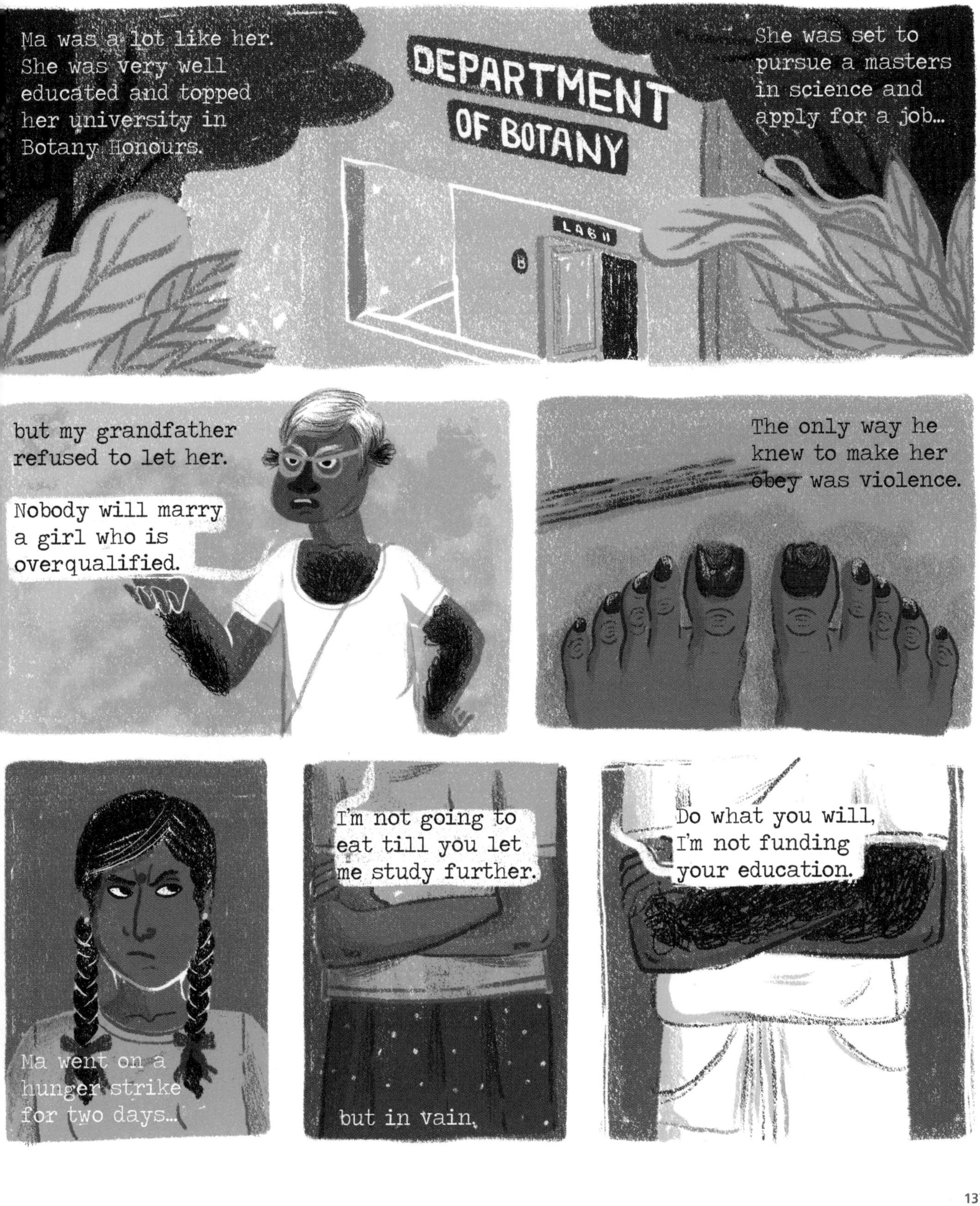
Ma was a lot like her. She was very well educated and topped her university in Botany Honours.
DEPARTMENT OF BOTANY
She was set to pursue a masters in science and apply for a job...
but my grandfather refused to let her.
Nobody will marry a girl who is overqualified.
The only way he knew to make her obey was violence.
Ma went on a hunger strike for two days...
I'm not going to eat till you let me study further.
but in vain.
Do what you will, I'm not funding your education.

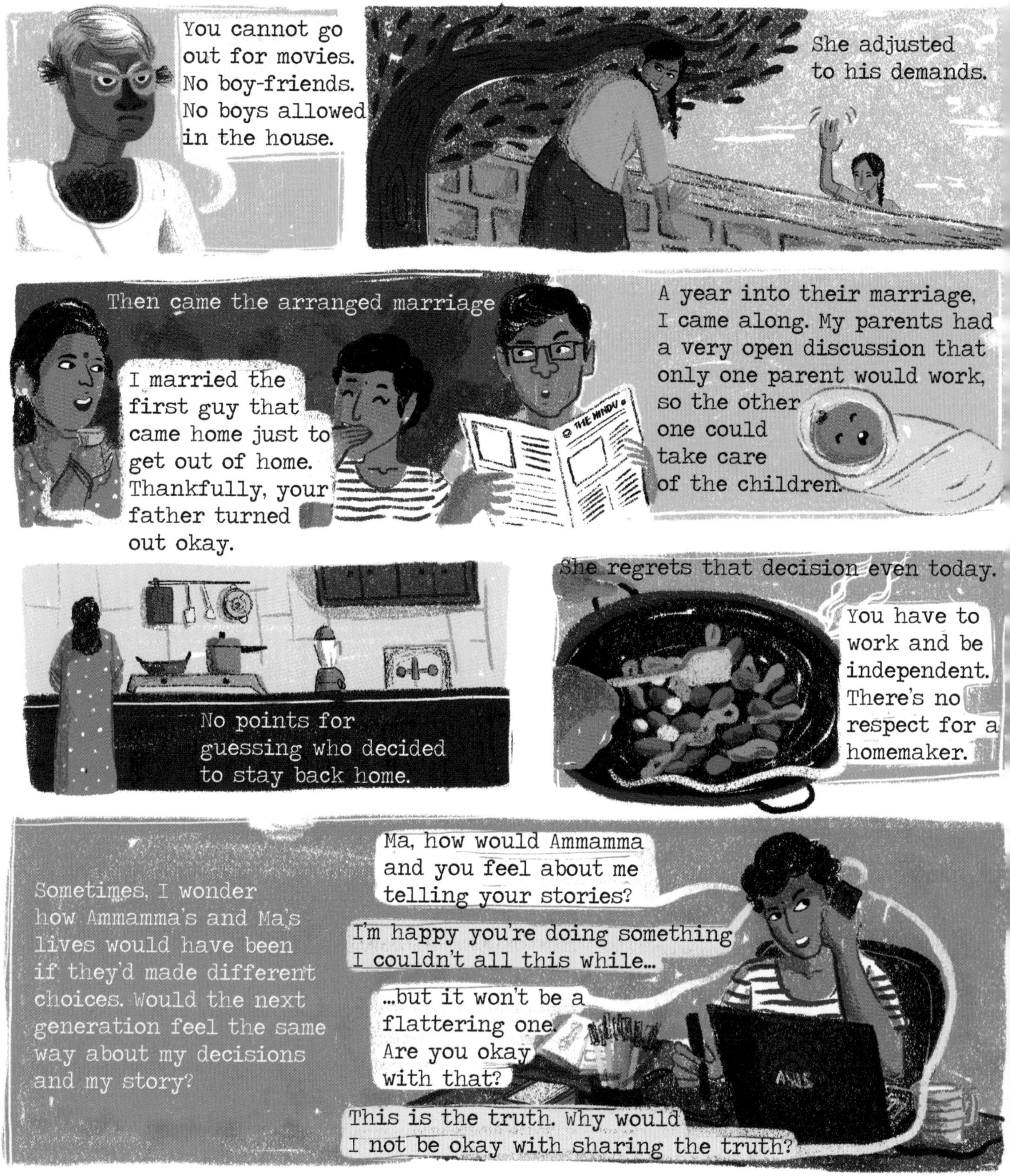
You cannot go out for movies. No boy-friends. No boys allowed in the house.
She adjusted to his demands.
Then came the arranged marriage
I married the first guy that came home just to get out of home. Thankfully, your father turned out okay.
THE HINDU
A year into their marriage, I came along. My parents had a very open discussion that only one parent would work, so the other one could take care of the children.
No points for guessing who decided to stay back home.
She regrets that decision even today.
You have to work and be independent. There's no respect for a homemaker.
Sometimes, I wonder how Ammamma's and Ma's lives would have been if they'd made different choices. Would the next generation feel the same way about my decisions and my story?
Ma, how would Ammamma and you feel about me telling your stories?
I'm happy you're doing something I couldn't all this while...
...but it won't be a flattering one. Are you okay with that?
This is the truth. Why would I not be okay with sharing the truth?

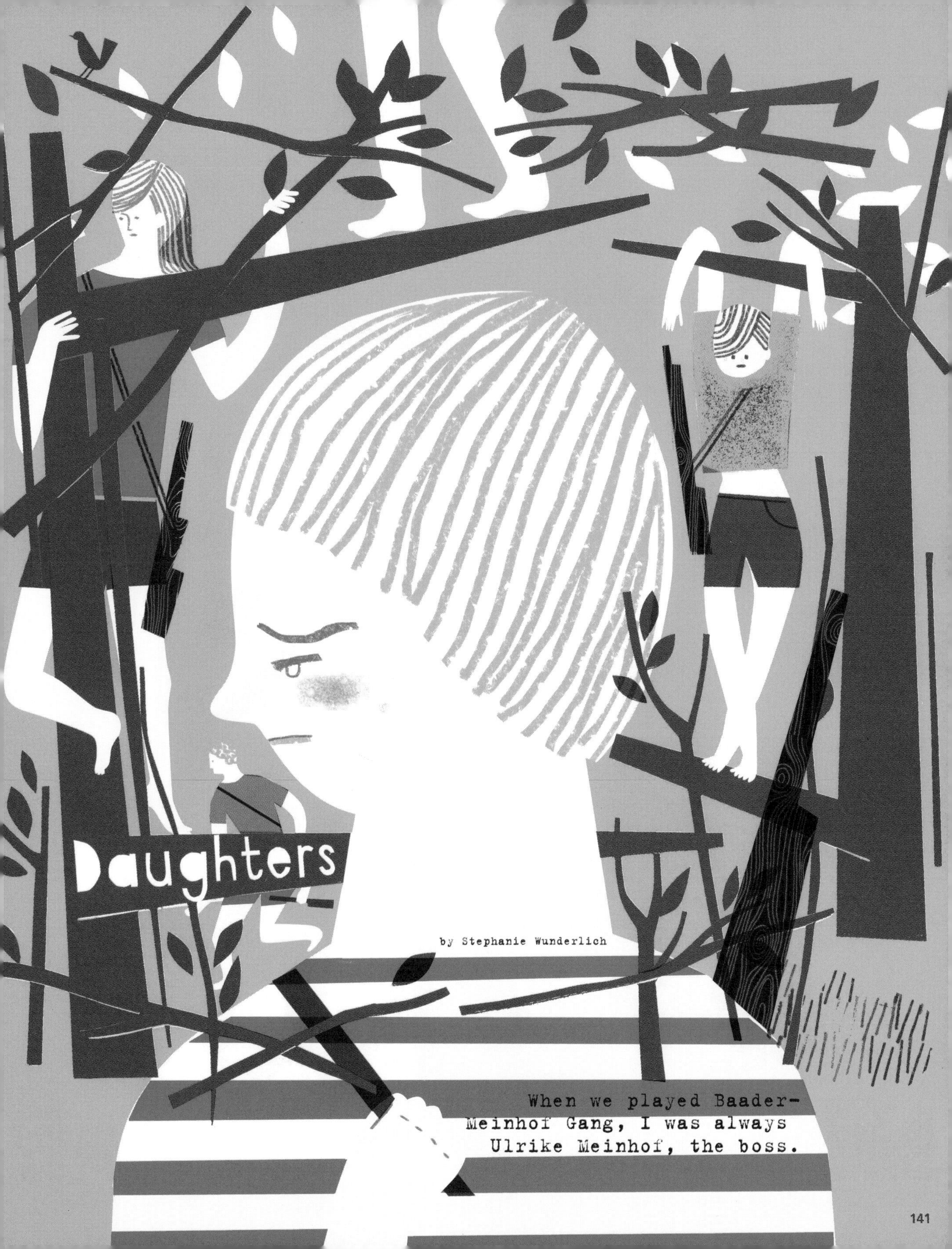

# Daughters

by Stephanie Wunderlich

When we played Baader-Meinhof Gang, I was always Ulrike Meinhof, the boss.

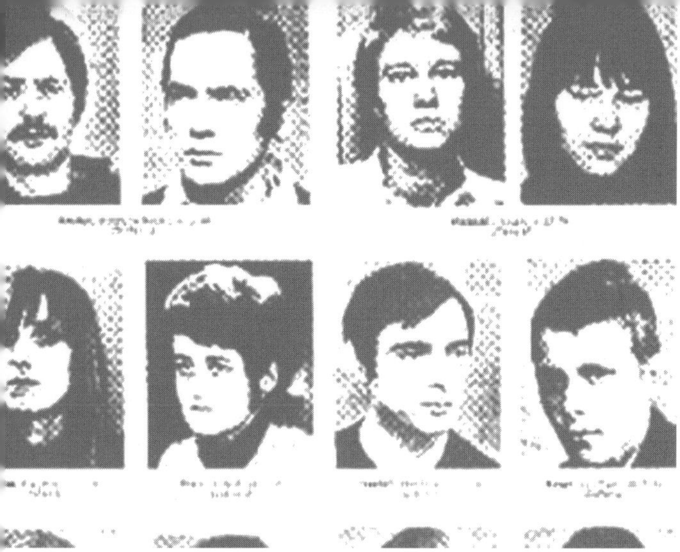

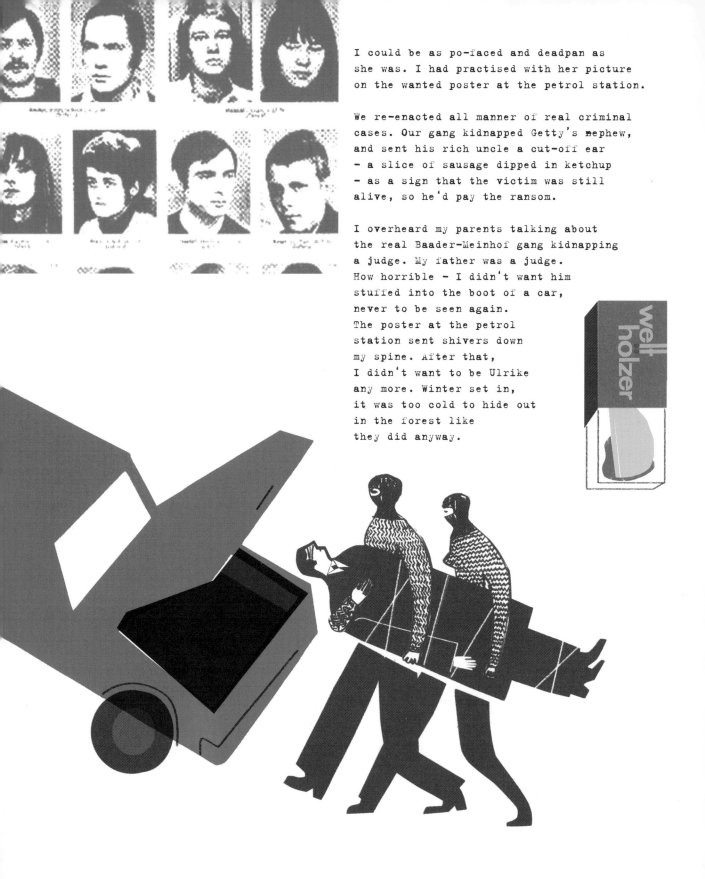

I could be as po-faced and deadpan as she was. I had practised with her picture on the wanted poster at the petrol station.

We re-enacted all manner of real criminal cases. Our gang kidnapped Getty's nephew, and sent his rich uncle a cut-off ear - a slice of sausage dipped in ketchup - as a sign that the victim was still alive, so he'd pay the ransom.

I overheard my parents talking about the real Baader-Meinhof gang kidnapping a judge. My father was a judge. How horrible - I didn't want him stuffed into the boot of a car, never to be seen again. The poster at the petrol station sent shivers down my spine. After that, I didn't want to be Ulrike any more. Winter set in, it was too cold to hide out in the forest like they did anyway.

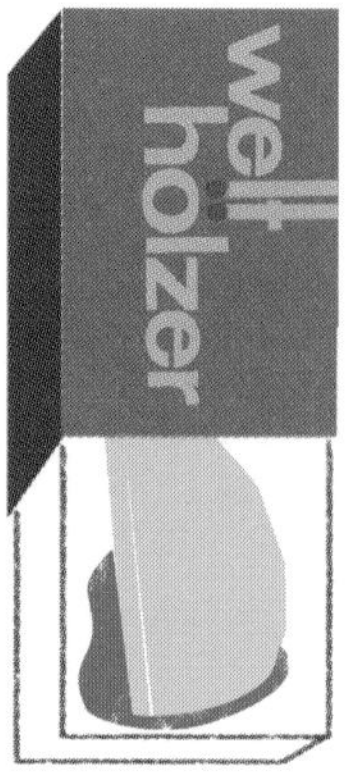
welt
holzer

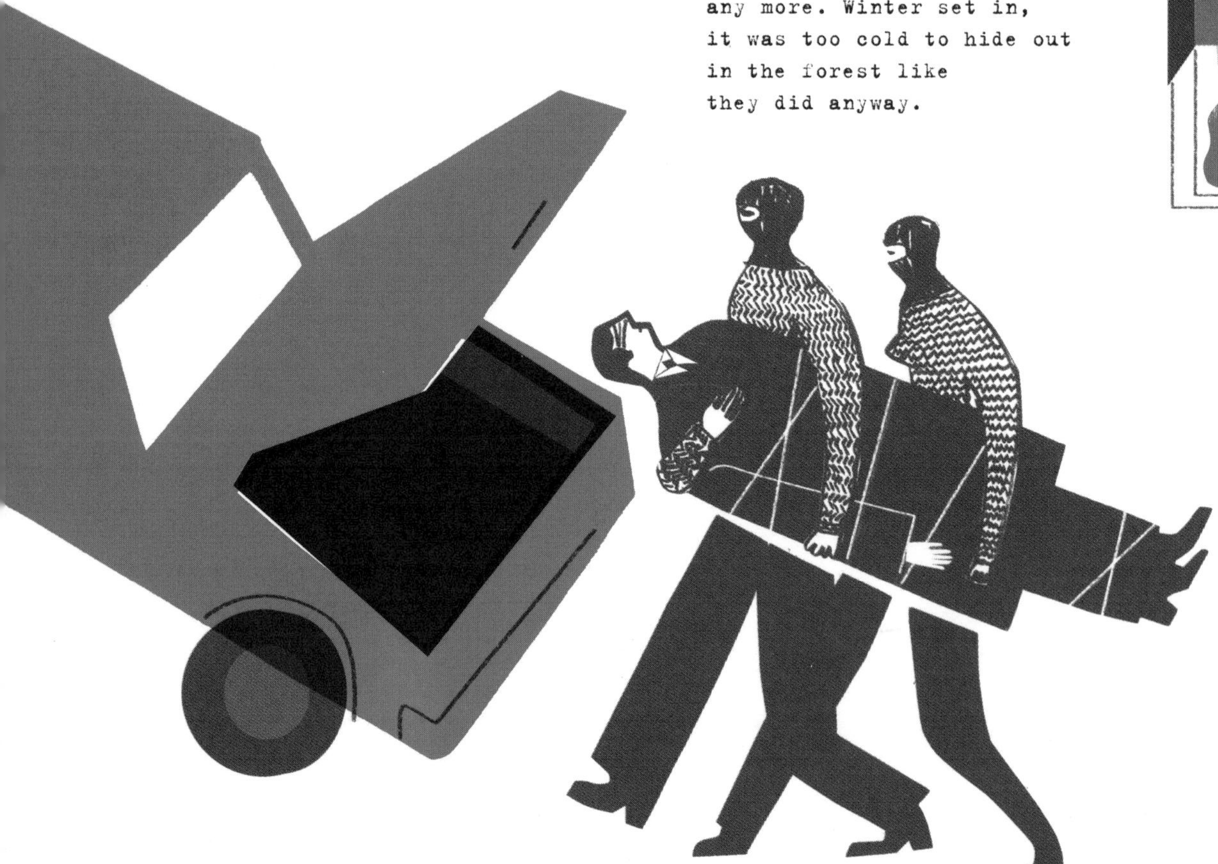

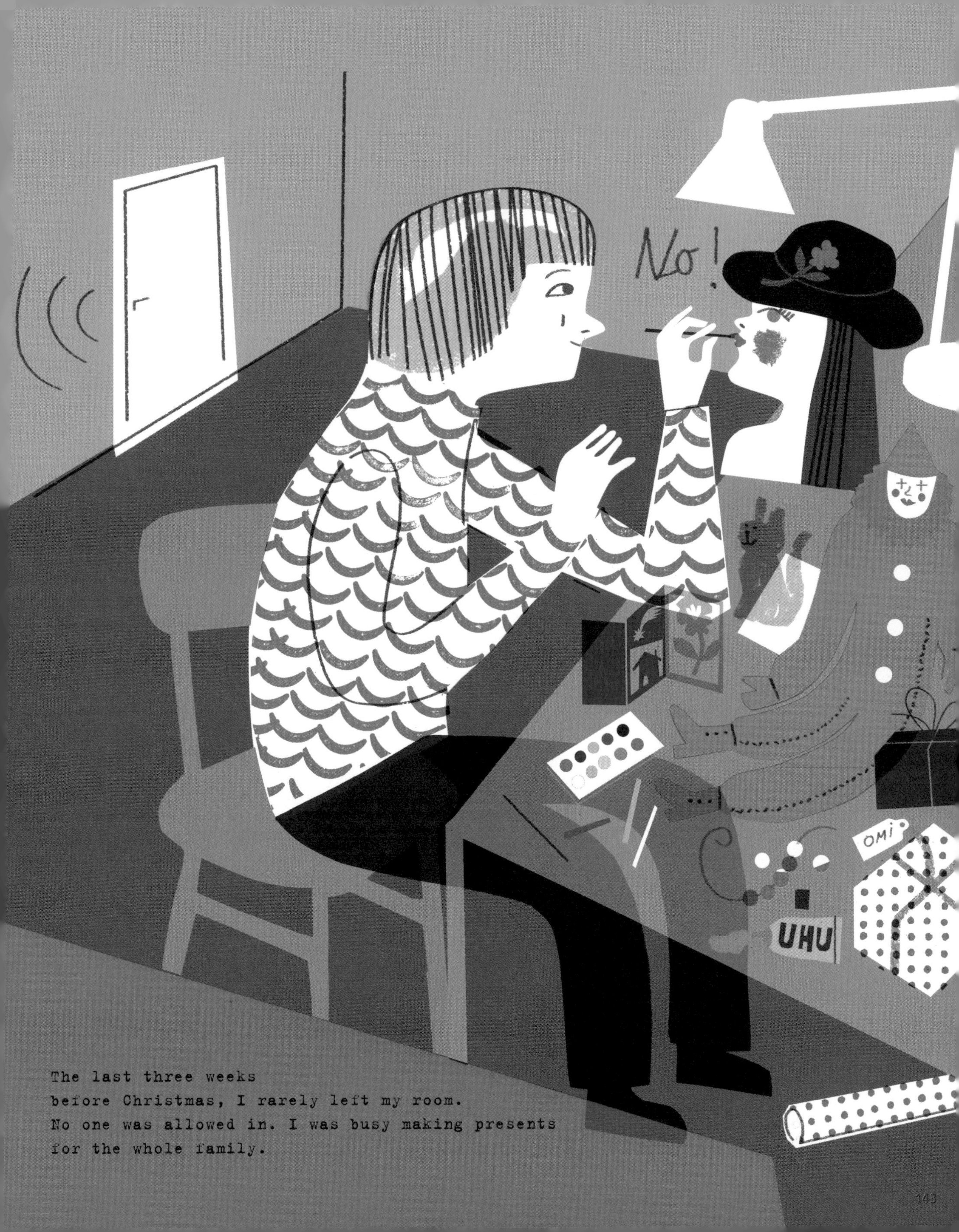
No!
OMi
UHU

The last three weeks
before Christmas, I rarely left my room.
No one was allowed in. I was busy making presents
for the whole family.

Those presents from long ago are still gathering dust in my mother's cupboard. My parents encouraged their kids' creative side.

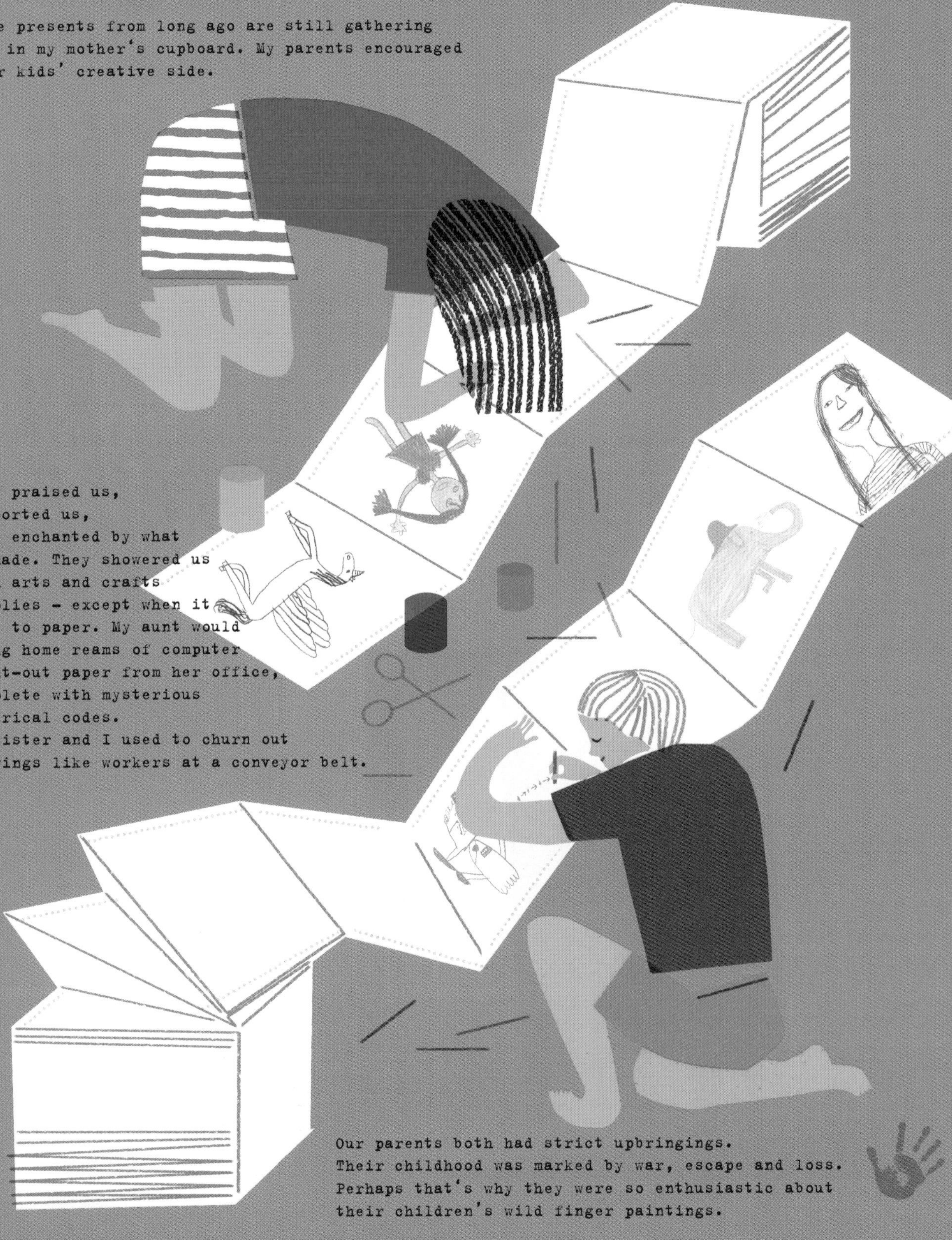

They praised us,
supported us,
were enchanted by what
we made. They showered us
with arts and crafts
supplies – except when it
came to paper. My aunt would
bring home reams of computer
print-out paper from her office,
complete with mysterious
numerical codes.
My sister and I used to churn out
drawings like workers at a conveyor belt.

Our parents both had strict upbringings.
Their childhood was marked by war, escape and loss.
Perhaps that's why they were so enthusiastic about
their children's wild finger paintings.

My beloved grandparents were responsible for instilling us with Prussian values: artistic talent was not one of them. Once, in front of the whole family, my grandfather asked his only grandson:

My dear boy, what would you like to be when you grow up?

Pardon me? Get a grip!

An artist.

He hit the table with his fist, making spoons jump and hollered:

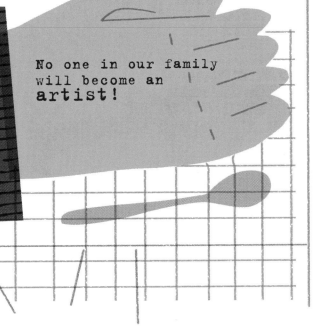

No one in our family will become an **artist**!

Grandfather never asked us girls what we wanted to be when we grew up. It would have been nice to be asked.

After the meal,
we girls had to help
Grandma with drying
the dishes.

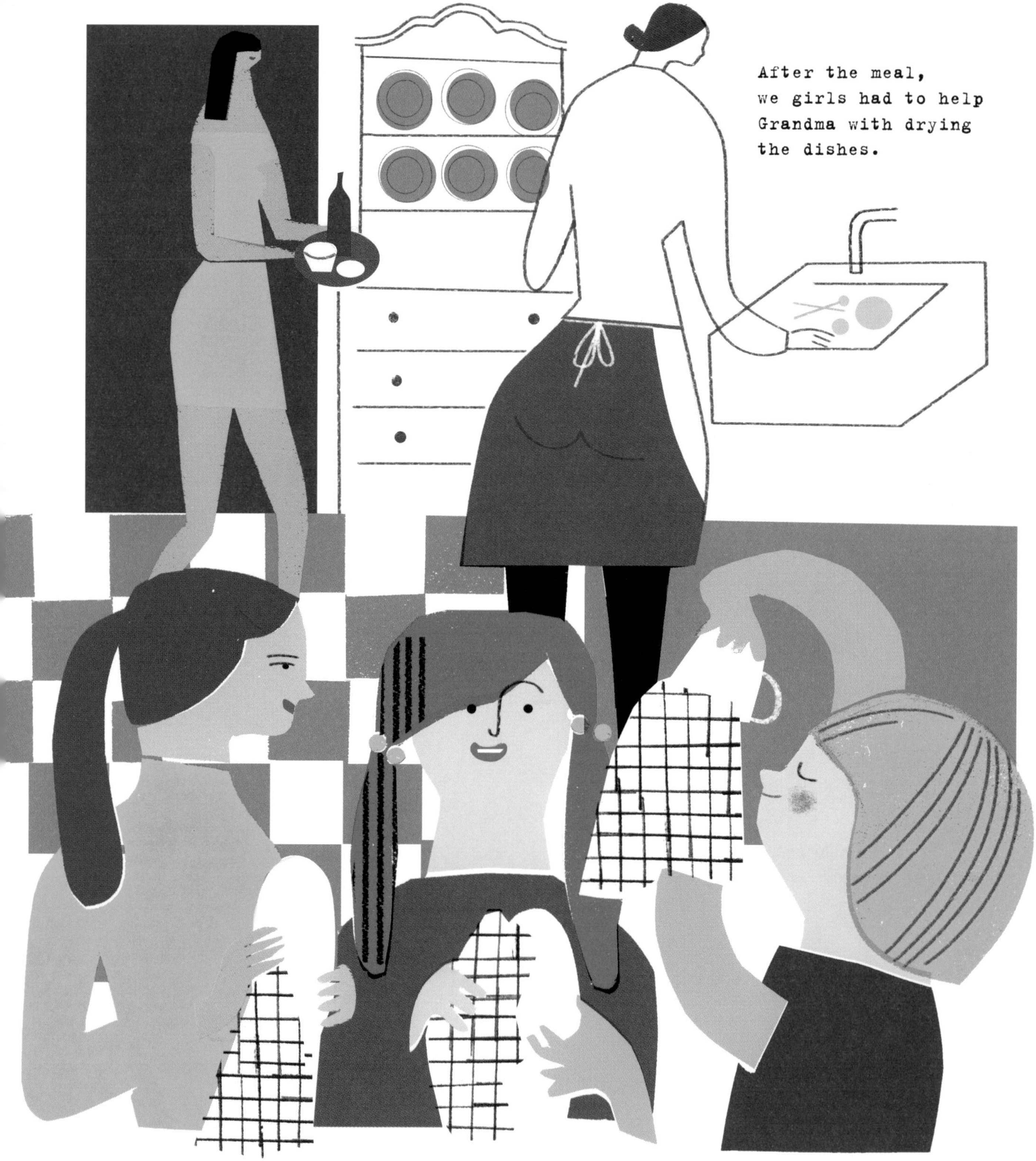

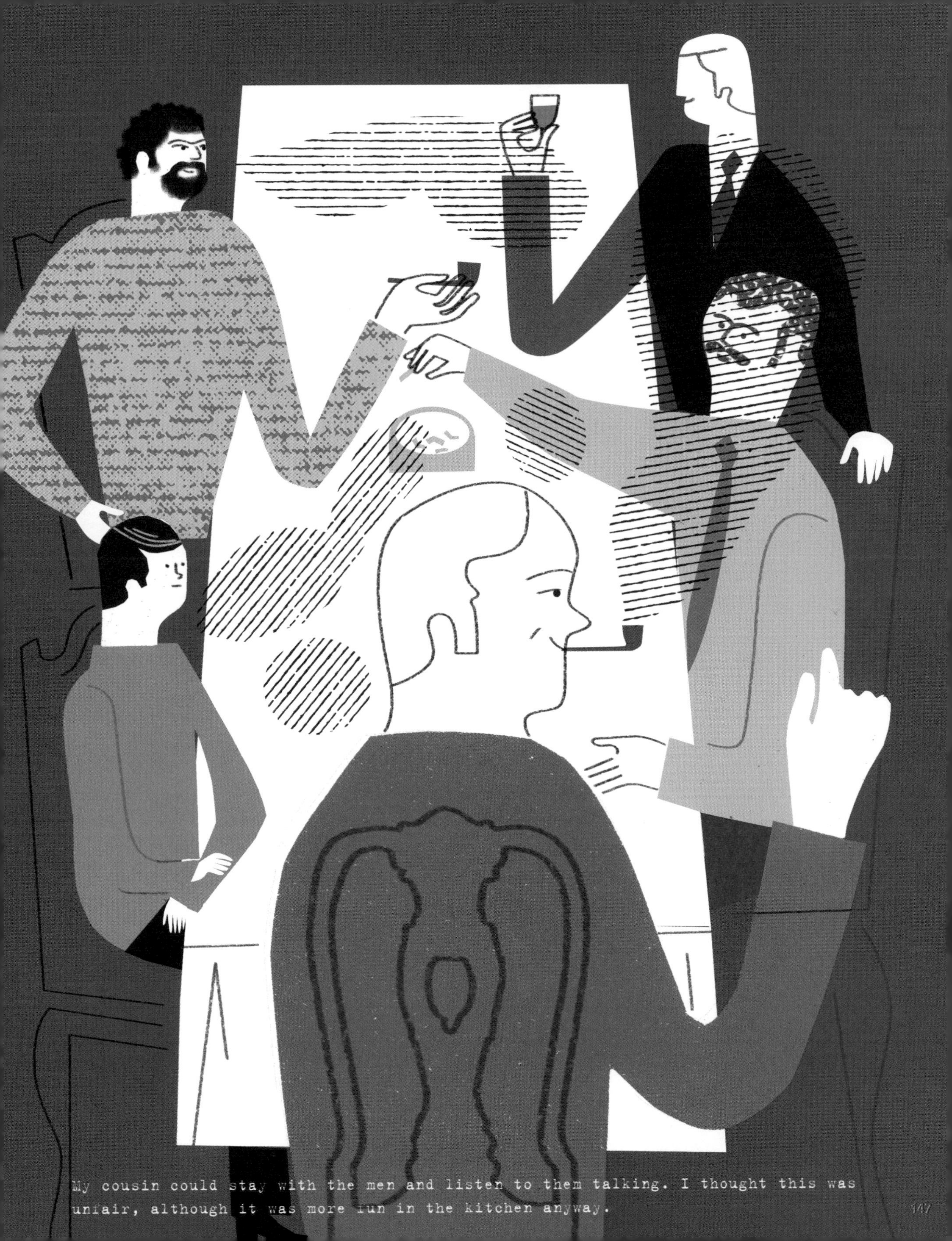

My cousin could stay with the men and listen to them talking. I thought this was unfair, although it was more fun in the kitchen anyway.

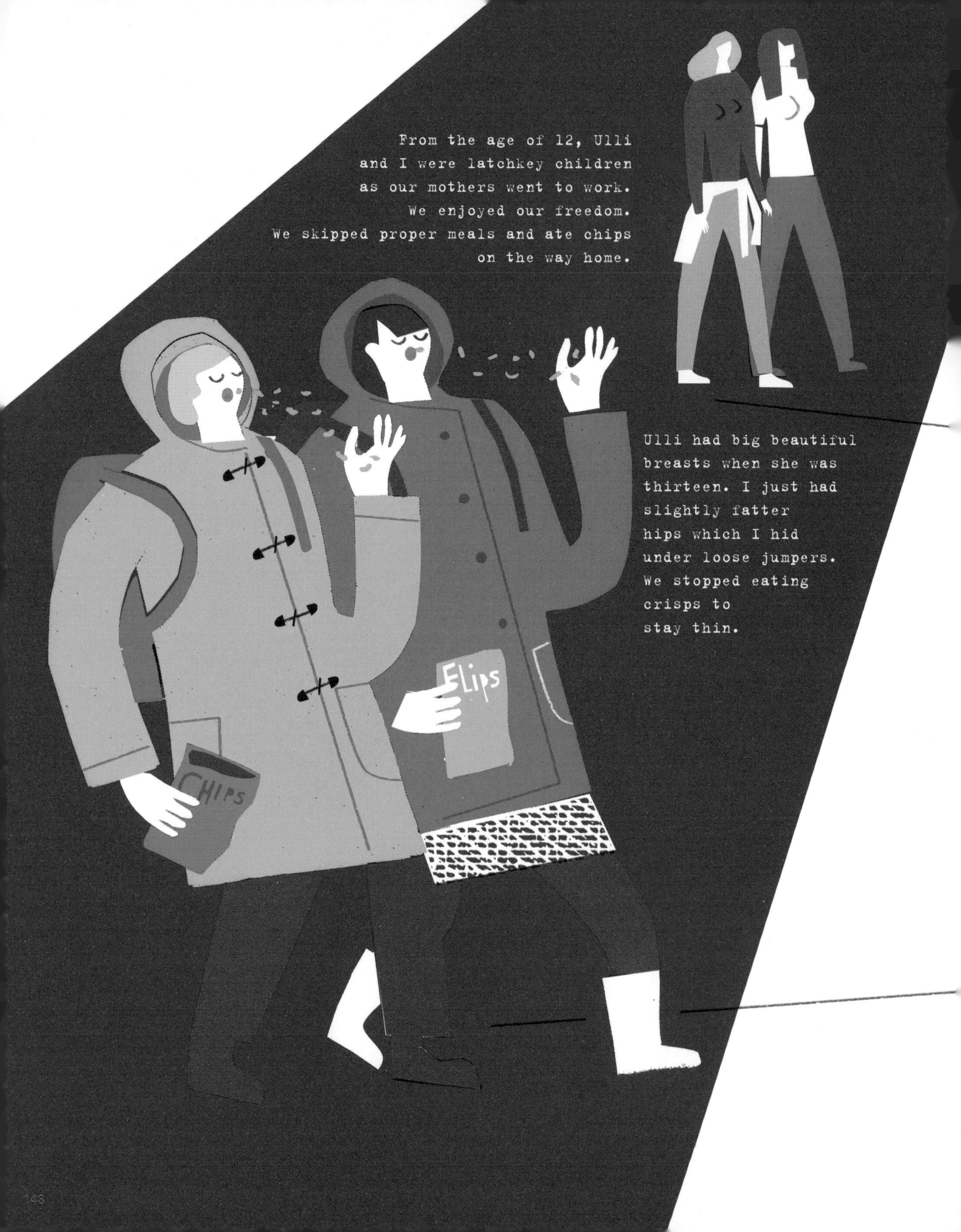
From the age of 12, Ulli and I were latchkey children as our mothers went to work. We enjoyed our freedom. We skipped proper meals and ate chips on the way home.
CHIPS
Ulli had big beautiful breasts when she was thirteen. I just had slightly fatter hips which I hid under loose jumpers. We stopped eating crisps to stay thin.

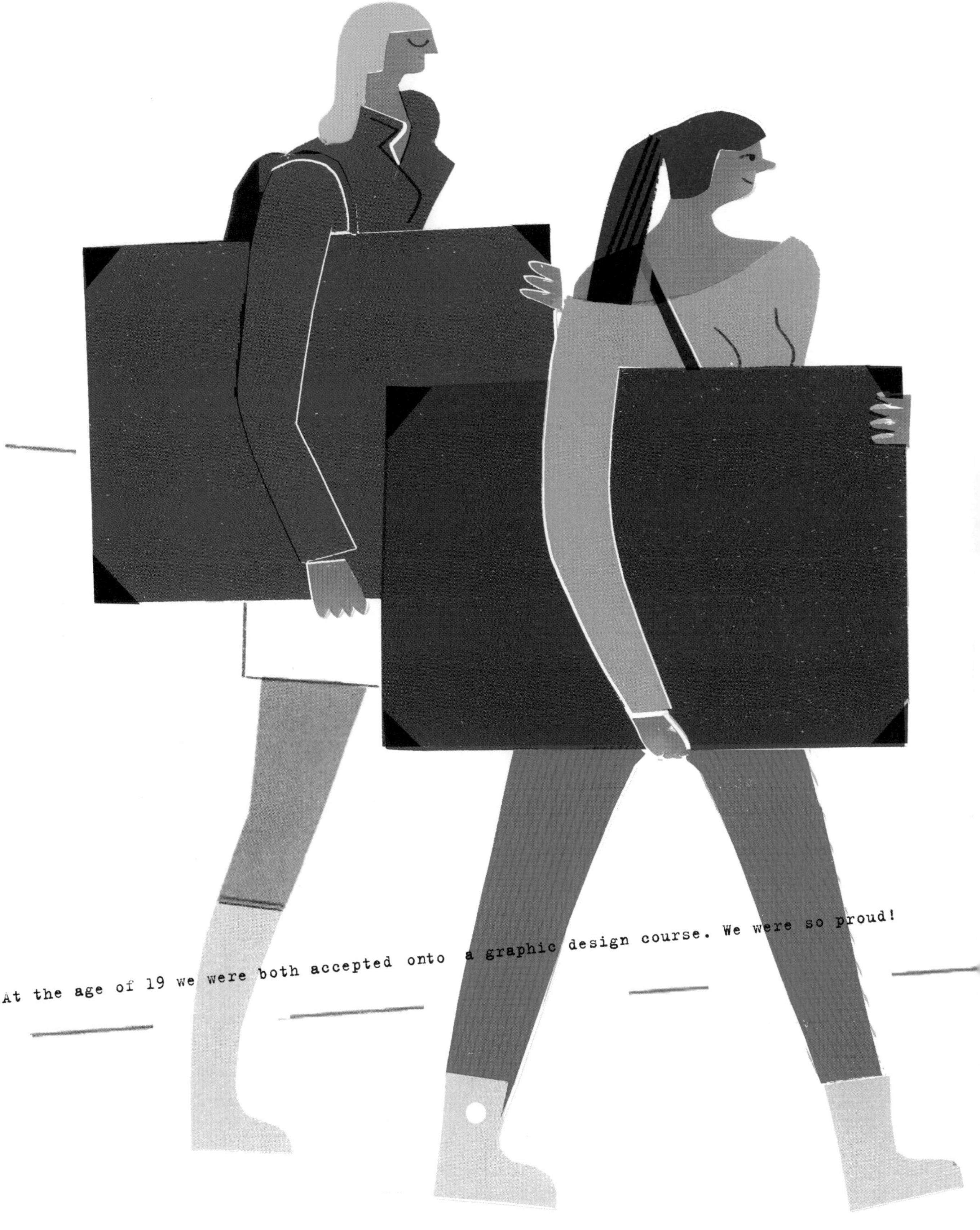
At the age of 19 we were both accepted onto a graphic design course. We were so proud!

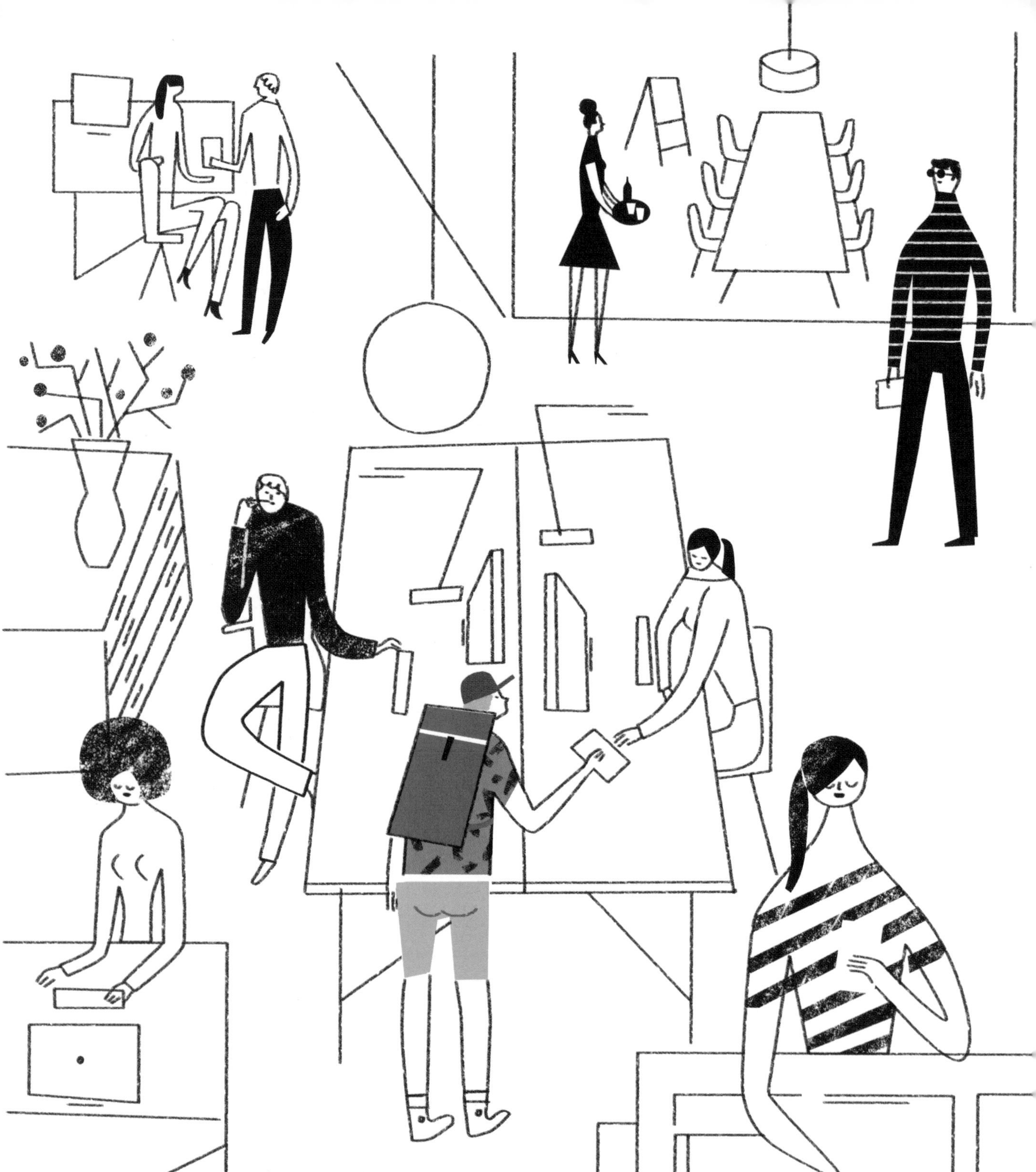

After graduating, I got a job at
a chic advertising agency.
All the furniture was white.
We weren't allowed to keep anything
personal on our desks. The bicycle
courier brought some colour into our
office life.

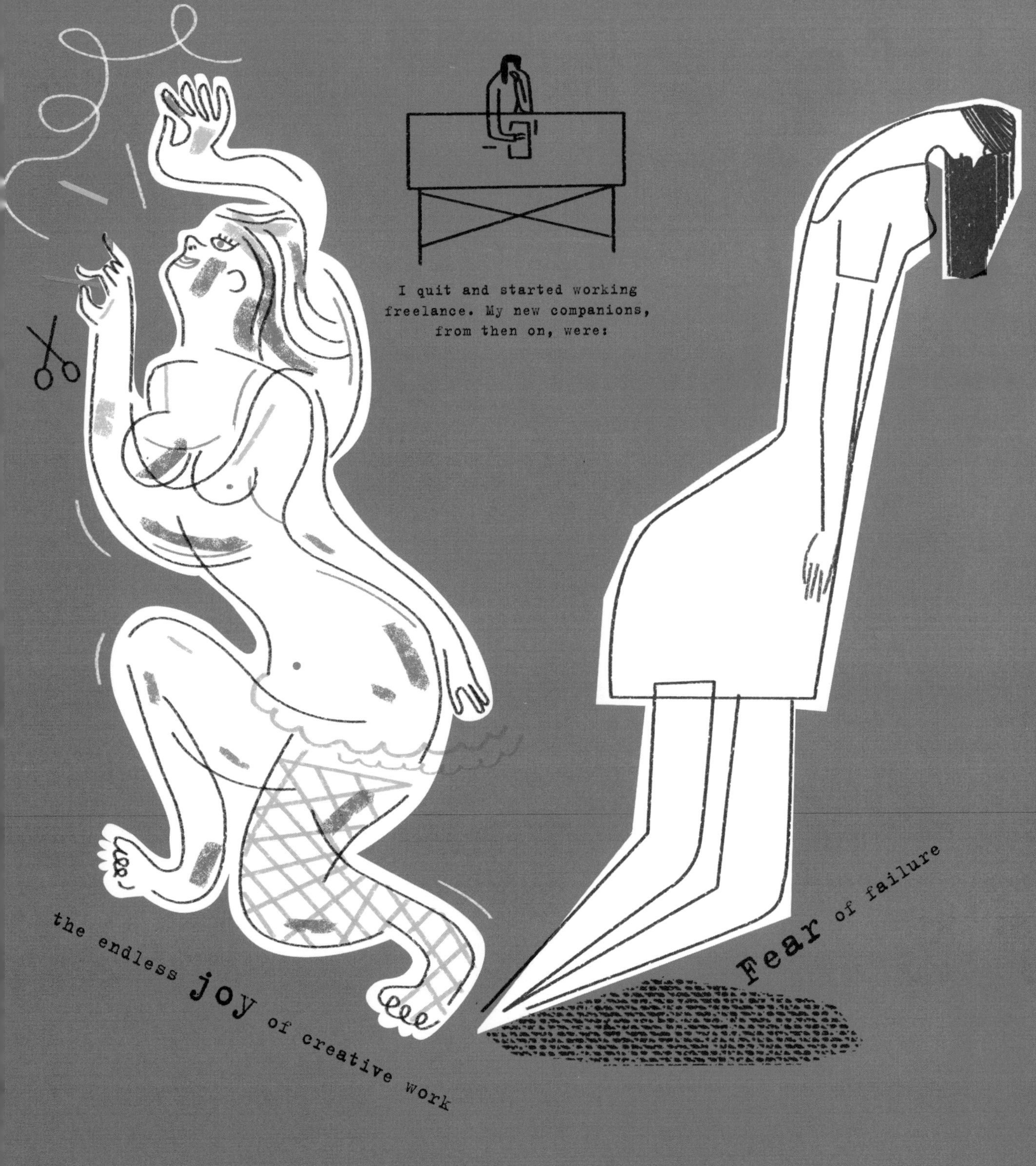
I quit and started working freelance. My new companions, from then on, were:
the endless joy of creative work
Fear of failure

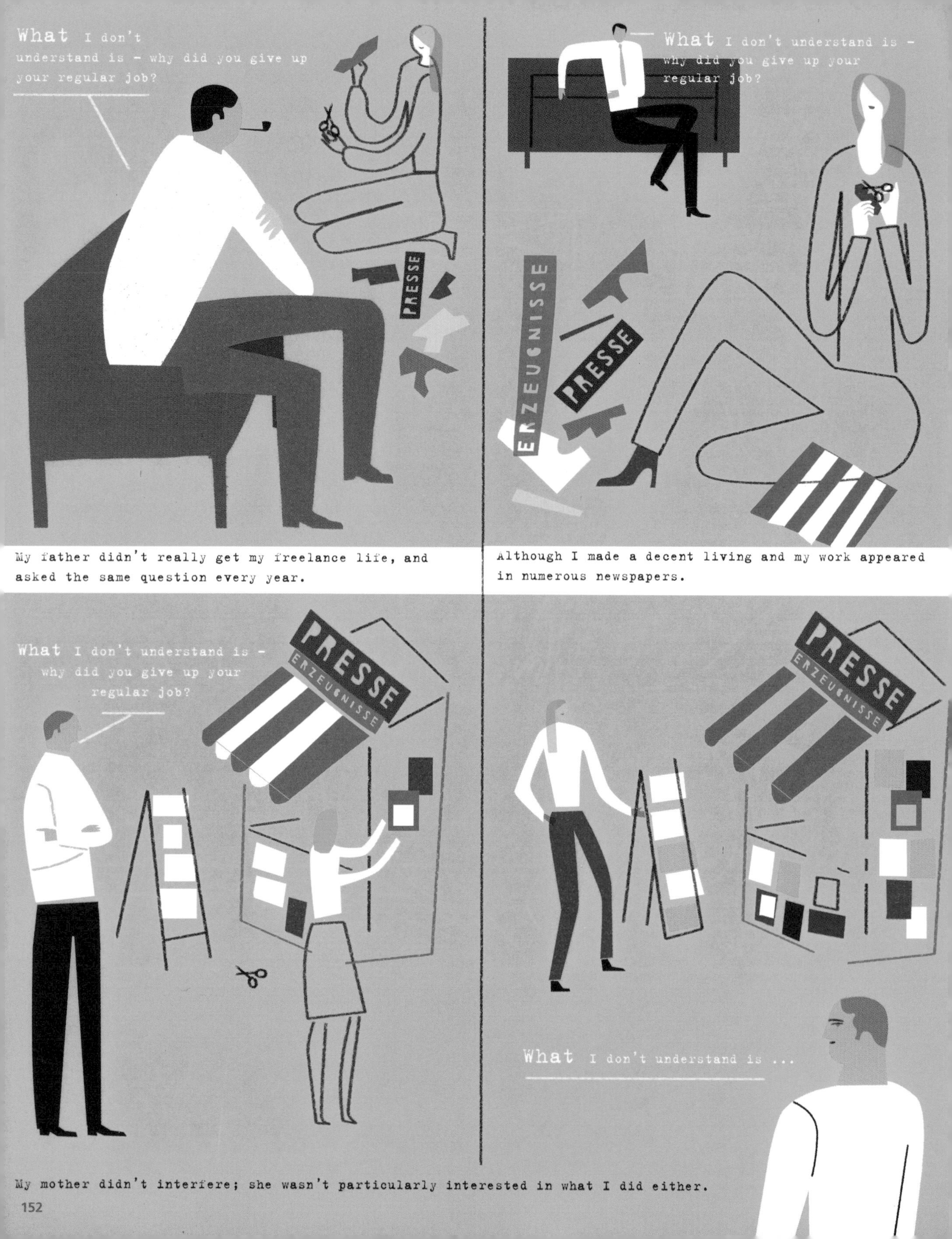

What I don't understand is – why did you give up your regular job?
PRESSE
My father didn't really get my freelance life, and asked the same question every year.
What I don't understand is – why did you give up your regular job?
ERZEUGNISSE
PRESSE
Although I made a decent living and my work appeared in numerous newspapers.
What I don't understand is – why did you give up your regular job?
PRESSE
ERZEUGNISSE
PRESSE
ERZEUGNISSE
What I don't understand is ...
My mother didn't interfere; she wasn't particularly interested in what I did either.

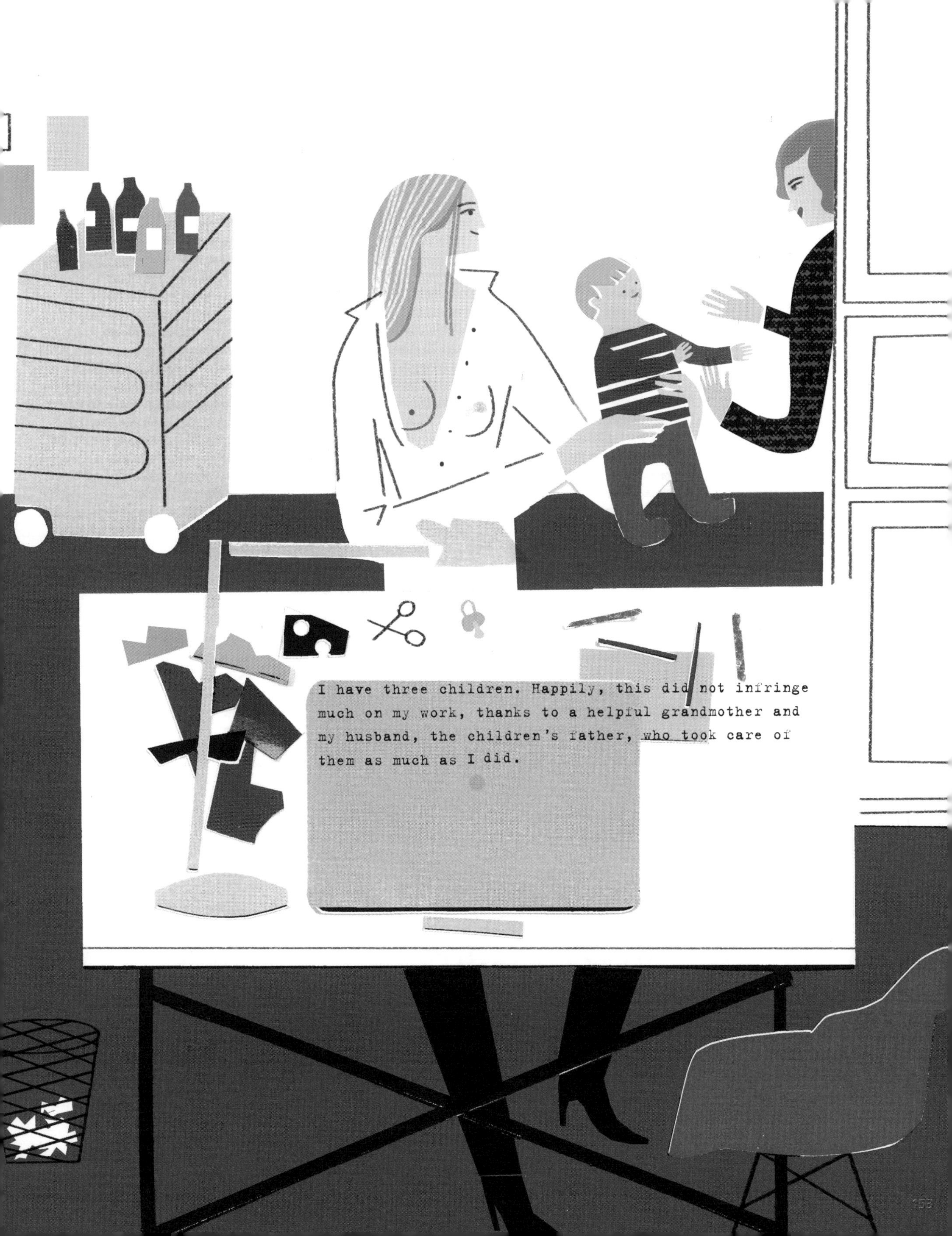

I have three children. Happily, this did not infringe much on my work, thanks to a helpful grandmother and my husband, the children's father, who took care of them as much as I did.

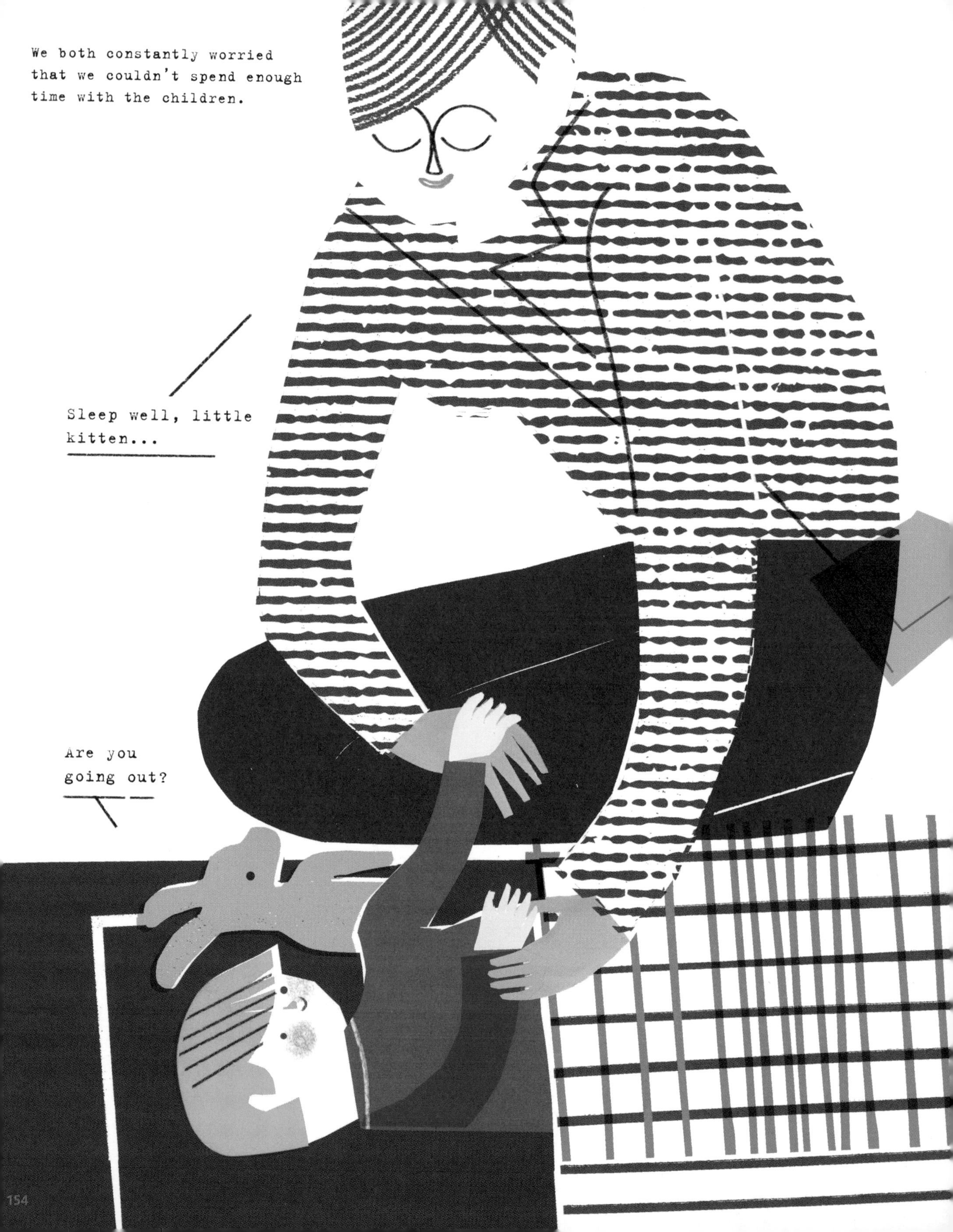
We both constantly worried that we couldn't spend enough time with the children.
Sleep well, little kitten...
Are you going out?

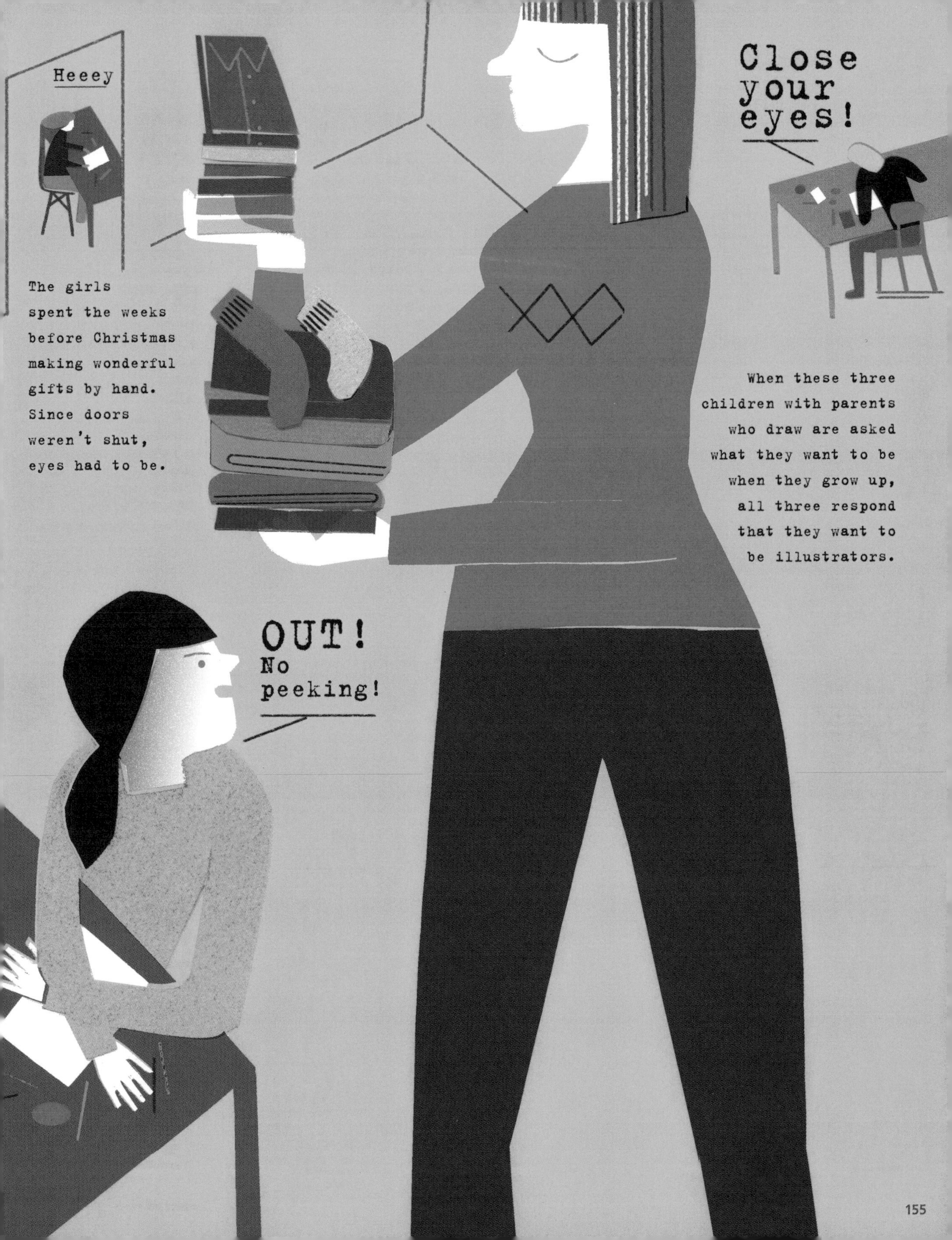
Heeey
Close your eyes!
OUT! No peeking!

The girls spent the weeks before Christmas making wonderful gifts by hand. Since doors weren't shut, eyes had to be.

When these three children with parents who draw are asked what they want to be when they grow up, all three respond that they want to be illustrators.

Then it's my turn to thump the table so hard that the spoons jump and holler:

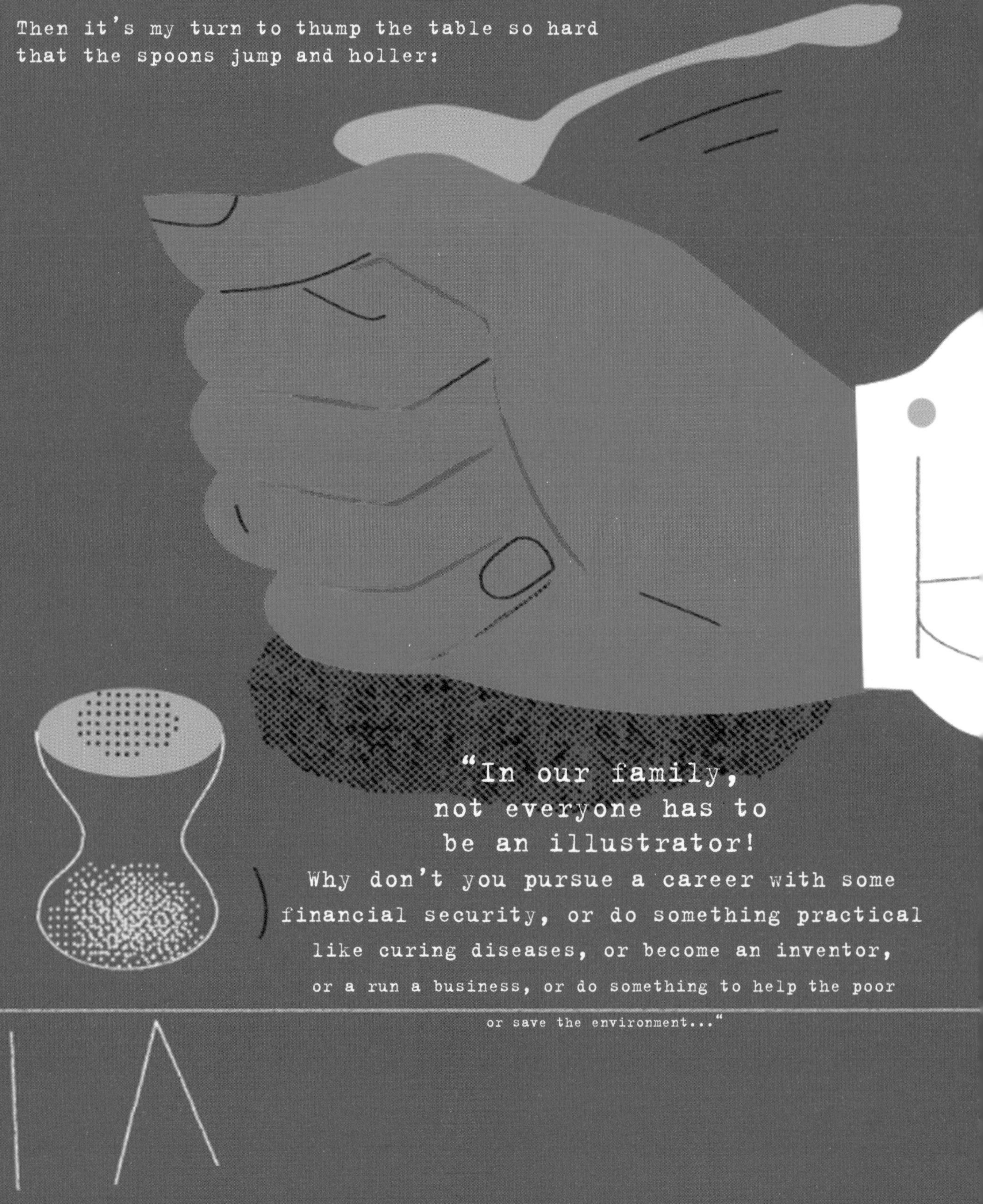

"In our family, not everyone has to be an illustrator! Why don't you pursue a career with some financial security, or do something practical like curing diseases, or become an inventor, or a run a business, or do something to help the poor or save the environment..."

## THE MAN I love

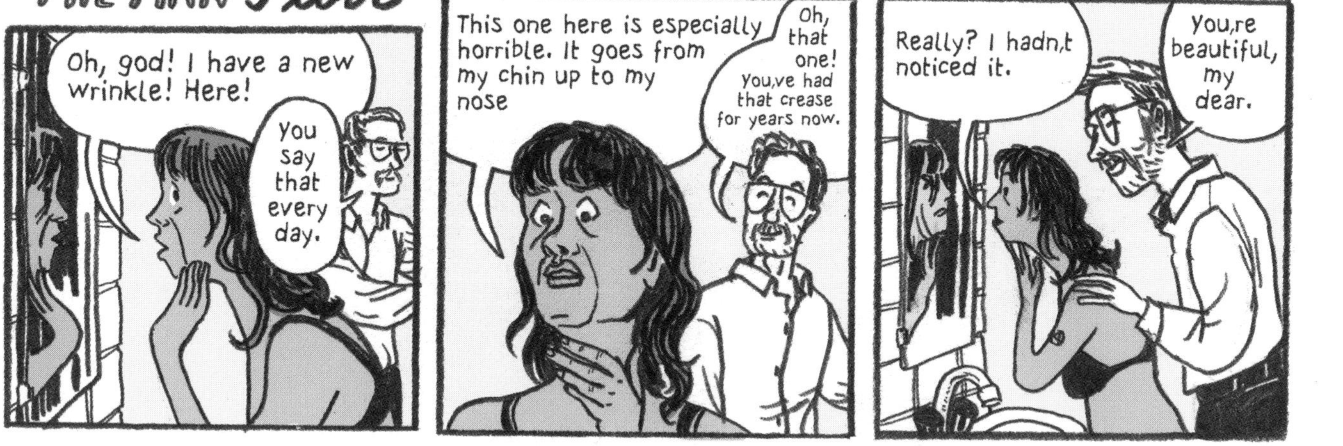
Oh, god! I have a new wrinkle! Here!
You say that every day.
This one here is especially horrible. It goes from my chin up to my nose
Oh, that one! You,ve had that crease for years now.
Really? I hadn,t noticed it.
You,re beautiful, my dear.

## New Dads

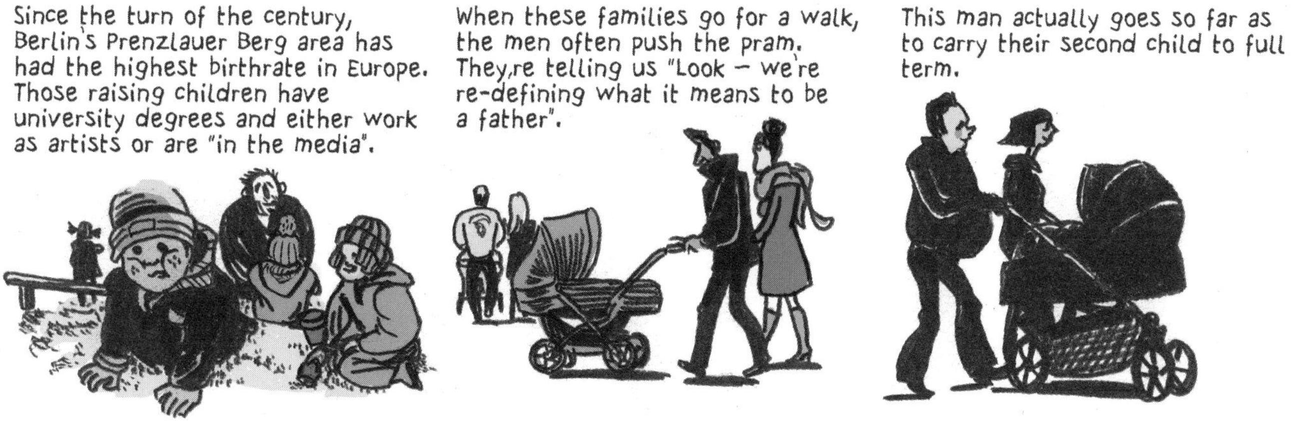
Since the turn of the century, Berlin's Prenzlauer Berg area has had the highest birthrate in Europe. Those raising children have university degrees and either work as artists or are "in the media".
When these families go for a walk, the men often push the pram. They,re telling us "Look – we're re-defining what it means to be a father".
This man actually goes so far as to carry their second child to full term.

## Bugaboo task force

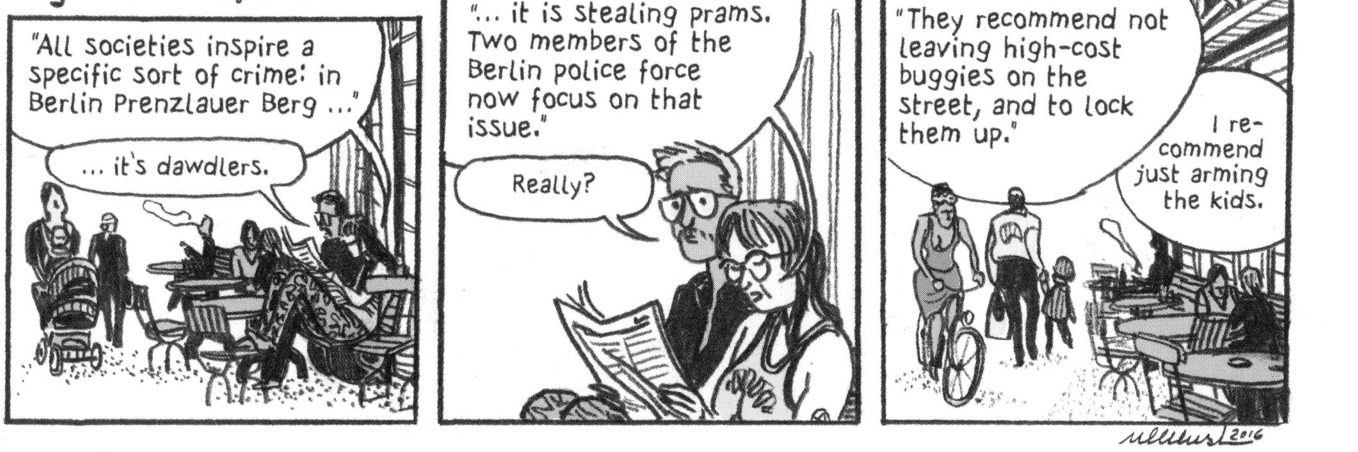
"All societies inspire a specific sort of crime: in Berlin Prenzlauer Berg ..."
... it's dawdlers.
"... it is stealing prams. Two members of the Berlin police force now focus on that issue."
Really?
"They recommend not leaving high-cost buggies on the street, and to lock them up."
I re-commend just arming the kids.
2016

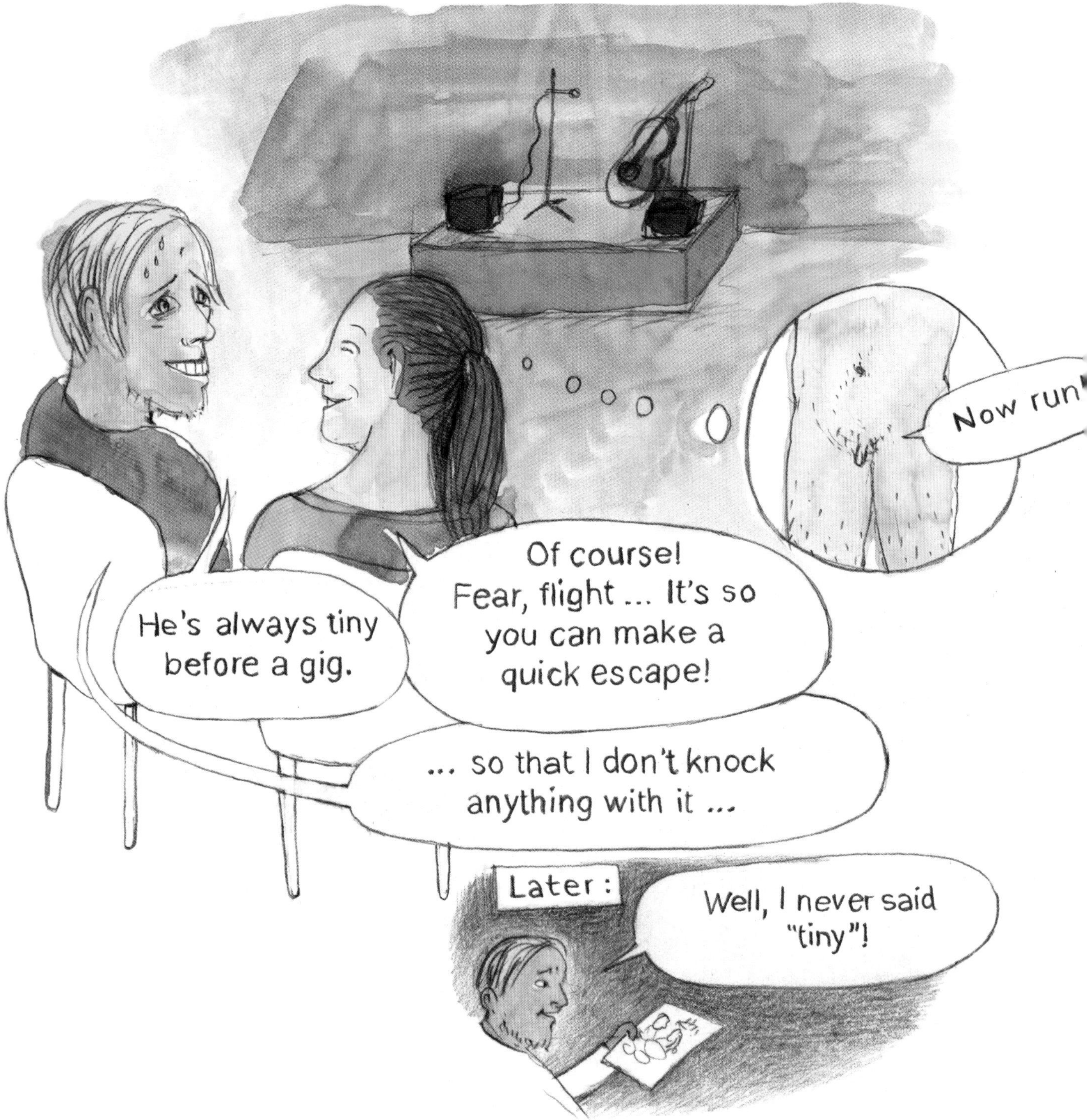
Now run!
He's always tiny before a gig.
Of course! Fear, flight ... It's so you can make a quick escape!
... so that I don't knock anything with it ...
Later:
Well, I never said "tiny"!

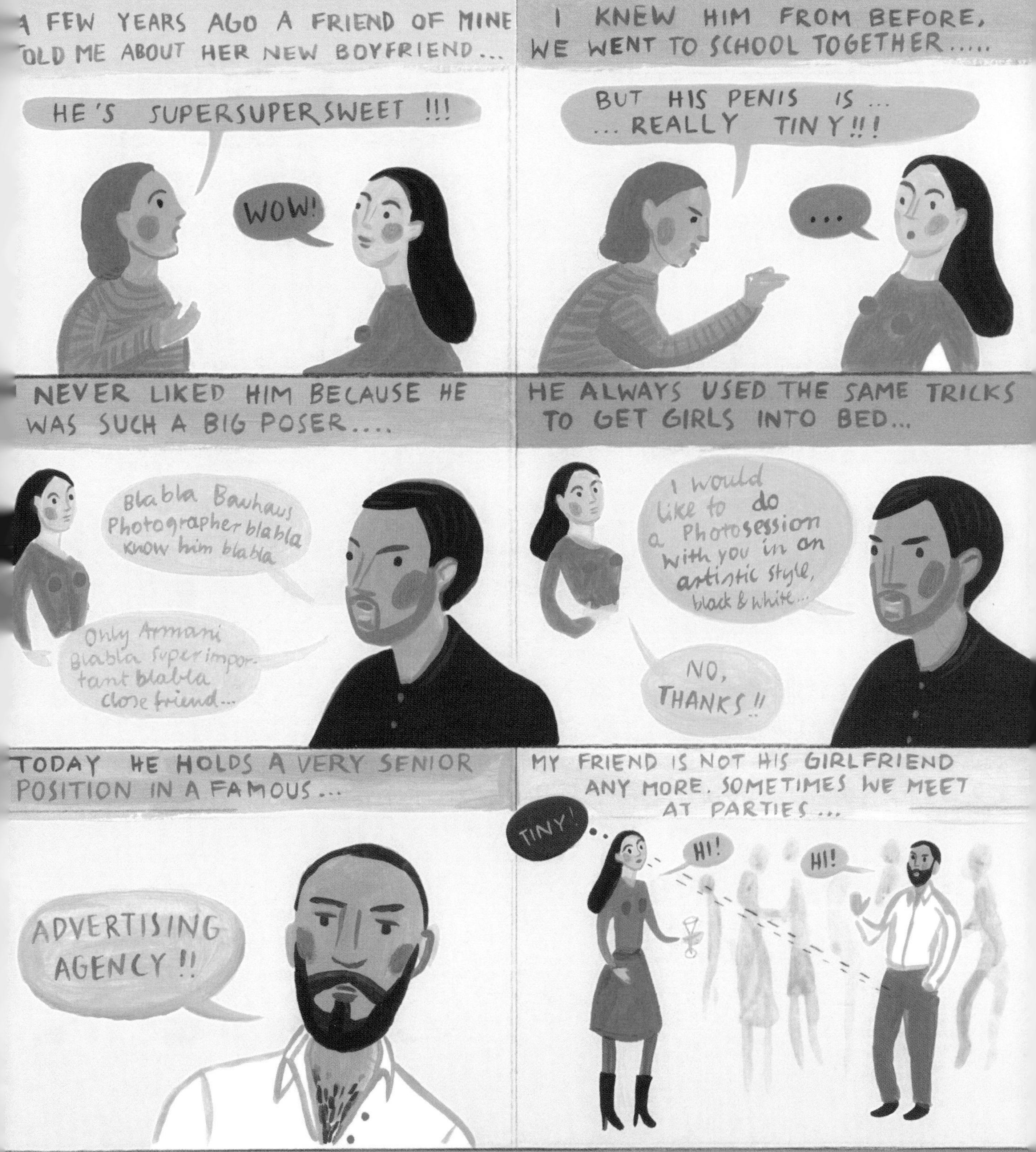
A FEW YEARS AGO A FRIEND OF MINE TOLD ME ABOUT HER NEW BOYFRIEND...
HE'S SUPERSUPERSWEET !!!
WOW!
I KNEW HIM FROM BEFORE, WE WENT TO SCHOOL TOGETHER.....
BUT HIS PENIS IS ... ... REALLY TINY!!!
...
NEVER LIKED HIM BECAUSE HE WAS SUCH A BIG POSER....
Blabla Bauhaus Photographer blabla know him blabla
Only Armani Blabla Superimpor-tant blabla close friend...
HE ALWAYS USED THE SAME TRICKS TO GET GIRLS INTO BED...
I would like to do a Photosession with you in an artistic style, black & white...
NO, THANKS!!
TODAY HE HOLDS A VERY SENIOR POSITION IN A FAMOUS...
ADVERTISING AGENCY!!
MY FRIEND IS NOT HIS GIRLFRIEND ANY MORE. SOMETIMES WE MEET AT PARTIES...
TINY!
HI!
HI!

# AN IDEAL BOYFRIEND

marialuisa

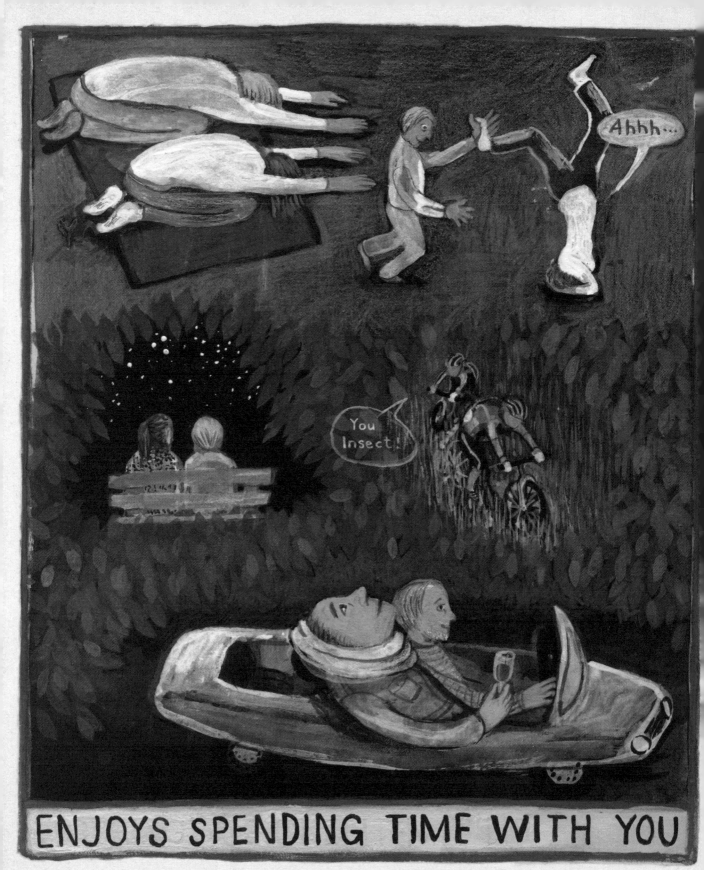

ENJOYS SPENDING TIME WITH YOU

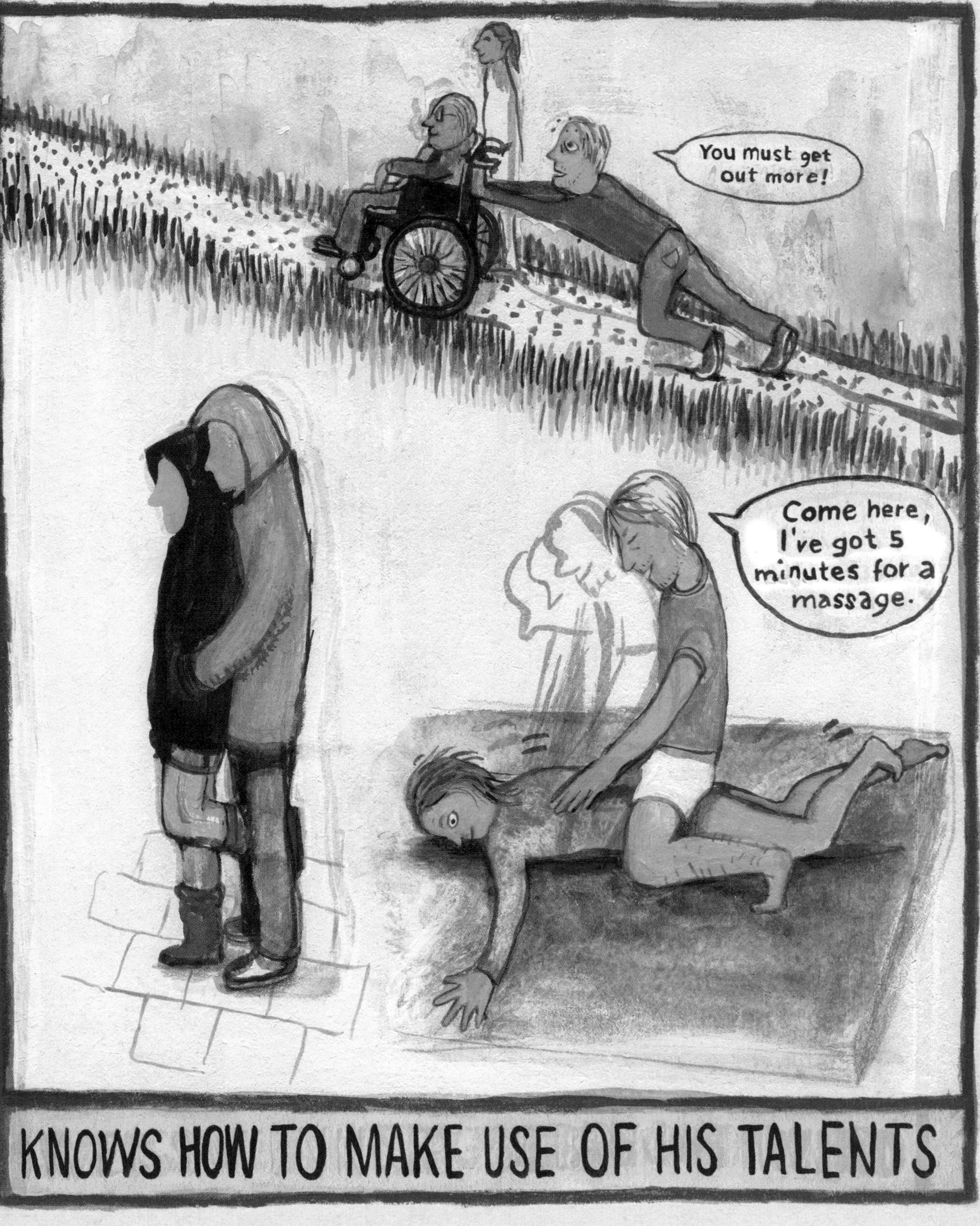
You must get out more!
Come here, I've got 5 minutes for a massage.
KNOWS HOW TO MAKE USE OF HIS TALENTS

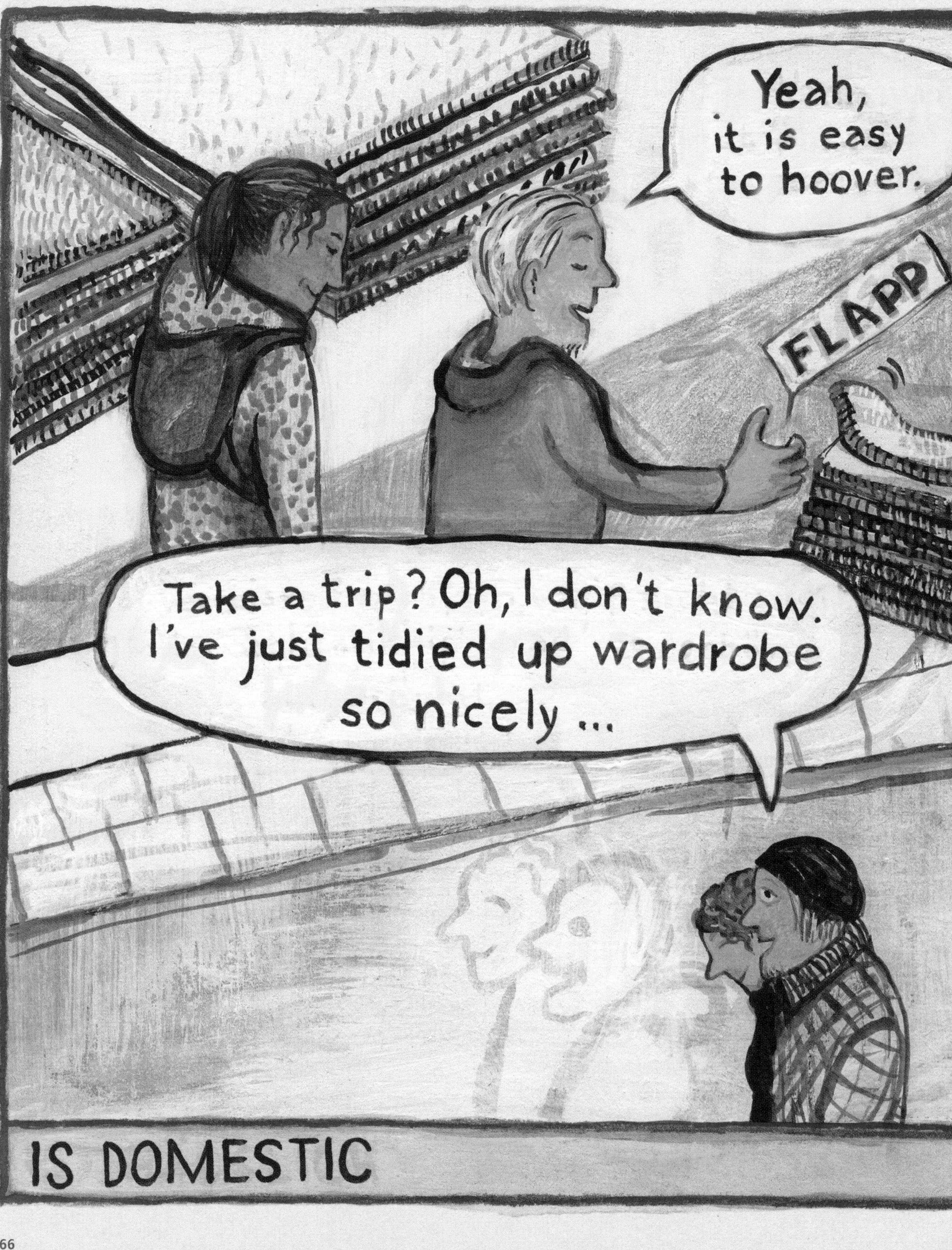
Yeah, it is easy to hoover.
FLAPP
Take a trip? Oh, I don't know. I've just tidied up wardrobe so nicely ...
IS DOMESTIC

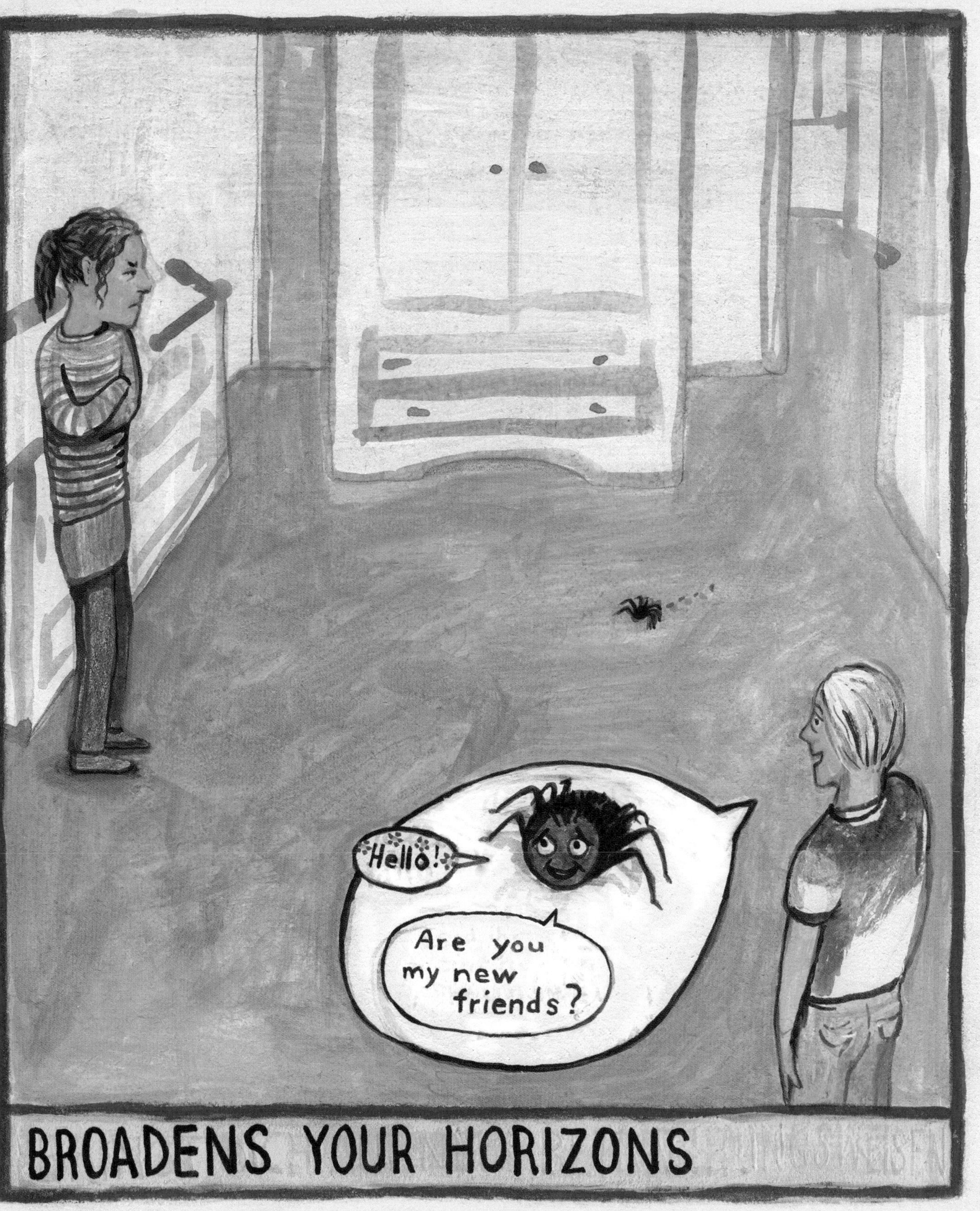
Hello!
Are you my new friends?
BROADENS YOUR HORIZONS

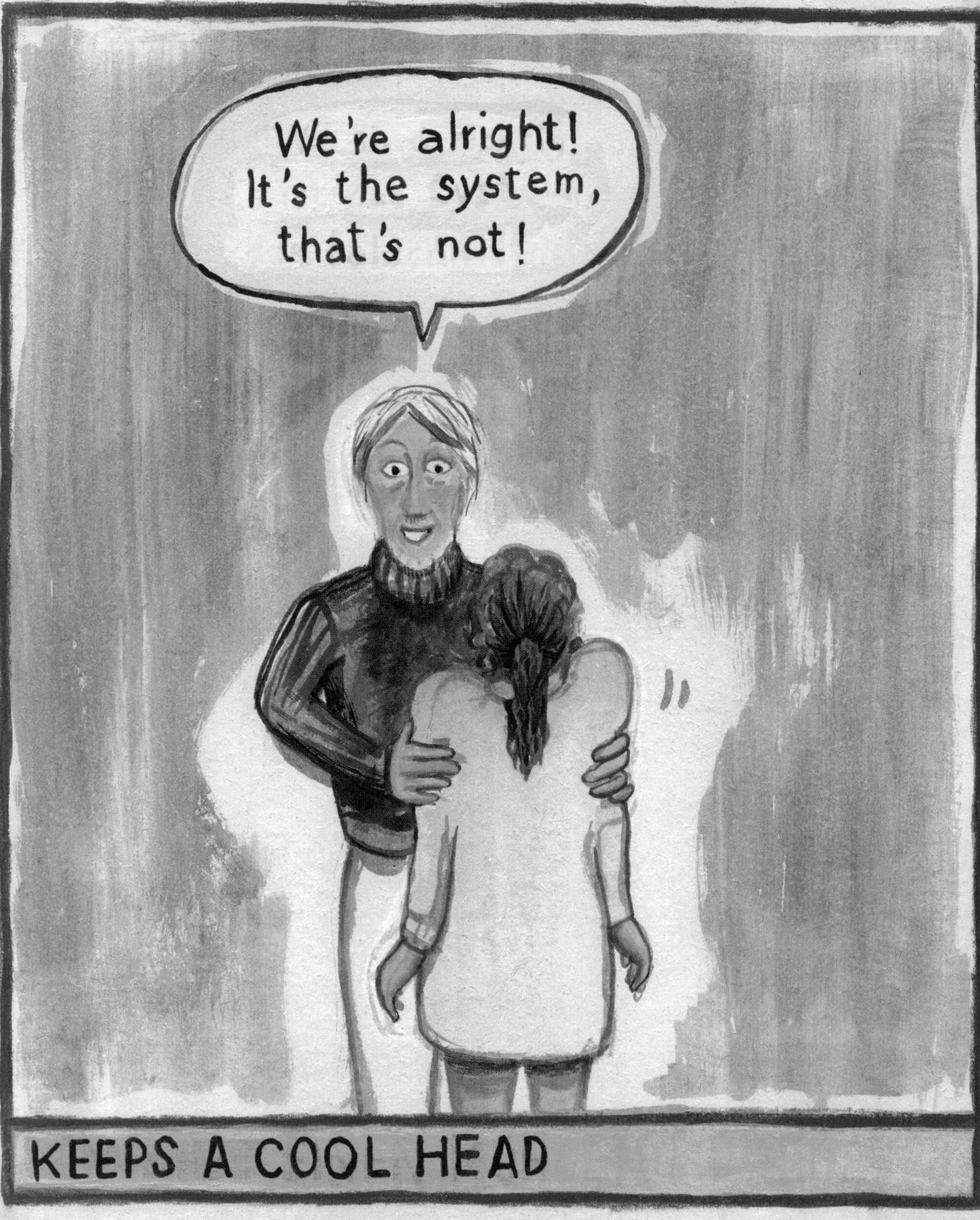
We're alright! It's the system, that's not!
KEEPS A COOL HEAD

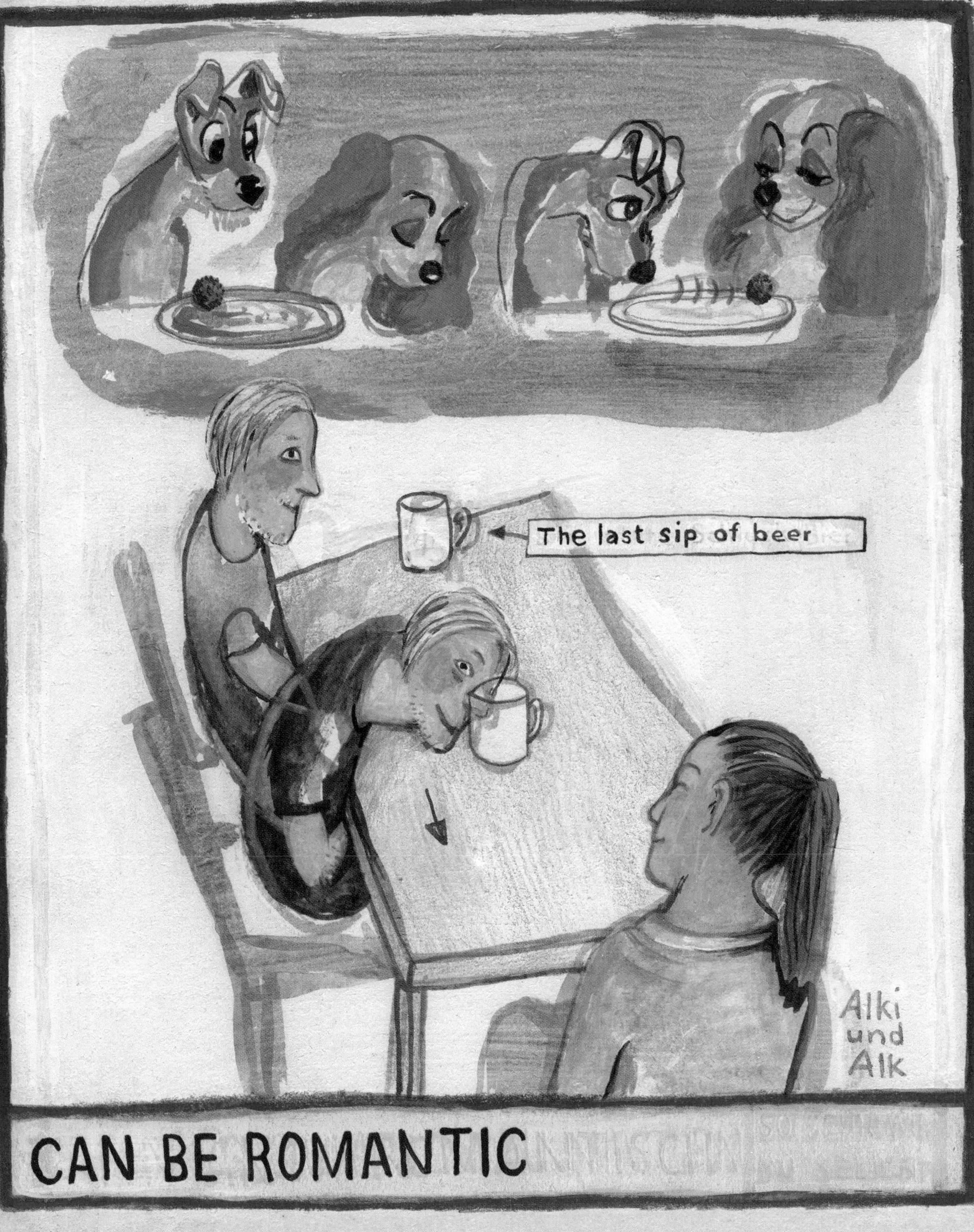
The last sip of beer
Alki
und
Alk
CAN BE ROMANTIC

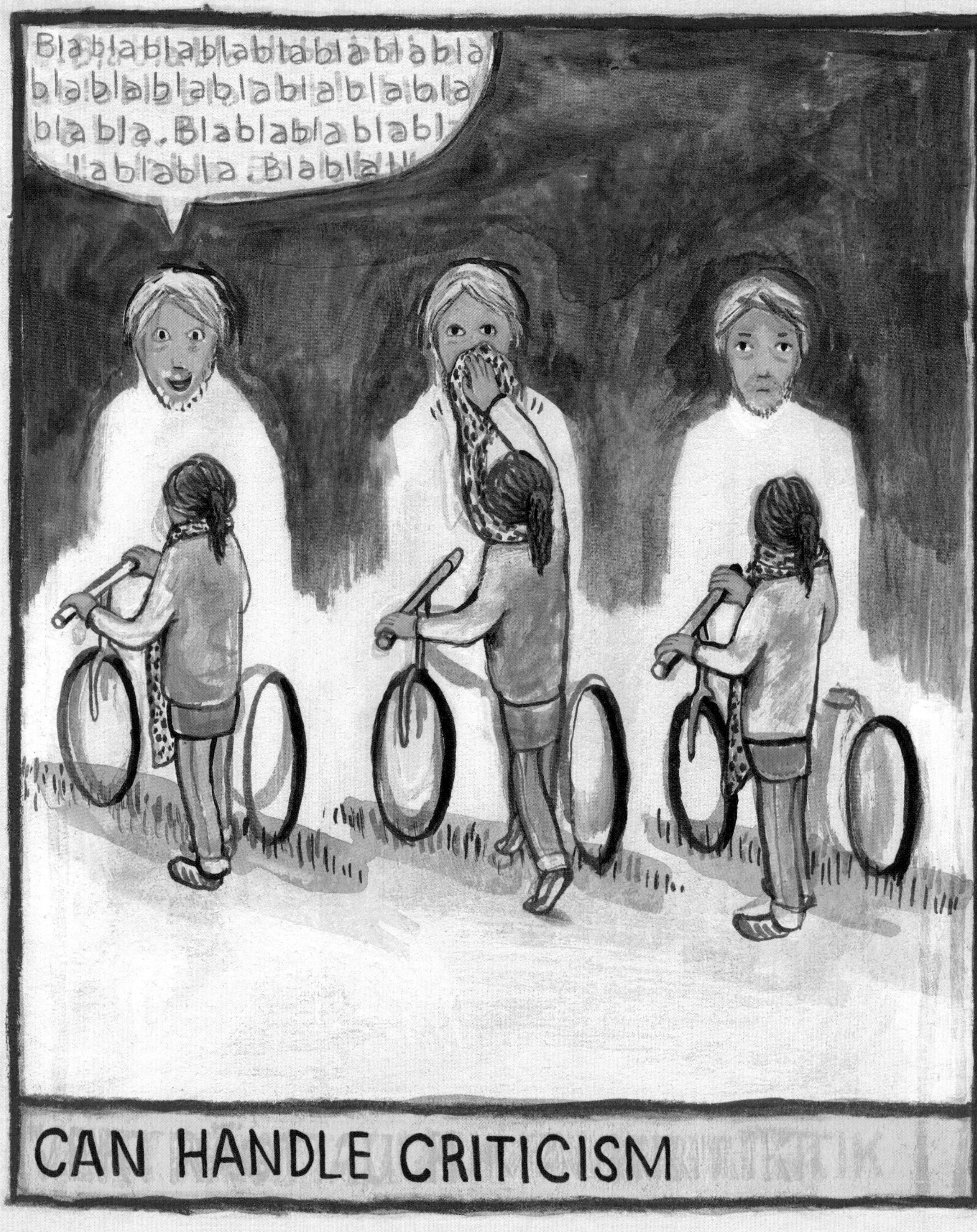
Blablablablablablablabla
blablablablablablablabla
blabla. Blablablablabl
lablabla. Blabla

CAN HANDLE CRITICISM

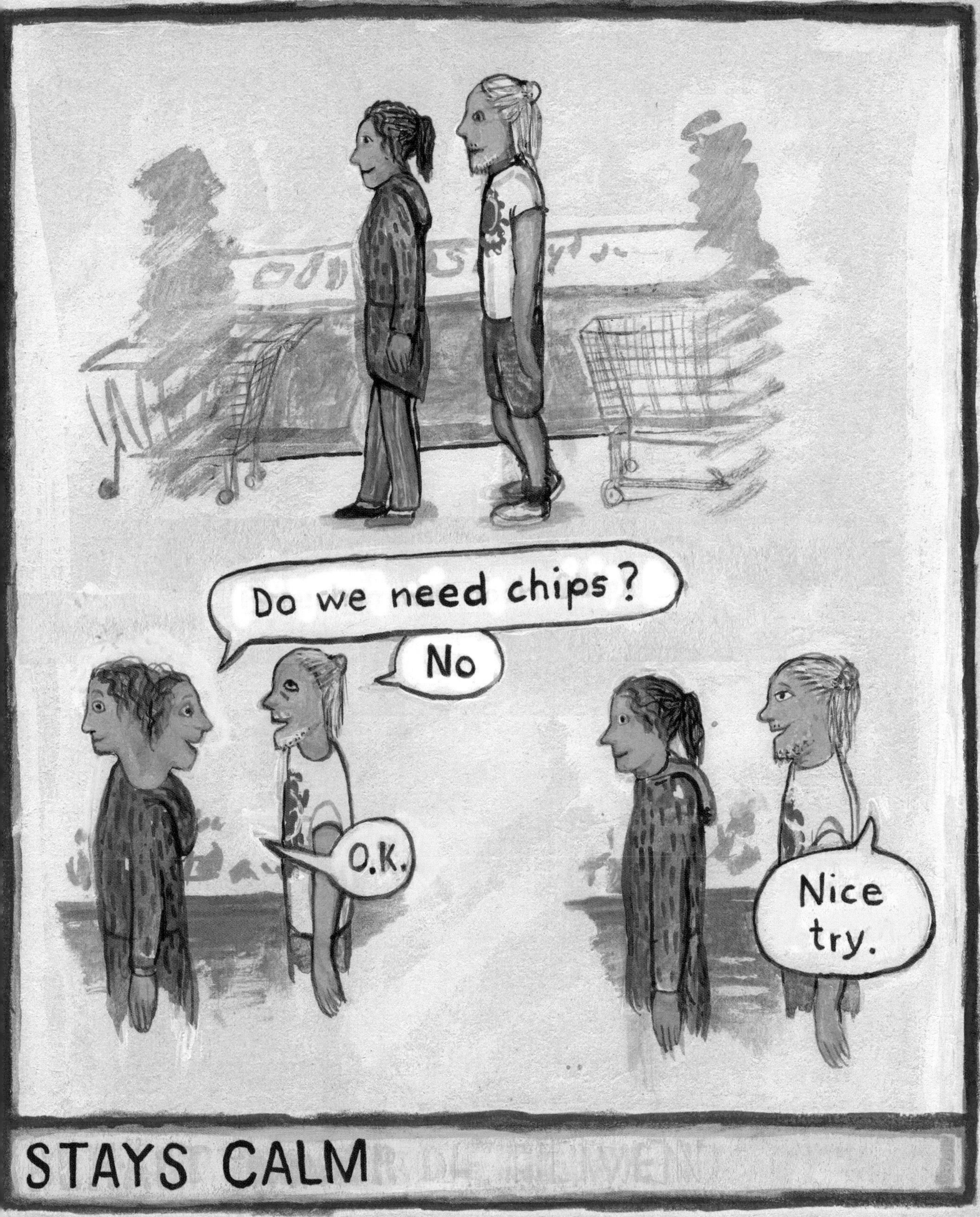
Do we need chips?
No
O.K.
Nice try.
STAYS CALM

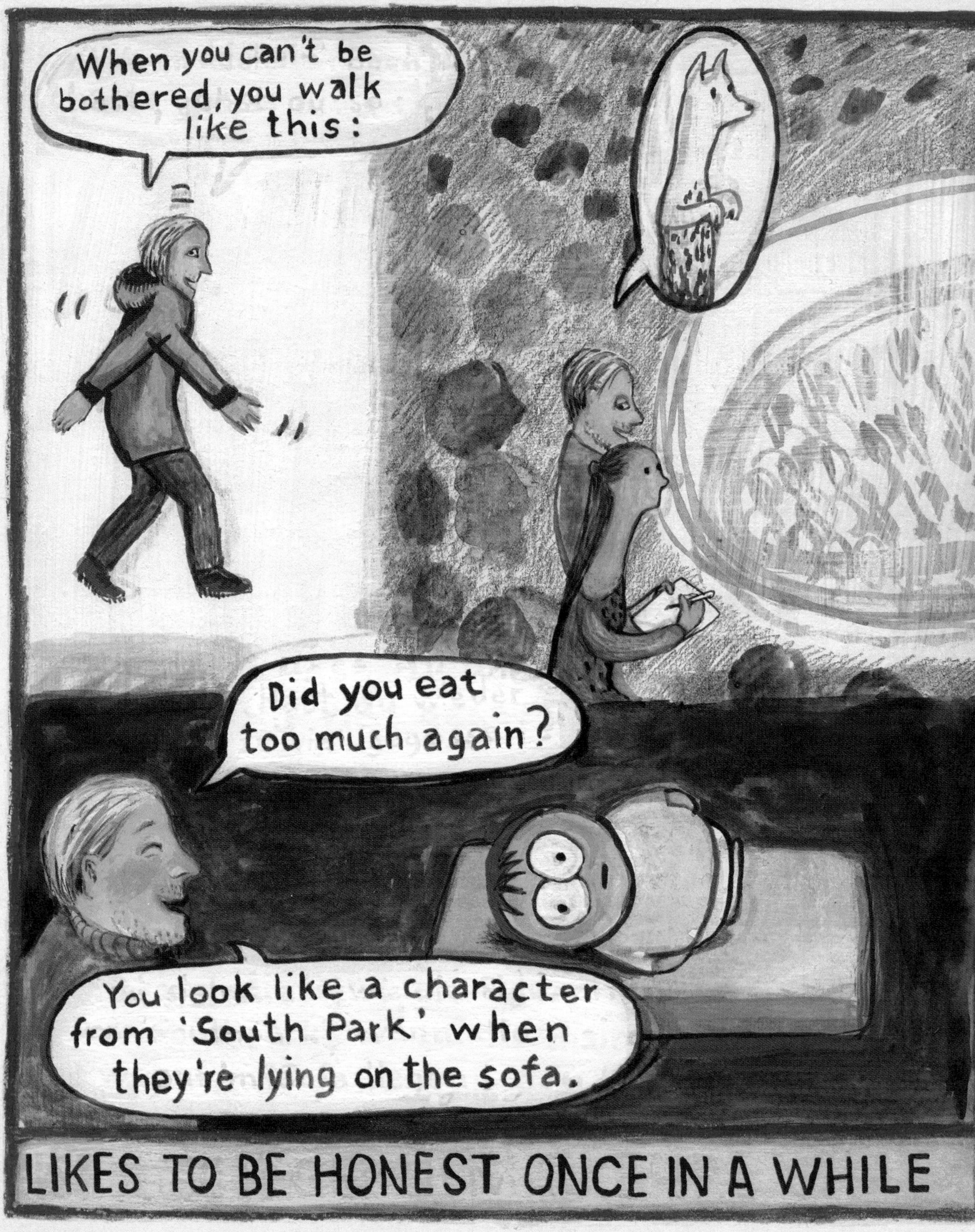
When you can't be bothered, you walk like this:
Did you eat too much again?
You look like a character from 'South Park' when they're lying on the sofa.
LIKES TO BE HONEST ONCE IN A WHILE

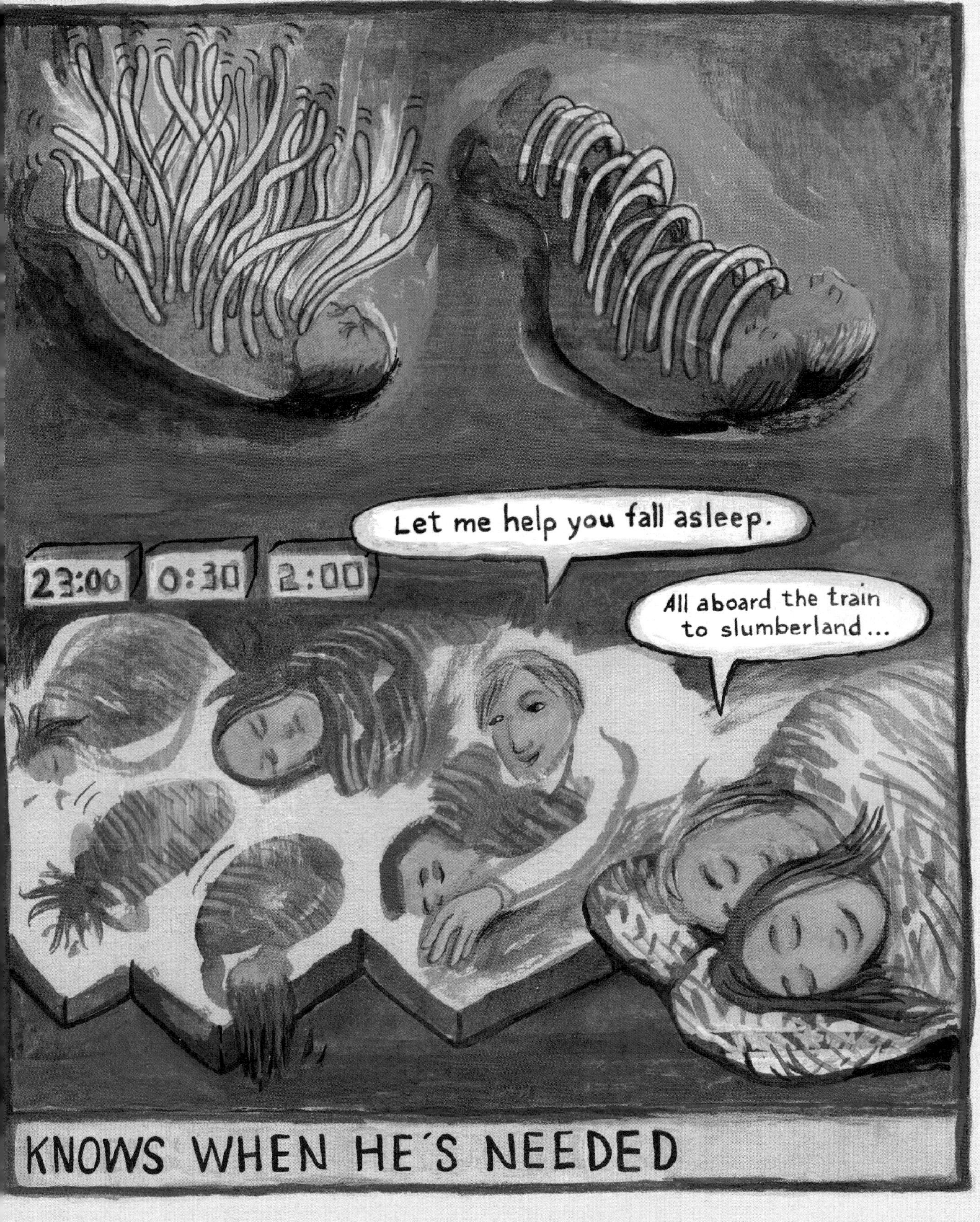
23:00
0:30
2:00
Let me help you fall asleep.
All aboard the train to slumberland ...
KNOWS WHEN HE´S NEEDED

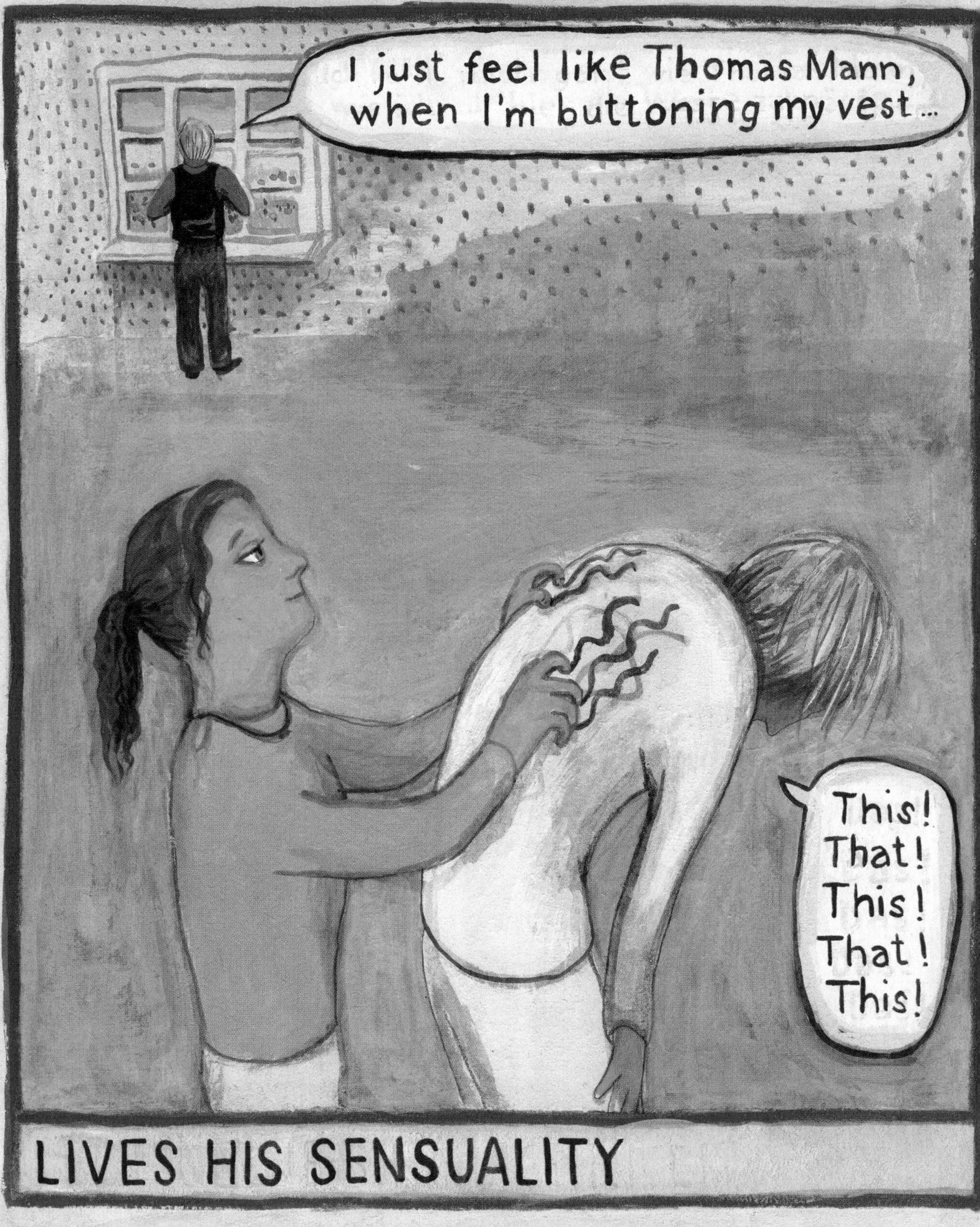

I just feel like Thomas Mann, when I'm buttoning my vest...
This! That! This! That! This!
LIVES HIS SENSUALITY

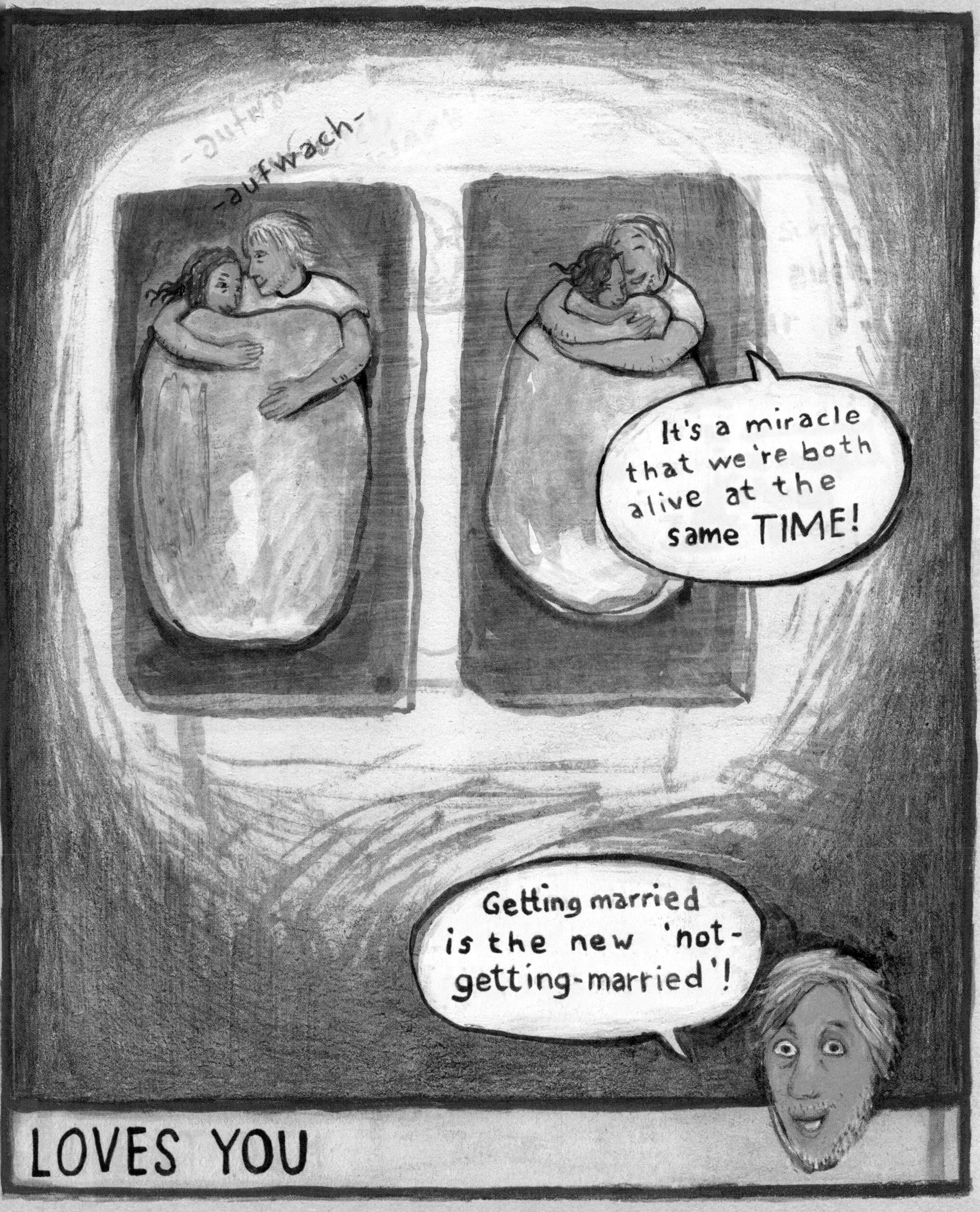
-aufwach-
It's a miracle that we're both alive at the same TIME!
Getting married is the new 'not-getting-married'!
LOVES YOU

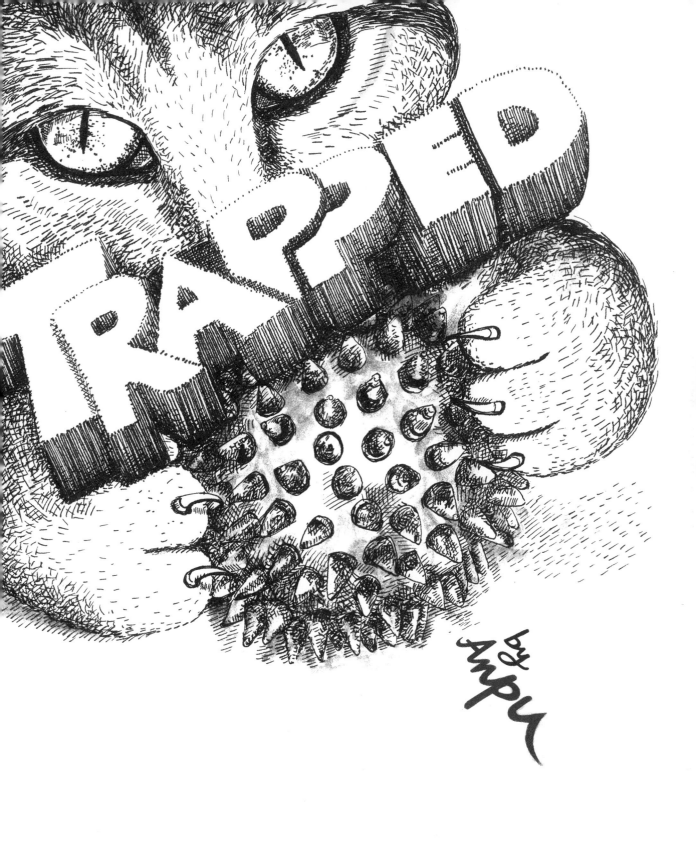

TRAPPED

by Anpu

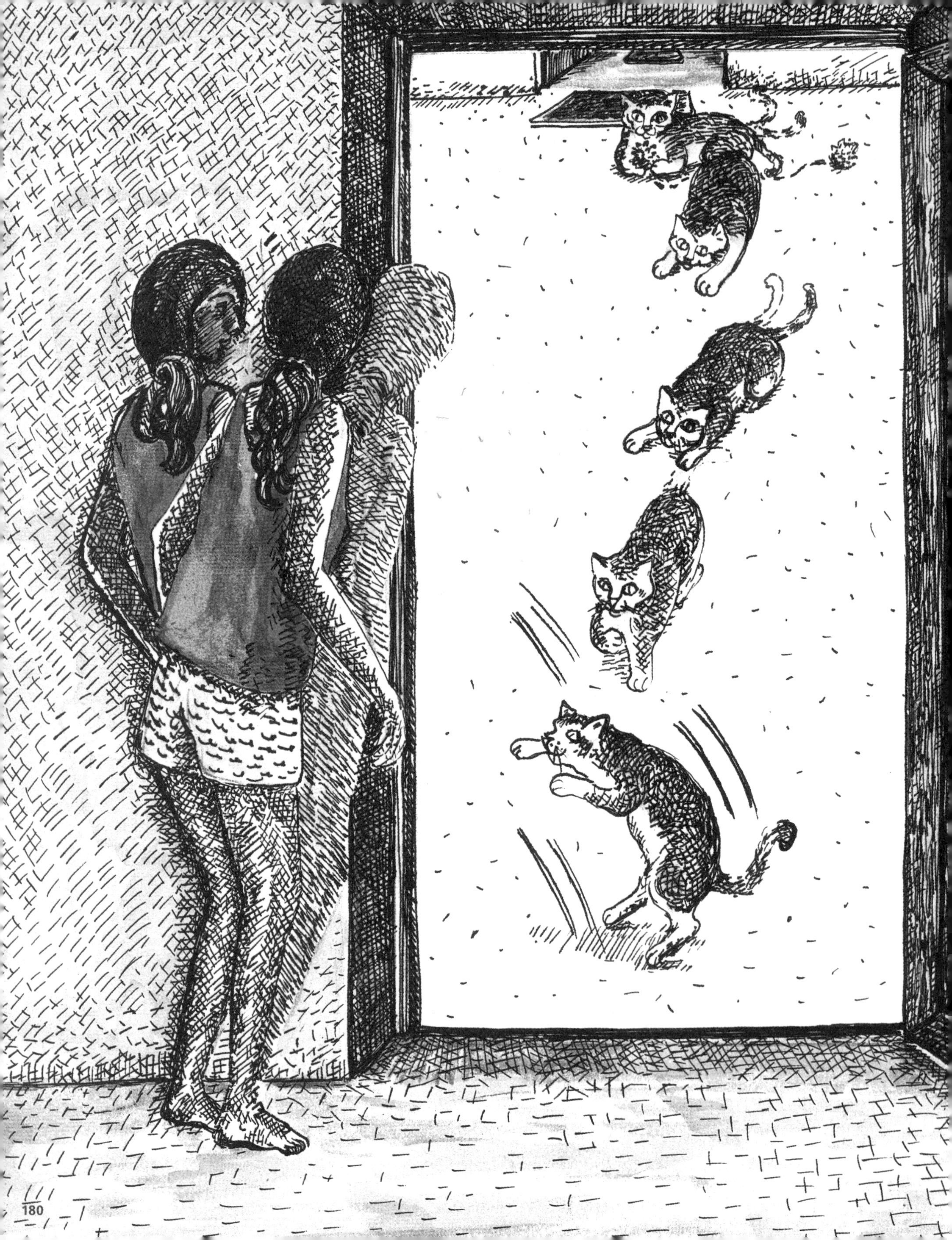

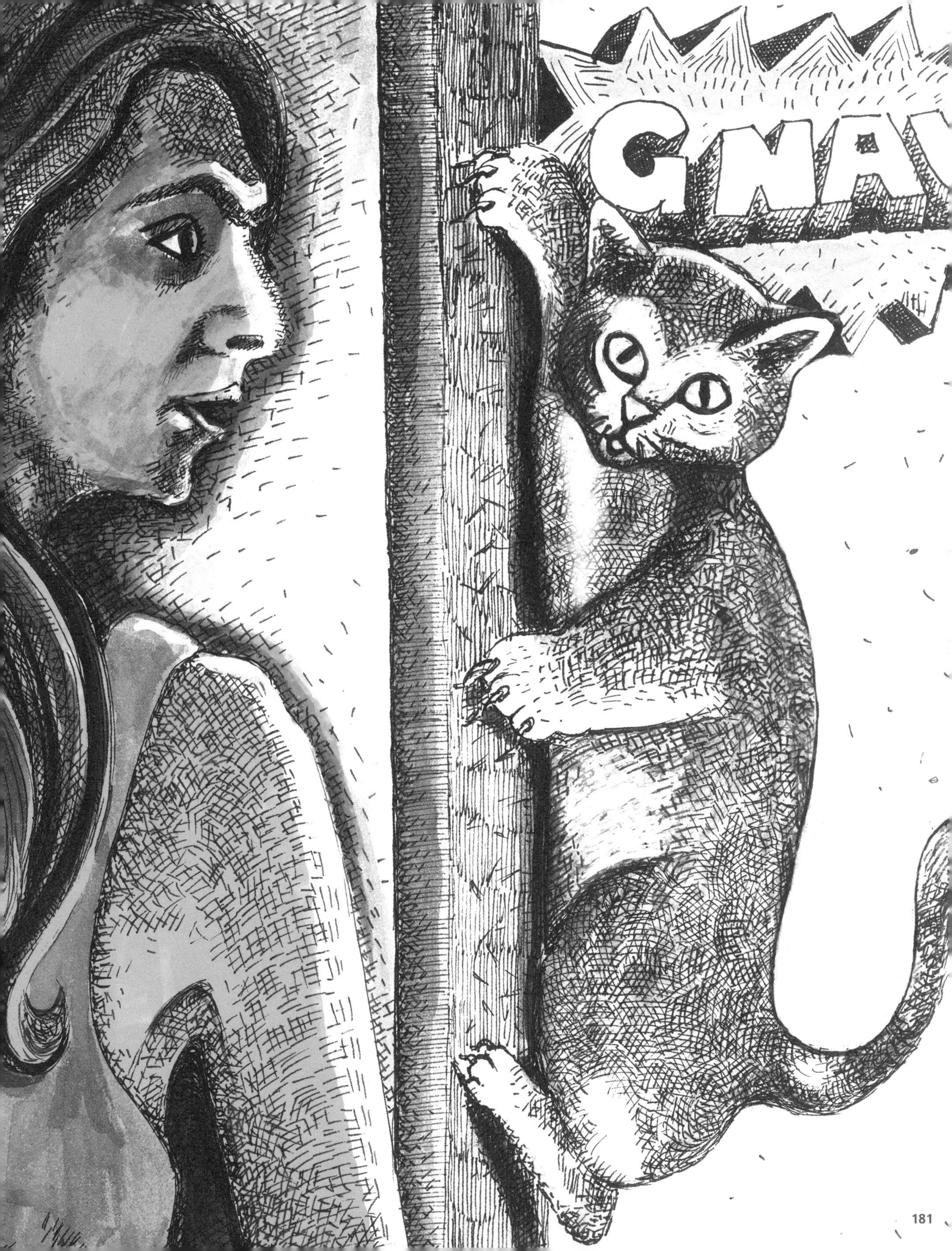
GMA

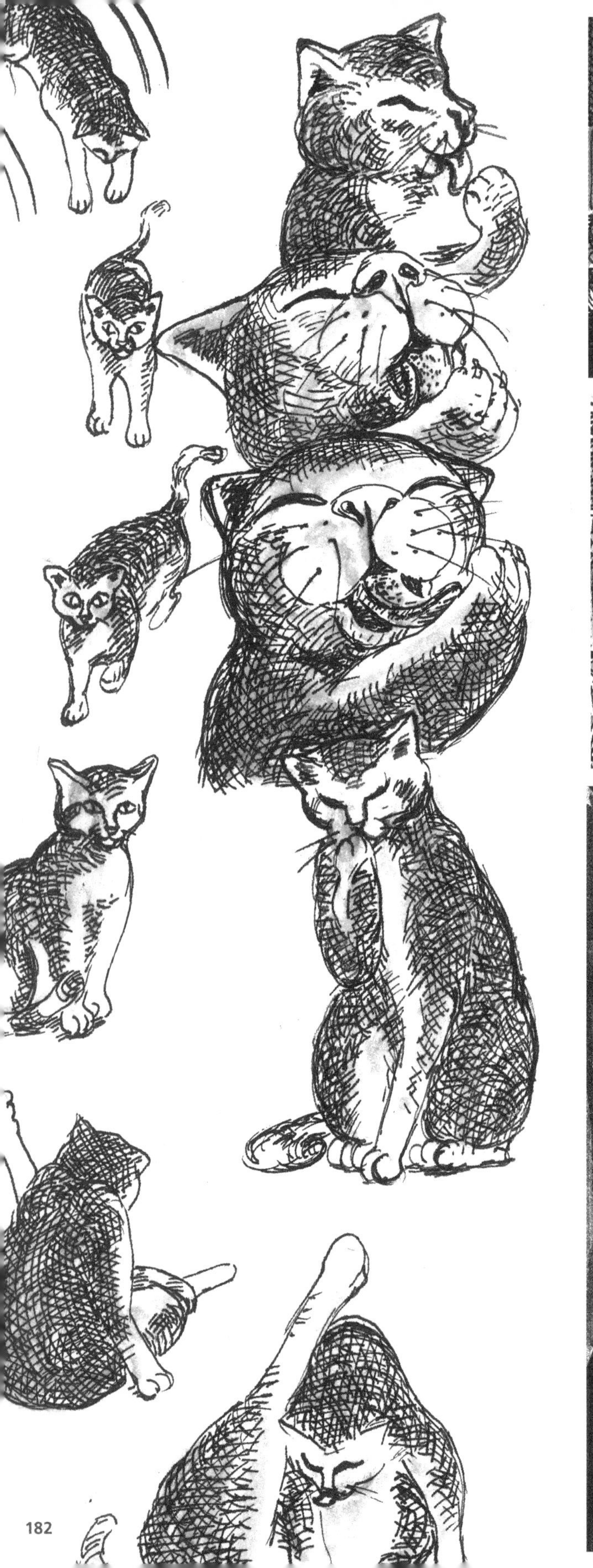

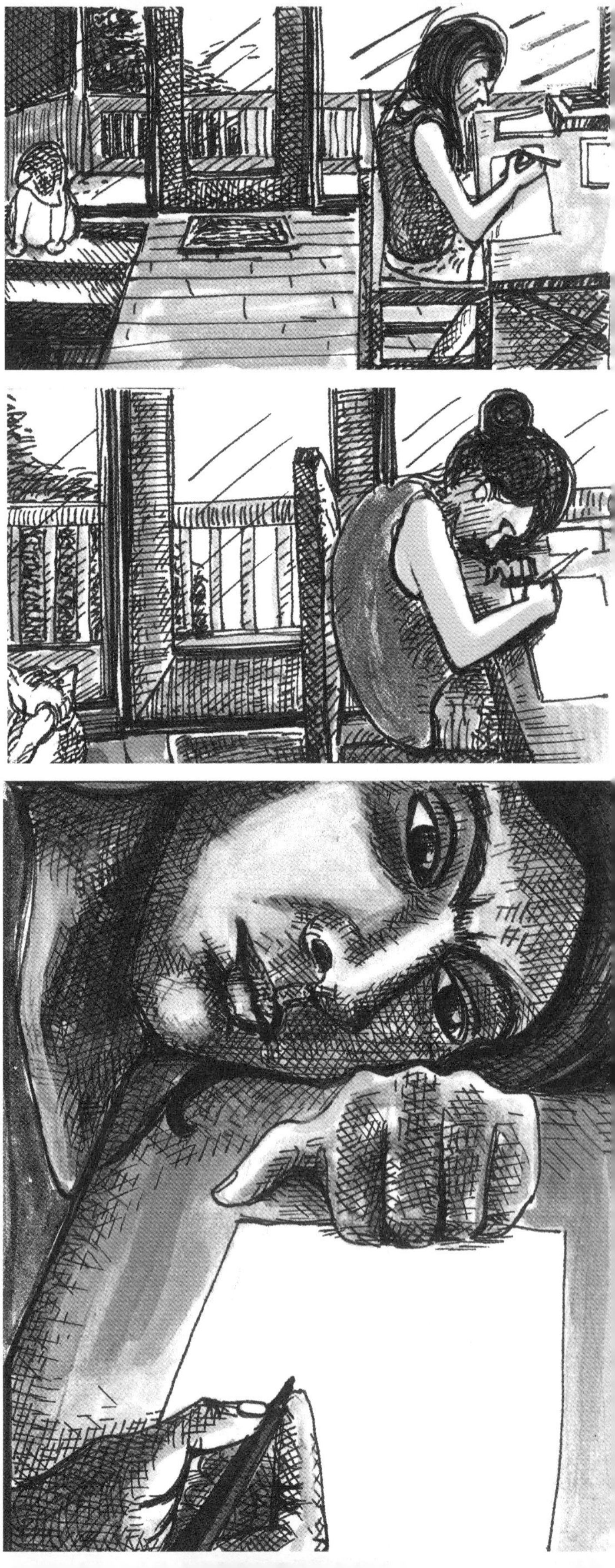

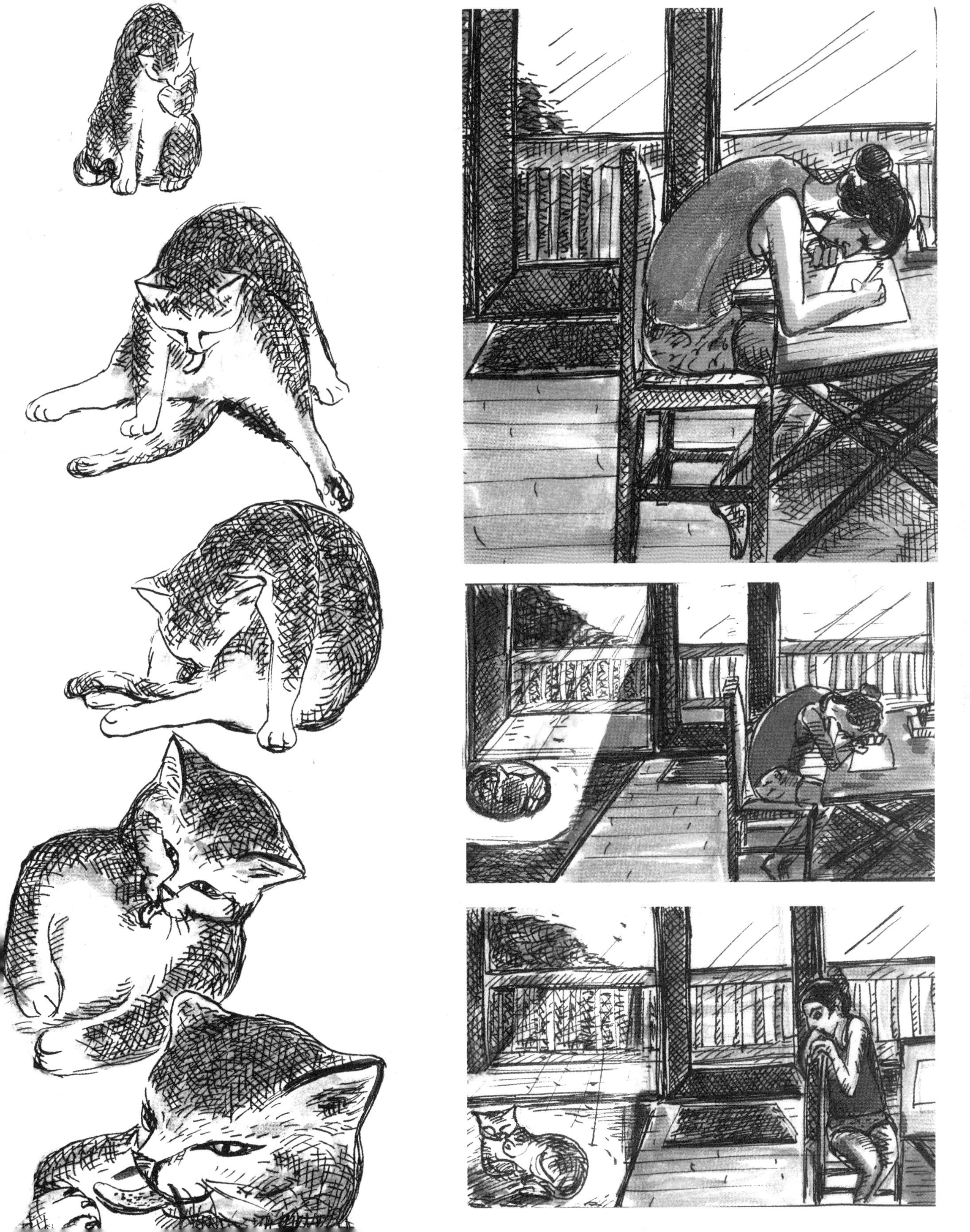

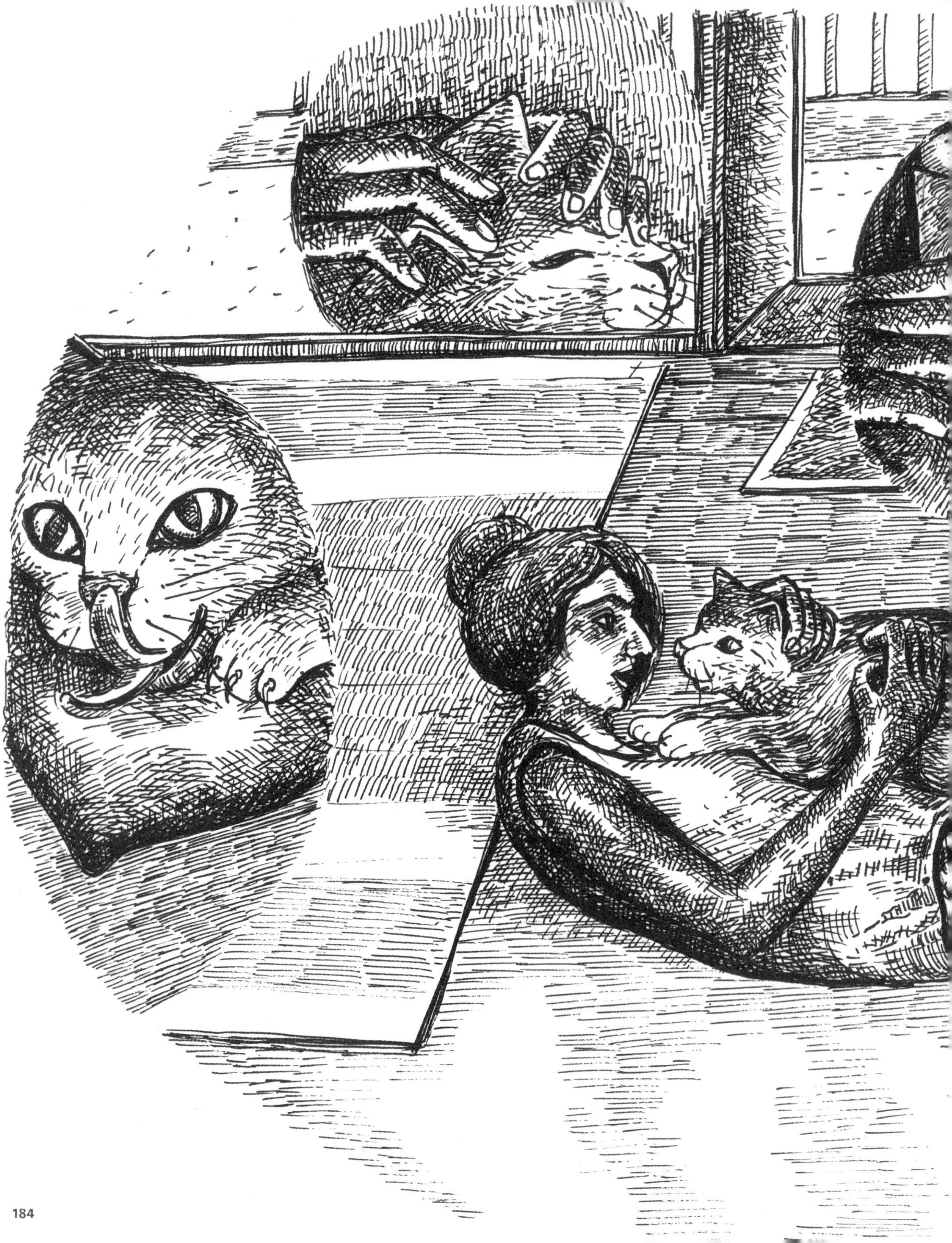

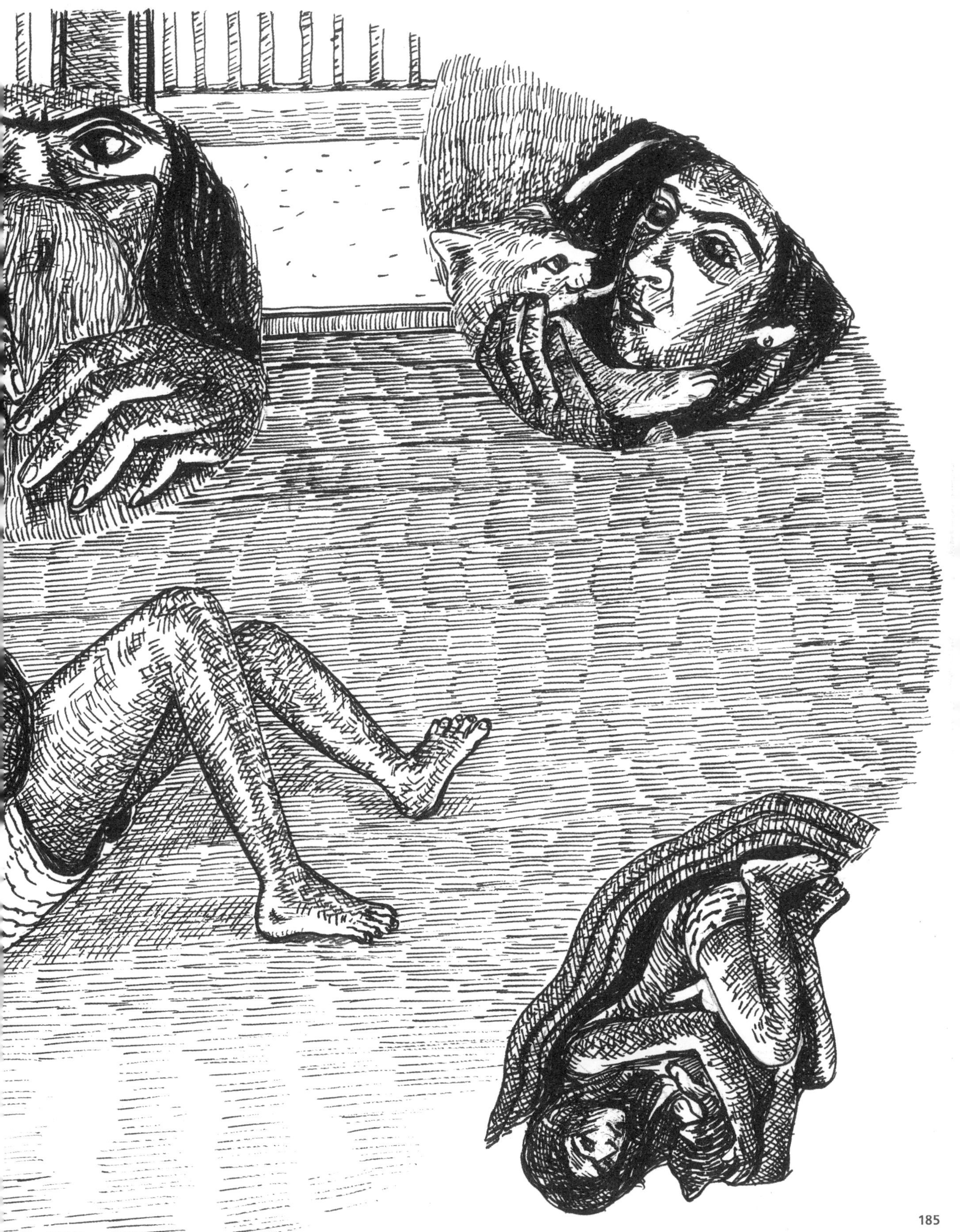

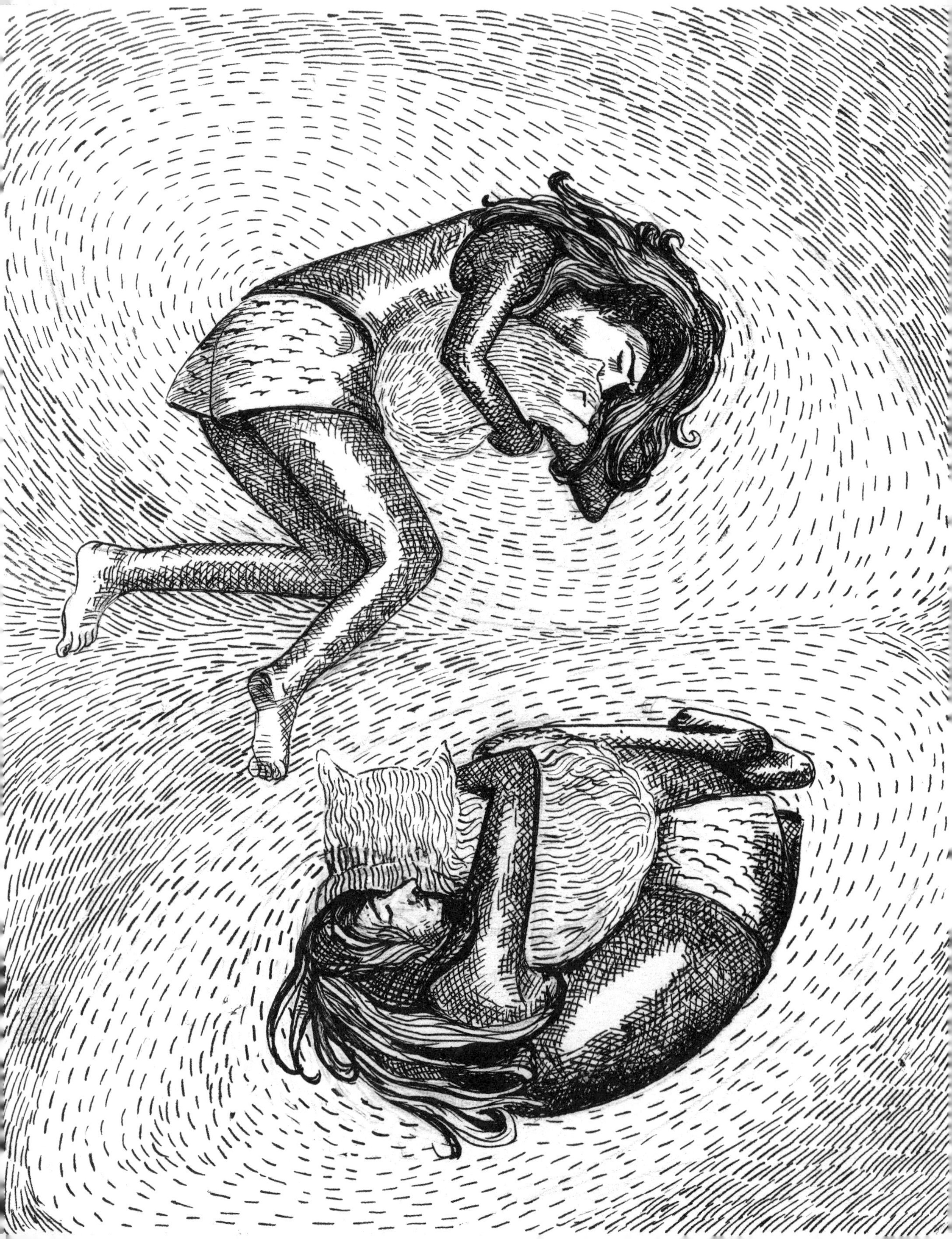

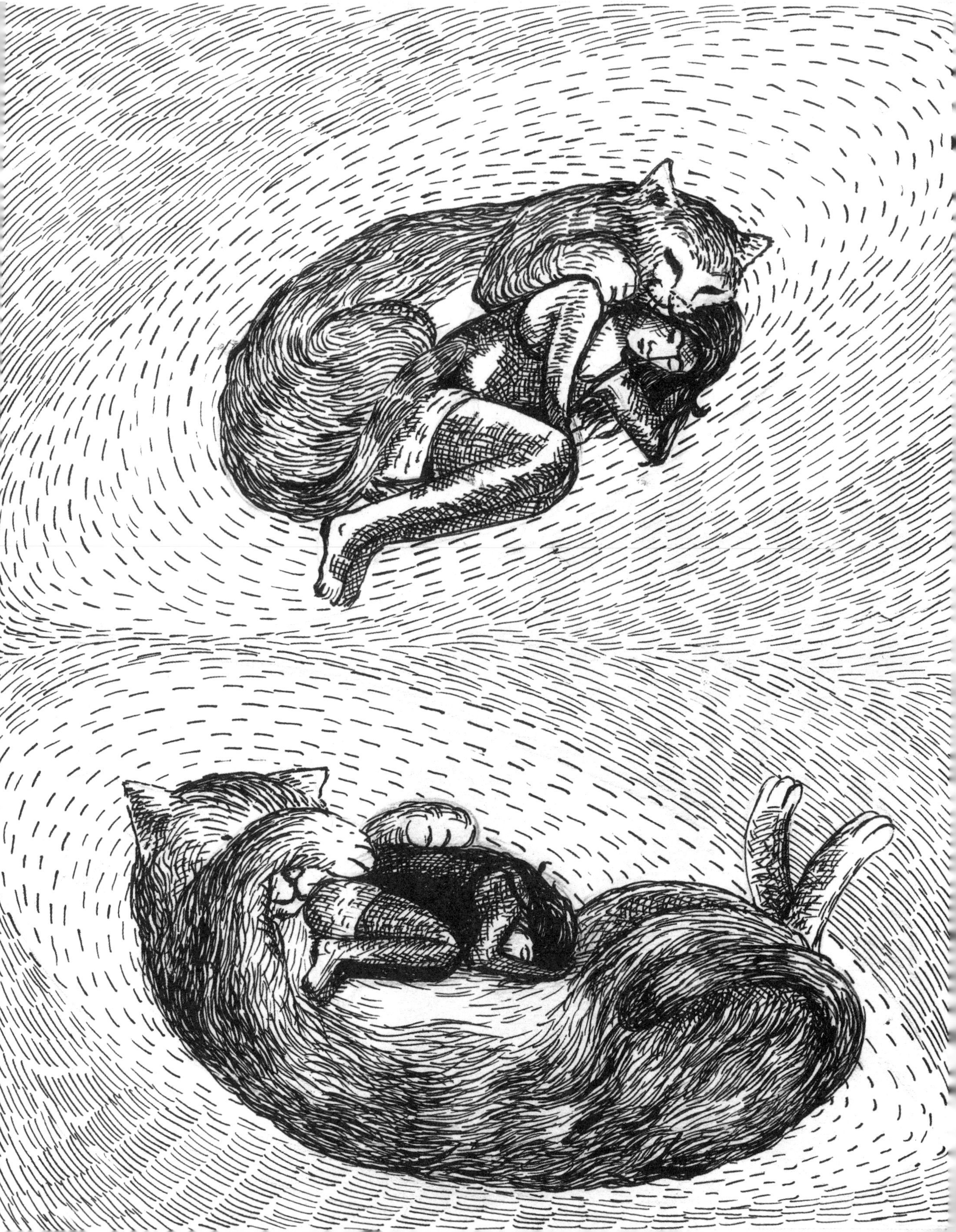

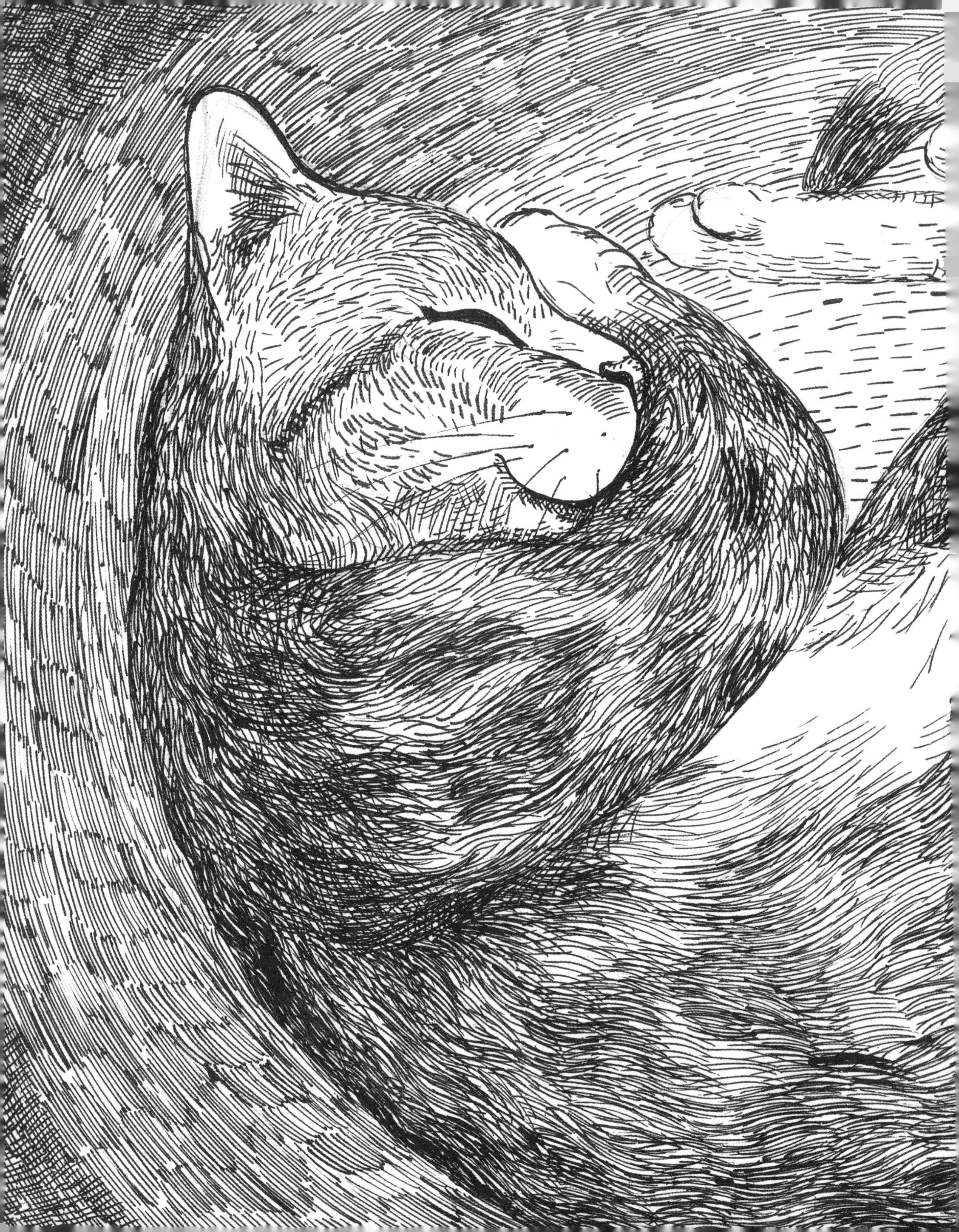

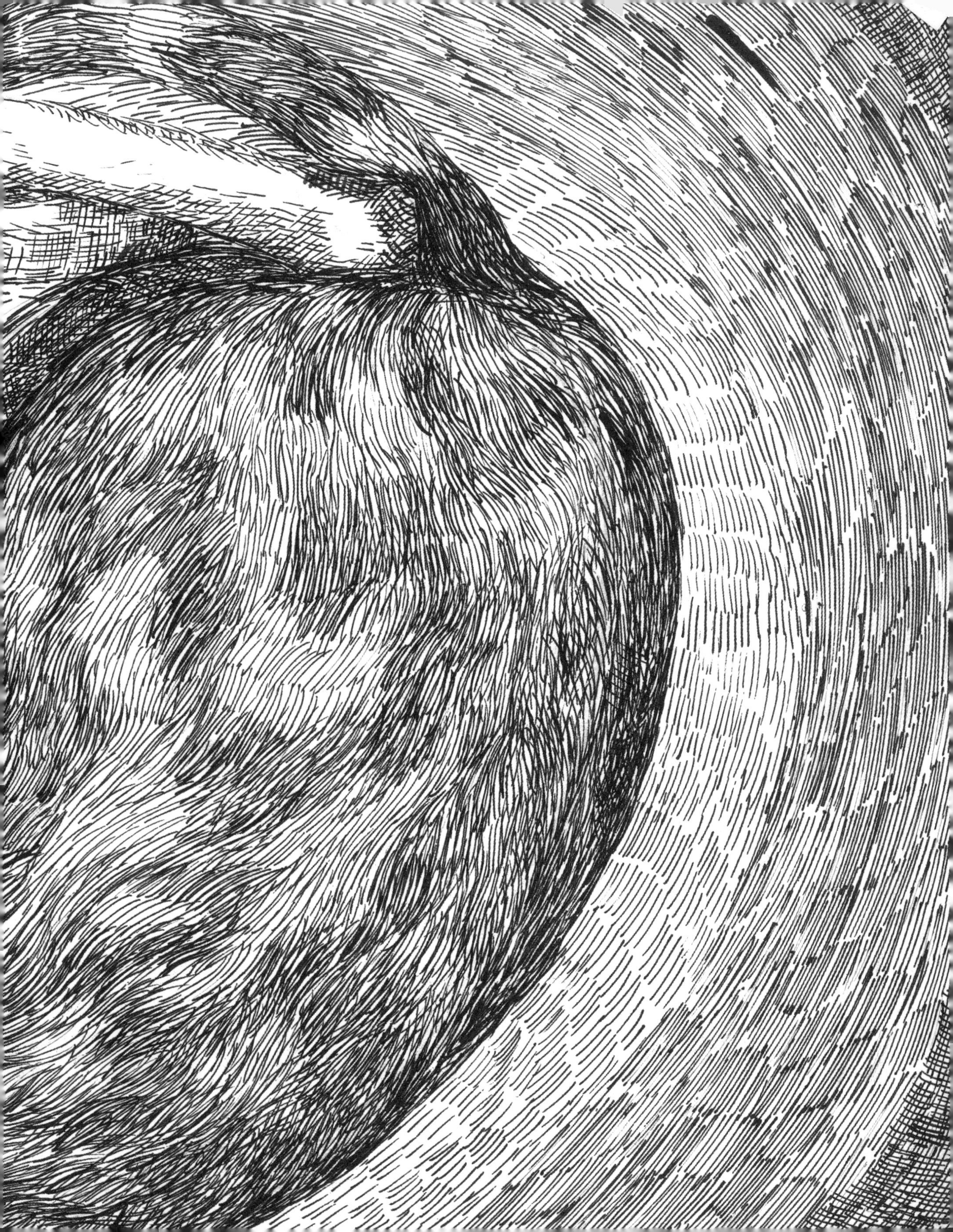

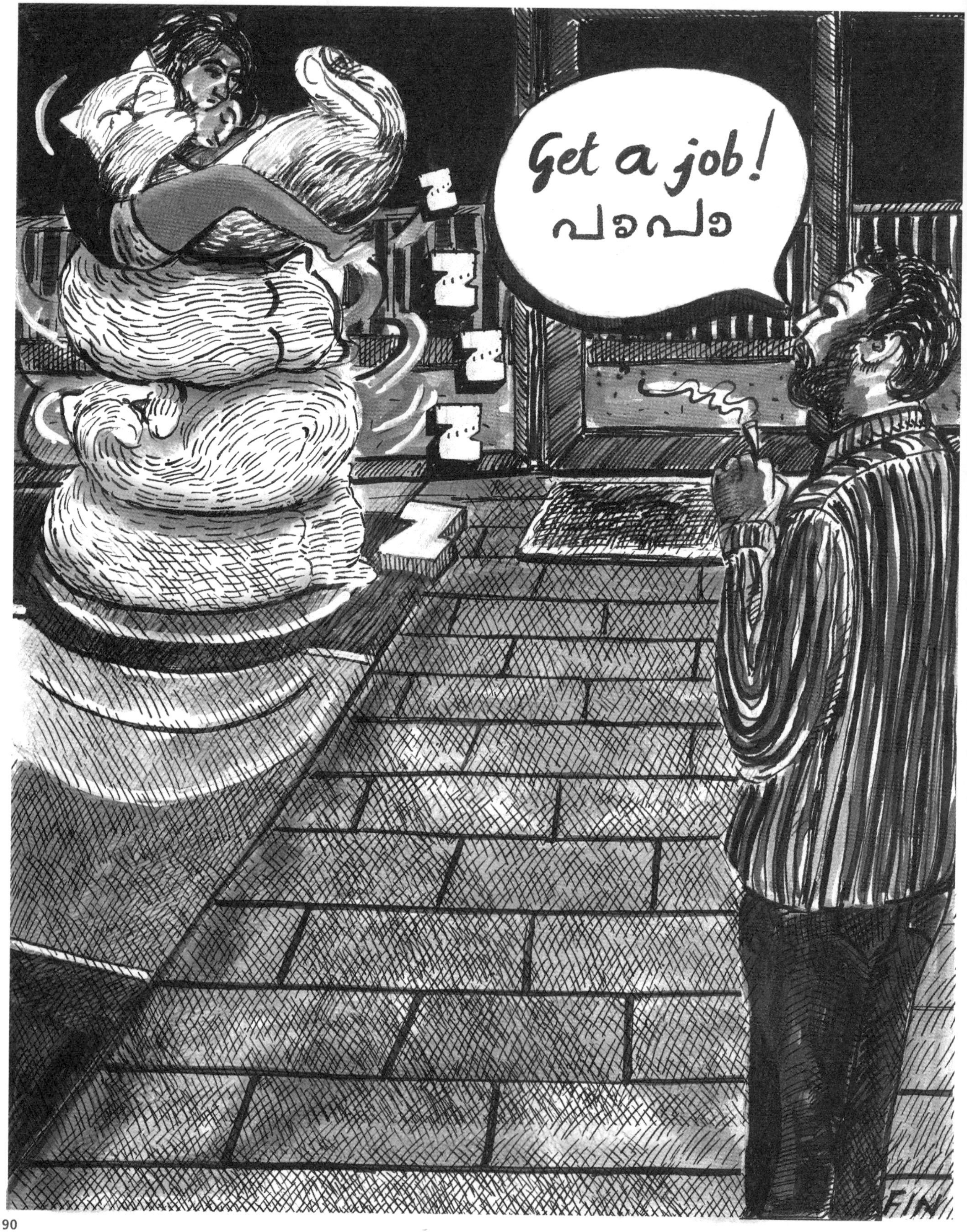
Get a job!
FIN

# Darko

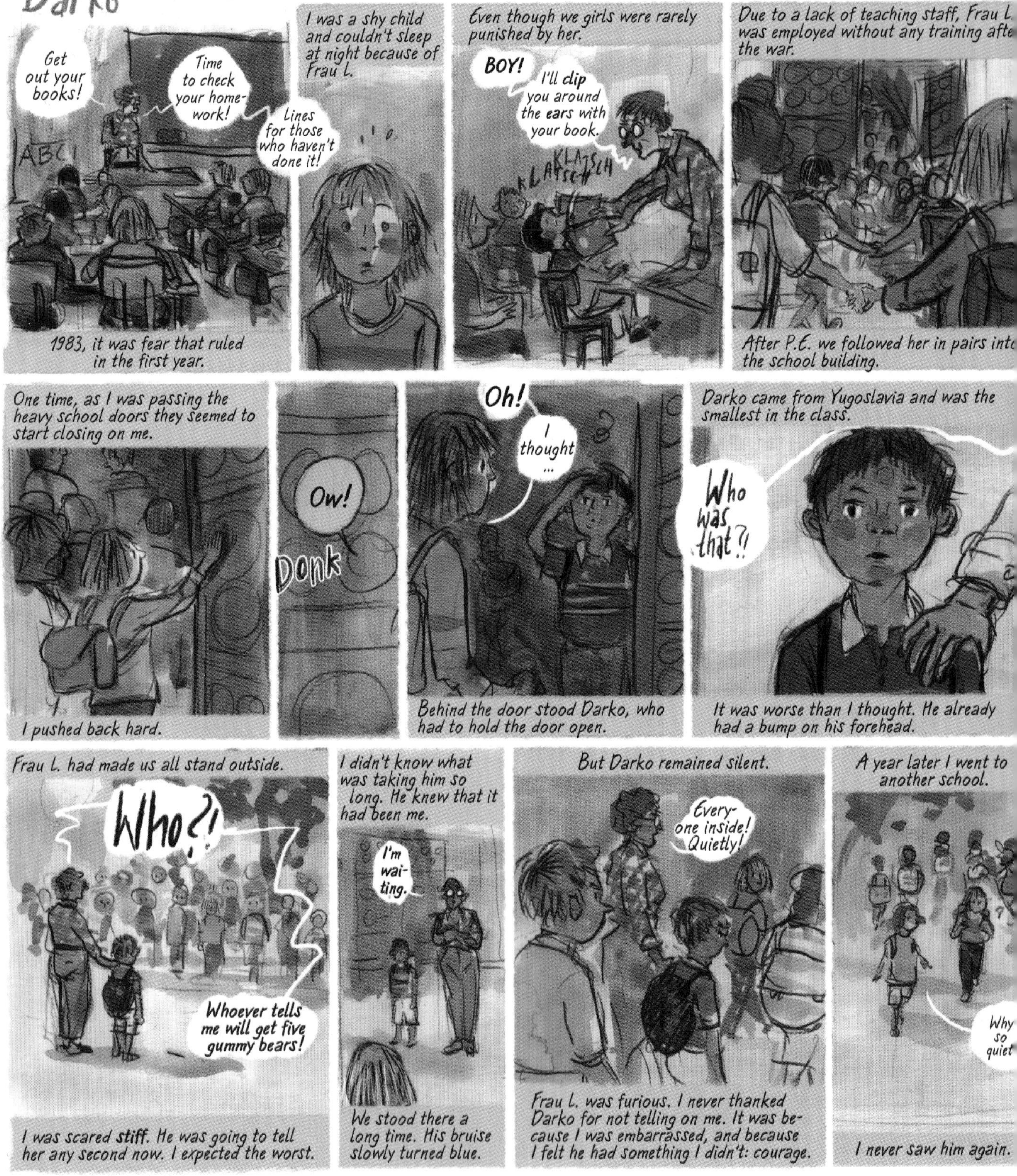
Get out your books!
Time to check your home-work!
Lines for those who haven't done it!
1983, it was fear that ruled in the first year.
I was a shy child and couldn't sleep at night because of Frau L.
Even though we girls were rarely punished by her.
BOY!
I'll **clip** you around the **ears** with your book.
KLATSCH KLATSCH
Due to a lack of teaching staff, Frau L. was employed without any training after the war.
After P.E. we followed her in pairs into the school building.
One time, as I was passing the heavy school doors they seemed to start closing on me.
I pushed back hard.
Ow!
DONK
Oh!
I thought ...
Behind the door stood Darko, who had to hold the door open.
Darko came from Yugoslavia and was the smallest in the class.
Who was that?!
It was worse than I thought. He already had a bump on his forehead.
Frau L. had made us all stand outside.
Who?!
Whoever tells me will get five gummy bears!
I was scared **stiff**. He was going to tell her any second now. I expected the worst.
I didn't know what was taking him so long. He knew that it had been me.
I'm wai-ting.
We stood there a long time. His bruise slowly turned blue.
But Darko remained silent.
Every-one inside! Quietly!
Frau L. was furious. I never thanked Darko for not telling on me. It was be-cause I was embarrassed, and because I felt he had something I didn't: courage.
A year later I went to another school.
Why so quiet
I never saw him again.

# Window

knew no fear until I was 22. I used to go out til dawn, walking
ome alone. But that changed this night.
TONK TONK TONK TONK
I heard the footsteps as I was almost at my door.
TONK
(Even today I cannot stand to have someone running up behind me.)
HEEEELP
The man grabbed me. I was briefly able to defend myself and I screamed as loud as I could. But he was stronger.
Then I was on the ground.
It seemed no one had heard me.
And I knew with clarity that it was over for me.
Fuck!
At that moment a window opened.
The attacker fled. My neighbour leapt barefoot onto the pavement.
Afterwards, he said:
"I woke up, looked out, saw nothing.
Then I thought, look again. Properly. I opened the window. Then I saw you lying there."
Him?
Him?
No.
Him?
No.
PRRING
No. He was a Fascist. Combat boots. Pale jeans.
vent to the police that same
ight, but without any result.
Even though I had escaped, it took months before I was able to walk along the street without panicking.
Suddenly everything terrible was possible. And no one would notice.
I went to say thank you to my neighbour again.
I was once attacked by a group of punks.
I was a rocker.
Then an old punk who was passing stepped in.
He said: so many against one – cowards! He saved me.
It became clear that I would have to pass that on one day.
Since then I look closely when I see something strange.
Looking twice is best.

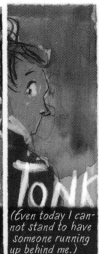

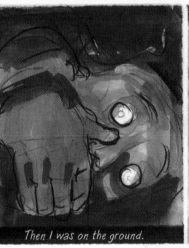

# Sleep

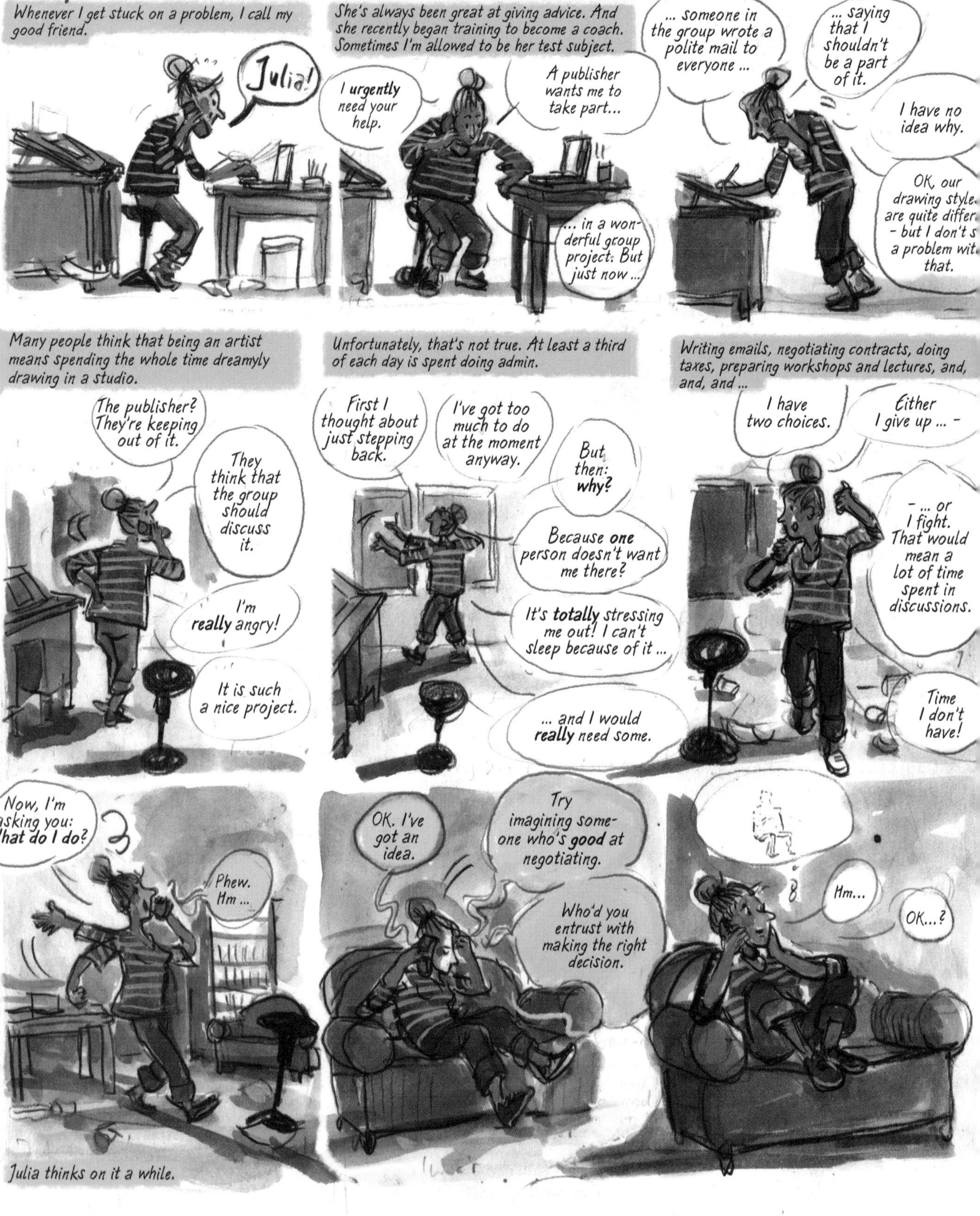

Whenever I get stuck on a problem, I call my good friend.
Julia!
She's always been great at giving advice. And she recently began training to become a coach. Sometimes I'm allowed to be her test subject.
I **urgently** need your help.
A publisher wants me to take part...
... in a wonderful group project. But just now ...
... someone in the group wrote a polite mail to everyone ...
... saying that I shouldn't be a part of it.
I have no idea why.
OK, our drawing style are quite differ - but I don't s a problem wit that.
Many people think that being an artist means spending the whole time dreamyly drawing in a studio.
The publisher? They're keeping out of it.
They think that the group should discuss it.
I'm **really** angry!
It is such a nice project.
Unfortunately, that's not true. At least a third of each day is spent doing admin.
First I thought about just stepping back.
I've got too much to do at the moment anyway.
But then: **why?**
Because **one** person doesn't want me there?
It's **totally** stressing me out! I can't sleep because of it ...
... and I would **really** need some.
Writing emails, negotiating contracts, doing taxes, preparing workshops and lectures, and, and, and ...
I have two choices.
Either I give up ... -
- ... or I fight. That would mean a lot of time spent in discussions.
Time I don't have!
Now, I'm asking you: **What do I do?**
Phew. Hm ...
Julia thinks on it a while.
OK. I've got an idea.
Try imagining someone who's **good** at negotiating.
Who'd you entrust with making the right decision.
Hm...
OK...?

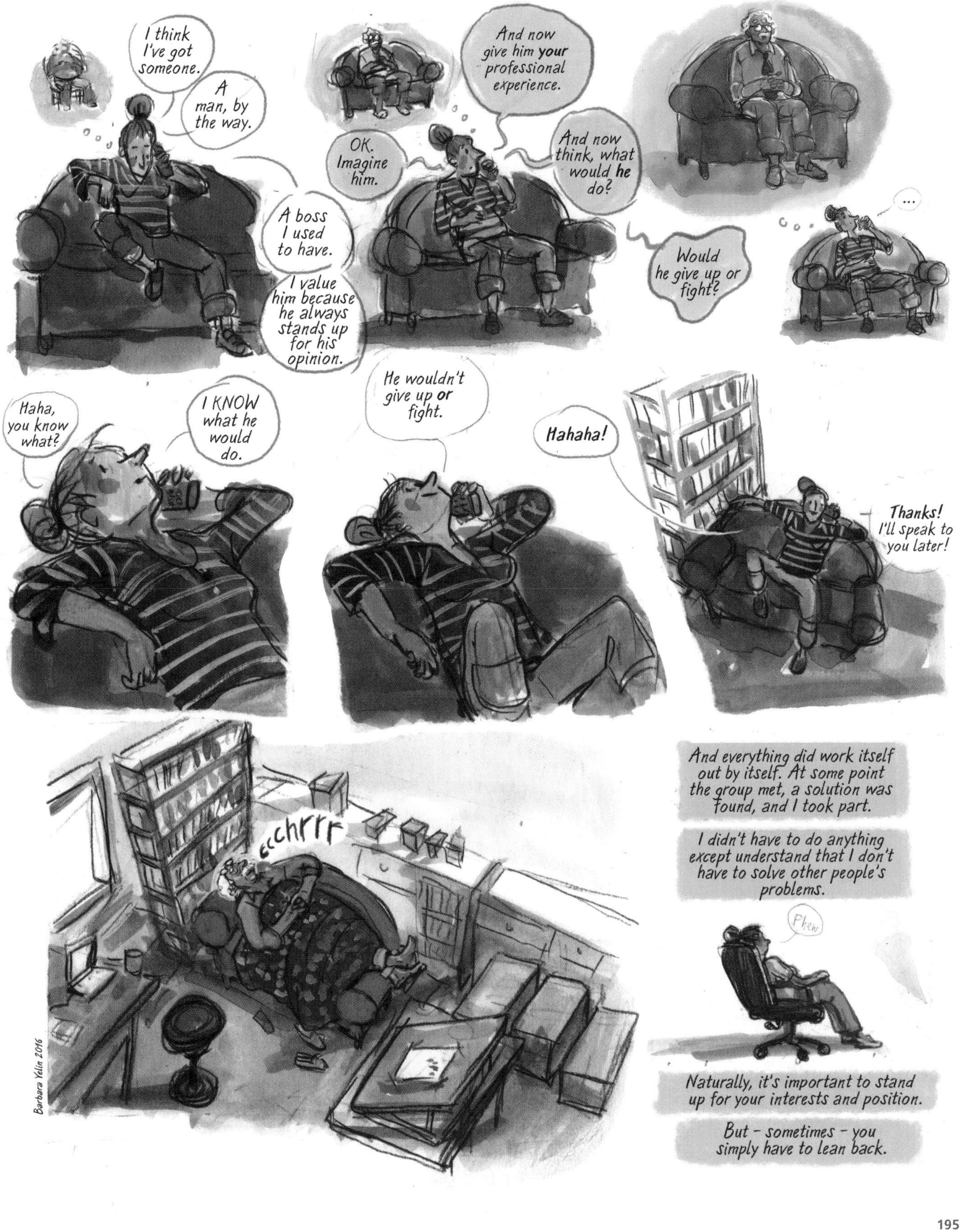
I think I've got someone.
A man, by the way.
A boss I used to have.
I value him because he always stands up for his opinion.
OK. Imagine him.
And now give him **your** professional experience.
And now think, what would **he** do?
Would he give up or fight?
...
Haha, you know what?
I KNOW what he would do.
He wouldn't give up **or** fight.
**Hahaha!**
**Thanks!** I'll speak to you later!
ccchrrr
Barbara Yelin 2016
And everything did work itself out by itself. At some point the group met, a solution was found, and I took part.
I didn't have to do anything except understand that I don't have to solve other people's problems.
Phew
Naturally, it's important to stand up for your interests and position.
But – sometimes – you simply have to lean back.

## A lack of independence (can be one's own fault?)

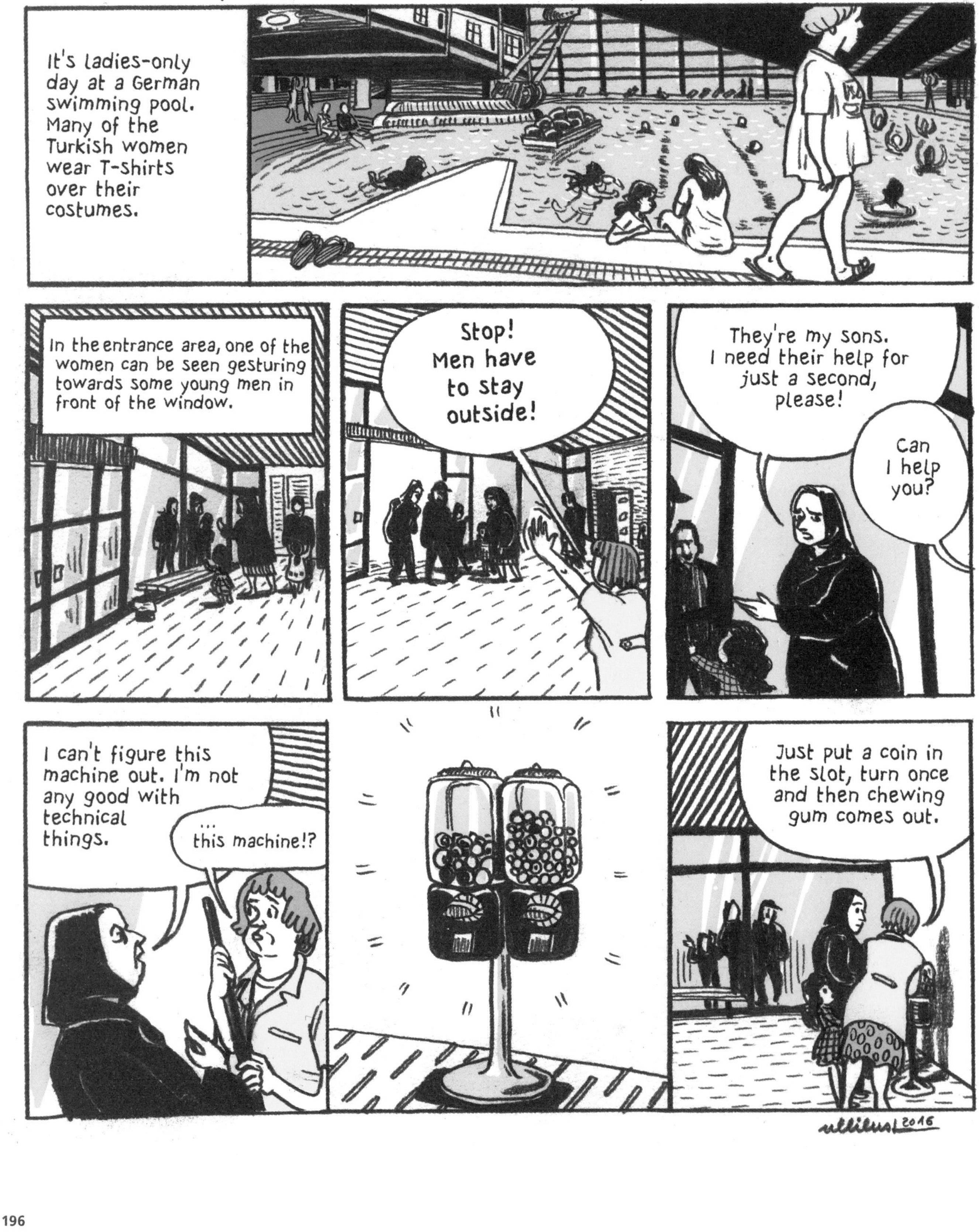
It's ladies-only day at a German swimming pool. Many of the Turkish women wear T-shirts over their costumes.
In the entrance area, one of the women can be seen gesturing towards some young men in front of the window.
Stop! Men have to stay outside!
They're my sons. I need their help for just a second, please!
Can I help you?
I can't figure this machine out. I'm not any good with technical things.
... this machine!?
Just put a coin in the slot, turn once and then chewing gum comes out.

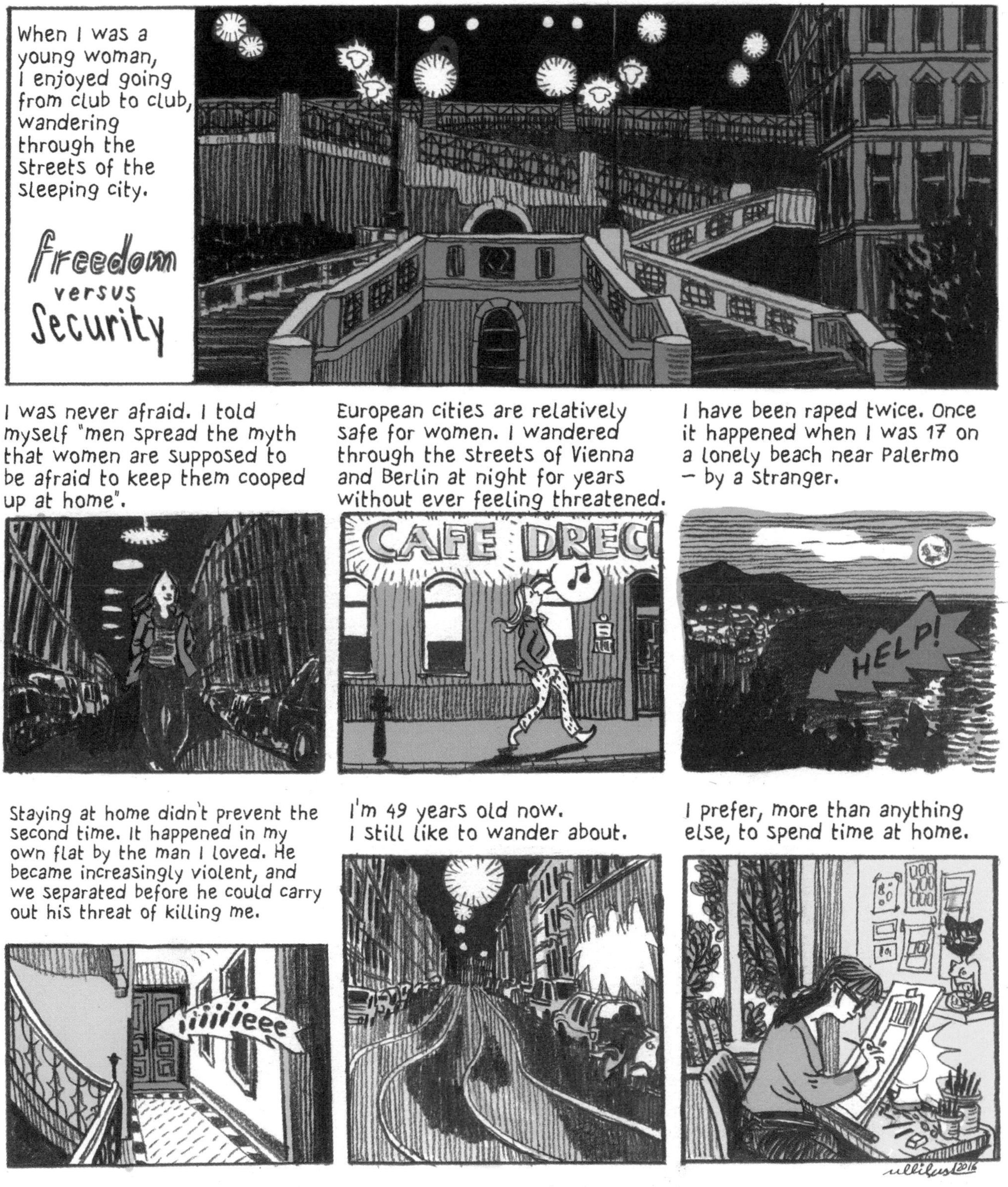
When I was a young woman, I enjoyed going from club to club, wandering through the streets of the sleeping city.
Freedom versus Security
I was never afraid. I told myself "men spread the myth that women are supposed to be afraid to keep them cooped up at home".
European cities are relatively safe for women. I wandered through the streets of Vienna and Berlin at night for years without ever feeling threatened.
CAFE DREC
I have been raped twice. Once it happened when I was 17 on a lonely beach near Palermo – by a stranger.
HELP!
Staying at home didn't prevent the second time. It happened in my own flat by the man I loved. He became increasingly violent, and we separated before he could carry out his threat of killing me.
iiiiieee
I'm 49 years old now. I still like to wander about.
I prefer, more than anything else, to spend time at home.
ullilust 2016

# EBONY & Ivory

Priya Kuriyan

THERE IS A PICTURE OF MY GRANDPARENTS THAT LIES WITHIN THE PAGES OF AN OLD FAMILY ALBUM. THE PICTURE IN ITSELF IS UNSPECTACULAR (IF YOU DON'T COUNT MY GRANDFATHER'S STRANGE BOW-TIE THAT IS); A MUNDANE PHOTOGRAPH OF A NEWLYWED COUPLE STARING STOICLY INTO A CAMERA. I THINK A LOT OF MY ASSUMPTIONS ABOUT THEIR MARRIAGE WERE BASED ON THAT PICTURE - THAT IT MUST HAVE BEEN LIKE THAT OF ANY OTHER MARRIED INDIAN COUPLE FROM THE 1940's---

THEY PROBABLY HAD A MARRIAGE ARRANGED BY THEIR PARENTS---

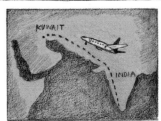

AFTER WHICH, LIKE MANY EDUCATED PEOPLE FROM KERALA, THEY MOVED TO THE MIDDLE EAST FOR WORK....

WHERE THEY HAD THREE LOVELY CHILDREN OF VARYING SKIN TONES--

ROSALIND, MY GRANDMOTHER WORKED AS A NURSE IN A HOSPITAL.

MATHEWS, MY GRANDFATHER, WAS A BANKER OF SOME SORT

AT A VERY YOUNG AGE, THE THREE KIDS WERE SENT OFF TO STUDY IN INDIA.

THEY WERE TO GROW UP UNDER THE GUARDIANSHIP OF AN AUNT FROM GRAND-FATHER'S SIDE.

THE KIDS GREW UP INTO STRAPPING YOUNG TEENS.

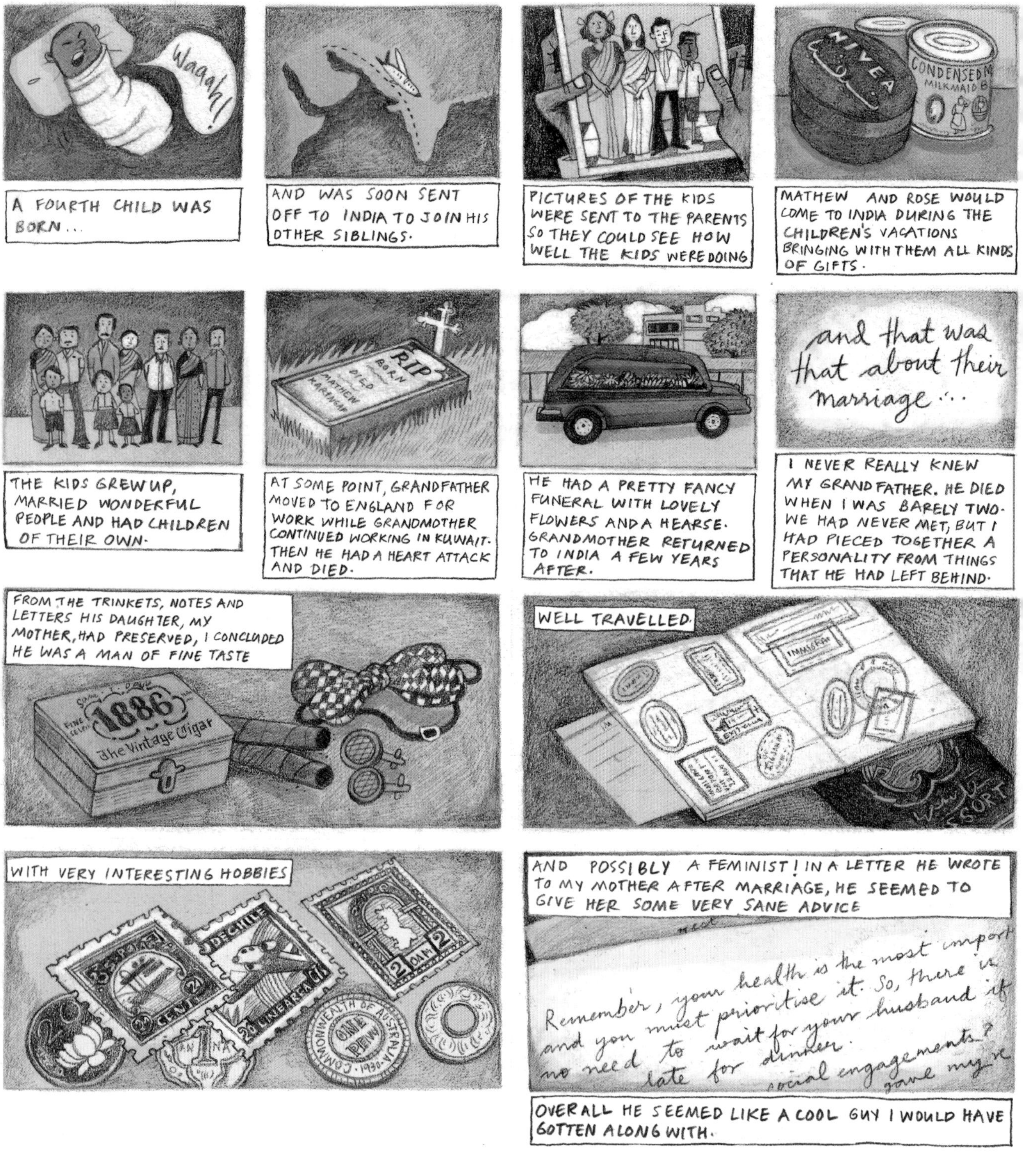
Waaah!
A FOURTH CHILD WAS BORN...
AND WAS SOON SENT OFF TO INDIA TO JOIN HIS OTHER SIBLINGS.
PICTURES OF THE KIDS WERE SENT TO THE PARENTS SO THEY COULD SEE HOW WELL THE KIDS WERE DOING
NIVEA
CONDENSED M
MILKMAID B
MATHEW AND ROSE WOULD COME TO INDIA DURING THE CHILDREN'S VACATIONS BRINGING WITH THEM ALL KINDS OF GIFTS.
THE KIDS GREW UP, MARRIED WONDERFUL PEOPLE AND HAD CHILDREN OF THEIR OWN.
RIP
BORN
DIED
MATHEW
KARAYAN
AT SOME POINT, GRANDFATHER MOVED TO ENGLAND FOR WORK WHILE GRANDMOTHER CONTINUED WORKING IN KUWAIT. THEN HE HAD A HEART ATTACK AND DIED.
HE HAD A PRETTY FANCY FUNERAL WITH LOVELY FLOWERS AND A HEARSE. GRANDMOTHER RETURNED TO INDIA A FEW YEARS AFTER.
and that was that about their marriage...
I NEVER REALLY KNEW MY GRANDFATHER. HE DIED WHEN I WAS BARELY TWO. WE HAD NEVER MET, BUT I HAD PIECED TOGETHER A PERSONALITY FROM THINGS THAT HE HAD LEFT BEHIND.
FROM THE TRINKETS, NOTES AND LETTERS HIS DAUGHTER, MY MOTHER, HAD PRESERVED, I CONCLUDED HE WAS A MAN OF FINE TASTE
1886
The Vintage Cigar
WELL TRAVELLED.
WITH VERY INTERESTING HOBBIES
ONE PENNY
COMMONWEALTH OF AUSTRALIA
AND POSSIBLY A FEMINIST! IN A LETTER HE WROTE TO MY MOTHER AFTER MARRIAGE, HE SEEMED TO GIVE HER SOME VERY SANE ADVICE
Remember, your health is the most import
and you must prioritise it. So, there is
no need to wait for your husband if
late for dinner
social engagements?
OVERALL HE SEEMED LIKE A COOL GUY I WOULD HAVE GOTTEN ALONG WITH.

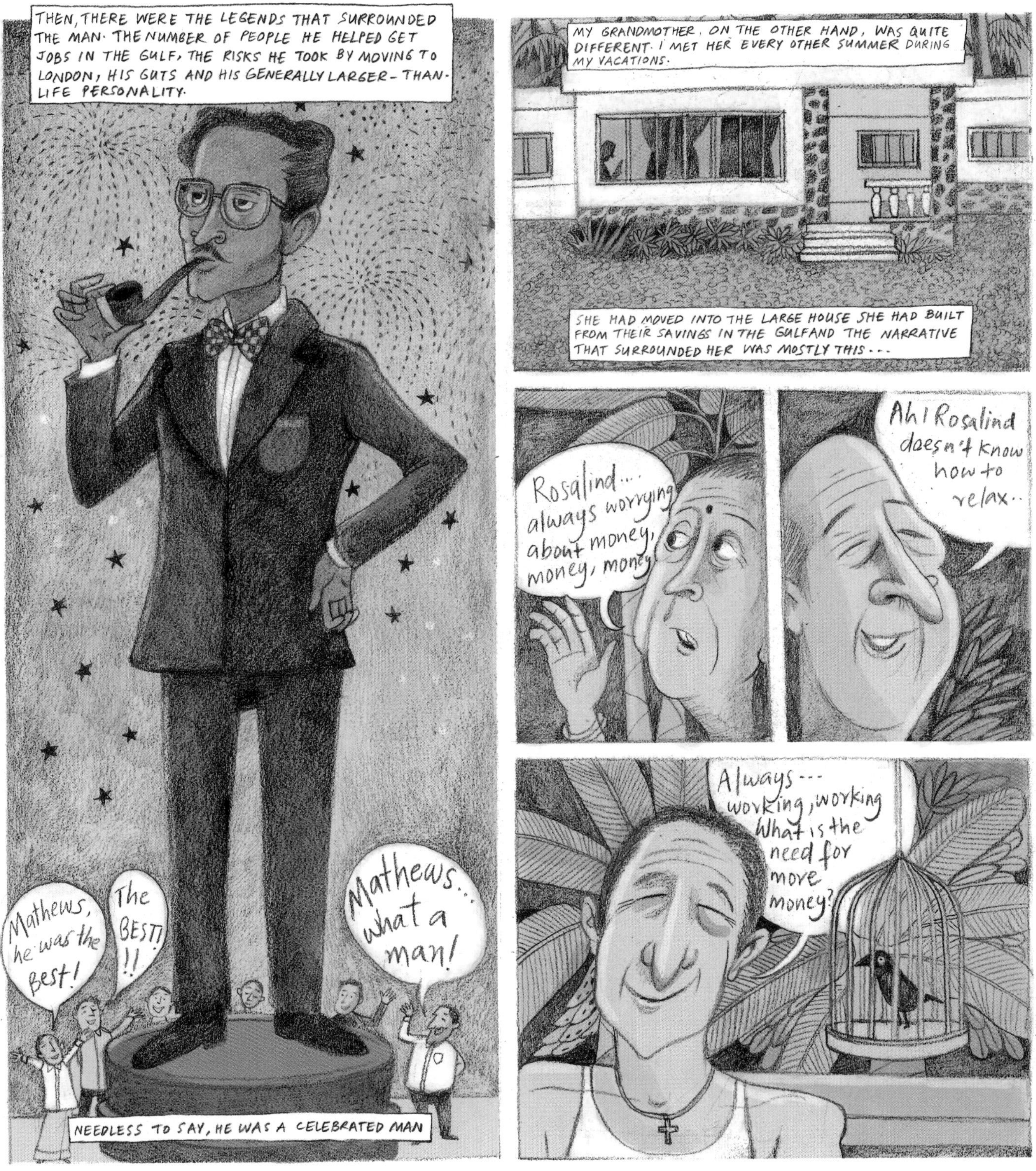
THEN, THERE WERE THE LEGENDS THAT SURROUNDED THE MAN. THE NUMBER OF PEOPLE HE HELPED GET JOBS IN THE GULF, THE RISKS HE TOOK BY MOVING TO LONDON, HIS GUTS AND HIS GENERALLY LARGER-THAN-LIFE PERSONALITY.
Mathews, he was the best!
The BEST! !!
Mathews... what a man!
NEEDLESS TO SAY, HE WAS A CELEBRATED MAN
MY GRANDMOTHER, ON THE OTHER HAND, WAS QUITE DIFFERENT. I MET HER EVERY OTHER SUMMER DURING MY VACATIONS.
SHE HAD MOVED INTO THE LARGE HOUSE SHE HAD BUILT FROM THEIR SAVINGS IN THE GULF AND THE NARRATIVE THAT SURROUNDED HER WAS MOSTLY THIS...
Rosalind... always worrying about money, money, money
Ah! Rosalind doesn't know how to relax..
Always... working, working What is the need for more money?

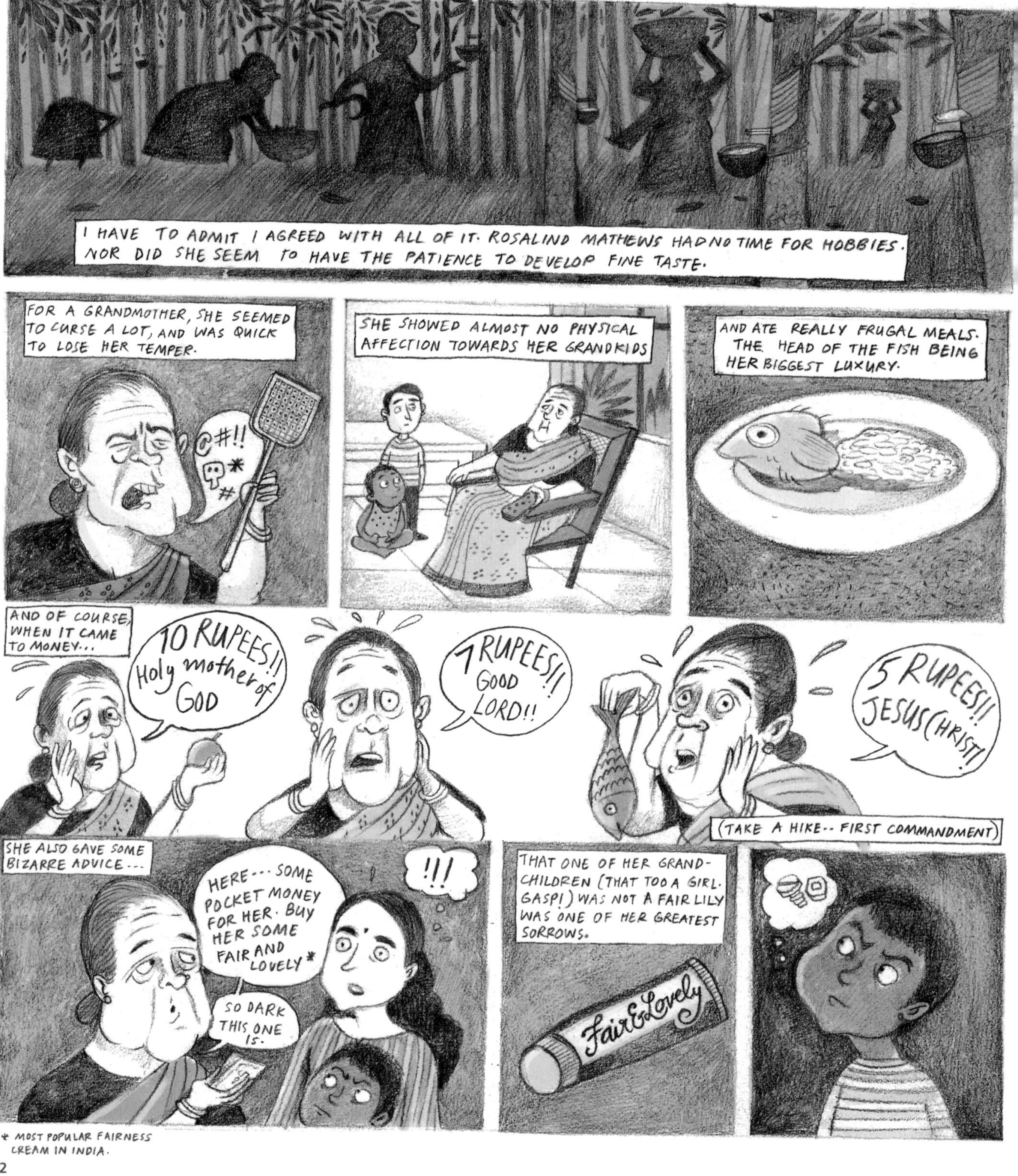
I HAVE TO ADMIT I AGREED WITH ALL OF IT. ROSALIND MATHEWS HAD NO TIME FOR HOBBIES. NOR DID SHE SEEM TO HAVE THE PATIENCE TO DEVELOP FINE TASTE.
FOR A GRANDMOTHER, SHE SEEMED TO CURSE A LOT, AND WAS QUICK TO LOSE HER TEMPER.
@#!! * #
SHE SHOWED ALMOST NO PHYSICAL AFFECTION TOWARDS HER GRANDKIDS
AND ATE REALLY FRUGAL MEALS. THE HEAD OF THE FISH BEING HER BIGGEST LUXURY.
AND OF COURSE, WHEN IT CAME TO MONEY...
10 RUPEES!! Holy mother of GOD
7 RUPEES!! GOOD LORD!!
5 RUPEES!! JESUS CHRIST!
(TAKE A HIKE.. FIRST COMMANDMENT)
SHE ALSO GAVE SOME BIZARRE ADVICE...
HERE... SOME POCKET MONEY FOR HER. BUY HER SOME FAIR AND LOVELY *
SO DARK THIS ONE IS.
!!!
THAT ONE OF HER GRANDCHILDREN (THAT TOO A GIRL. GASP!) WAS NOT A FAIR LILY WAS ONE OF HER GREATEST SORROWS.
Fair&Lovely

* MOST POPULAR FAIRNESS CREAM IN INDIA.

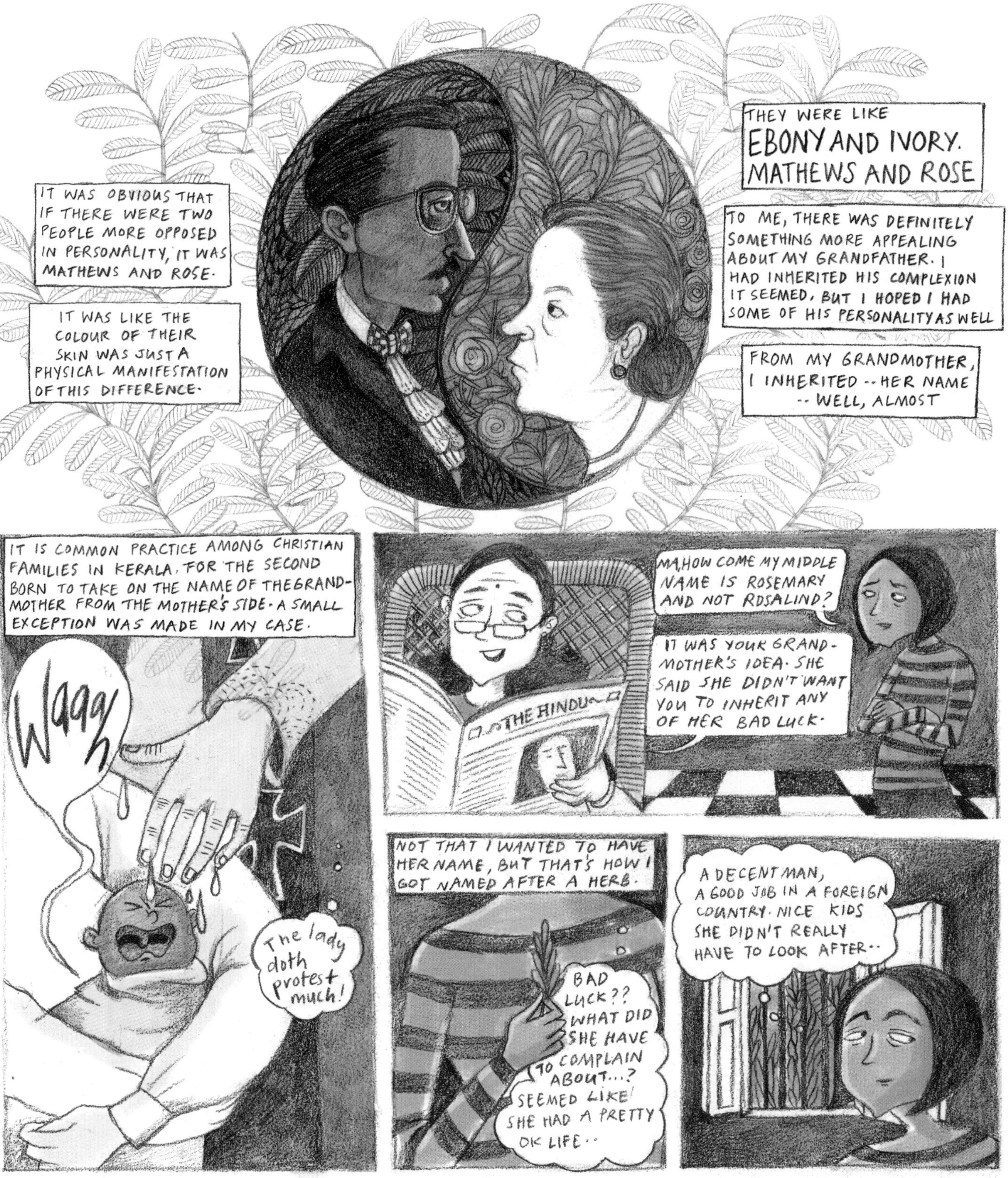
THEY WERE LIKE EBONY AND IVORY. MATHEWS AND ROSE
IT WAS OBVIOUS THAT IF THERE WERE TWO PEOPLE MORE OPPOSED IN PERSONALITY, IT WAS MATHEWS AND ROSE.
IT WAS LIKE THE COLOUR OF THEIR SKIN WAS JUST A PHYSICAL MANIFESTATION OF THIS DIFFERENCE.
TO ME, THERE WAS DEFINITELY SOMETHING MORE APPEALING ABOUT MY GRANDFATHER. I HAD INHERITED HIS COMPLEXION IT SEEMED, BUT I HOPED I HAD SOME OF HIS PERSONALITY AS WELL
FROM MY GRANDMOTHER, I INHERITED -- HER NAME -- WELL, ALMOST
IT IS COMMON PRACTICE AMONG CHRISTIAN FAMILIES IN KERALA, FOR THE SECOND BORN TO TAKE ON THE NAME OF THE GRANDMOTHER FROM THE MOTHER'S SIDE. A SMALL EXCEPTION WAS MADE IN MY CASE.
Waaa!
The lady doth protest much!
MA, HOW COME MY MIDDLE NAME IS ROSEMARY AND NOT ROSALIND?
IT WAS YOUR GRANDMOTHER'S IDEA. SHE SAID SHE DIDN'T WANT YOU TO INHERIT ANY OF HER BAD LUCK.
THE HINDU
NOT THAT I WANTED TO HAVE HER NAME, BUT THAT'S HOW I GOT NAMED AFTER A HERB.
BAD LUCK?? WHAT DID SHE HAVE TO COMPLAIN ABOUT...? SEEMED LIKE SHE HAD A PRETTY OK LIFE..
A DECENT MAN, A GOOD JOB IN A FOREIGN COUNTRY. NICE KIDS SHE DIDN'T REALLY HAVE TO LOOK AFTER..

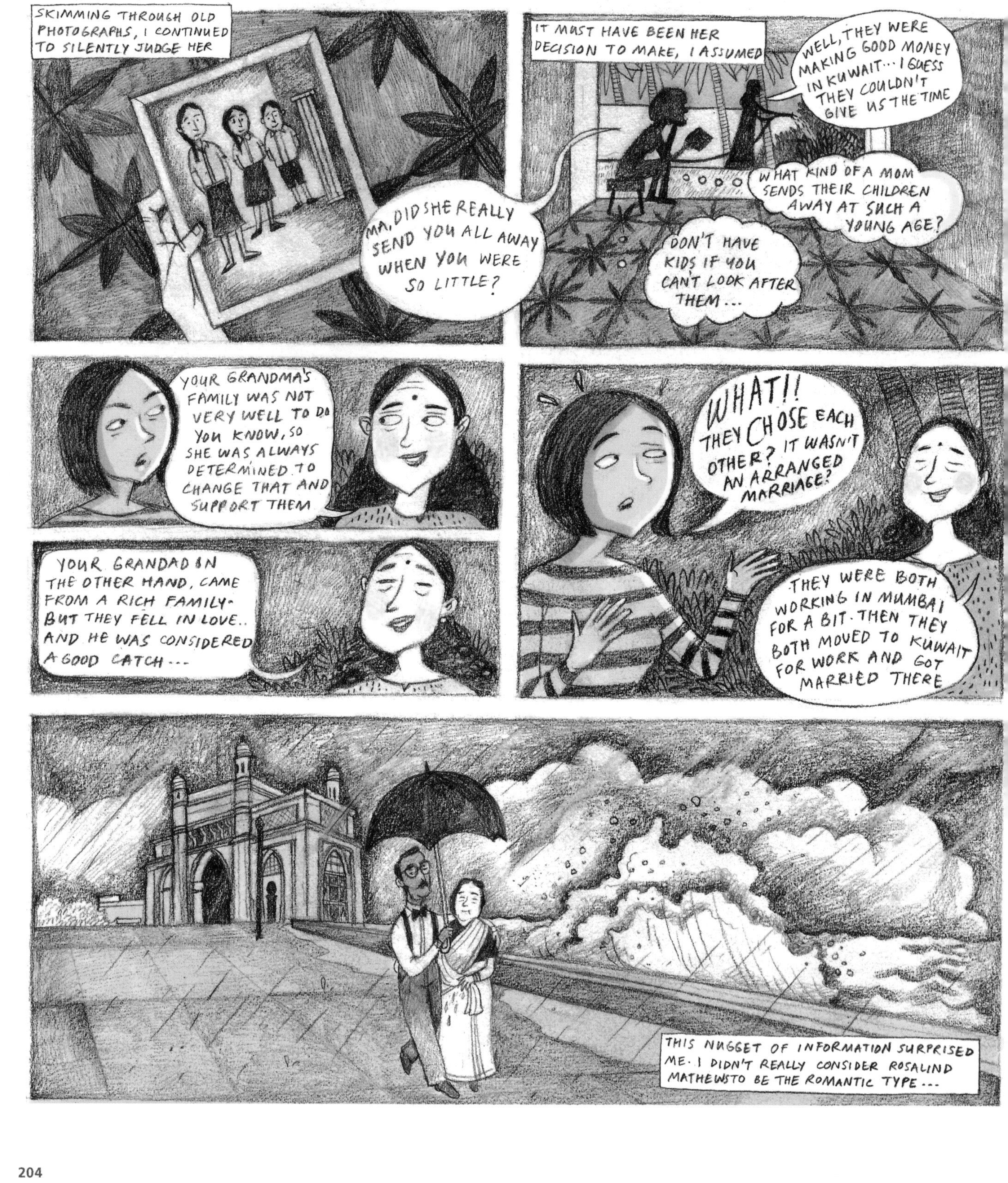
SKIMMING THROUGH OLD PHOTOGRAPHS, I CONTINUED TO SILENTLY JUDGE HER
MA, DID SHE REALLY SEND YOU ALL AWAY WHEN YOU WERE SO LITTLE?
IT MUST HAVE BEEN HER DECISION TO MAKE, I ASSUMED
WELL, THEY WERE MAKING GOOD MONEY IN KUWAIT... I GUESS THEY COULDN'T GIVE US THE TIME
WHAT KIND OF A MOM SENDS THEIR CHILDREN AWAY AT SUCH A YOUNG AGE?
DON'T HAVE KIDS IF YOU CAN'T LOOK AFTER THEM...
YOUR GRANDMA'S FAMILY WAS NOT VERY WELL TO DO YOU KNOW, SO SHE WAS ALWAYS DETERMINED TO CHANGE THAT AND SUPPORT THEM
YOUR GRANDAD ON THE OTHER HAND, CAME FROM A RICH FAMILY. BUT THEY FELL IN LOVE.. AND HE WAS CONSIDERED A GOOD CATCH...
WHAT!! THEY CHOSE EACH OTHER? IT WASN'T AN ARRANGED MARRIAGE?
THEY WERE BOTH WORKING IN MUMBAI FOR A BIT. THEN THEY BOTH MOVED TO KUWAIT FOR WORK AND GOT MARRIED THERE
THIS NUGGET OF INFORMATION SURPRISED ME. I DIDN'T REALLY CONSIDER ROSALIND MATHEWS TO BE THE ROMANTIC TYPE...

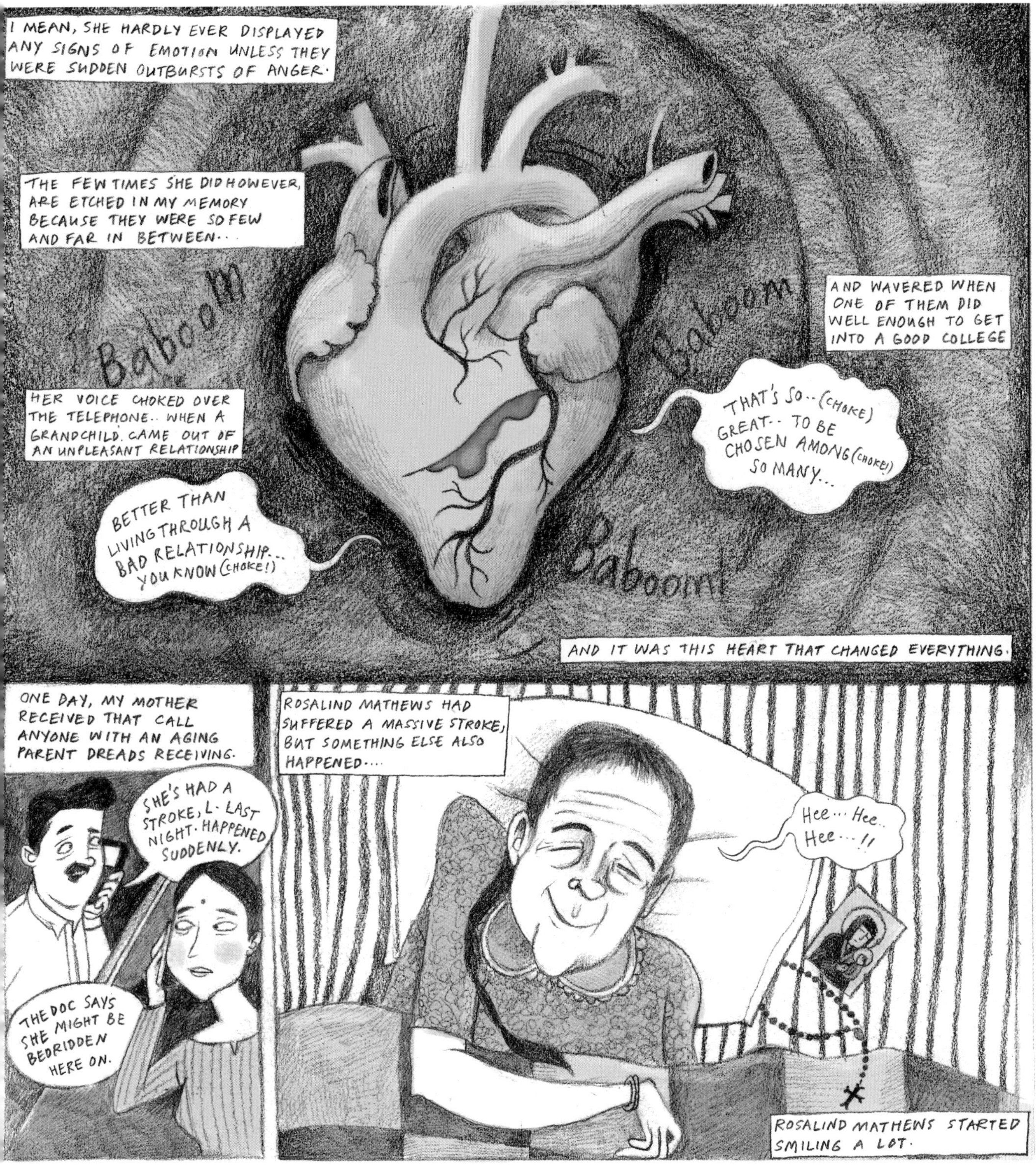
I MEAN, SHE HARDLY EVER DISPLAYED ANY SIGNS OF EMOTION UNLESS THEY WERE SUDDEN OUTBURSTS OF ANGER.
THE FEW TIMES SHE DID HOWEVER, ARE ETCHED IN MY MEMORY BECAUSE THEY WERE SO FEW AND FAR IN BETWEEN...
Baboom
Baboom
Baboom!
HER VOICE CHOKED OVER THE TELEPHONE.. WHEN A GRANDCHILD CAME OUT OF AN UNPLEASANT RELATIONSHIP
BETTER THAN LIVING THROUGH A BAD RELATIONSHIP... YOU KNOW (CHOKE!)
AND WAVERED WHEN ONE OF THEM DID WELL ENOUGH TO GET INTO A GOOD COLLEGE
THAT'S SO.. (CHOKE) GREAT.. TO BE CHOSEN AMONG (CHOKE!) SO MANY...
AND IT WAS THIS HEART THAT CHANGED EVERYTHING.
ONE DAY, MY MOTHER RECEIVED THAT CALL ANYONE WITH AN AGING PARENT DREADS RECEIVING.
SHE'S HAD A STROKE, L- LAST NIGHT. HAPPENED SUDDENLY.
THE DOC SAYS SHE MIGHT BE BEDRIDDEN HERE ON.
ROSALIND MATHEWS HAD SUFFERED A MASSIVE STROKE, BUT SOMETHING ELSE ALSO HAPPENED....
Hee... Hee.. Hee...!!
ROSALIND MATHEWS STARTED SMILING A LOT.

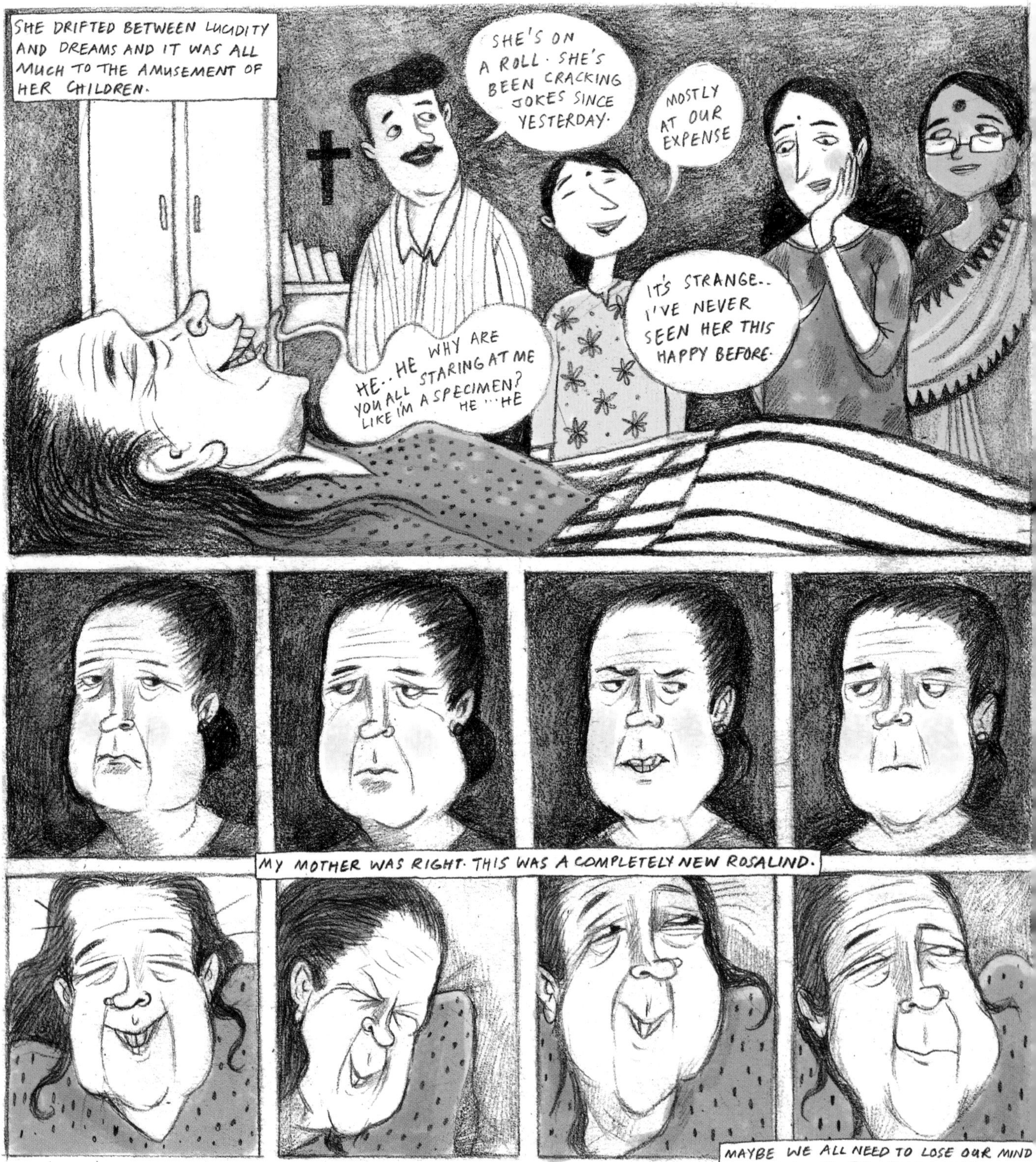
SHE DRIFTED BETWEEN LUCIDITY AND DREAMS AND IT WAS ALL MUCH TO THE AMUSEMENT OF HER CHILDREN.
SHE'S ON A ROLL. SHE'S BEEN CRACKING JOKES SINCE YESTERDAY.
MOSTLY AT OUR EXPENSE
HE.. HE WHY ARE YOU ALL STARING AT ME LIKE I'M A SPECIMEN? HE ... HE
IT'S STRANGE.. I'VE NEVER SEEN HER THIS HAPPY BEFORE.
MY MOTHER WAS RIGHT. THIS WAS A COMPLETELY NEW ROSALIND.
MAYBE WE ALL NEED TO LOSE OUR MIND A LITTLE BIT TO BE TRULY HAPPY.

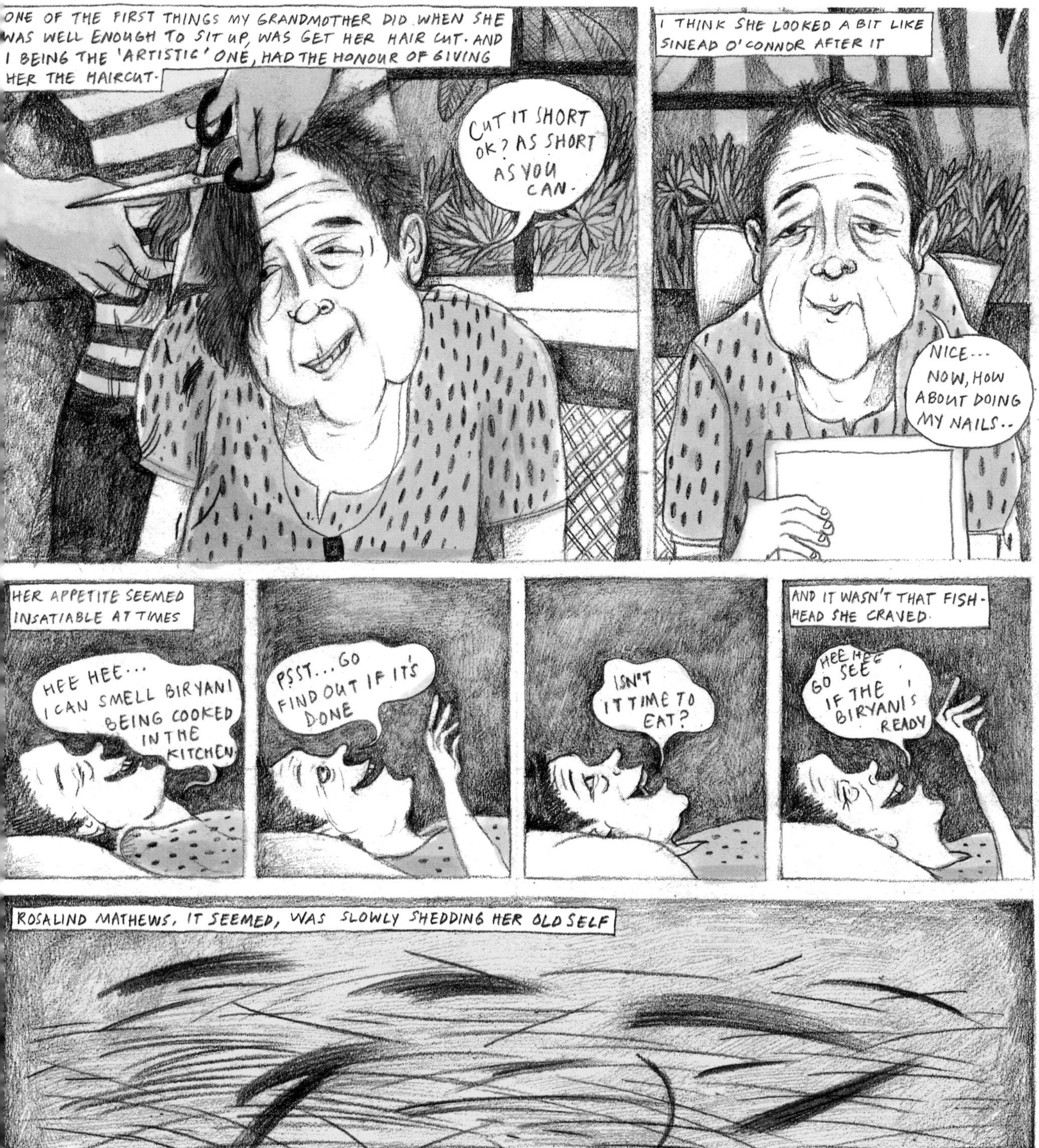

ONE OF THE FIRST THINGS MY GRANDMOTHER DID WHEN SHE WAS WELL ENOUGH TO SIT UP, WAS GET HER HAIR CUT. AND I BEING THE 'ARTISTIC' ONE, HAD THE HONOUR OF GIVING HER THE HAIRCUT.
CUT IT SHORT OK? AS SHORT AS YOU CAN.
I THINK SHE LOOKED A BIT LIKE SINEAD O'CONNOR AFTER IT
NICE... NOW, HOW ABOUT DOING MY NAILS..
HER APPETITE SEEMED INSATIABLE AT TIMES
HEE HEE... I CAN SMELL BIRYANI BEING COOKED IN THE KITCHEN
PSST... GO FIND OUT IF IT'S DONE
ISN'T IT TIME TO EAT?
AND IT WASN'T THAT FISH-HEAD SHE CRAVED.
HEE HEE, GO SEE IF THE BIRYANI'S READY
ROSALIND MATHEWS, IT SEEMED, WAS SLOWLY SHEDDING HER OLD SELF
FOR THE FIRST TIME, SHE ALSO STARTED SPEAKING TO HER CHILDREN ABOUT HER MARRIAGE

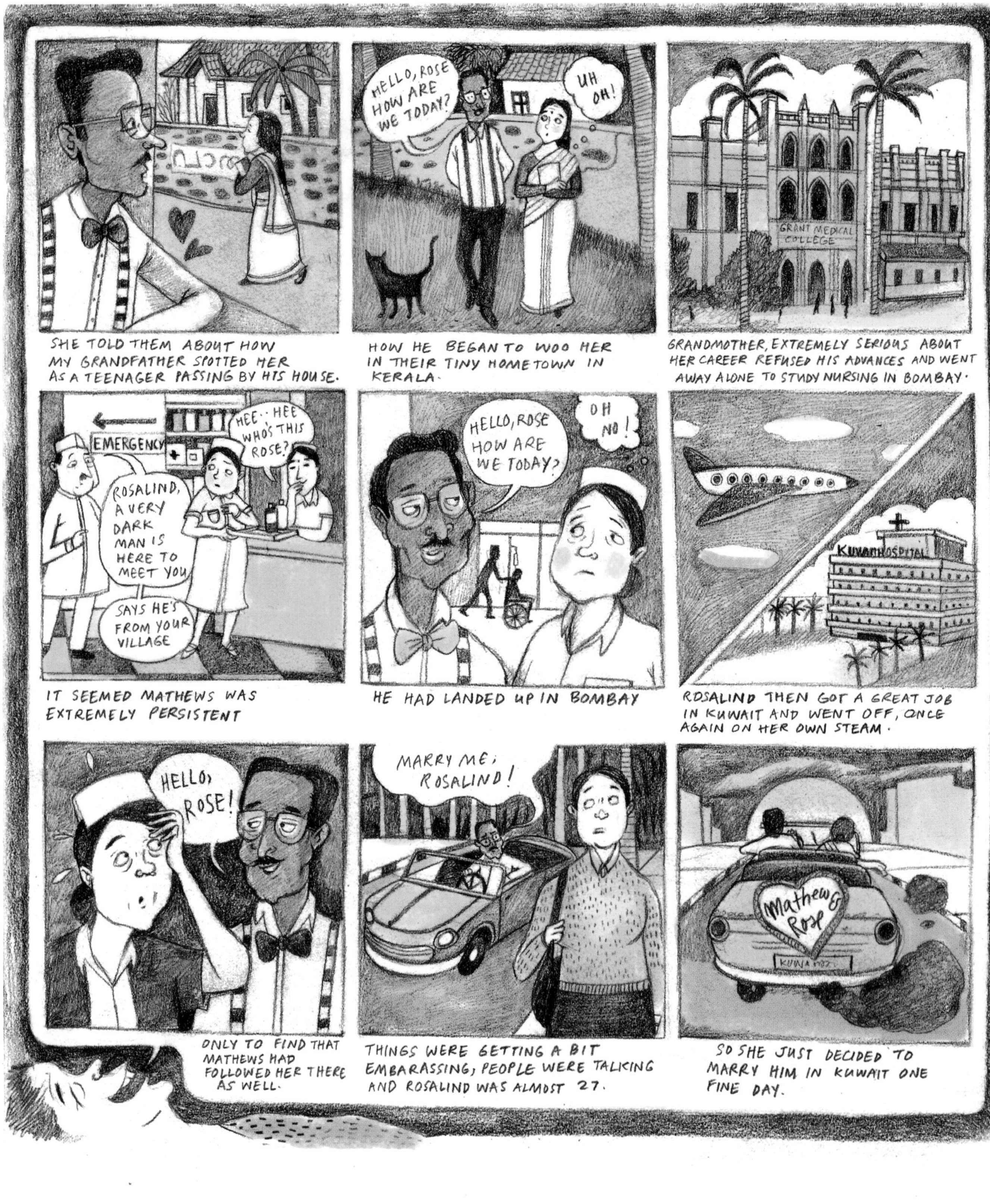
SHE TOLD THEM ABOUT HOW MY GRANDFATHER SPOTTED HER AS A TEENAGER PASSING BY HIS HOUSE.
HELLO, ROSE HOW ARE WE TODAY?
UH OH!
HOW HE BEGAN TO WOO HER IN THEIR TINY HOMETOWN IN KERALA.
GRANT MEDICAL COLLEGE
GRANDMOTHER, EXTREMELY SERIOUS ABOUT HER CAREER REFUSED HIS ADVANCES AND WENT AWAY ALONE TO STUDY NURSING IN BOMBAY.
EMERGENCY
HEE.. HEE WHO'S THIS ROSE?
ROSALIND, A VERY DARK MAN IS HERE TO MEET YOU
SAYS HE'S FROM YOUR VILLAGE
IT SEEMED MATHEWS WAS EXTREMELY PERSISTENT
HELLO, ROSE HOW ARE WE TODAY?
OH NO!
HE HAD LANDED UP IN BOMBAY
ROSALIND THEN GOT A GREAT JOB IN KUWAIT AND WENT OFF, ONCE AGAIN ON HER OWN STEAM.
HELLO, ROSE!
ONLY TO FIND THAT MATHEWS HAD FOLLOWED HER THERE AS WELL.
MARRY ME, ROSALIND!
THINGS WERE GETTING A BIT EMBARASSING, PEOPLE WERE TALKING AND ROSALIND WAS ALMOST 27.
Mathews Rose
SO SHE JUST DECIDED TO MARRY HIM IN KUWAIT ONE FINE DAY.

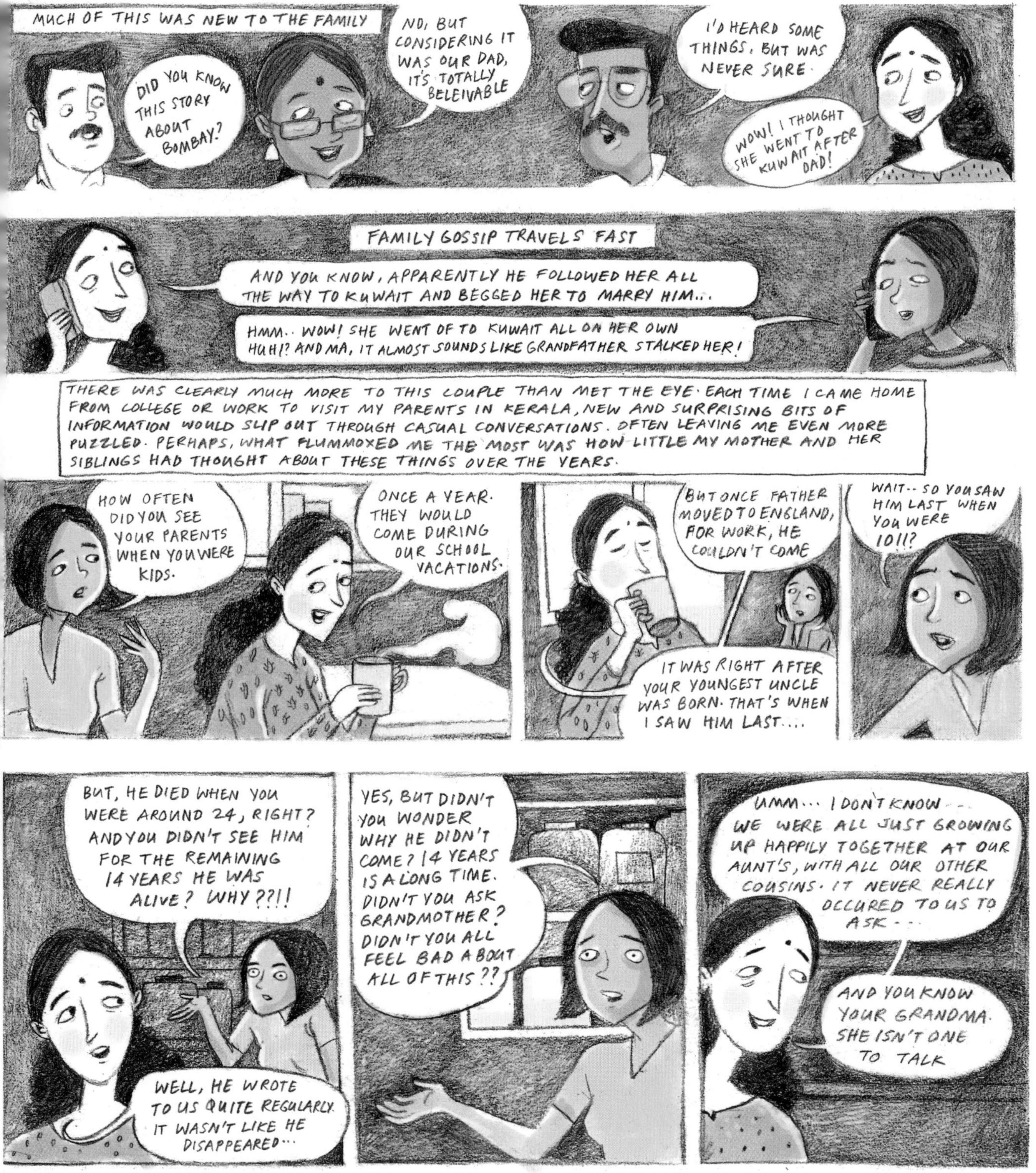
MUCH OF THIS WAS NEW TO THE FAMILY
DID YOU KNOW THIS STORY ABOUT BOMBAY?
NO, BUT CONSIDERING IT WAS OUR DAD, IT'S TOTALLY BELEIVABLE
I'D HEARD SOME THINGS, BUT WAS NEVER SURE.
WOW! I THOUGHT SHE WENT TO KUWAIT AFTER DAD!
FAMILY GOSSIP TRAVELS FAST
AND YOU KNOW, APPARENTLY HE FOLLOWED HER ALL THE WAY TO KUWAIT AND BEGGED HER TO MARRY HIM...
HMM.. WOW! SHE WENT OF TO KUWAIT ALL ON HER OWN HUH!? AND MA, IT ALMOST SOUNDS LIKE GRANDFATHER STALKED HER!
THERE WAS CLEARLY MUCH MORE TO THIS COUPLE THAN MET THE EYE. EACH TIME I CAME HOME FROM COLLEGE OR WORK TO VISIT MY PARENTS IN KERALA, NEW AND SURPRISING BITS OF INFORMATION WOULD SLIP OUT THROUGH CASUAL CONVERSATIONS. OFTEN LEAVING ME EVEN MORE PUZZLED. PERHAPS, WHAT FLUMMOXED ME THE MOST WAS HOW LITTLE MY MOTHER AND HER SIBLINGS HAD THOUGHT ABOUT THESE THINGS OVER THE YEARS.
HOW OFTEN DID YOU SEE YOUR PARENTS WHEN YOU WERE KIDS.
ONCE A YEAR. THEY WOULD COME DURING OUR SCHOOL VACATIONS.
BUT ONCE FATHER MOVED TO ENGLAND, FOR WORK, HE COULDN'T COME
IT WAS RIGHT AFTER YOUR YOUNGEST UNCLE WAS BORN. THAT'S WHEN I SAW HIM LAST....
WAIT.. SO YOU SAW HIM LAST WHEN YOU WERE 10!!?
BUT, HE DIED WHEN YOU WERE AROUND 24, RIGHT? AND YOU DIDN'T SEE HIM FOR THE REMAINING 14 YEARS HE WAS ALIVE? WHY ??!!
WELL, HE WROTE TO US QUITE REGULARLY. IT WASN'T LIKE HE DISAPPEARED...
YES, BUT DIDN'T YOU WONDER WHY HE DIDN'T COME? 14 YEARS IS A LONG TIME. DIDN'T YOU ASK GRANDMOTHER? DIDN'T YOU ALL FEEL BAD ABOUT ALL OF THIS ??
UMM... I DON'T KNOW... WE WERE ALL JUST GROWING UP HAPPILY TOGETHER AT OUR AUNT'S, WITH ALL OUR OTHER COUSINS. IT NEVER REALLY OCCURED TO US TO ASK...
AND YOU KNOW YOUR GRANDMA. SHE ISN'T ONE TO TALK

SOMEHOW, I COULDN'T WRAP MY HEAD AROUND ALL THIS. MAYBE IT WAS JUST A VERY DIFFERENT TIME. THINGS WERE QUIETLY TAKEN FOR GRANTED. HAD IT BEEN NOW...

What's on your mind

feeling blue 😔
Hubby can't make it for vacay again

POST

NAAH! I DOUBT ROSALIND WOULD EVER DO THAT!

COME TO THINK OF IT, I COULDN'T REMEMBER HER MENTIONING GRANDFATHER EVEN ONCE... NOT ONCE..

HMMM.. MAYBE HIS POPULARITY IRKED HER A BIT?

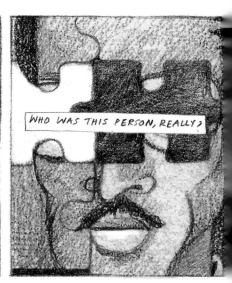

WHO WAS THIS PERSON, REALLY?

ROSALIND MATHEWS LONG SILENCE AROUND THIS, MADE THIS PUZZLE EVEN MORE INTRIGUING

BUT LITTLE DID WE KNOW WHAT WAS COMING NEXT

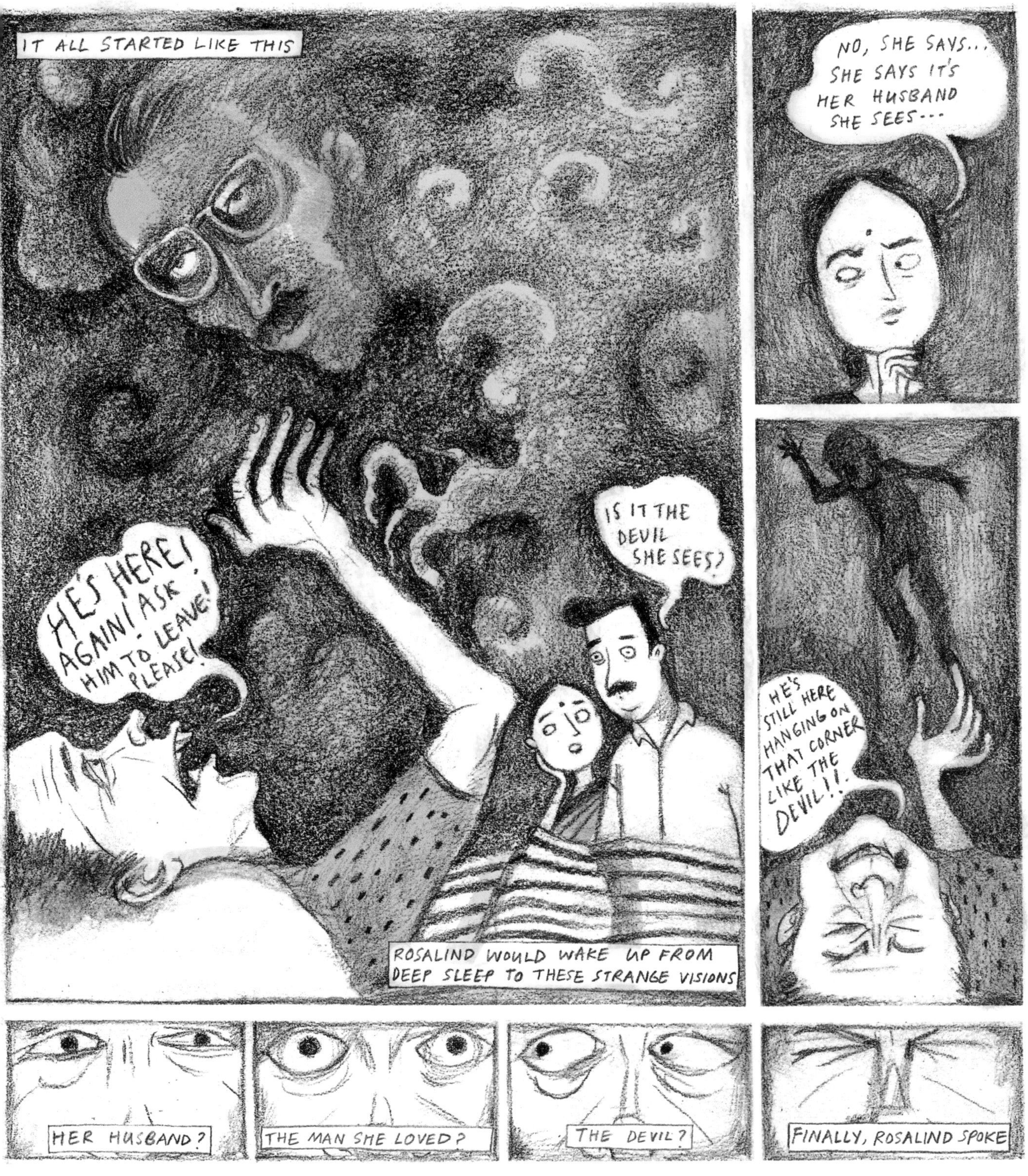
IT ALL STARTED LIKE THIS
HE'S HERE! AGAIN! ASK HIM TO LEAVE! PLEASE!
IS IT THE DEVIL SHE SEES?
ROSALIND WOULD WAKE UP FROM DEEP SLEEP TO THESE STRANGE VISIONS
NO, SHE SAYS... SHE SAYS IT'S HER HUSBAND SHE SEES...
HE'S STILL HERE HANGING ON THAT CORNER LIKE THE DEVIL!!
HER HUSBAND?
THE MAN SHE LOVED?
THE DEVIL?
FINALLY, ROSALIND SPOKE

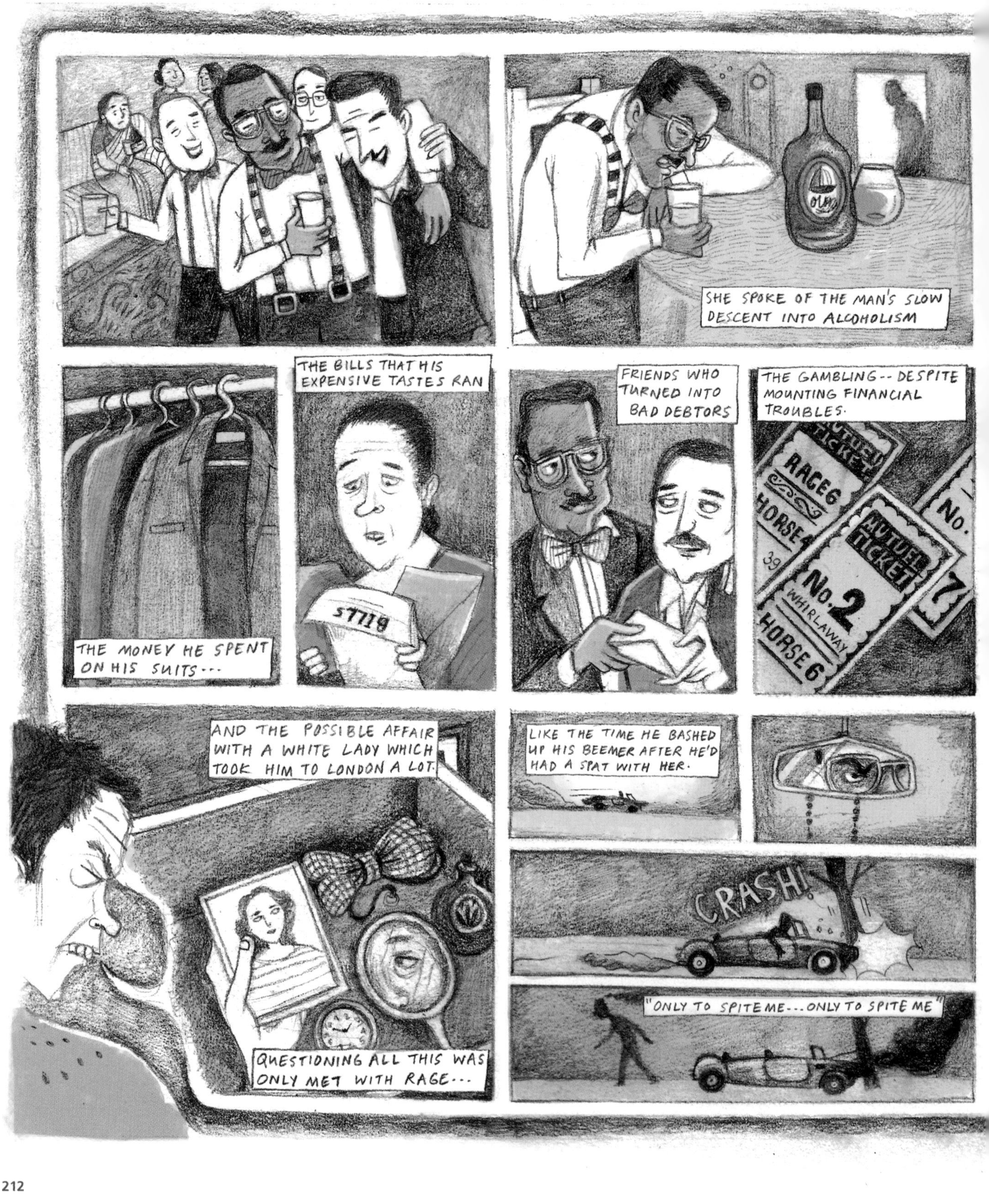
SHE SPOKE OF THE MAN'S SLOW DESCENT INTO ALCOHOLISM
THE MONEY HE SPENT ON HIS SUITS...
THE BILLS THAT HIS EXPENSIVE TASTES RAN
BILLS
FRIENDS WHO TURNED INTO BAD DEBTORS
THE GAMBLING -- DESPITE MOUNTING FINANCIAL TROUBLES.
RACE 6
HORSE 4
MUTUEL TICKET
No. 2
WHIRLAWAY
HORSE 6
No.
AND THE POSSIBLE AFFAIR WITH A WHITE LADY WHICH TOOK HIM TO LONDON A LOT.
LIKE THE TIME HE BASHED UP HIS BEEMER AFTER HE'D HAD A SPAT WITH HER.
CRASH!
"ONLY TO SPITE ME... ONLY TO SPITE ME"
QUESTIONING ALL THIS WAS ONLY MET WITH RAGE...

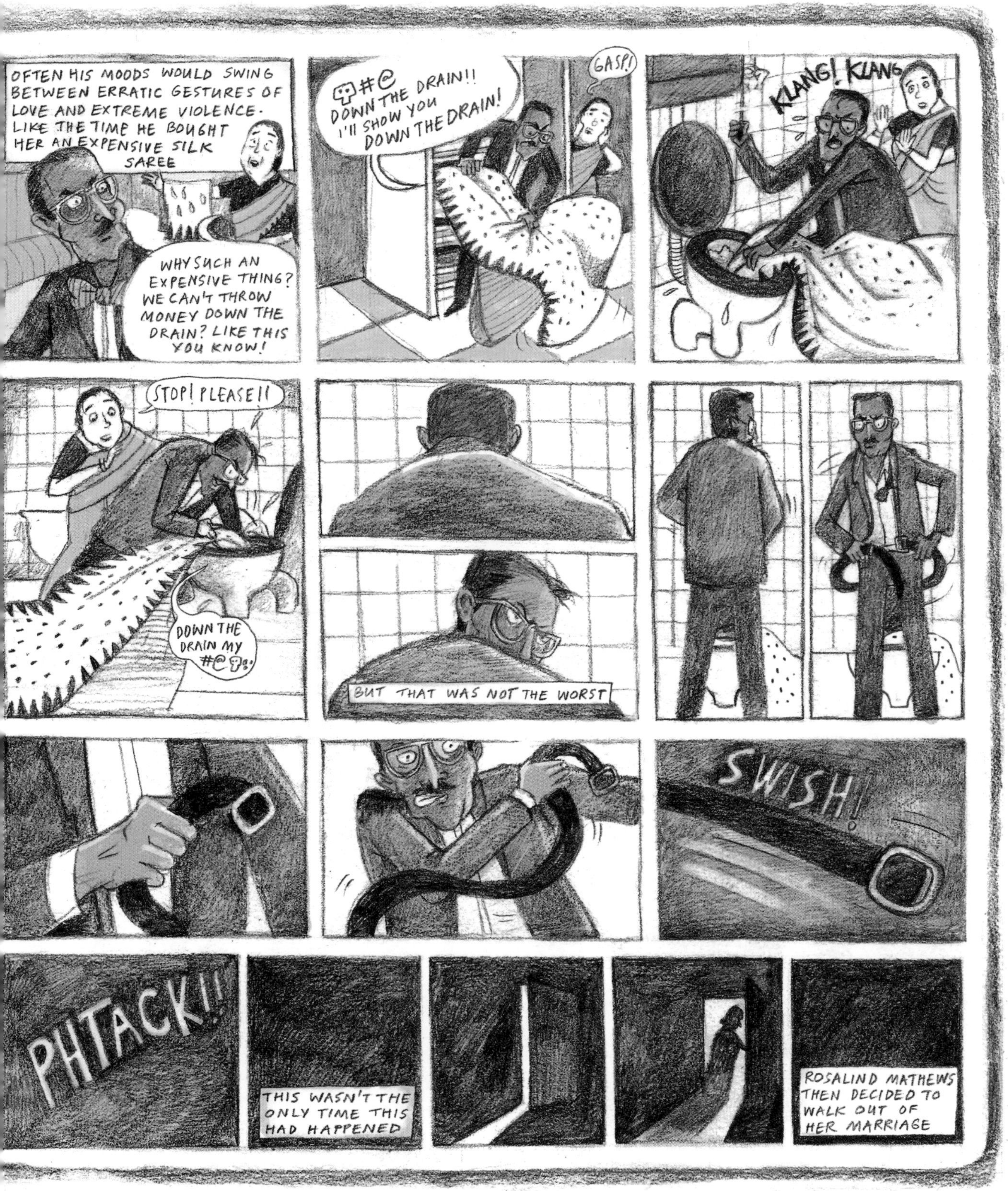

OFTEN HIS MOODS WOULD SWING BETWEEN ERRATIC GESTURES OF LOVE AND EXTREME VIOLENCE. LIKE THE TIME HE BOUGHT HER AN EXPENSIVE SILK SAREE
WHY SUCH AN EXPENSIVE THING? WE CAN'T THROW MONEY DOWN THE DRAIN? LIKE THIS YOU KNOW!
#@ DOWN THE DRAIN!! I'LL SHOW YOU DOWN THE DRAIN!
GASP!
KLANG! KLANG
STOP! PLEASE!!
DOWN THE DRAIN MY #@
BUT THAT WAS NOT THE WORST
SWISH!
PHTACK!!
THIS WASN'T THE ONLY TIME THIS HAD HAPPENED
ROSALIND MATHEWS THEN DECIDED TO WALK OUT OF HER MARRIAGE

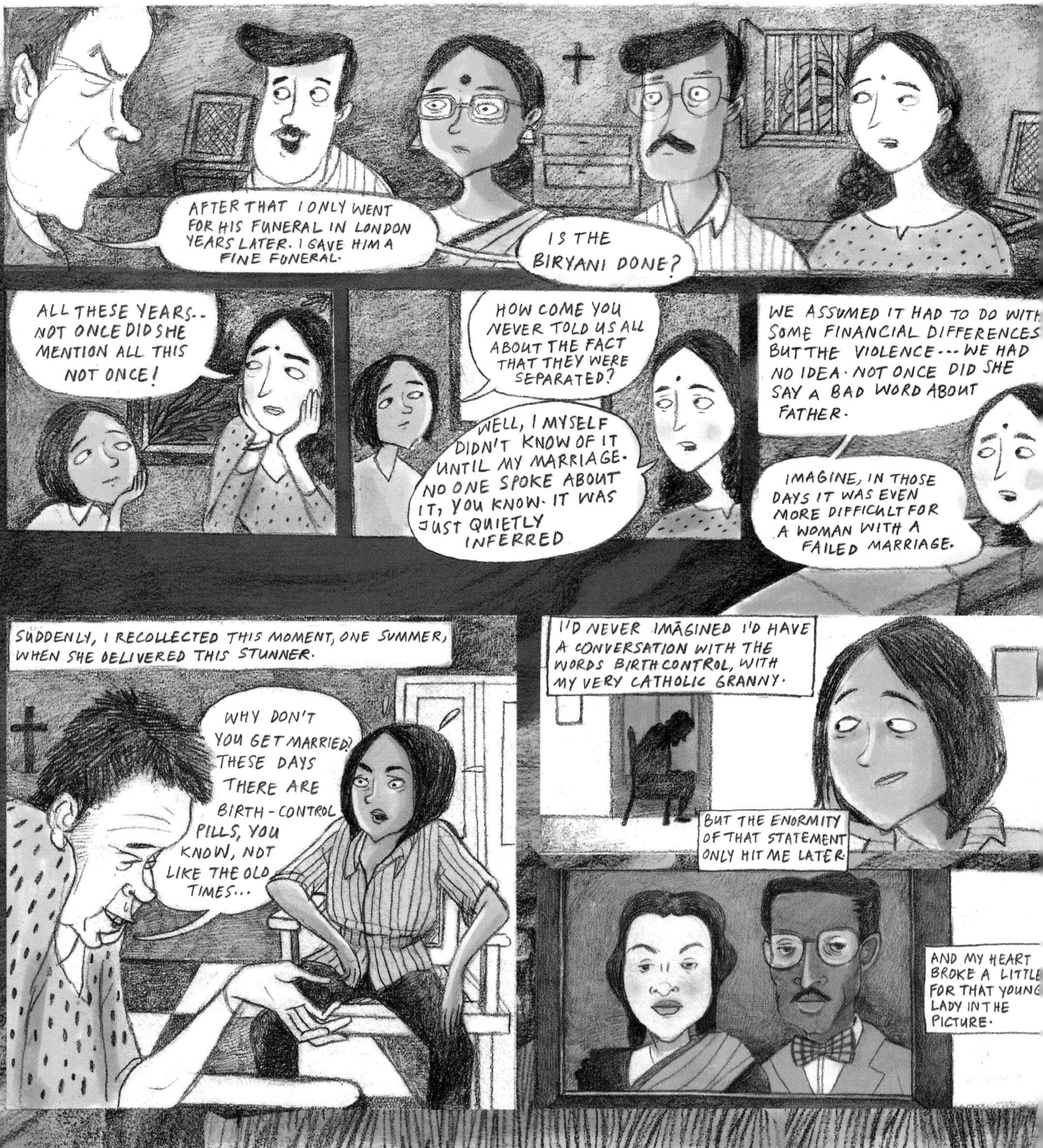

AFTER THAT I ONLY WENT FOR HIS FUNERAL IN LONDON YEARS LATER. I GAVE HIM A FINE FUNERAL.
IS THE BIRYANI DONE?
ALL THESE YEARS.. NOT ONCE DID SHE MENTION ALL THIS NOT ONCE!
HOW COME YOU NEVER TOLD US ALL ABOUT THE FACT THAT THEY WERE SEPARATED?
WELL, I MYSELF DIDN'T KNOW OF IT UNTIL MY MARRIAGE. NO ONE SPOKE ABOUT IT, YOU KNOW. IT WAS JUST QUIETLY INFERRED
WE ASSUMED IT HAD TO DO WITH SOME FINANCIAL DIFFERENCES BUT THE VIOLENCE... WE HAD NO IDEA. NOT ONCE DID SHE SAY A BAD WORD ABOUT FATHER.
IMAGINE, IN THOSE DAYS IT WAS EVEN MORE DIFFICULT FOR A WOMAN WITH A FAILED MARRIAGE.
SUDDENLY, I RECOLLECTED THIS MOMENT, ONE SUMMER, WHEN SHE DELIVERED THIS STUNNER.
WHY DON'T YOU GET MARRIED? THESE DAYS THERE ARE BIRTH-CONTROL PILLS, YOU KNOW, NOT LIKE THE OLD TIMES...
I'D NEVER IMAGINED I'D HAVE A CONVERSATION WITH THE WORDS BIRTH CONTROL, WITH MY VERY CATHOLIC GRANNY.
BUT THE ENORMITY OF THAT STATEMENT ONLY HIT ME LATER.
AND MY HEART BROKE A LITTLE FOR THAT YOUNG LADY IN THE PICTURE.

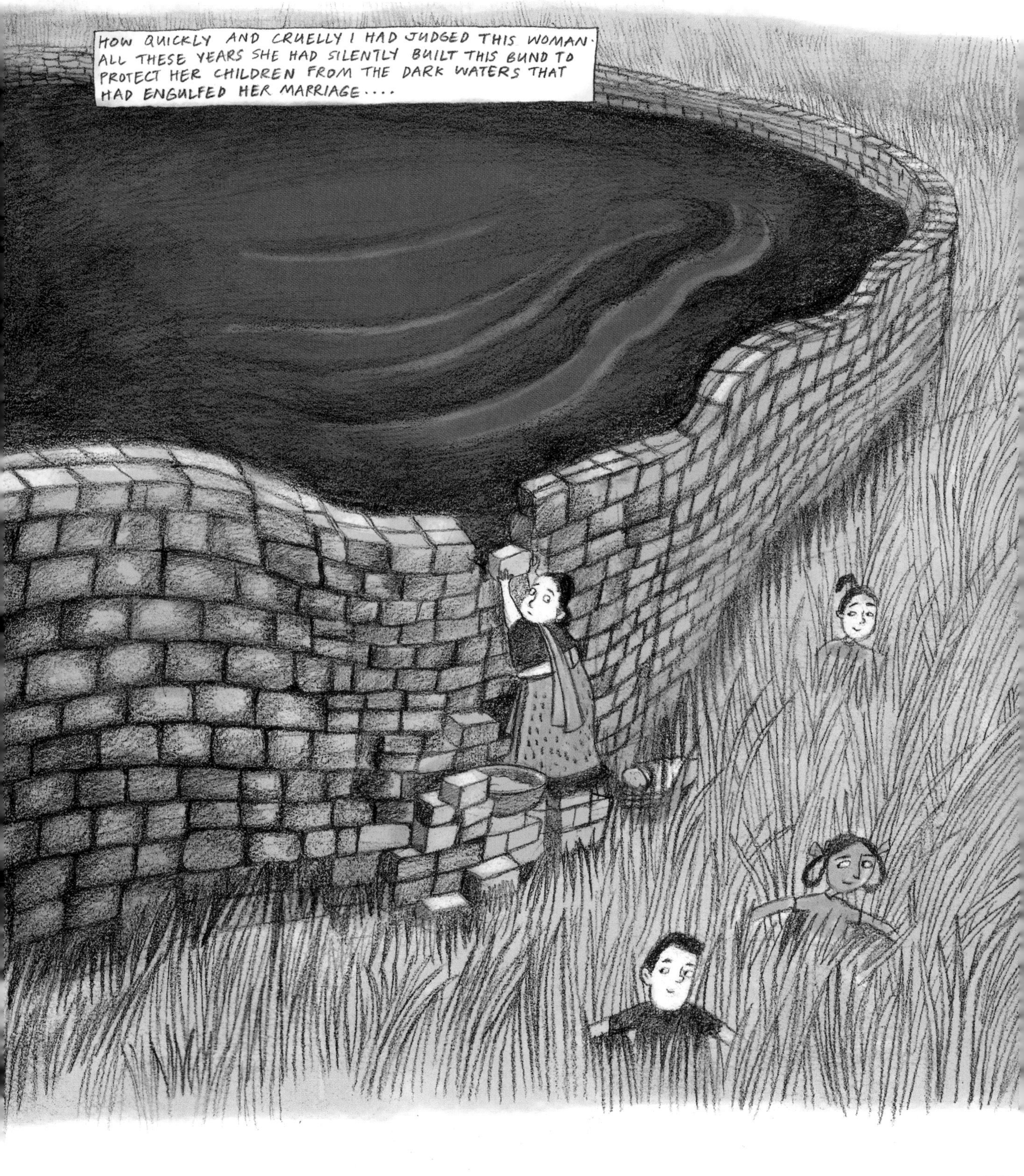
HOW QUICKLY AND CRUELLY I HAD JUDGED THIS WOMAN. ALL THESE YEARS SHE HAD SILENTLY BUILT THIS BUND TO PROTECT HER CHILDREN FROM THE DARK WATERS THAT HAD ENGULFED HER MARRIAGE....

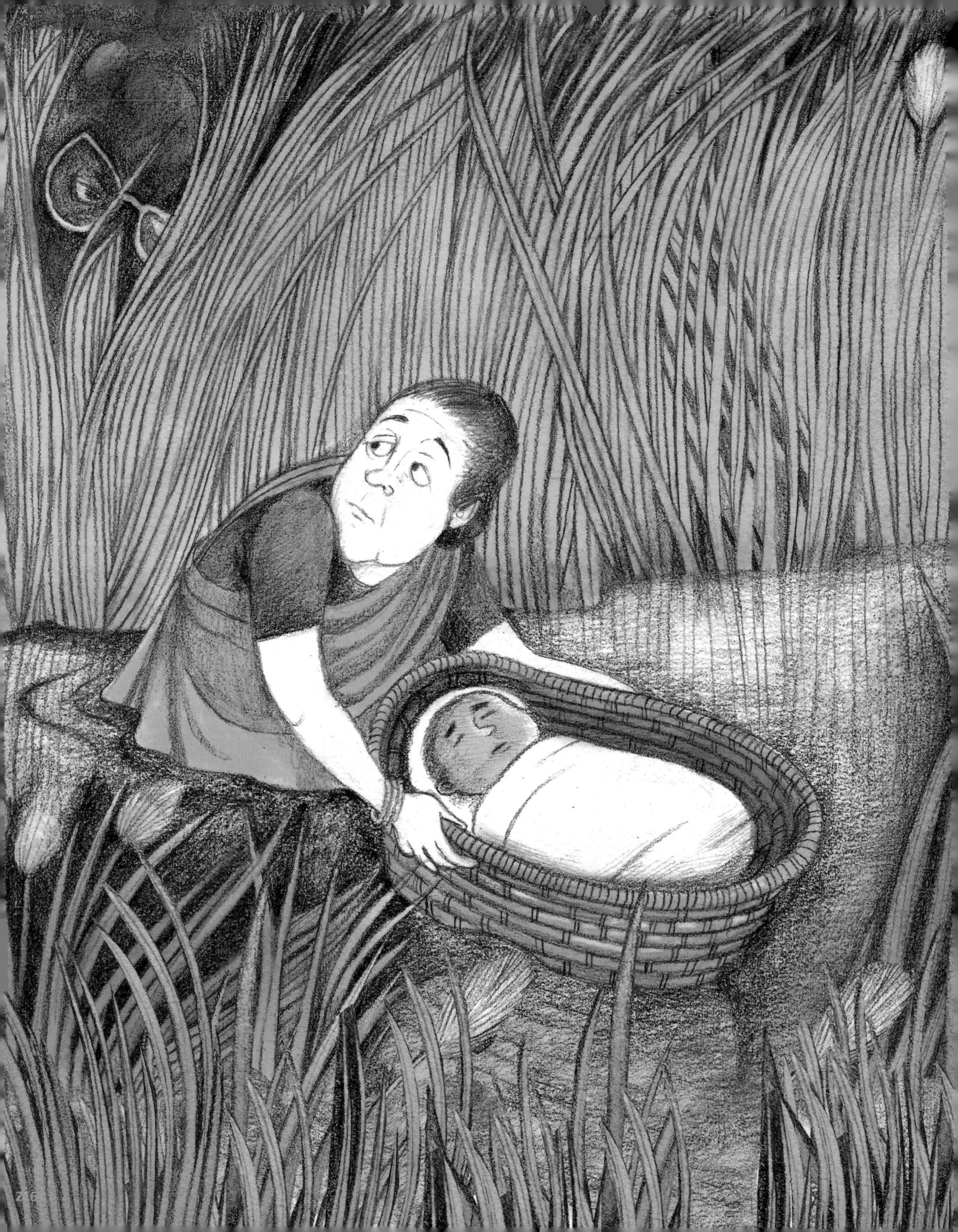

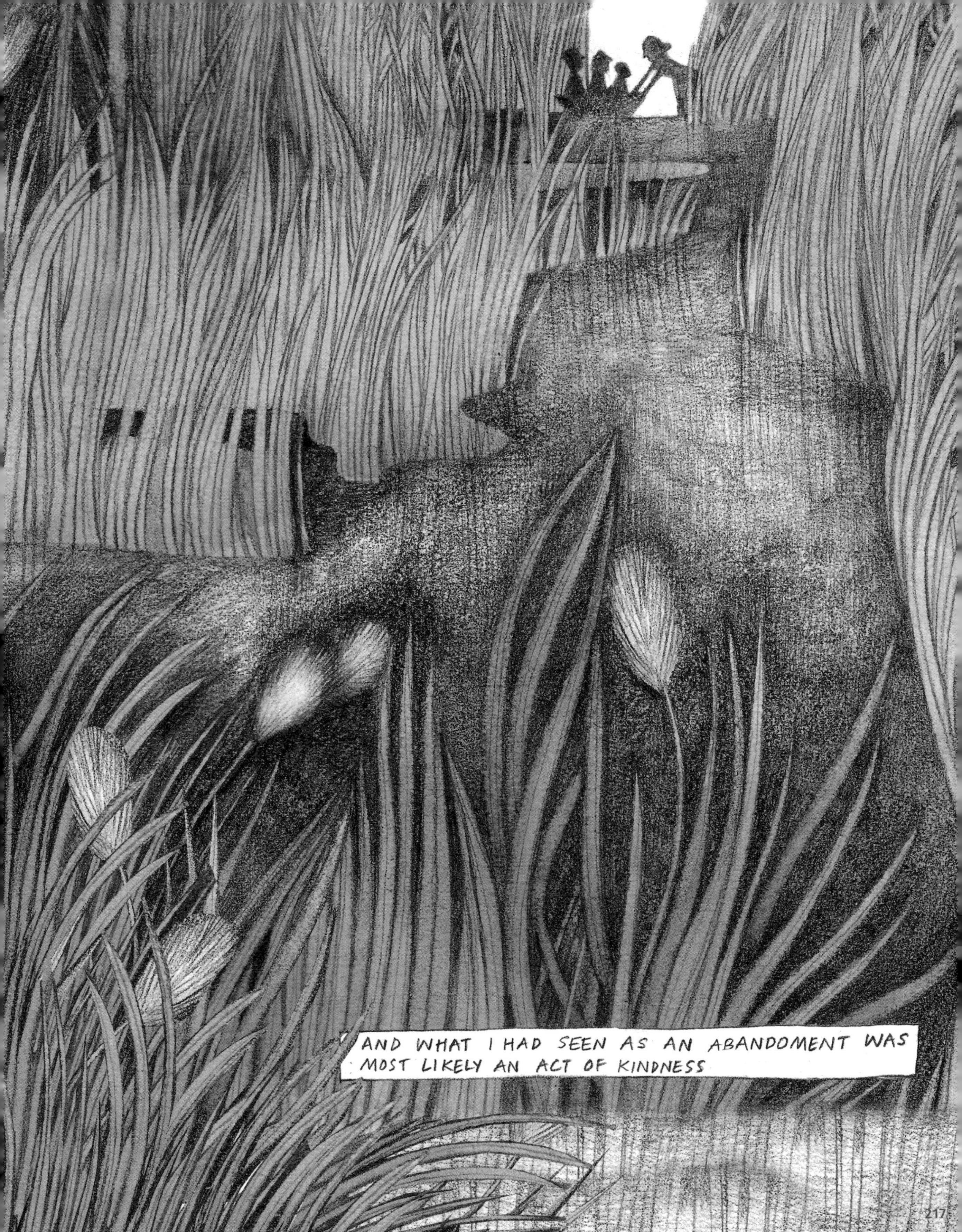
AND WHAT I HAD SEEN AS AN ABANDOMENT WAS MOST LIKELY AN ACT OF KINDNESS

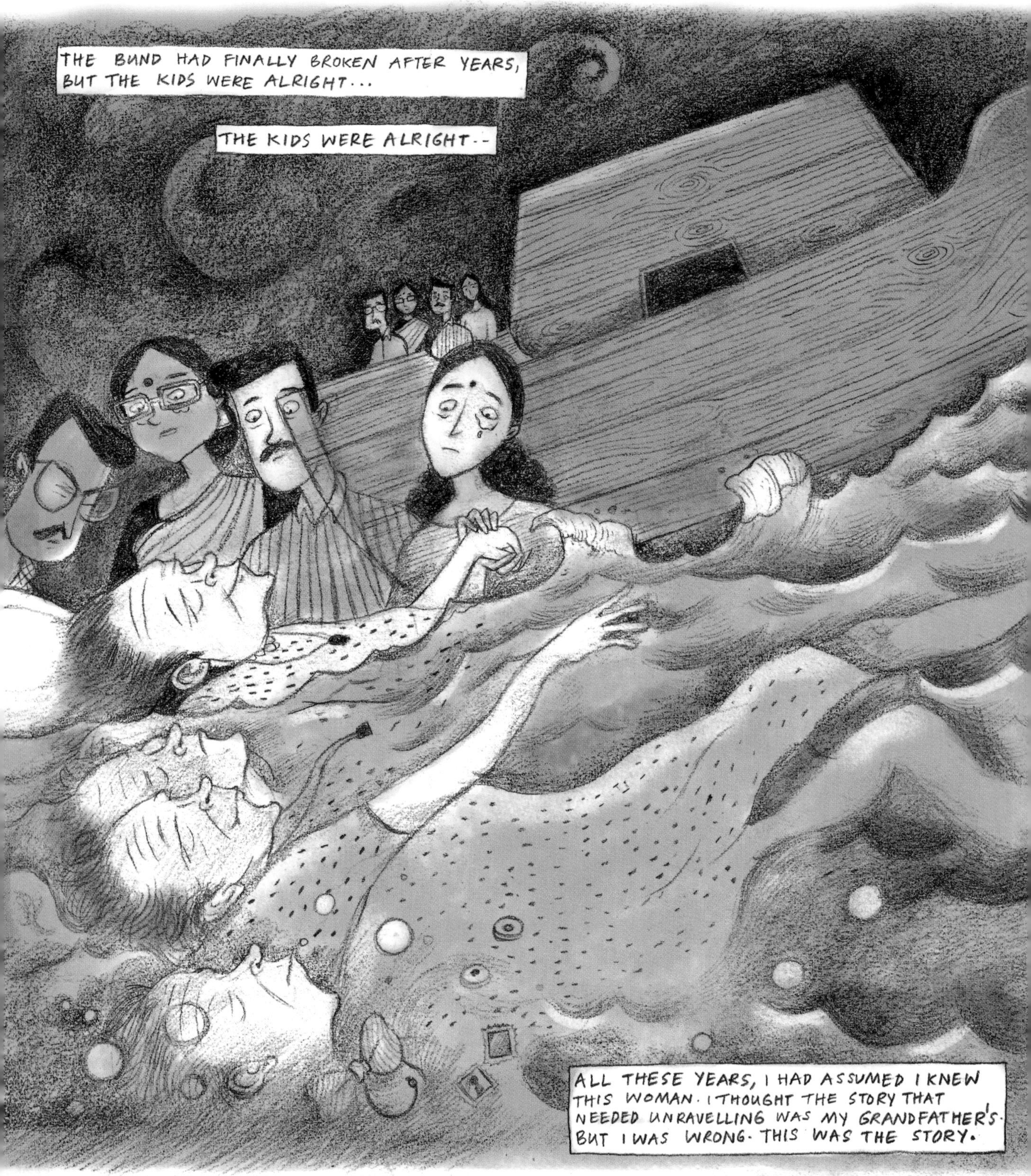
THE BUND HAD FINALLY BROKEN AFTER YEARS, BUT THE KIDS WERE ALRIGHT...
THE KIDS WERE ALRIGHT..
ALL THESE YEARS, I HAD ASSUMED I KNEW THIS WOMAN. I THOUGHT THE STORY THAT NEEDED UNRAVELLING WAS MY GRANDFATHER'S. BUT I WAS WRONG. THIS WAS THE STORY.

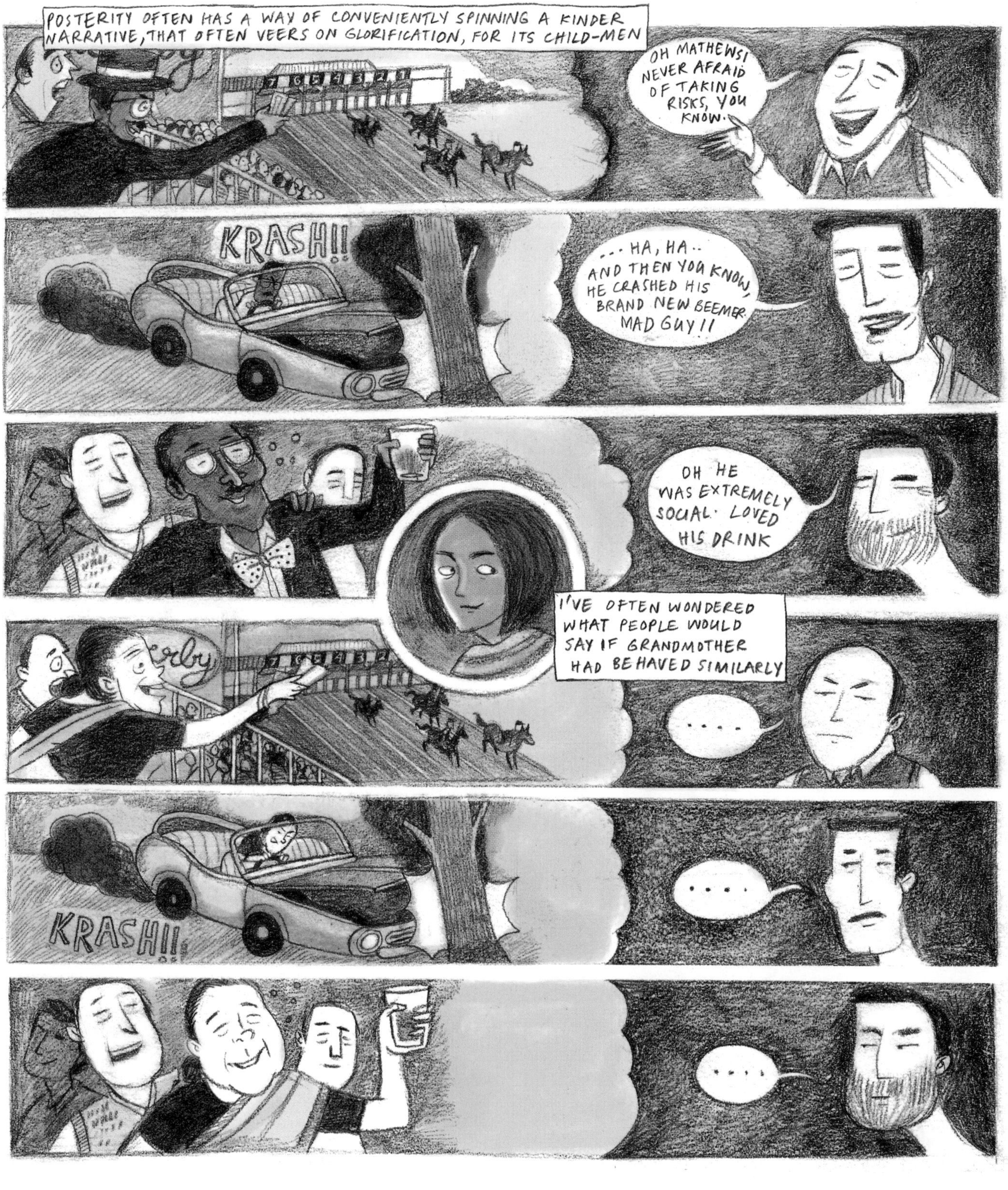
POSTERITY OFTEN HAS A WAY OF CONVENIENTLY SPINNING A KINDER NARRATIVE, THAT OFTEN VEERS ON GLORIFICATION, FOR ITS CHILD-MEN
OH MATHEWS! NEVER AFRAID OF TAKING RISKS, YOU KNOW.
KRASH!!
... HA, HA.. AND THEN YOU KNOW, HE CRASHED HIS BRAND NEW BEEMER. MAD GUY!!
OH HE WAS EXTREMELY SOCIAL. LOVED HIS DRINK
I'VE OFTEN WONDERED WHAT PEOPLE WOULD SAY IF GRANDMOTHER HAD BEHAVED SIMILARLY
.....
KRASH!!
....
....

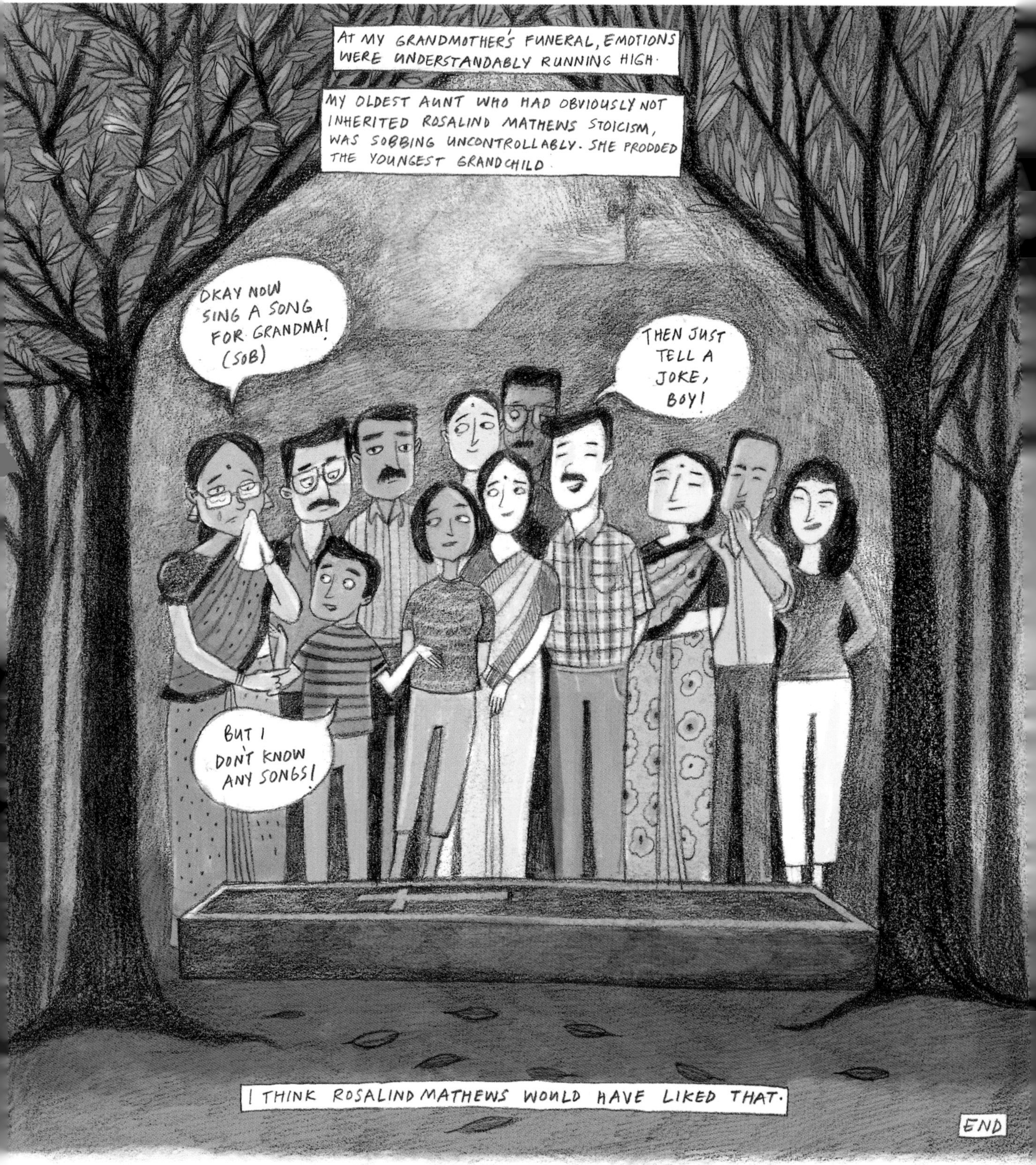
AT MY GRANDMOTHER'S FUNERAL, EMOTIONS WERE UNDERSTANDABLY RUNNING HIGH.
MY OLDEST AUNT WHO HAD OBVIOUSLY NOT INHERITED ROSALIND MATHEWS STOICISM, WAS SOBBING UNCONTROLLABLY. SHE PRODDED THE YOUNGEST GRANDCHILD.
OKAY NOW SING A SONG FOR GRANDMA! (SOB)
BUT I DON'T KNOW ANY SONGS!
THEN JUST TELL A JOKE, BOY!
I THINK ROSALIND MATHEWS WOULD HAVE LIKED THAT.
END

## Contributors

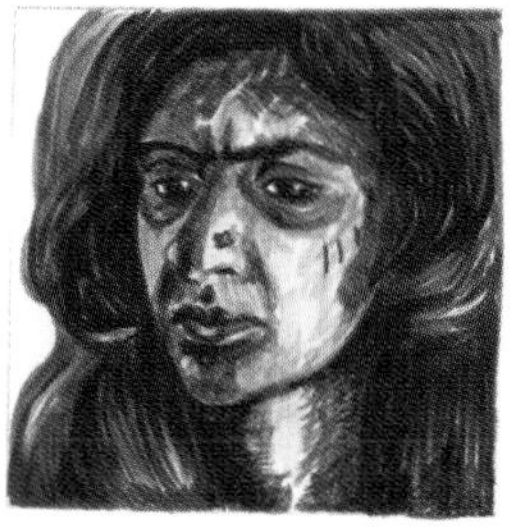

**Anpu Varkey** (1980) A voyeur, a drifter who is addicted to heights, time travel and insipid barren landscapes. Anpu Varkey is a painter of surfaces, from canvases and paper to walls and pavements. She has been painting in the large scale format for over a decade. Having lived in Bremen for a couple of years, she was highly influenced by the urban street art and DIY culture that was prevalent in the studio space she shared. She moved to Delhi in 2011 and has co-organised and participated in street art projects within the city and around India. Her first comic *Jaba* was self-published in 2014: it traces a day in the life of her cat. **anpuvarkey.wordpress.com**

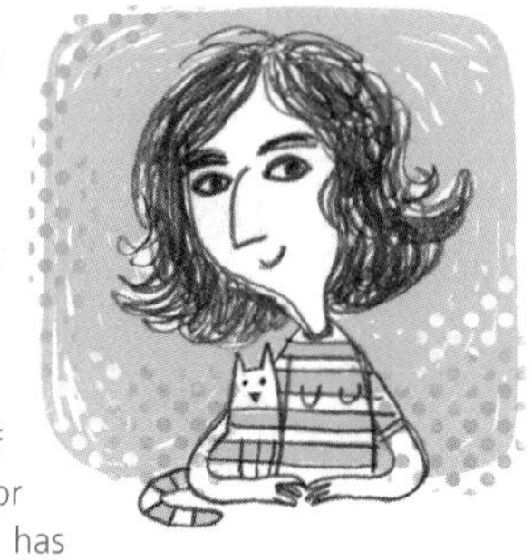

**Archana Sreenivasan** (1978) is an illustrator based in Bangalore, India. She works mostly with publishing houses and magazines, illustrating children's books, book covers and editorial pieces. She has also worked on a few comic illustration projects. Don't ask about her cat, or she won't stop talking. **archanasreenivasan.com**

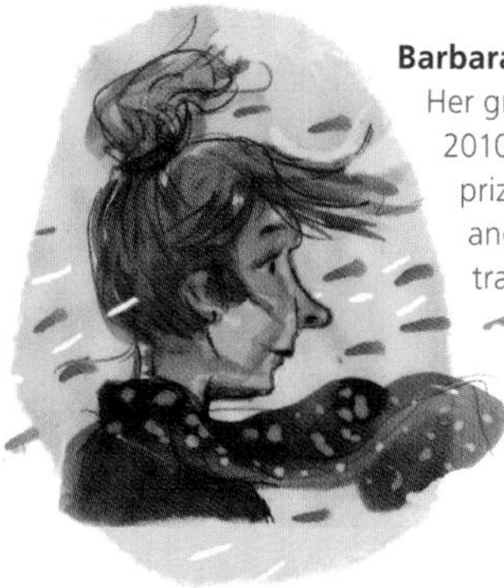

**Barbara Yelin** (1977) studied illustration at the Hamburg University of Applied Sciences. Her graphic novel *Gift* (2014) with author Peer Meter was published by Reprodukt, Berlin 2010, as was her most recent book *Irmina* (2014), which has been awarded a number of prizes and translated into French and English. On assignments as a workshop instructor and comics blogger for the Goethe-Institut and other cultural associations, she has travelled and taught in places such as Kosovo, Cairo, Delhi and Tel Aviv. She now lives and works in Munich.
**barbarayelin.de**

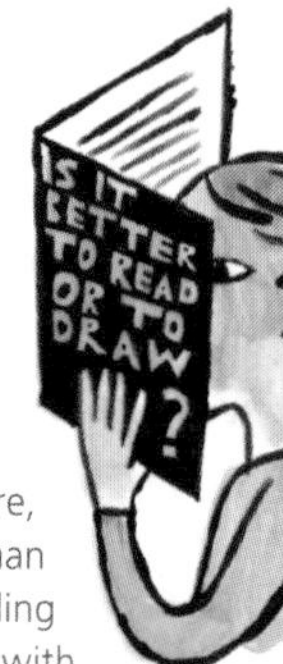
IS IT BETTER TO READ OR TO DRAW ?

**Katrin Stangl** (1977) studied at the Academy of Visual Arts in Leipzig. She creates images for both her own and other people's texts using a wide variety of techniques. Katrin has received numerous awards for her prints and illustrations. She lives with her family in Cologne.
**katrinstangl.de**

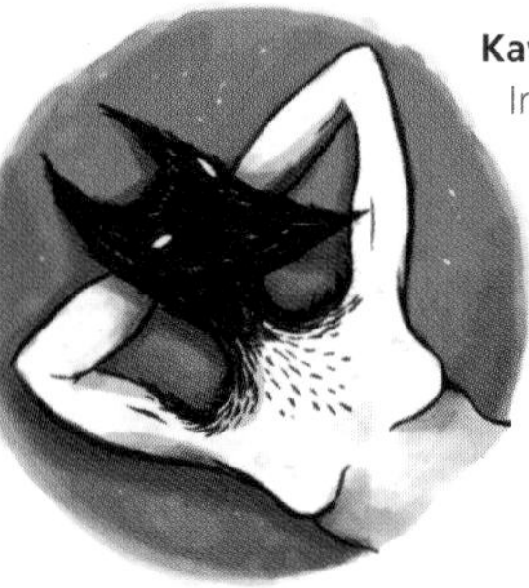

**Kaveri Gopalakrishnan** (1988) is an independent comic-maker and illustrator from Bangalore, India. Her short story 'Basic Space' (2015) is a part of the *Drawing the Line* anthology by Zubaan Books (India) and AdAstra Comix (Northern America). Kaveri regularly micro-blogs while travelling between city and countryside, making short, personal comics on themes of our relationship with nature, self-understanding and urban spaces. She is creator of online webcomic series UrbanLore Comics and '#NewAgeWisdomEtc'.
**kaverigeewhiz.tumblr.com**

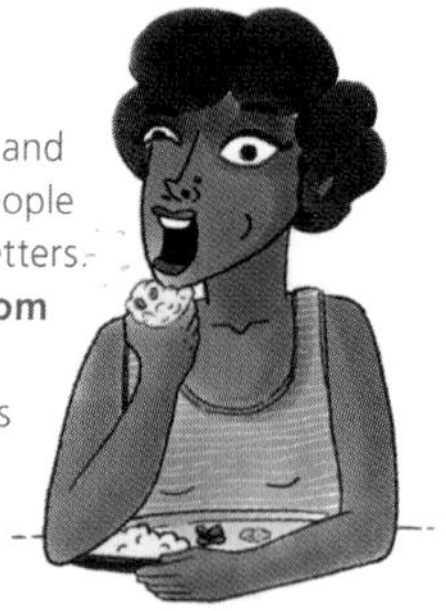

**Kruttika Susarla** is an illustrator, graphic designer and comic-maker currently living and working out of New Delhi. In her personal time she likes sketching people outdoors and/or drawing letters.
**kruttika.com**

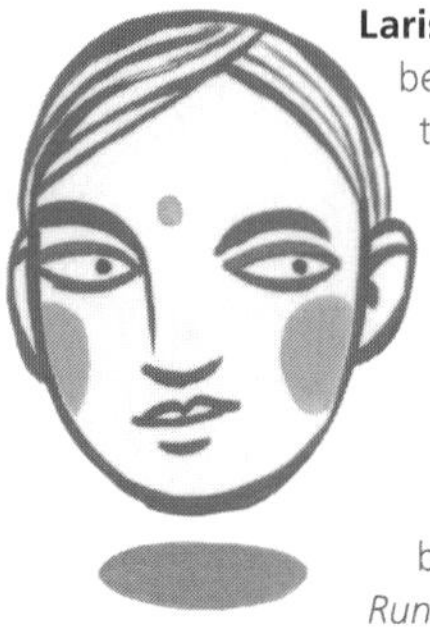

**Larissa Bertonasco** (1972) works as a freelance illustrator and graphic artist in Hamburg and has been part of SPRING since its foundation. In 2014 she initiated the workshop 'Drawing attention' together with Ludmilla Bartscht and Priya Kuriyan in New Delhi, which was attended by 15 Indian cartoonists focussing on gender issues. The book *Drawing the Line* and also the collaboration with Indian illustrators for this anthology originate in this encounter.
**bertonasco.de**

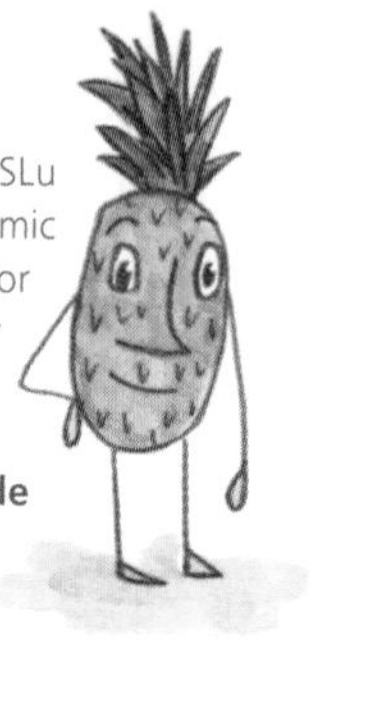

**Ludmilla Bartscht** (1981) studied visual communication and illustration at the UdK Berlin, HSLu Luzern (CH) and HAW Hamburg, attaining a degree there in 2012. She is co-editor of a number of comic magazines. In 2008, she was awarded the Max und Moritz award at the Comic-Salon in Erlangen for best student publication and in 2012-13 she drew a daily comic called 'Der Findling' for the *Frankfurter Rundschau*. Working as a fine artist, illustrator, cartoonist and lecturer, she has participated in exhibitions both in Germany and abroad. She has been a member of SPRING since 2009 and lives in Freiburg.
**ludmilla-bartscht.de**

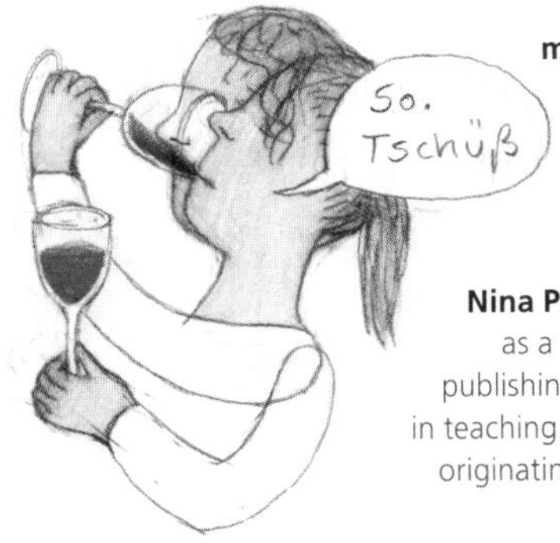
So. Tschüß

**marialuisa** (1974) was born in Buenos Aires. She studied illustration at HAW Hamburg. Her artistic approach varies between a rather free and a more narrative drawing style. Since 2001, her drawings have appeared in books, newspapers as well as numerous exhibitions, both in Germany and abroad. She has been an integral part of SPRING since it was founded. marialuisa lives and works in Hamburg. **marialuisa.de**

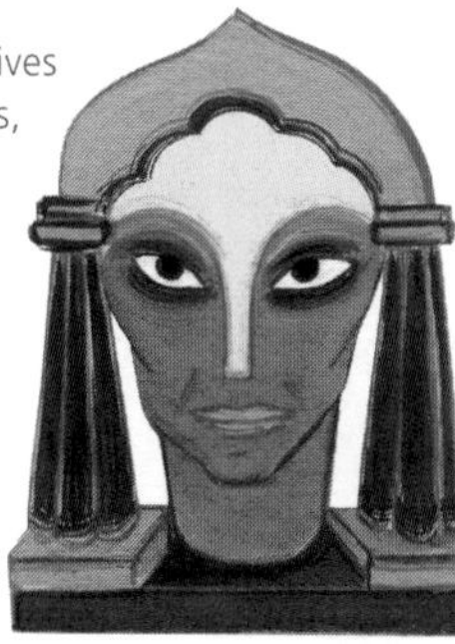

**Nina Pagalies** (1971) was born in Hamburg, studied at HFK Bremen and lives as a freelance illustrator in Berlin. She works across media for magazines, publishing houses and various cultural institutions, and regularly participates in teaching. Her current project is a digital city game ibook series for the iPad, originating in the work of the award-winning website www.wortwusel.net. **pagalies.com**

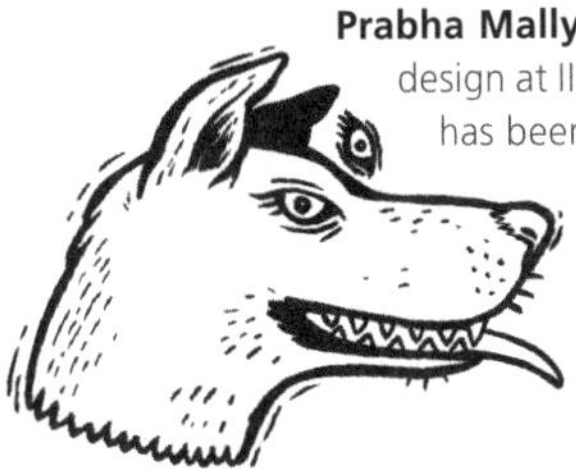

**Prabha Mallya** (1984) spent her childhood in Goa. She studied visual communication design at IIT Kanpur, India, and illustration at SCAD, Savannah, USA. Since 2009, she has been illustrating books and creating short comics for various magazines and anthologies. She lives in Stanford, California, and is frequently spotted in and around Bangalore. **crabbits.wordpress.com, fishkitty.tumblr.com**

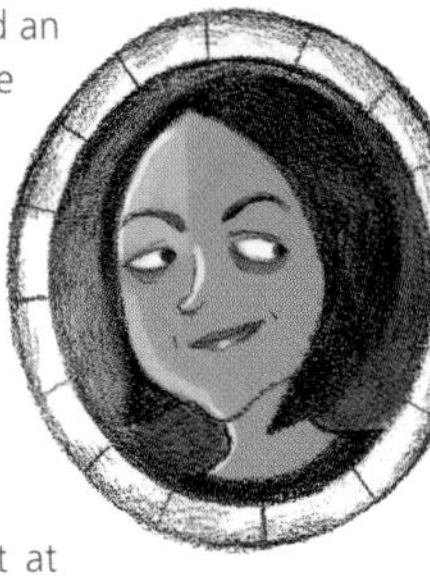

**Priya Kuriyan** is a children's book illustrator, comic book artist and an animator. A graduate of the National Institute of Design, Ahmedabad, she has directed educational films for the Sesame Street show (India) and the Children's Film Society of India. She has illustrated numerous children's books for various Indian publishers. Apart from contributing to comic book anthologies like the *Pao* anthology (Penguin Books) and *Eat the Sky, Drink the Ocean* (Zubaan), her work has appeared in newspapers like *The Indian Express, Hindu Business Line* and *India Today*. She currently lives in New Delhi, filling her sketchbooks with funny caricatures of its residents. **kuriyanmakeskomics.tumblr.com, priyakuriyan.blogspot.com**

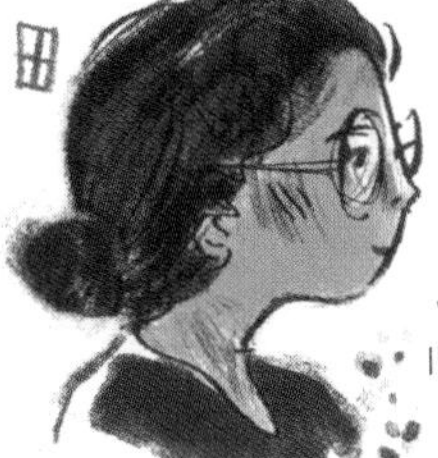

**Reshu Singh** (1991) is an illustrator and visual artist. She studied Applied Art at College of Art, New Delhi. Since graduating in 2012, she has worked at Turmeric Design (a graphic design studio in New Delhi) where she has drawn murals, designed interior graphics and illustrated book covers. Her story, 'The Photo', appeared in *Drawing the Line* (Zubaan, 2015), and was subsequently part of the exhibition 'Comix Creatrix: 100 Women Making Comics' at the House of Illustration in London. She enjoys working with ink and all possible ways of mark-making. **reshusingh.com**

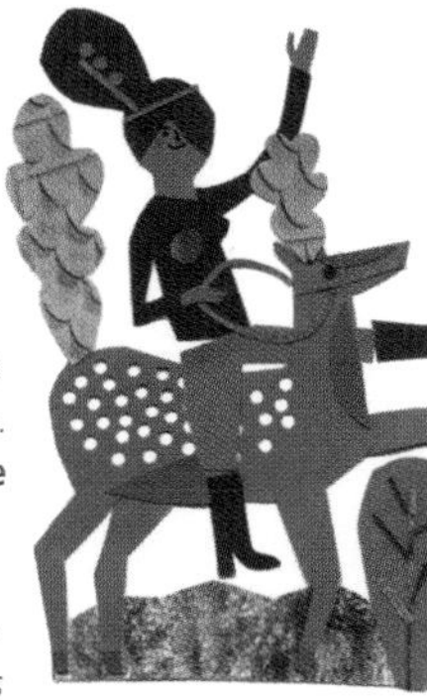

**Stephanie Wunderlich** studied Communication Design at both FH Augsburg and ISIA Urbino and graduated with a degree in communication design. Based in Hamburg, she works as a freelance illustrator for international magazine and book publishers. She also teaches illustration, currently at the University of Applied Science Hamburg. Her favourite medium is paper collage. She creates her illustrations using digital as well as analog techniques (scissors and glue). She has received awards from Art Directors' Club Germany, American Illustration and 3x3 Magazine. **wunderlich-illustration.de**

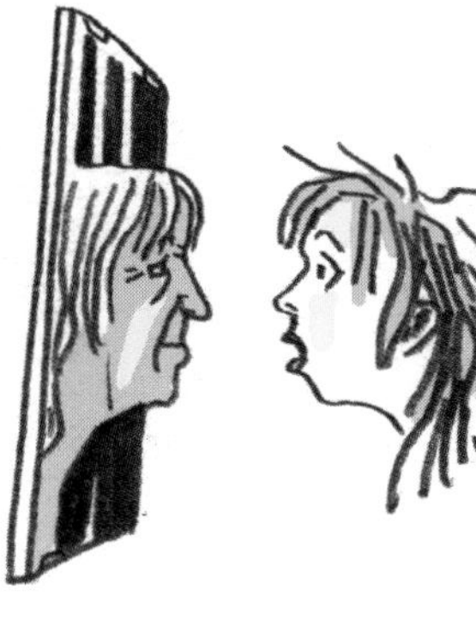

**Ulli Lust** (1967) moved to Berlin in 1995, where she studied graphic design and now lives as a cartoonist. Her published work includes pieces of graphic journalism featuring observations on modern life. Her most successful graphic novel *Today is the Last Day of the Rest of Your Life* has been translated into ten languages and won several awards. In 2013 *Flughunde,* an adaptation of the eponymous novel by Marcel Beyer, was released by Suhrkamp Verlag. Besides drawing comics she runs the screen-comic-publisher www.electrocomics.com, which publishes e-books and online comics by an ever-increasing group of international cartoonists. Since 2013 she is a professor for comics and illustration at the University of Applied Sciences and Arts of Hannover. **ullilust.de, electrocomics.com**

**SPRING** magazine was founded in Hamburg, Germany, in 2004 by a collective of women artists. Every year since then, the group has published a theme-based anthology, consisting of an unusual combination of comics, illustration and free drawing, using a wide variety of visual narrative techniques. **SPRING** is independent and non-commercial. Since its beginning, the group has consisted only of women and has become a important network for women artists in Germany.

**ZUBAAN** is an independent feminist publishing house based in New Delhi with a strong academic and general list. It was set up as an imprint of India's first feminist publishing house, Kali for Women, and carries forward Kali's tradition of publishing world-quality books to high editorial and production standards. Zubaan means tongue, voice, language, in Hindustani. Zubaan publishes work in the areas of humanities and social sciences as well as fiction, general non-fiction and books for young adults under its Young Zubaan imprint.

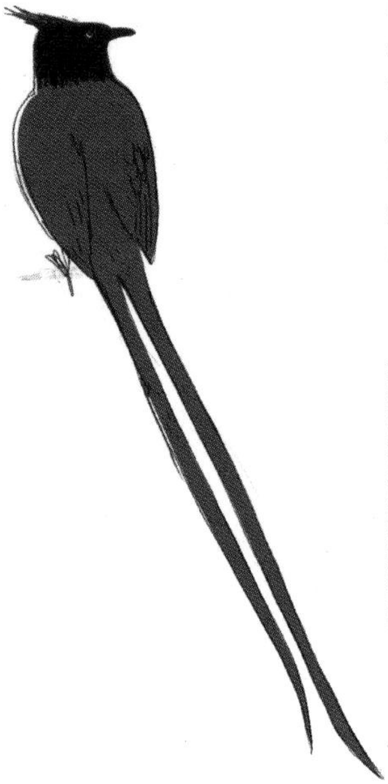

zubaan

Zubaan Publishers Pvt. Ltd.,
128B Shahpur Jat, First Floor
New Delhi 110049, India
Email: contact@zubaanbooks.com
Website: www.zubaanbooks.com

The publishers gratefully acknowledge the support of
Goethe-Institut / Max Mueller Bhavan New Delhi.

GOETHE INSTITUT
MAX MUELLER BHAVAN



Cover design: Priya Kuriyan
Additional illustrations: Ludmilla Bartscht (p 2), marialuisa (pp 4, 160), Prabha Mallya (pp 3, 9), Barbara Yelin (p 6), Archana Sreenivasan (p 8).

Translation:
Nadja Gebhardt, Berlin
Deborah S. Phillips, Berlin
Michael Waaler, Hamburg

Layout and Production:
Sandra Meifarth, Berlin
Anita Roy, Wellington, UK

Printed and bound at: Replika Press Pvt. Ltd.

ISBN: 978-93-85932-24-3



**www.zubaanbooks.com**
**www.springmagazin.de**